PRAISE FOR ELLEN MEISTER

Take My Husband

STARRED REVIEW

"A darkly comedic farce . . . Understanding that marriages can't always weather decades' worth of ebbs and flows, Meister's protagonist makes a strong case for communicating one's wants and needs early and loudly."

—*Booklist*

The Rooftop Party

"A wickedly entertaining rom-com / murder mystery from start to finish. It promises to be a contender for beach read of the year."

—Bookreporter

"Meister creates an engaging mystery in the unique setting of the home shopping world. It's as fun to watch Dana piece together the clues as it is to see the behind-the-scenes details of her life as a TV host. Dana juggles a relationship, family drama, and a high-profile job, making her likable and easy to root for. Meister imbues her (and many other characters) with a quick wit and plenty of laughworthy lines. Perfect for readers who like their mysteries light on the murder but heavy on the humor."

—*Kirkus Reviews*

T0182790

Love Sold Separately

"Witty, clever, and full of original characters, it kept me up reading way past my bedtime! A great romp of a read."
—Candace Bushnell, bestselling author of *Sex and the City* and *Is There Still Sex in the City*

Dorothy Parker Drank Here

"Meister's Dorothy Parker is just as sharp, witty, and pleasantly mean as fans would expect. Her humanity shines through, though, along with her humor . . . a surprisingly emotional novel. Not even death can keep Dorothy Parker down in this sad and funny story."
—*Kirkus Reviews*

"If you're not a fan of Parker's or Meister's already, you soon will be."
—Bookreporter

Farewell, Dorothy Parker

"Meister skillfully translates the rapier-like wit of the Algonquin Round Table to modern-day New York . . . [with] pathos, nuanced characters, plenty of rapid-fire one-liners, and a heartrending denouement."
—*Publishers Weekly*

The Other Life

"How many wonder what their life would be like if they chose a different path? This inimitable tale is mesmerizing . . . executed flawlessly."
—New York Journal of Books

"A provocative and unique tale of the road not taken. You won't want to miss this one!"

—Sarah Addison Allen, *New York Times* bestselling author of *The Girl Who Chased the Moon*

Divorce Towers

ALSO BY ELLEN MEISTER

Take My Husband

The Rooftop Party

Love Sold Separately

Dorothy Parker Drank Here

Farewell, Dorothy Parker

The Other Life

The Smart One

Secret Confessions of the Applewood PTA

Divorce Towers

A NOVEL

ELLEN MEISTER

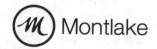

Published by Montlake, Seattle

www.apub.com

Amazon, the Amazon logo, and Montlake are trademarks of Amazon.com, Inc., or its affiliates.

ISBN-13: 9781662520891 (paperback)
ISBN-13: 9781662520907 (digital)

Cover design by Caroline Teagle Johnson
Cover images: © ianmcdonnell / Getty; © Darya Komarova / Getty; © OSTILL / Getty; © Koen Van Damme / Stocksy

Printed in the United States of America

For Pete

Oh, life is a glorious cycle of song,
A medley of extemporanea;
And love is a thing that can never go wrong;
And I am Marie of Roumania.
—Dorothy Parker

Chapter 1
ADDISON

Addison Torres stared down at the cracked screen on her phone, ignoring the announcements at the Delta Air Lines terminal. She crossed her long legs at the ankle, settling in. This was her routine when flying—hang back until the last minute to minimize the wait, the jostling, and the aggressive maneuvering for a spot in the overhead bin. But then she remembered. She wouldn't have to push to the back of the plane—she was holding a first-class ticket.

She had, of course, objected. It was a ridiculous waste of money. She was Addy from the block, after all. A Queens native who was far too proud to covet such luxuries. Or to admit to it, anyway.

Addison glanced up to see the expensively dressed first-class passengers already moving toward the gateway, acting like they didn't notice the large mass of humanity pressing in from the periphery. She grabbed the handle of her wheeled bag and fell in behind the privileged assembly.

They were ruly, nonchalant, delicately perfumed. Addison knew from experience that most of them weren't nearly as confident as they pretended to be. Even the smug ones. Or, more precisely, *especially* the smug ones. Out of habit, she tried to determine who was single and who wasn't, but stopped the thought in its tracks. That part of your life is over, she told herself.

Three weeks ago, Addison had been fired from the best and worst job she'd ever had, working for Manhattan's premier matchmaker to the rich and richer. On the best days, it was glorious, as Addison realized she was preternaturally good at putting people together, with almost a sixth sense about it. But the worst days were torture, as her boss was so toxic she made Miranda Priestly look like Mr. Rogers. Also, Addison had discovered it's not a great idea to sleep with one of your clients. Particularly if you're engaged.

And that's why she was here, flying out to Los Angeles to start a new life. She had thrown a hand grenade into the old one.

Despite herself, Addison's eyes swept the crowd in front of her, landing on an astonishingly good-looking guy with glossy dark hair and a body so sculpted you could see the muscles through his expensive cotton shirt. But he was ostentatiously thumbing through a script, which Addison knew was pure theater. Classic douchebag. The only thing missing was a pair of sunglasses on the top of his head. Of course, she wanted to sleep with him. And that, in a sticky, salty, bottom-of-the-bag pistachio nutshell, was her problem. She was a genius at finding matches for other people, but when it came to herself, she was about as sharp as a soup spoon.

The guy sensed her watching and looked up, catching her eye. He gave her a small, charming smile that seemed to say *I think you're cute too.* Addison blew out a breath and shook her head—her way of saying *It's not happening, dude.* He gave her an easy shrug, and she understood that too. He was telling her she couldn't blame a guy for trying.

She went back to her cracked screen and opened the boarding pass, positioning it so the barcode could scan beneath the fissure. One of these days—if the job worked out—she would be able to afford a new phone. In the meantime, she held it toward the gate agent, then walked down the Jetway ramp to board.

Once on the plane, she spotted her seat and saw that McScripty—who was clearly an actor, though she didn't recognize him—was in the same row but on the other side of the aisle, with a wide seat and a console between them. It was a relief. She avoided his eye and focused on her destination but was waylaid by a sliver-thin blond woman who bolted into the aisle just as Addison was about to pass. Apparently, this human splinter had to do some emergency rearranging of her stored items, holding up a planeload of people trying to board. It took longer than it should, and Addison let out an impatient sigh. McScripty caught it and smiled again, giving a sympathetic eye roll. She was close enough to see his perfect teeth, but then she noticed his nose was a little heavy and off center. Still gorgeous, but maybe not as handsome as he thought he was. Addison knew she was still a long way from talking herself out of her attraction for him, but she was determined. After all, she had promised herself this would be the year of celibacy. Twelve full months without sex. She was certain it would cure her of her habit of self-destruction. Also, it was a conscious sacrifice to protect the innocent, who didn't deserve her recklessness. It wouldn't make up for what she had done to her fiancé, Marco, whose heart she had shattered with her infidelity. But at least it would keep her from a repeat performance.

The splinter lady finally sat down and put her pink Birkin bag in her lap, and Addison was able to pass and take her seat a few rows back, by the window.

Almost immediately, McScripty leaned across the empty seat next to him and spoke to her.

"You know who that was?" he asked conspiratorially, nodding toward the blond woman.

"No clue," she said.

"Isabel Nemeroff." His eyes went wide, as if he were disclosing something astonishing. But the name meant nothing to Addison.

"I'm sorry, I don't—"

"Sony Pictures?" he offered, looking quite certain it would ring a bell.

"I'm from Queens," she said, eager to dispel any notion that she was somehow in his world.

He registered surprise. "I was sure you were an actress."

Addison nearly laughed, wondering how often he'd used that line before. For a moment, though, she considered the possibility that he was being sincere. Not completely far fetched. First, there was the context—a New York–to–Los Angeles flight. But also, her looks. At nearly five-ten, with broad shoulders and genetically excellent posture, Addison could be imposing. That—together with her rich, dark hair, worn swept to the side and just past shoulder length—made people think she was prettier than she actually was. One guy she dated had the nerve to be honest about it. *You know, you're very sexy and kind of pretty, but not that pretty.*

She glanced back at McScripty and decided he was playing her. In fact, she knew just what he expected. She was supposed to ask if *he* was an actor, at which point he would tell her about the script he was reading and how his career was about to crack wide open.

Instead she said, "Just a regular person with a rich uncle and a first-class ticket."

"Nothing wrong with having a rich uncle," he said with what looked like a sneaky grin.

Addison huffed, annoyed. She couldn't be sure, but she thought he winked. Was he suggesting that *uncle* was a euphemism for *sugar daddy*? Arnie Glass was seventy-five years old. Besides, he was her actual uncle. Or rather her great-uncle. The insinuation irked her.

And also, she had begged her uncle to get her a seat in coach, insisting she didn't need to fly first class. But Arnie Glass—who was one of her last living relatives—wouldn't hear of it, and so here she was.

The guilt weighed on her. And it wasn't just about the first-class ticket. Her uncle was such a good man, and Addison wasn't sure she deserved his generosity. She had called him when her life blew up, explaining that she'd been fired from her job, then Marco had walked out. And all of it—every last bit—was her own damned fault. She'd anticipated a lecture from him on getting her act together and living up to the expectations her parents would have had, but he had said, "Sweetheart, come out to Los Angeles and get a fresh start. I can even get you a job at my condo. They're looking for a concierge, and you'd be perfect for it."

That was when she had started crying. The very idea that he wanted to help her was almost too much to bear. Addison's parents had been

4

gone over ten years, and she had stopped expecting anyone to love her this much. When she protested, through her hiccuping sobs, that she wasn't sure she was qualified to be a concierge, he scoffed, insisting he was good friends with the building manager and had enough pull to get her the job. Most of all, he was confident she'd knock it out of the park.

"I'm calling my assistant right now," he'd said, "and telling her to buy you a ticket."

From there, everything happened in an excited blur—the single Zoom interview, the emailed contract, the packing of boxes and disposal of furniture. And now here she was, being hit on by some LA type who probably wasn't accustomed to rejection.

"Well, I'm sure you need to get back to your script," she said, and opened the e-reader app on her phone. Before he could protest, a large man in a suit took the aisle seat between them, cutting off their communication. Perfect, she thought. It would keep her out of trouble.

She didn't see McScripty again until she was exiting the plane's lavatory and almost ran smack into his chest. Clearly, he'd been waiting for her. Now, she was close enough to smell his cologne, make out the rounded contours of his highly developed pectorals.

"I wanted to apologize," he said. "I think I offended you earlier."

His eyes were even darker than hers—almost black—and powerfully seductive. But she was determined not to succumb. She held his gaze. "You did."

He looked surprised by her bluntness. She got that a lot. But normally, Addison didn't see any use for polite lies. If someone offended you, there was no reason to pretend otherwise.

"Can I make it up to you?" he asked.

She laughed. "I'm over it."

"I'm really not as bad as you think," he said with a coy smile.

He had punched the word *bad*, clearly expecting some flirty banter, but Addison wasn't having it. "Let me get this straight," she said. "You say something to offend me, and then you use it as a ploy to hit on me?"

He blinked. "You really think I'm an asshole."

5

His tone was defensive, as if he was challenging her to take it back with something like *Oh, no—not at all! It was just a big misunderstanding.* But she simply shrugged and said, "And you think I'm an idiot, so I guess we're even." Then she gave him a wide smile, sidled past him, and went back to her seat, confident she'd blocked any chance of another come-on from him. She had gone full bitch, and he wasn't going to seek her out in baggage claim and beg to start over, looking for a chance to exchange contact info.

She was right, of course, and as she pulled her biggest suitcase off the conveyor belt, she couldn't help feeling just a little disappointed. But Addison told herself it was for the best. Given another shot with this guy, she just might have made an excuse to sleep with him, telling herself she could restart her twelve-months-of-celibacy clock afterward.

Dragging her luggage through the glass doors, Addison was met with the chaotic sunshine of a Los Angeles afternoon and the snarl of LAX traffic. She saw Dr. Arnold Glass, retired plastic surgeon, waving out the window of his BMW, ignoring the neon-vested female security guard trying to get him to move his car from the curb. When she screeched her whistle at him, Arnie turned and said something that clearly disarmed her, as she let her whistle drop and gave out a laugh. God, he was a charmer.

Arnie turned toward Addison. "Sweetheart!" he shouted. "Welcome!"

Her heart nearly melted at the sight of him, but before she could respond, there was McScripty again, passing between them on his way to the crosswalk, catching the attention of several women as he sauntered by. Uncle Arnie followed her gaze, and when his eyes landed on the object of her scrutiny, he registered surprise.

"Dante?" he said to the man.

McScripty turned to him, and they exchanged a few friendly words she couldn't make out. But she definitely heard what her uncle said next.

"Can I give you a lift?"

Chapter 2

There was only so long Addison could stay glued in place. So when her uncle got out of his car, she approached and greeted him, ignoring McScripty as he threw his bag into the open trunk.

"Addison, sweetheart," Arnie said, giving her a warm hug. "I'm so glad you're here."

"Me too," she said, nearly choking on a lump of gratitude. There was simply no way to express what she felt.

But of course, she didn't need to. Uncle Arnie studied her face for an appreciative moment, then wrested the biggest suitcase from her grip and hoisted it into the car. She would have put up a fuss, but she knew how much pride he took in retaining his youthful vigor. At seventy-five, he was lean but solid, a little shorter than Addison, with a low center of gravity that seemed to radiate power. Like her mother's family, she thought, compact and hardy, able to withstand long winters in the shtetl. Addison was built like her Puerto Rican father—lanky, but with imposing shoulders.

Arnie ran his hand through his wavy silver hair, which he wore long and thick. Addison assumed it served as a mating call to women his age, a symbol of his virility.

She picked up her second-largest bag, and McScripty tried to pull it from her hands. "I got it," she argued. It was one thing to placate her sweet uncle's ego. She wasn't going to indulge this guy's preening.

Still, he went back to the trunk and insisted on helping Arnie engineer the puzzle of fitting in all the luggage. Every guy she'd ever known thought he had a unique genius for car-trunk geometry.

"Addison, this is Dante D'Amico," Arnie said over his shoulder as he slid in her last bag. He slammed the trunk closed, turned back to her, and opened his arms in wonder. "He lives in the building!"

Arnie seemed so utterly delighted by the coincidence that Addison forced a tight smile and put out her hand. Inside, she roiled. Nothing about this was okay. She was starting a new job, a new life. She had vowed to behave herself. And here was this devastating guy she'd wanted to fuck since the moment she saw him posturing with that stupid script. And he would be living under the same roof in Beekman Towers.

Why couldn't things ever be easy?

Dante took her hand, and the warm touch—electrified by his smirk—was almost too much.

"Well," he said. "That was a meet-cute."

God, this guy was as LA as a cheesy soundtrack. She tried to pull away, but he held tight, putting his other hand over their grip. It was a practiced move by a man who understood the art of seduction, for now they were joined, flesh to flesh, and it felt like foreplay. She looked down at his strong hands and, despite herself, became aware of their pulses connecting and throbbing somewhere south of her navel. Trouble. This guy knew exactly what he was doing.

"Arnie," Dante said, still staring into Addison's eyes, "your niece was the most beautiful woman on that plane."

"You were on the same flight!" Arnie gushed. "Marvelous. You two are going to be great friends."

"I hope so," Dante said, finally releasing her hand.

Trying to ground herself, she touched the tiny heart pendant hanging around her neck, and he seemed to notice the gesture, which gave her a shiver. They got into the car—Addison in the front and Dante in the back—and inched into the excruciating LAX traffic. She tried to settle herself into the comfortable leather seat, angling the AC vent away from her face.

Arnie chattered as he drove, explaining to Dante that Addison would be their building's new concierge and to Addison that Dante was a talent agent who racked up more frequent flier miles than anyone he knew, going back and forth between New York and Los Angeles. An agent, she thought, of course. Not an actor but the guy who powered their careers.

As her uncle talked and drove, going from one freeway to another and then exiting, Addison looked out the window, trying to reconcile that this was her new home—this bright, sunny place with its palm trees and incongruous architecture. She imagined all the buildings were empty, as it seemed the entire population was on the road. With a gut squeeze of anxiety, she reminded herself that if she was going to make a life here, she'd need to learn how to drive.

Arnie's cell phone rang—loudly—through the car's Bluetooth speaker. He tapped the screen in the middle of the dashboard, which identified the caller as Sage.

"Hey, baby," he said to her.

Baby? Addison studied his face. Did Arnie have a girlfriend named Sage? That sounded too young. *Way* too young. He should be with a woman who had a name like Sheila. Or Marilyn. Or even Pamela or Kimberly.

"Hey, Papa Bear," said a very girlish young woman's voice. "I thought you were coming over."

Oh, no, Addison thought. This was worse than she had imagined. The caller sounded almost like a child. And with four marriages under his belt, Arnie had an even worse track record than she did. But at least his wives had been more or less age appropriate.

"I told you," Arnie said to Sage. "I had to pick up my niece from the airport. She's going to be our new concierge."

The girl giggled. "I forgot! I'm a little stoned."

"In that case I'll be over as soon as I can," he replied with a chuckle, inducing even more girlish laughter.

Addison gave him a frank look of disapproval, and Arnie responded with an apologetic shrug. But he didn't seem terribly ashamed.

"Sage," he said, "my niece is in the car with me. Say hello to Addison."

"Hi, Addison," the girl squeaked.

Addison said hello back, and then Dante leaned forward to pipe in "Hey, Sage."

"Arnie," the girl whined, "I thought you said *niece*."

"For God's sake," Addison mumbled, surmising this girl was a natural airhead, weed or no weed.

Arnie continued grinning, unfazed, resilient in his ebullience. Addison recognized the mood. When a man knew he was getting laid, his focus was shatterproof.

"Dante is in the car too," he said to Sage. "Ran into him at the airport."

"Dante!" Sage said with a gasp, as if she couldn't imagine more delightful news, and Addison sensed they had some kind of history, or at least a pattern of flirtation.

Arnie got off the phone, telling the girl he would come by in about an hour. Addison folded her arms.

"I take it you don't approve," he said.

"How *old* is she?" Addison herself was twenty-nine and clocked this girl as younger.

Her uncle sped through a yellow light, only to reach a red one. "I'm a lonely old guy, and she's very sweet," he said, braking.

"Uncle Arnie, you haven't been lonely a day in your life."

"I think *lonely* is a euphemism," Dante said from the back.

Addison sighed, getting the gist. "Fine," she said, "but I'm sure there are plenty of age-appropriate women who would be happy to . . . scratch that itch."

"Oh, he's got those too," Dante said. "Every divorcée over fifty wants a piece of Dr. Arnie."

"Is that true?" Addison asked her uncle.

"What can I say? I'm a single guy who wants to be married. It's a vibe women react to."

"You really want to get married again?" she asked.

"I *like* being married."

"Obviously," Dante said, and there was enough attitude in his tone for Addison to understand he probably had at least one failed marriage under his own belt. "Too bad you can't find the right woman."

"*That,*" Addison said, pointing at the car's Bluetooth speaker, "is not the right woman." She thought about the job she'd left and knew that, given the chance, she could find her uncle's soulmate—a woman of substance who would bring out the best in him. And it sure as hell wouldn't be some stoner young enough to be his granddaughter.

"Trust me, I have no intention of proposing to Sage. But she's a fun gal." At that, he started digging around in his shirt's breast pocket while holding the steering wheel with one hand.

"Everything okay?" Addison asked.

"Absolutely, sweetheart. I just . . . I thought I had a vitamin in here."

Addison watched as her uncle went from his breast pocket to his pants pocket, swerving a bit as he frantically searched.

"Be careful!" she said, alarmed at how close they came to veering out of their lane.

"Found it," he muttered, pulling a small pill from his pocket and popping it into his mouth. He put both hands back on the wheel, and Addison studied his profile.

"Uncle Arnie," she said, concerned, "what did you just take?"

"Nothing to worry about. It's just . . . medicine."

"You said it was a vitamin."

"I think it was a little-blue-pill kind of vitamin," Dante said from the back seat.

Addison looked at him and understood. *Viagra.* She should have known. "You could have just told me," she said to her uncle. "I'm not a child."

Arnie shrugged. "I didn't want to make you uncomfortable."

"At least promise me she's not a minor."

He put his hand to his heart. "Of course not!"

Addison glanced back for confirmation, and Dante nodded. "She's not as young as she sounds," he said. "Just into that whole little-girl vibe. Already married and divorced a daddy figure."

"Oh, great," Addison muttered, making no effort to hide the sarcasm.

Arnie looked in his side-view mirror and changed lanes. "Viagra's been a game changer for fellas my age," he mused.

"There's actually a guy in our building who deals it," Dante chimed in.

"Why would someone buy Viagra from a dealer," Addison asked, "when they can get it online . . . or from CVS?"

"I guess they're embarrassed to ask their doctor for a prescription."

"But the black market is okay?" Addison shook her head and wondered what she was getting herself into with this job.

"That's unsafe and illegal." Arnie tsked, clearly in doctor mode. "Who's the guy?"

Dante told him the name, and Arnie tightened his brow in concentration. "I don't think I know him."

"Skinny and pale, with a hair transplant?" Dante prompted.

Arnie nodded as if he was conjuring an image. "Has a girlfriend with a Brazilian butt lift and a bad eye job?"

Addison listened, wondering if everyone in Los Angeles was identified by the cosmetic work they'd had done or if it was just the culture of this small slice of overpriced real estate.

"That's him," Dante said to Arnie, and then addressed Addison again. "Your uncle is kind of a legend in the building. He's got the dirt on everyone's plastic surgery."

"And that comes up a lot?" she asked.

Arnie shrugged. "Some guys are just obsessed with knowing if a woman's boobs are real. So they come to the doc for answers."

Addison blew out a breath, considering all she had just learned. Viagra dealers. Breast-implant investigators. Old men sleeping with stoned young women. This wasn't what she had expected. Addison had imagined the very expensive Beekman Towers as the Beverly Hills version of a Sutton Place co-op—a property where the überwealthy lived, played, and kept themselves high above the general riffraff of society.

"Isn't anybody in the building happily married?" she asked.

"No one in the building is married, *period*," Dante explained.

"What do you mean?"

"Arnie," Dante said, "you didn't tell her?"

"It never came up."

"*What* never came up?" Addison pressed.

Arnie made a hand gesture toward Dante, encouraging him to speak. So he did.

"Addison," he said, leaning forward, "the Beekman's reputation is pretty notorious in LA. It's where affluent people move when their marriage falls apart and their spouse kicks them out." He sat back, apparently satisfied with his explanation.

Addison glanced out the window, taking this in. She'd been anticipating job duties like making dinner reservations for privileged couples at high-end restaurants and arranging to have their dry cleaning delivered. But if Dante was right, it was something else entirely. She would, essentially, be camp counselor to the rich, glamorous, and horny.

"Is this true?" she asked her uncle.

Arnie turned into the circular driveway in front of the building, where two uniformed doormen stood guard. He put the car in park and turned to her. "Why do you think they call it Divorce Towers?"

Chapter 3

Divorce Towers? What, exactly, would people expect from a concierge in such a place? Addison thought about the job she just left as assistant to an upscale matchmaker—where she had been consumed with the private lives of the obscenely wealthy—and wondered if she had inadvertently stepped into a funhouse-mirror version of her previous life.

She tried to quiet a rising panic telling her this was a huge mistake and that she should have stayed in Queens and taken a job at the Wendy's drive-through. Stop it, she coached herself. You are going to make this work. You have to.

They exited the car, and Arnie introduced her to two doormen in white-trimmed blue uniforms, one parking valet in a Beekman polo shirt, and a muscled porter who had been summoned to take her bags. Addison braced herself for wariness, understanding she would need to win their trust. She was, after all, the new girl—someone who had gotten the job through a connection. But everyone seemed so . . . pleasant. They were open, friendly, trusting. This would take some getting used to.

The glass doors slid silently apart, beckoning them toward the cool, dry, glistening interior. With her uncle on one side and Dante on the other, Addison stepped into the cavernous lobby, and her jaw nearly unhinged at the grandeur of it all. Every inch was gleaming and exquisite, a study in shades of . . . beige. Milky beige. Sandy beige. Holy Temple beige. On either side was a wall of water, cascading in straight sheets over such smooth marble it barely made a sound. Still, it reminded Addison that a trip to the bathroom would be prudent sooner rather than later. She looked up at the high ceiling, and it struck her that it was tall enough to accommodate a low-flying blimp, though navigating past the white crystal chandeliers might be a challenge.

"Fuck me," she whispered, in reverential awe.

"If you insist," Dante said under his breath. "Just give me five minutes to shower."

Before she could respond, a woman sang out from across the lobby. "Arnie! You bad boy! I was at the gym all morning, and you never showed up."

From a distance, the woman looked like an emaciated Julia Roberts, with double-D breasts accentuated by a skintight white top and tanned ropy arms.

"I was picking my niece up at the airport," Arnie called back, his voice carrying across the expanse.

The woman approached and gave him a playful swat on the arm. "I guess you're excused, then," she said, before coming in for a full-contact hug.

Addison studied the exchange, wondering if this aerobics junkie—who clearly had a thing for Arnie—was a good match. She was probably in her early fifties—much younger than her uncle, but certainly more age appropriate than the baby-voiced stoner waiting for him upstairs. This was the type he often went for—with silicone breasts and expensive tastes—but Addison understood he needed someone with more depth, a woman who could challenge him intellectually. She wondered if she could find someone like that for him in this place and decided it was worth a try. What better way to repay him for all he'd done for her?

She glanced over to see Arnie was grinning, clearly delighted by the woman's flirty embrace. "Louise, meet Addison, our new concierge."

"Oh, Arnie, she's darling!" Louise gushed, and moved in to hug Addison. "You're going to love it here, dear. And look—you're already surrounded by the two handsomest men in the building."

"Good to see you, Louise," said Dante.

"Watch out for this one," the woman cautioned Addison, with the wag of a finger bearing an enormous, diamond-encrusted ruby.

"Don't worry," Addison said. "I know a player when I see one."

Louise laughed like it was the funniest thing she'd ever heard, but Addison was dead serious and wondered if her personal style might be a little too frank for LA.

She thought about her Zoom interview with Ms. Frankie Wilcox, the no-nonsense building manager who would be her new boss. Frankie seemed to appreciate Addison's forthrightness, so at least there was that.

The Tower A elevator doors swished open, and an elderly woman with bright-orange hair and a matching cane hobbled out. She caught sight of the assemblage and smiled, her tiny eyes twinkling. "Arnie!" she cried. "I haven't seen you all week."

"Looking beautiful, Sally. How are you feeling?"

"Ready for action," said the old woman. She gave a shimmy for emphasis.

Arnie chuckled. "I know just how you feel," he said, turning serious, and Addison realized the Viagra would be kicking in soon and he was probably eager for his date with Sage.

Sally gave a hoarse laugh. "Pity you're too old for me, Doc. Now, Dante, on the other hand . . ."

"I'm flattered," Dante responded, hand to heart. "But you might be too much woman for me, Sally."

"I don't doubt that, dear boy."

"One of these days we'll find you a handsome young stud," Arnie offered. He turned to Addison to fill her in on Sally Conrad's background, explaining that she had been a film star in her younger days and had once done a love scene with Marlon Brando.

The conversation was interrupted by the click of high heels, causing all heads to pivot toward two designer-clad forty-something women entering the building. They both wore short skirts and ankle boots, revealing sleek, polished legs. They looked so similar that, for a moment, Addison wondered if they were sisters. Then she realized the resemblance was more about their outfits and matching lips, which seemed overplumped with filler.

The taller one clocked Dante's presence and gave the other a nudge. Addison immediately sensed one of them had slept with him. Maybe both.

"Hey, Dante," called the shorter one, her voice husky with seduction.

He barely had time to respond before the women gasped and giggled, noticing her uncle.

"Dr. Arnie!" cooed the tall one.

"Hi, Dr. Arnie!" echoed the other, her voice rising several octaves.

Dante gave Addison a look that seemed to say *See what I mean about your uncle?* And she knew he was right. Women adored him.

Arnie beamed in delight at the attention of the lip sisters. "The whole room just lit up!" he called to them, and Addison understood his appeal. Arnie adored women. All of them. Old. Young. Beautiful. Not so beautiful. He reveled in their very presence.

As they stood and chatted in the lobby over the next several minutes, more people came and went. Some of them greeted Dante; all of them greeted Arnie. Well, except for one mysterious woman who tried to hide her face under a hat as she scurried by. Addison caught a glimpse and noted that she was as striking as Tyra Banks and couldn't imagine why such a beauty wouldn't want to flaunt her looks.

At last, Arnie announced he needed to give Addison a tour and get her settled in.

"Don't you have . . . *plans?*" Dante asked pointedly.

Arnie dismissed the importance with a wave of his hand. "Addison comes first," he said, putting his arm around her.

She was about to thank him when Dante cut in. "Why don't you let me show her around? It'll give us a chance to get acquainted."

"You sure you don't mind?"

"A pleasure."

Arnie looked at his niece. "Sweetheart? That okay with you?"

It wasn't, but she didn't want to cramp her uncle's style. "As long as he understands I've got pepper spray in my purse and I know how to use it," she said.

In truth, it wasn't Dante she didn't trust but herself. Keeping her hands off this guy was not going to be easy. Scaring him away, she thought, might be her best option.

But Arnie and Dante laughed, assuming it was meant as a joke, and it was settled.

"Where do you want to start?" Dante asked after Arnie had left. "The spa? The pool? The gym? My place?"

Addison sighed. "I think I should meet Frankie Wilcox," she said, eager to score early points with the new boss. Besides, she assumed Frankie would make short shrift of Dante, sending him away so she could take over the tour herself.

"She's been filling in at the concierge desk," he said. "Follow me."

Addison told him she needed to make a pit stop first, and Dante led her to the restrooms, behind a partition wall at the rear of the lobby.

She rushed past him into the ladies' room, which was even more opulent than she expected, its gleaming marble floor reflecting the soft light of the crystal chandeliers. There was a lounge area in the corner, with a shell pink velvet chaise. It looked so soft, so inviting, that Addison suddenly realized how tired she felt and was tempted to lie down for a nap. But she did her business, washed up at the gold-plated faucets, and ran a brush through her dark hair as she examined her reflection. She didn't look as worn out as she felt, but maybe some Hollywood type had designed the lighting to make it especially flattering. Addison slid some lipstick across her mouth—lately she'd been inspired by AOC to go for bright red—and decided she looked damned good for someone who'd just traveled across the country. She took off her denim jacket, which she thought was too casual for meeting her boss, and smoothed out the silky black shell, which showed off her strong shoulders. She was ready.

But once again, on exiting the lavatory, she nearly ran smack into Dante.

"Whoa," he said, taking in her freshened appearance. "All that for me?"

"Don't flatter yourself."

He moved in closer and ran his knuckles down the flesh of her upper arm, sending a charged shiver straight through to her center. His dark eyes bored into hers, but Addison's gaze drifted to his dusky lips, which were hot as hell. She imagined kissing him, and the pulse of desire tugged at her. Damn. Why did her body always have to betray her like this?

He seemed to sense what she was thinking, and his own eyes traveled to her mouth, then to her throat and onward as his pelvis pushed forward, nearly making contact.

"I want to kiss you," he said.

"You can't."

"Why not?"

"Because," she said, "we'll only wind up fucking."

"And?" he pressed, his eyes pleading.

"And I'm celibate."

Dante went silent. Then, he laughed—loud and hard—exposing those gorgeous white teeth. "You strike me as the least celibate person I've ever met."

"That's the point," she said. "I need to practice impulse control." Of course, she wasn't going to tell him the whole story—that she had a habit of sabotaging any relationship that seemed promising. And while she understood it was all tied to losing her parents so young, that self-awareness did nothing to stop her from bulldozing the people who least deserved it. Until she could figure all this out, it was best to go cold turkey.

"For how long?" he asked. "Because I'm a patient man."

"A year."

"Okay, not that patient."

She put a hand on his chest to push him away, but he was as immovable as a boulder. "Seriously, Dante, you don't want to get mixed up with me."

"Can't you at least give me one kiss?" he asked, moving his face toward hers.

She turned her head to avoid mouth-to-mouth contact, and that's when she saw a woman turn the corner to use the restroom. The shocked stranger stopped in her tracks as they locked eyes, and Addison was rocked by a jolt of recognition. This wasn't a stranger at all. They had met in Addison's Queens kitchen. Only the woman had been here, in Beverly Hills, speaking to her through a Zoom call.

It was Frankie Wilcox.

Chapter 4
ARNIE

Dirty old man.

The phrase had never bothered Arnie. It conjured an image of some lecherous creep who went after underage girls, and that wasn't his style. To him, women didn't hit their stride until they passed forty and blossomed into full sensuality. That's what he found sexy—maturity and experience. Given the choice between a strong, charismatic fifty-year-old who knew a thing or two and some ersatz teenybopper with daddy issues, he'd go for the real woman every time.

But Sage was sweet and funny—with the body of a *Playboy* centerfold—and absolutely mad about sex. So who was he to turn her down?

Except that when he showed up at her apartment that day, it felt wrong. The girl suddenly seemed so very young. He knew it had something to do with the arrival of his niece. But mostly it was about the email he'd just received from Paulette, his ex-wife. Or more precisely, his second ex-wife. There had been two more after her. If he was honest with himself, those next marriages failed because he'd been trying to find a replacement. But there was only one Paulette. What a woman.

She was, unfortunately, widely misunderstood. Most people thought she was a crazy bitch—selfish, greedy, and mean. Of course, he could see their point—especially when he thought about the incident with the glass coffee table—but there was so much more to her. She was vital, passionate, fiercely intelligent. Life with Paulette was never dull. So even though he'd often felt like he was locked in a cage with a tiger, they had been exhilarating years, and he had never stopped loving her. Not when she cheated on him. Or when she cheated on him again. Or even when she ran away with the Italian.

But all that was over, according to her. The marriage had fallen apart. She had thrown Sergio out and was getting ready to leave Milan and come back home in a couple of months. She'd mentioned nothing about where she planned to live, but she did say she had always wondered if leaving Arnie was a mistake. *Love ya*, she'd written at the end.

Now, Arnie imagined making room for her in his condo. He'd clean out one of the closets and replace the black leather sofa. (She hated black furniture. Also white shoes, cheap wine, politics, smokers, gum chewers, chatty waiters, football, and dogs.) They could pick up right where they left off. He felt himself getting aroused at the thought, but he wasn't going to use Sage to scratch that itch. Her youth felt suddenly indecent.

"You sure you don't want to do it?" Sage said when he told her he'd changed his mind.

"I'm sure, baby."

"'Cause I can probably get you hard, Papa Bear." She tried to reach for his crotch, and he backed away.

"It's not that," he said. As a physician, Arnie knew the phosphodiesterase type five inhibitor in his system would be providing more than adequate blood flow to his penis for several hours, and he would have no trouble getting an erection. Viagra was a hell of a breakthrough.

"What's wrong?" she asked.

They were standing in her living room, which was decorated in neutral colors, with two oversize zebra-striped chairs flanking the sofa, and Arnie glanced past her at the terrace, where he could see a pair of slender legs crossed at the ankles on a lounge chair. That was another weird thing about this fling with Sage. She lived with her mother, a divorcée from Encino.

"I just have a lot on my mind," he said.

"We could do something else," Sage offered. "You want to get high? Or maybe you can watch me—"

"No, no," he interrupted, "let's go to the pool."

Sage clapped her hands. "I'll get my sunscreen."

A short while later, they were in their bathing suits on the deck by the rooftop pool, relaxing on cushioned lounges while the panorama of Beverly Hills pulsed in the distance.

As Sage took selfies and got busy posting them or doing god knows what on her phone, Arnie surveyed the poolside, trying to determine if there was anyone age appropriate for her. In the middle of a weekday there weren't many people around, but he did notice that young computer nerd from Tower A doing laps. Arnie had heard rumors that he was some kind of boy genius—a tech entrepreneur that got ripped off by his girlfriend, who was in cahoots with his business partner. Might explain why he always seemed so angry.

Sage, of course, didn't glance his way, but she did look up when David Haber, the thick-necked anesthesiologist from 704, walked by. Arnie had known him for a long time—a decent guy, and rarely serious, even after his wife left him. Sage sat up straighter, arching her back.

"Will you do me?" she asked Arnie as she waved her tube of La Mer sunscreen at him.

She'd said it loud enough for Haber to hear, which, Arnie supposed, was the point. She was looking for another daddy who might be more eager for sex.

"Sure, baby," Arnie said, squirting a puddle of the pricey lotion into his palm.

Haber turned toward them, and Arnie followed the sweep of his eyes. First, of course, they landed on Sage in her bright-pink bikini. Then they clocked his silver-haired colleague smoothing lotion across the girl's silky back.

"Dr. Glass," Haber said, "I've never seen a man enjoy retirement more."

"Carpe diem," Arnie replied.

"Tish, I love it when you speak French," Haber quipped, doing a passable impression of Gomez Addams.

"My mom speaks French," Sage piped in, sounding awed by the coincidence.

"It was Latin, babe," Arnie said. "He was joking." He introduced the two, and Haber moved closer to shake the girl's hand.

"Sage," Haber repeated. "I think I met your sisters, *Rosemary* and *Thyme*."

She swatted his leg. "Oh! You're *funny!*"

"I'll be here all week."

"Don't you live here?" Sage asked, confused.

Arnie sighed. The girl wasn't stupid. She was just young, and maybe a little high.

"It's an old joke," Haber explained. "Kind of like Dr. Glass."

Arnie laughed. Because if you couldn't have a sense of humor about yourself, what was the point? Besides, he liked Haber, and if the guy wanted to flirt with Sage, he wasn't going to get in his way.

Arnie announced that he needed a dip in the pool and offered his lounge to Haber, who was only too happy to take his place.

After two easy laps, Arnie toweled himself off and waved goodbye to Sage and her new papa bear. Then he tried to make his way back to his apartment to compose a carefully worded response to Paulette. But before he even reached the elevator, he was waylaid by a woman from Tower A—an interior decorator with a million-dollar smile—who was eager to show him her new breast implants.

"For a professional opinion," she said with a wink, and this time, there was no reason to reject the overture. After all, this didn't feel like robbing the cradle. This was a woman. An eager, mature, experienced, sex-loving woman who knew what she wanted—and that included half the male residents of Beekman Towers and, Arnie suspected, at least a few staff members. As long as he played it safe, what better way to distract himself while waiting for Paulette to return? Besides, no sense letting the Viagra go to waste.

Chapter 5
ADDISON

"Boundaries," Frankie Wilcox was saying as they sat in her office.

"Of course," Addison said. "I have no—"

Frankie held up a hand. "I don't even need to hear it," she said. "Just remember that it's your job to define the boundaries. Some of the residents are going to think you're their friend, and you're not."

You mean like you and Arnie? Addison was tempted to say, because she knew they were morning coffee buddies. But Addison decided it was best not to call her boss a hypocrite before the job even started.

Besides, Addison loved the idea of boundaries, since keeping a professional distance from the personal lives of the residents would make the job so much easier. Right now, though, she just wanted to explain that Dante had come on hard, but she had done the right thing and was in the midst of rebuffing him when Frankie rounded the corner. Not only that, but she had taken a vow of celibacy for a full year, and she was actually proud of herself that she had stuck to her plan and wasn't in his apartment right now, fucking his brains out. Because the old Addison would have. Still, she knew this sentiment wasn't exactly the way to score points with her new boss.

"I'm really sorry, Frankie" was all she could say.

Her boss nodded. "As long as it doesn't happen again. *Ever.*"

And that was that. At least for now. Addison understood she would need to prove herself to this woman, which would mean staying as far away from Dante as possible.

As Frankie Wilcox pulled new-employee forms from her desk and went over the job, the hours, the rules, the hierarchy, and the expectations, Addison studied her neat features and efficient demeanor. Though not more than five foot three, she had the commanding presence of Michelle Obama, whom she resembled, but with fuller cheeks and short hair. And she dressed like a TV newswoman, in an expensive pale-blue suit over a simple white shell. As manager, Frankie Wilcox was the only building employee who wasn't required to wear a uniform. Addison's consisted of a red blazer she was expected to wear over her own clothes, and she understood she would stand out like the Montauk Point Lighthouse, sitting at the long beige table at the back of the massive beige lobby.

A short time later, Frankie's assistant, Raphael, who doubled as a personal trainer, was summoned to show Addison to her apartment and get her settled in. Tomorrow she would begin her orientation.

"New Yorker?" Raphael asked as he led her to the elevator.

"Is it that obvious?"

He seemed to size up her outfit with a sniff. "You're forgiven," he said, "as long as you don't think that makes you better than anyone else . . ."

"Of course not!"

Raphael laughed. "I'm messing with you, girl."

She laughed, too, appreciating the camaraderie, and followed him into the elevator. "What floor am I on?"

He answered by pushing the button marked **INDOOR POOL**—clearly one level down from the lobby—and Addison wondered if she'd be sleeping in the back of a locker room. Fortunately, when the doors swished open, he brought her to the opposite end of the hallway, where there was a sign that read **CONCIERGE SUITE**.

"Gorgeous or what?" Raphael asked with a dramatic flourish after he used his key to let them in. With his hip jutted and his arms spread, he seemed to be talking more about himself than the apartment.

She was tempted to agree. He was handsome as hell, with symmetrical features, smooth dark skin, and exquisitely sculpted muscles. Like the *David* if he'd gone to the gym. Also, he was gay. Addison was grateful he'd made that so clear. There'd be no sexual tension.

She surveyed the furnished apartment, which was semisubterranean and smelled faintly of chlorine. If she listened carefully, she could hear echo-y voices wafting over from the indoor pool. Still, it was a sweet setup for free digs, with a large living room open to a gleaming, brand-new kitchen, and a separate bedroom that was compact but still bigger than the one she'd had in Jackson Heights. Windows set close to the ceiling let in just enough light to keep it from feeling underground. The furnishings were bland but attractive, like they belonged in a hotel room. Addison was grateful the beige decor was broken up by splashes of soft blue. Once she unpacked the boxes she'd had shipped—which someone had neatly stacked along the walls—it just might feel like home.

"I'm trying to calculate how much this would cost in Manhattan," she said.

He scoffed. "When you consider what they want from you, honey, it ain't a bargain."

She nearly scoffed back, as she'd just spent two years at a high-stress job and knew that if she set boundaries as Frankie had instructed, this would be easy by comparison—even if it wasn't as buttoned up as she'd expected. "Seems pretty nine-to-five," she said.

He laughed. "Oh, please."

Addison squinted at him, trying to discern whether he was a troublemaker, instigating drama. "I'm all ears."

Raphael approached the counter between the kitchen and the living room, where there was an enormous gift basket of fruit, nuts, cheese, and other goodies. He pulled off a card stapled to the cellophane and held it toward her. "You going to read this?"

"Why don't you do it?" she prodded, knowing it was exactly what he wanted to hear. The guy was as nosy as the camera in a reality show.

He opened the tiny envelope and pulled out the card. "It's from Arnie Glass. Just says *Welcome, Addison.*" He looked disappointed it wasn't something more salacious. "That your grandpa?"

"Uncle."

"Wonder if he knows what you're in for."

Addison folded her arms. "Seems like you're trying to scare me, Raphael."

"Not scare you, baby girl, *warn* you." He pulled open the cellophane and took out an apple. "Mind?" he asked, holding it up.

"Do I have a choice?"

"Not really," he said, biting into it. "Frankie tell you about the bat phone?"

Bat phone? She gave him a quizzical look.

"This thing," he continued, pointing to an old-fashioned business phone on the kitchen counter. "It's a direct line to the concierge desk."

"Landline?" she asked.

"A relic, right? But the residents love it. If they need you when you're off duty, they press a button, and it rings like the place is on fire."

"The phone rings in my *apartment?*" she asked, trying to wrap her head around this information. Because surely they couldn't just call her whenever they wanted.

Raphael chuckled. "It's not complicated. You're on call twenty-four seven."

"That can't be right," she said, imagining being woken in the middle of the night for . . . What? A spa appointment? A dinner reservation? It didn't make sense.

"Why do you think you and Frankie are the only two employees with apartments in the building?"

She dismissed this with a wave of her hand, certain he was just trying to stir up trouble. No one would need a concierge in the middle of the night. "If I set boundaries, I'm sure folks will be respectful of my schedule."

Raphael laughed so hard he bent at the waist. "You sweet thing," he said, wiping his tears. "You don't know what it's like to work for rich people."

At that, a giant lump formed in her throat because she knew exactly what it was like. A while later, when Raphael left and shut the door behind him, Addison wondered if she'd made a terrible mistake.

As she unpacked, though, she convinced herself it was fine and that the phone would probably ring only once in a blue moon, when there was some kind of emergency. She'd simply follow Frankie's advice and folks would respect her. That's all there was to it.

By the time she got the bedroom set up and ate a light meal, thanks to the gift from Uncle Arnie, Addison was exhausted. She stripped to her underwear and fell into bed, grateful the day was over. As she drifted off, Addison congratulated herself for landing such a cushy gig. So what if these folks were rich, spoiled, and thirsty? It wasn't anything she couldn't handle.

Hours later, when she was jolted awake by a harsh, persistent ringing, Addison bolted up in bed, her heart pounding. Disoriented, she took a moment to remember where she was and to understand the source of the noise. The bat phone! But who would be calling her before she had even started? And how on earth did that phone have such a loud, piercing ringer?

Bleary, she stumbled out of bed in the dark and made her way to the kitchen, where she flicked on a light. She was still groggy enough to be confused when she realized the phone was silent. The sound was her doorbell. Someone was pressing the buzzer.

Still in her underwear, Addison approached the door.

"Who is it?" she called, but couldn't hear the response. She opened the door just a crack to see who was there.

Dante.

Chapter 6

"What are you doing here?" Addison asked, trying to hide her body behind the door.

"Oh, good," he said, catching a glimpse, "you were expecting me." Dante's smirk bloomed into a full smile, revealing a single dimple, and it was killer. Why did this guy have to be so damned good looking?

Addison narrowed the door opening. "Funny," she said dismissively. "You need to leave. Now."

"But I brought champagne." He held up a bottle of Dom Pérignon. "To welcome you aboard."

"Thanks anyway."

"Come on," he said. "Put on some clothes and let me in. I promise I'll be a perfect gentleman."

"Is anyone in the hall?" she asked, concerned that even his presence outside her door could land her in deep shit with Frankie. "Did someone see you?"

"Don't worry. I'm like a ninja."

"Doesn't that mean you can vanish without a trace?"

"Come on," Dante insisted. "I'm sure you could use a friend here. Someone to give you the inside dirt on this place."

"You almost cost me my job," she said, though she figured he'd already surmised that. After he'd tried to kiss her, he'd clocked Frankie's presence and backed off, making a quick and appropriate exit.

Dante frowned, looking genuinely contrite. "I'm sorry," he said. "Really. If I'd known Frankie was around the corner . . ."

She gave a nod, acknowledging his sincerity.

"Can't you please let me make it up to you?" He held up the bottle again. "This is expensive stuff."

"I don't doubt it. I just—"

"I can fill you in on important gossip even your uncle doesn't know."

That stopped her, because she understood how helpful it could be to start the job fully armed and had hoped to find time to pump Arnie for information. Even so, she knew her uncle's insights would be skewed by his lust-colored perceptions of the opposite sex. And Frankie certainly wasn't going to be honest with her about the idiosyncrasies of the residents. Her one other connection, Raphael, was an in-house gossip hound, but she could tell he had a flair for the dramatic. Dante seemed just cynical enough to give it to her straight.

"Like what?" she asked.

He bit his lip in concentration, trying to find something to share. Then his eyes went bright, and he leaned in. "Did you notice that tall woman in the blue hat?"

Addison recalled the willowy beauty who had rushed by on her way to the elevator. "The one who looks like Tyra Banks?"

He nodded. "She's a celebrity in her own right but thinks no one here knows who she is."

"And you do?"

"In my business, you've got to have an eye for faces."

Of course, she thought. As a talent agent, he probably spent half his day looking at headshots. "Well?" she pressed. "Who is she?"

Dante dangled the champagne bottle again. "I'll tell you over a drink."

Addison sighed. This guy knew just how to play her, because now she was burning to know who the mystery woman was. Still, she should probably shut the door and put an end to this. It was the smart thing to do.

But maybe not, she thought. Maybe this was a good opportunity to test her resolve. If she could sit alone in a room with this smoldering guy and not jump him, she'd sail through a year of celibacy with no problem. The bigger issue was Frankie, because if she found out Addison had Dante in her room even for an innocent conversation, she'd be furious.

Be smart, Addison told herself. You need this job. You can't afford to get fired again. Not now, when you have no friends, no fiancé, not even an apartment to call your own.

She looked into Dante's handsome face, ready to send him away. But when he flashed that dimple again, she wondered if Frankie would really fire her over such a small infraction. No way, she decided—not when she didn't practice what she preached. Besides, there was almost no chance she'd find out.

"You sure no one saw you?" Addison asked.

"Positive."

She searched his eyes for deception. "And how do I know you'll behave yourself?"

"You have my word."

Addison narrowed her gaze, wondering exactly how good his word was. She thought for a minute, sizing him up, then remembered the vibe she'd picked up in the car that he had at least one divorce under his belt. "You got kids?" she asked.

He cocked his head. "That's a funny question."

"I want you to swear on the life of someone you love." In her experience, even the most hardened liars stopped short of swearing on a kid's life if they weren't sincere.

"No kids," he said. "But I can swear on my mother's life. How's that?"

He seemed earnest, but Addison hesitated yet again, thinking about Logan Kinkaid, the client she'd slept with. It was such complete stupidity. They'd been in his apartment, discussing a terrible date he'd had with a woman her boss had chosen for him. Addison's job had been to debrief him, determine what had gone wrong, and take notes for finding a better match. But the conversation went on for over two hours, turning so intimate it suddenly felt like they had an almost spiritual connection. Once he put his hand on her thigh, nothing else existed. Not even Marco, her fiancé.

And here was Dante, hotter than either one of them. But she had learned from her mistakes and felt certain she could resist him. Besides, she really wanted to know about the woman in the blue hat.

Dante looked at her expectantly, and she took a deep breath, committing to her decision.

"Is anyone out there?" she asked.

He glanced up and down the hall, then shook his head.

"Okay, hang on." She shut the door and got dressed, throwing on a pair of jeans and a faded T-shirt before running a brush through her bed-tangled hair.

"Hurry," she whispered, opening the door. "But just one drink, and then you're out."

"I promise," he said, but held up two crossed fingers.

Addison didn't laugh. "Don't make me regret this," she said, and shut the door after him.

Dante looked around while Addison went into the kitchenette to find glasses. Since she hadn't yet unpacked the housewares boxes, she had to rely on whatever the management had provided, and began opening cabinets. There was nothing with a stem, so she grabbed her only choice—two oversize tumblers. She brought them to the living room area, where Dante was pulling the champagne cork from the bottle. It eased out with a distinct pop, followed by a shimmer of French carbon dioxide of impeccable vintage.

He took the glasses from Addison and laughed at the size. "Thirsty?"

"If I was thirsty I would have brought out the bowls."

Dante chuckled as he poured them each a drink. Then he held up his glass. "To being thirsty," he said with a wink. When Addison didn't laugh, he turned more serious. "To your new job . . . and new friends."

At that, she tipped her glass toward his, making contact. Addison took a sip and closed her eyes as the bubbles played on her tongue and slipped down her throat. It was sublime.

When she looked up, Dante was studying her, delighted. "You're welcome," he said.

She laughed. "Don't get carried away with yourself."

He smiled and sat down on the sofa. "So, were you a concierge in New York?"

Addison sat next to him, leaving nearly two feet of space. "I don't want to talk about me."

"Don't be so stubborn."

She studied his hand holding the glass—masculine despite the manicured perfection—and forced herself to look away. "Fine," she said, taking another sip of champagne. "I was not a concierge. I was assistant to a matchmaker." Addison hadn't planned on divulging that particular piece of information, but she figured Dante wouldn't make an issue of it. Back home, she'd had a few friends who got angry when she refused to try to find them a match. They didn't understand how the process worked and assumed she could materialize a perfect man, combing through Piper's database for her personal use to produce a guy with the face of Ryan Reynolds, the body of Jason Momoa, the wallet of Elon Musk, and the devotion of Pete Buttigieg.

"You serious?" Dante asked.

"I know. It sounds ridiculous when there are about a billion websites for meeting people. But there are wealthy types on the East Coast who wouldn't dream of swimming in those waters. So they go to see Piper Leroy."

"Your boss?"

"Ex-boss."

"What happened?" he said. "Did you quit or . . ."

"Never mind. Tell me about the woman in the blue hat."

"Did you like it, though?" he pressed. "Fixing people up like that?"

"Now who's being stubborn?"

"Just answer the question," he said. "I'm genuinely curious. It's a weird-as-hell job."

"Sometimes," she said. "Sometimes I liked it, when the clients weren't assholes. And I was pretty good at it. But Piper was a piece of work, so . . ." She shrugged.

"So here you are," he said.

"So here I am," she repeated, omitting the critical details about her self-destructed life, ignoring the vision of Marco's pained face. She held up her glass as if it were another toast, and he tipped his tumbler against hers. They both drank.

"Now tell me about the mystery woman," she continued.

"That," he said, picking up the bottle and pouring more champagne into Addison's glass, "would be Maya."

"Maya," she echoed.

"Maya Mayfield."

"Why does that sound familiar?"

"Ever hear of a reality show called *Single File?*"

"Of course. It was huge for a while." Addison hesitated, and then, in a flash, it came to her. "Oh my god! Maya Mayfield! She and Brianna were the first lesbian couple on the show. It was such a big deal."

"Bingo."

"I can't believe I didn't recognize her. She's all over social media." Addison could picture her posts on Instagram. The beautiful wedding photos with Brianna. Lots of memes about the magic of love and honesty.

"She built a hell of a brand for herself," Dante said.

"So why is she suddenly so secretive?"

"I don't know for sure," he said, "but I have a good guess."

"Tell me."

Dante took another sip of his champagne, and Addison couldn't help watching the movement of his beautiful throat. He was clean shaven, but she could tell he had the kind of dark beard that would start to sprout a shadow within hours. She caught a whiff of his cologne and felt herself growing warm. Stop it, she told herself. You will not lust for this man. You will not.

He put down his glass and looked at her. "She's here alone. In Divorce Towers."

Addison focused, but it didn't seem like a very big deal. "So her marriage fell apart. Like exactly fifty percent of the population. Not sure that's a reason for someone to go underground. Unless . . ." She trailed off as she began connecting the dots.

"Unless," he prompted.

"Unless they've built a reputation as a relationship guru and their followers are completely invested in their own wonderful marriage."

He raised his glass to acknowledge her deduction.

Addison took out her phone, opened Instagram, and navigated to Maya's page. Even through her cracked screen, she could tell it was the same woman. Addison also noted that the page was still loaded with images of Maya and Brianna together.

"Have you told anyone else?" she asked.

"No reason to."

"Good," Addison said, feeling suddenly protective of a woman who'd had a bad breakup and needed some space. "Keep it to yourself."

"I can be very discreet," he said pointedly, then gave her a lingering look, his eyes traveling from her neck to her mouth and then back to her eyes.

"I'll keep that in mind," she said, regretting it almost immediately.

His eyes took her in again. "In case you have a change of heart about us?"

"I won't," she said quickly, knowing her resolve was weakening. She thought about his mouth on her throat, about that bed in the other room, about the heat of his flesh.

"You might," he said, as if reading her mind.

Addison stood. "Maybe you should go."

He reached out for her hand, rubbed his thumb against it. "Maybe I should stay."

His touch was almost too much, and her body responded with pulsing heat that started in her center and wriggled southward. She wanted to press against him, desperate and breathless. But no. She would stick with the plan. A year of celibacy. And then . . . all bets were off.

"Don't," she said, pulling her hand away.

"Are you sure?"

She paused, not sure at all. "I don't know."

He stood and moved closer, running his knuckles gently across her clavicle. She shivered. "Then why don't you let me stay," he whispered into her neck.

Her neck. Why did he have to go for her neck? It was her erogenous Achilles' heel. She hesitated, so eager to feel his mouth on her flesh she leaned into him.

"No," she said out loud as she stopped herself. Addison pushed him away and walked toward the door. She needed to get this over with quickly, or she'd run out of strength. "Goodbye, Dante."

He waited a long beat, staring at her, but she wouldn't look him in the eye. "If that's what you want," he finally said.

"Please. Just go."

He stood for another long moment, his expression softening. Then he gave her the same easy shrug he'd offered at the airport. "Benefits or not, I hope we can be friends," he said.

She gave a nod, and in the few steps it took for him to get from the sofa to the door, something in Addison shifted. She saw the trajectory of their relationship playing out in dozens of scenes just like this one, with frustration and desire building to an impossible crescendo. Eventually, they would hook up. It was inevitable. So why not get it over with right now? If she slept with him tonight, she'd get him out of her system and could start her twelve-month clock again tomorrow. It all seemed so very logical.

He opened the door, and she slammed it shut.

"Changed your mind already?" he asked, turning back to her.

Addison answered by putting her lips on his. He responded with the tenderest kiss, pulling her toward him. It was sweet, teasing. She pressed against his firm body, and then their mouths were open, tongues intertwined. His lips found her neck, and his hands reached for her bottom and drew her even closer. Addison was dizzy with desire.

She wanted him.

As his lips traveled down her collarbone in tiny kisses, she was so desperate for more mouth-to-skin contact that she pulled off her shirt. His hands found the silk of her back as his tongue traced its way down her chest toward the top of her bra.

"Bedroom," she whispered, but before they could move, a horrible ringing penetrated the room, shocking them apart.

"Is that a landline?" he asked.

Let's just ignore it, she thought and kissed him again, trying to resurrect the mood as the ringing stopped and started again.

"Fuck," she said, pulling away, because fraternizing with Dante might earn her a stern warning or even house arrest, but ignoring a resident would surely be a capital offense.

"You have to get that?" he asked when he saw her expression.

Addison sighed. "It's the bat phone."

"What does that mean?" he asked.

"It means," she said, pushing open the door, "that you have to leave."

Chapter 7

Still in her bra and jeans, Addison took a second to steady herself. She smoothed her hair, as if it might help her sound more professional, then grabbed the ringing phone. "Hello?" she said, in what she hoped was a polished yet friendly tone.

"Hello?" said a man's confused voice.

"Can I help you?"

"Is this Frankie?" he asked.

"It's Addison," she said. "I'm the, uh . . . the new concierge."

"You're not supposed to answer 'Hello.' You're supposed to answer 'Concierge. How may I help you?'"

Addison sighed. It was after midnight, and this guy was lecturing her on phone etiquette. "Sorry," she said. "It's my first day. Is everything okay?"

"No," he seethed. "It's not. They're at it again."

"Excuse me?"

"The sex fiends."

Addison glanced at the door, concerned for a brief second that this was about her and Dante. But of course that was ridiculous. "Are these your neighbors?"

"I know sex is a normal human function, and I don't begrudge anyone having vigorous relations, but I didn't buy a luxury condo to listen to that kind of violent bacchanalia coming through the walls in the middle of the night."

"Violent?" she asked. Surely that couldn't be right.

"You need to come up and tell them to stop. It's not my job," he said.

It's not my job, either, Addison thought. Not yet, anyway. And at this point, she had no idea what kind of protocol Frankie would insist on in such a situation. But she didn't think it was wise to wake her new boss with something like this in the middle of the night, and unfortunately, this weird guy was too angry to blow off.

"Of course," she said, hoping he was exaggerating and that it would be easy to placate him once they were face to face. "I'll be right up. Just let me get some information." Addison grabbed a pen and got his name and apartment number.

"You'd better hurry," he said before hanging up.

Addison knew exactly how impatient rich people could be, so she snatched her T-shirt from the floor, pulled it on, and dashed to the elevator. Inside, she pushed the button for the eleventh floor, where she would find Zach Brody in unit 1102. "Come on, come on," she whispered under her breath, watching the elevator make its ascent.

When the doors opened and she looked around, Addison realized she had made a mistake. She was in Tower B, and Zach Brody was in Tower A. She would have to take the elevator back to the ground floor, cross the marble lobby, and get on the other elevator. If this guy was anything like Piper Leroy's clients, he would be in a righteous fury by the time she arrived.

Sure enough, when the elevator doors swished open on Zach Brody's floor, a furious young man was pacing in front of it. He was tall and lean, with a boyish face and a clump of sandy-colored hair that splayed out like it was trying to make an escape. To Addison, he looked more like a petulant techie from the Geek Squad than a multimillionaire who could afford to live in Beekman Towers.

"Mr. Brody?" she said. "I'm Addison."

"What took you so long?" he demanded, then looked her up and down as his expression hardened. Addison wondered what on earth she might have done to warrant this reaction.

"And why aren't you wearing a red blazer?" he continued. "You're supposed to be wearing a red blazer."

Ironically, she was dressed almost exactly the same as he was, in a faded green T-shirt and jeans. But he was right—she should have worn the blazer. It would have projected an air of authority, especially if she had to knock on someone's door in the middle of the night. She hoped it wouldn't come to that.

Zach led her down the hall and opened the door to his apartment. Addison stepped inside the cavernous space and had to force herself not to gawk. The place was striking, with an open floor plan against the backdrop of a wall of windows, the night sky twinkling in such pristine splendor it almost seemed like Hollywood magic. The decor was modern without being cold—a mixture of self-assured blues and greens, accented with natural wood and large, dramatic plants. Zach Brody had either exquisite taste or a special genius for hiring the right decorator.

"What a beautiful apartment," she said. "It's—"

"This way," he interrupted, and led her to his bedroom.

It was a big square space—with the same massive windows and view as the living room—made cozy with darker colors. His rumpled bed was against an interior wall that no doubt abutted his next-door neighbor's unit.

"Listen," he commanded, pointing at the wall.

Addison cocked her head and heard nothing except the quiet scrape of some furniture.

"I don't—"

"Give it a second," he said.

They stood there by his bed and sure enough, a few moments later she heard a low moan in a man's voice.

"You like that?" asked an accented woman.

Another groan.

"You want more, don't you?" said the woman's voice.

"Please!"

"Louder!" she commanded.

"Please!" begged the man.

"I can't hear you."

Maybe he should tell her to take out her earbuds, Addison wanted to joke, but she suspected Zach Brody didn't have a keen sense of humor. And in this situation, she couldn't blame him. No one wanted to hear that coming through their bedroom wall.

"Please, Mommy!" the man screamed. "Please!"

Mommy? Addison hoped this was just some weird-as-fuck role-playing. There was more noise then, and possibly a slap, followed by strange gurgling.

"Well?" Zach said, folding his arms.

"You're absolutely right," Addison consoled. "You shouldn't be subjected to this."

"I was sleeping," he said. "They woke me up."

"I'm very sorry that happened. I'll have a word with the residents first thing in the morning." She said a silent prayer that he wouldn't insist on immediate action. Not that she was intimidated by the idea of meeting the fetishists. Addison knew that even the kinkiest people could be perfectly reasonable human beings. Hell, she'd had a friend in college who paid her tuition by working as a dominatrix, and she was one of the sweetest and smartest people Addison knew. But the very idea of confronting these folks in the middle of their activities made her cringe.

Zach Brody's jaw went hard as stone. "You're not waiting until the morning," he seethed.

"They've quieted down," she said cheerily. "I'm sure they won't wake you again."

"They'll be at it all night. They've done it before. And I have a meeting in the morning."

Addison tried to think of something else to say so she could get a dialogue going with this guy and soften him. Also, she was pretty sure the gurgling meant the freak in 1104 was done with tonight's adventure and that if she chatted with Zach Brody long enough, the neighbors would settle down and go to sleep.

"This has happened before?" she asked.

"Twice."

"And you reported it to Frankie?"

"To the other one," he said. "Jenna. I don't know what she said to them, but it stopped for a while."

Addison knew he was referring to the last concierge, who ran off to Vegas with one of the residents for a quickie marriage before moving to Sonoma. At the moment, a cushy life in wine country didn't seem like such a bad idea.

After listening for another few seconds, Addison concluded that the neighbors had indeed quieted for the night and was about to say so when a fleecy white ball of fur appeared from under the bed. But it was no ordinary cat. It was a lushly coated designer feline that went perfectly with the decor. Zach bent to scoop her up, and the animal seemed to go liquid in his arms.

"You okay, Betty?" he cooed, petting the cat's head.

Addison bit her lip. "Like Betty Boop?"

"Like Betty *Snyder*," he said defensively. "She doesn't even know who Betty Boop is."

"But she knows who Betty Snyder is?" Addison asked, wondering if he was the type who credited his cat with human intelligence. "*I* don't even know who Betty Snyder is."

Zach was staring down at the cat, his mouth moving the tiniest bit into a near smile.

"Oh!" she said. "You were joking."

"Yes," he said, matter-of-factly.

"Okay, so who's Betty Snyder?"

"Google it."

Really? Google it? Addison felt like she had stumbled into the middle of some antagonistic social media thread. But she simply said, "Sure, I'll get right on that."

He folded his arms, looking impatient. "I'm serious. You might find it edifying."

"I'll take it under consideration," Addison said, trying to find his gentler side again. "But can I ask if she's Persian? Such a beauty." She didn't know much about cats except what she had learned from her old boss, who had three of them. Also that she was extremely allergic. A tickle formed in her throat.

"Yes," Zach said, rubbing his cheek against the cat's soft head. "And she needs her sleep too."

As Addison stifled a sneeze, the woman's voice came through the wall again.

"Stop that!" she yelled, and there was a sharp sound, like a belt. Or maybe a whip.

"I can't help it," said the man.

"You're a bad boy!" the woman shouted.

"I am!" wept the man. "I am!"

Zach looked at Addison. "You have to do something," he said, and Addison swallowed against a lump of dread because she knew he was right.

Chapter 8

After leaving Zach Brody's apartment, Addison straightened her shoulders and approached the neighbor's door, trying to arrange her face in a pleasant expression. Just be straightforward, she told herself. No judgment. It's all about keeping the peace.

She pressed the buzzer and prayed she wouldn't be greeted by a woman in a black leather cat suit and stiletto boots.

For a moment, she heard nothing. Then there was movement inside the apartment, though she couldn't make out any footsteps. At last, the faint voice of an elderly woman asked, "Who's there?"

"Concierge," Addison answered.

The door swung open, and Addison found herself looking down at a pale-haired woman in a motorized wheelchair. She had to be at least eighty years old, with a large head atop a body so tiny it almost seemed as if the chair could swallow her whole. This couldn't be the "Mommy" woman with the whip . . . could it?

"I, uh . . . ," Addison stammered.

"Oh, shit," came the husky reply. "Are they at it again?"

Addison blinked. The voice. The language. It was all so incongruous. But it was a relief to know this wasn't the dominatrix she'd heard.

"I'm Addison Torres, the new concierge. I just wanted to make sure everything was all right. One of the residents heard some . . . sounds."

The woman shook her head. "I was reading and took my hearing aids out. Otherwise I would have told them to quiet down."

"I see," Addison said, though she didn't. Who was the woman living with? And why did they think it was okay to indulge in their kinky role-play with this frail old lady in the next room? "Are you all right?"

"Yes, cookie," the woman said with a laugh. "Absolutely." She held out a bony hand. "Regina English. Nice to meet you. Come in."

Addison gently shook the woman's papery hand and considered whether she should accept the invitation. It would be more official if she stayed outside and asked to have a word with the offending parties at the doorway. Wasn't that just the kind of boundary-setting Frankie had warned her about? On the other hand, maybe this elderly lady needed some intervention, and Addison was the only person who could provide it.

"We're harmless," the woman said. "I promise."

Addison hoped that was true and followed her inside. "I'm very sorry to bother you, Mrs. English," she said, shutting the door behind her.

"It's Dr. English," the woman corrected, leading Addison farther into the living room. "But you can call me Regina."

"Medical doctor?" Addison asked.

"Yes—retired psychiatrist."

Addison nodded, impressed, and realized this was no helpless little old lady. A woman of her generation couldn't have made it through medical school without a good dose of grit.

Storing away the information, she looked around the condo, which seemed pretty normal. There were no torture racks or handcuffs, no shelves of dildos. In fact, the place had a museum-like quality, as if the expensive antiques and framed paintings were on display for the public. Addison half expected to see signs for a gift shop.

"Can I get you something?" the woman asked her. "A cup of tea? A cocktail?"

A cocktail? Addison almost laughed at the offer, picturing a night of pounding back mojitos with Dr. Regina English. "I'm fine, thanks," she said, and listened for the kind of noises she'd heard from Zach's place. "I think I should speak with—"

"Yes, of course. Have a seat." She pointed toward an overstuffed leather sofa. "I'll be right back."

As the doctor whirred out of the room and down the hall, Addison remained standing, hoping to project an air of authority despite her attire. She heard a knock on an interior door.

The doctor coughed to clear her throat. "Geoffrey," she called.

There was some murmuring then, and a few moments later Regina English wheeled back into the living room.

"My son will be right with us," she said.

Her son. Of course. Who else would it be? Addison tried playing psychiatrist herself, reflecting on a grown man who lived with his diminutive yet powerful mother, and had a weird oedipal fetish that manifested in bondage and discipline.

"I've spoken with him about it in the past," the doctor continued.

"Excuse me?"

"The loud fornicating. I've always encouraged Geoffrey to live a full and satisfying sex life. What better way to celebrate being human? The only caveat is being mindful of the neighbors."

This was the conversation she had with her *son*? Addison wondered how it was possible Beverly Hills rich people were even weirder than Manhattan rich people. She shook her head to clear the thought away and changed the subject.

"I like your paintings," she said.

"You'll have to tell Geoffrey," said Dr. English. "These are his—he's an art dealer."

Of course he is, Addison thought. It's just the kind of pseudojob a trust fund guy would have. She had a client like that in New York—he listed his profession as *collector*, but really he just bought expensive toys with his inherited fortune.

"Which one is your favorite?" Regina English continued.

Addison glanced around, trying to find one that moved her. They were all modern and abstract, and she wondered if the question was a kind of Rorschach test. She imagined pointing to the blue one only to hear the doctor say *Aha! You think you need to keep recreating the trauma of your parents' death, so you sabotage your most important relationships. Tell me more about how you cheated on your fiancé.*

Her eyes landed on a large geometric color-blocked painting over the sofa in a familiar style. "Is that a real Rothko?" she asked. Addison knew the artist's paintings sold for tens of millions of dollars—a fact she had learned from her ex-boss Piper, who had one client wealthy enough to afford an original.

"It is," said the doctor, looking impressed that Addison had identified it. "Were you involved in the arts?"

"I just knew someone back in New York who had one."

"New York," the doctor repeated, as if it was a bit of fascinating information. "An exciting city for a young person."

"Absolutely," Addison agreed. She sensed the shrink was probing for more information, but didn't want to offer anything.

"Must have been hard to leave your family."

It would have been, Addison thought, if my parents were alive. Instead she just said, "Not really."

The doctor waited a long beat, as if expecting Addison to elaborate. Finally she asked, "Why did you decide to leave?"

Boundaries, Addison coached herself. Do not open up to this woman. "Time for a new career, a change of scenery." There. Perfectly vague.

Regina English nodded, as if the response was loaded and worthy of thought. "What was the old career?"

Addison sighed at the direct question—a hard one to wriggle out of without being rude. "I was in a service industry," she said, and when the doctor's eyebrows lifted, Addison had a mental facepalm moment. She had made it sound like she managed a massage parlor. Or freelanced as a dominatrix.

"I worked for a matchmaker who had some very upscale clients," she clarified, and hoped it wasn't a mistake to divulge this.

The doctor looked intrigued. "What interesting work. How did you decide who to match with whom?"

"Various methods."

"Such as?"

The woman was not easily discouraged. But at this point, Addison couldn't see any reason to hold back. "Some of it was scientific," she said. "We had long questionnaires for clients to fill out. But a lot of it was just talking to people and getting to know them."

"So we have something in common—you did a lot of listening."

"I guess I did."

"Were you good at the job?"

"Honestly?" Addison asked, hedging so as not to seem too immodest.

"Of course," said the doctor. "I always want honesty."

Addison smiled. "Then yes, I rocked it. At least most of the time. How about you? Were you a good psychiatrist?"

"I rocked it, as well," she said. "Most of the time. But right now I wish I had some of your matchmaking skills."

"Why's that?"

"My darling nurse. Beautiful person inside and out. She deserves to find love."

Addison offered a tight smile, hoping the woman was not going to ask her to find a match for her nurse. "A lot of people have luck with dating sites," she said.

At that, Addison heard footsteps and looked up to see a freshly showered man enter the room. He was sixtyish and tall, with an unfortunate chin, one small hoop earring, and short silver bangs plastered to his forehead like Julius Caesar's. The frames of his oversize eyeglasses had a checkerboard pattern—very pop art. Addison assumed this was meant to convey a sophisticated sense of irony. And wealth. But the effect was cartoonish.

"Addison Torres," said the older woman, "may I present my son, Geoffrey English."

He gave Addison's hand a firm shake, showing no sign of embarrassment. "You're the new concierge," he said.

"Tomorrow's my first official day," she said with a smile. "And I'm sorry to bother you at this hour, but one of your neighbors . . ."

"My apologies," he said. "My lady friend and I—"

"It's okay," Addison interrupted, not wanting to hear any kind of explanation. "I just need to ask you to keep it a little quieter."

"Of course," he said. "You have my word. Also, please understand . . ." He looked back toward the closed bedroom door and lowered his voice. "She's not a prostitute."

Addison stared for a moment, taking in the information. He didn't seem to care that she knew he'd begged to be hurt and called the woman "Mommy," as long as she didn't think he paid for it. "It's . . . I . . . ," Addison stammered, wondering how to respond. "I didn't think—"

"I'm actually very much in love with her."

"Oh, for heaven's sake, Geoffrey," said his mother. "Be realistic."

Geoffrey folded his arms and turned to Addison. "My mother thinks my lady friend is too good for me," he explained.

Addison didn't know where to look. But she did know one thing—she did not want to be in the middle of this.

"I never said that," Dr. English cut in. "But you must know she doesn't return your feelings."

"Maybe not yet," he told her.

"Dearest," she said, "I only want you to be happy, and you're chasing an impossible dream."

Addison cleared her throat. "Okay, well. I don't want to take up any more of your evening."

"It was lovely to meet you," Dr. English said. "Please stop by any time."

Great, Addison thought, my new BFFs. But she just gave a wave, and left.

Chapter 9
ARNIE

Arnie loved the early morning. He loved knowing a full day was stretched out before him, full of nothing but possibilities. He loved waking at sunrise, taking in the newspapers that had been left at his doorstep by one of the porters, and hurrying to the gym before it got busy with people streaming in for exercise classes and one-on-ones with the personal trainers.

Now more than ever, Arnie was determined to keep up with his workout schedule so he'd be in the best possible shape when his ex, Paulette, arrived back in the US. Today, however, he'd need to cut it a little short, as he was making breakfast for his niece on her first official day as concierge of Beekman Towers.

Arnie pushed through the glass doors to the building's gym and saw that only three other people had arrived before him to work out—all women. Not a bad way to start his day.

"Good morning!" he called, and everyone looked up.

"Hi, Arnie!" said Louise Wagner from the elliptical.

"Yoo-hoo!" sang Fran Kennedy, who was next to her.

"Hey, Doc," grunted Barbara Conti, who was doing crunches.

Arnie was delighted that they seemed genuinely happy to see him. He enjoyed flirting with pretty women, even when he knew it wouldn't lead anywhere. With Louise, of course, it could. They'd slept together once—or was it twice?—and it struck him there was an open invitation to her bed. But he knew he needed to tread carefully with her, as she was looking for a boyfriend and he didn't want to get embroiled in anything that might end badly. Arnie never liked hurting anyone's feelings.

Fran Kennedy, on the other hand, already had a boyfriend and was not interested in sleeping with Arnie. Still, it was pretty clear that she wanted him to be more attracted to her than to Louise. She was that competitive with her friend.

Barbara Conti had a full-time job, so he didn't see her around much. But when he did, it wasn't easy to look away from her pouty lips. He probably spent more time thinking about them than he should.

Arnie accepted a towel from the gym attendant and got on the treadmill to start his warm-up, wondering what Paulette would make of all this. Surely she'd be jealous—maybe even furious. She'd want his eyes on her and her alone. But of course she rarely awoke before noon, so he'd be able to continue these workouts, thinking about her warm body in his bed. And when they made ferocious love, she'd know she had all of him—heart, mind, and body.

But for now, Arnie was a free man, and he was damn well going to take advantage of that fact. He looked again at Barbara and those pillowy lips.

Louise dismounted from the elliptical and stepped onto the tread-mill next to Arnie. Fran followed quickly behind, taking the machine on the other side of him. Arnie felt almost drunk in a haze of estrogen. He grinned.

"I was telling Fran about your pretty niece," Louise said.

"So darling of you to get her a job here," Fran added.

He turned his treadmill up to a slow jog and answered their curious questions about Addison. Was she single . . . Wasn't she the one whose parents had died so tragically . . . What did she do in New York . . . Did he think she might be interested in Dante?

"That's her business," he said, as if he didn't love gossiping every bit as much as they did. "I don't think she's going to want her uncle Arnie involved in her social life."

The women moved on to other dishy news about the building and then asked Arnie if he was going to stick around for Raphael's Pilates class. He explained that he had to cut it short today and would be leaving after his leg workout.

He was in midgrunt, working out his quads, when he saw an unfamiliar woman enter the gym—always an intriguing moment for Arnie. This lovely lady had short dark hair, a long neck, and the posture of a ballet dancer. He pegged her as late forties, and she had the tension around her eyes of someone who was recently divorced. Arnie finished his reps, ran his hand through his hair, and wiped himself dry. He approached as she was examining the exercise equipment.

"Hello," he said, extending his hand like a politician. "Arnie Glass."

She looked surprised by the intrusion but recovered quickly. "Melody Forrest," she said, shaking his hand firmly. Her voice was strong.

"Now that's a poetic name."

She grinned. "Makes it easier to remember."

"*I'm* certainly not going to forget it." He offered her his most charming smile. "Did you just move in?"

"I did, I did," she said quickly, and he could tell she buzzed with an inner electricity—the kind of energy that was hard to tame. "How did you know?"

Arnie shrugged. "I haven't seen you before."

"He's the mayor!" Louise called over from the treadmill.

Melody looked surprised. "The mayor?"

"She's kidding," he said. "But I know almost everyone in the building, so . . . I guess that makes me Mayor Arnie."

She considered that with a tilt of her head, studying his face. "Let me know if you need help with your next campaign," she said, her eyes sweeping his entirety.

Arnie took a sharp inhale. This woman was interested. And she was hot.

"Are you in politics?" he asked, noting that she had the frenetic energy of a Kellyanne Conway.

She shook her head. "Public relations."

In his plastic surgery practice, he'd had a few patients who'd worked in PR, and they were all dynamos. Arnie shifted his weight, intrigued.

"You must work very hard," he said.

"That's why it's good to know the gym isn't too crowded at this hour. I can fit in my workouts before going to the office."

"Well, if you ever need a tour around the building, I'm your man."

"I'm off *today*," she said, a tease in her voice.

This lady didn't kid around—she was ready, willing, and able. He liked that. A lot. And sure, he understood she was probably eager to get revenge on her ex for whatever had driven their marriage apart, but Arnie was okay with that. Hell, it was practically the motto of Divorce Towers: Don't get even. Get laid.

"Why don't you stop by around ten?" he said. "I'm unit 605, Tower B."

"Be ready for me," she cooed, and floated out of the room like she was riding a current.

Arnie stood for a moment, watching her leave. Then he went back to his workout in a gym that had suddenly turned much, much steamier.

Chapter 10

Later, as he whisked pancake batter to prepare for Addison's arrival, Arnie was still thinking about Melody Forrest. She seemed like a vixen—just the kind of woman to keep him occupied while he awaited the return of his one true love. He threw a drop of water on the skillet, and it sizzled. Arnie closed his eyes and let his imagination take over as he envisioned Melody pushing her way into his apartment, hungry and aggressive. He held tight to his fantasy until the moment Addison rang the buzzer. That, he believed, was his superpower—the ability to turn it on and off like a light switch. Well, one of his superpowers. Arnie liked to think of himself as a man of many talents. But for right now, he was simply Uncle Arnie. And he adored his darling niece more than he could ever express. She was like the daughter—or, more accurately, granddaughter—he never had.

He opened the door to see her standing there in her red concierge blazer. "Sweetheart!" he gushed. "Happy first day of work! You look marvelous."

Addison returned his hug. "Thank you, Uncle Arnie."

He led her into the kitchen, which was modern and sleek, with slate gray cabinets and moody lighting, like a page from *Architectural Digest: Rich Bachelor Edition*.

Arnie began spilling batter onto the griddle with practiced expertise, and Addison offered to help. When he shooed her away, she poured herself a cup of coffee and took a seat at the wide island. Arnie moved aside his newspapers as well as the imitation Fabergé egg Paulette had bought for him in the 1980s, when such things were a symbol of status and taste. It had been a gift to celebrate the opening of his new private practice, and she had placed it on the corner of the desk in his office, where patients could admire it while they consulted with him about their needs and concerns. Now, it had a prominent position on his kitchen counter, and he thought about Paulette every time he looked at it—and even more so since getting her email. She'd be so pleased he'd kept it all these years.

He went back to flipping the pancakes.

"You excited?" he asked over his shoulder. "Nervous?"

"A little of both, I guess."

"You'll knock it out of the park. And today will be fun. Frankie is great—she'll show you around, introduce you to the residents."

Addison sipped her coffee. "I already slummed with a couple of them last night."

He detected a note of cynical amusement in her voice, and he turned to study her face. "Oh?" he asked, raising an eyebrow.

Addison proceeded to tell him about the indignant phone call she'd gotten from Zach Brody.

"He's a sad one," Arnie said.

"Why's that?"

"From what I've heard, he founded some tech company that was on the brink of success when his partner and girlfriend stole the business and ran away with his money."

"That's shitty, but it's not like he's destitute," Addison said. "I saw his apartment."

"Granted, he's not starving, but he was poised to make *billions*."

Addison shook her head, clearly taking it all in, and Arnie knew she was trying to process the disappointment of being a mere millionaire. She sipped her coffee; then her brow went tight in concentration.

"Did you ever hear of Betty Snyder?" she asked.

"Does she live in the building?"

"Hang on," Addison said and took out her phone. She spent a few seconds tapping at her cracked screen, then muttered, "Well, that tracks. She was an early computer scientist. Worked on something called ENIAC. It was—"

"The first computer. I know, kiddo."

"He named his cat after her. It's kind of sweet, but also off-the-charts nerdy."

He smiled, amused. "You're going to meet a lot of interesting characters here."

"Last night was definitely a head start," she said, and went on to recount what she had heard through the wall of Zach's bedroom.

"Some people forget they have neighbors." Arnie clucked.

"To me, the weirdest part was that the man wanted to be sure I understood he wasn't paying for it."

Not weird at all, Arnie thought—a guy needed to know he could attract a woman. And he needed the world to know it too. "It's the male ego," he explained as he slid three pancakes onto a plate and placed it in front of his niece.

"His mother sure didn't help that cause. She said the lady is out of his league."

"Ouch," he said. "Was she gorgeous or something?"

Addison picked up the maple syrup and doused her pancakes. "I didn't get to meet her. But he insisted she's the love of his life."

Arnie nodded, taking in the phrase *love of his life*. He had wanted to tell Addison about Paulette's return, and this struck him as a perfect segue.

"Speaking of . . . ," he said, taking a stack of pancakes for himself. "Guess who I heard from." He sat opposite Addison and poured a careful amount of syrup over his breakfast.

She studied his face for a good long beat. "Lara?" she guessed, naming his fourth wife.

He exhaled. "Lara has moved on."

"Oh, god," she said. "Not Paulette?"

He stabbed a wedge-shaped bite of pancakes. "She's coming back to the States."

"Oh, Uncle Arnie," Addison chided. "That's not—"

"She broke up with the Italian!" he explained, certain she could understand this was excellent news—a dream come true. "She'll be in town by Christmas, and I think she wants me to take her back."

"And you *want* to take her back?"

"Of course!"

"But it was a terrible relationship."

"Oh, honey, no."

Addison looked stricken. "She sent you to the hospital! You nearly lost an eye."

"That was an accident," he insisted. It had been a terrible fight. Paulette had worked herself into a jealous rage after a friend's wife asked for his opinion on her breast implants. It led to a litany of suspicions she'd been storing up for months. When she brought up Cancún—the vacation he'd turned down—things went from bad to worse. He'd never given her a good excuse for why he didn't want to go, but that was only because he was embarrassed to tell her about the diarrhea he'd had the last time he'd been to Mexico. She knew he was hiding something and assumed the worst—that he was having an affair with the new receptionist in his office. She pounded at his chest, screaming *Admit it, you fucking bastard! Admit it!*

Then he made the biggest mistake of all. He told her to calm down. Women hated that—especially Paulette—and she drew her hand back to slap him across the face. Trying to duck, he tripped over the leg of a chair and fell into the glass coffee table, which shattered. There was so much blood Paulette had to throw out the rug. Arnie still had scars by his right eye and across his left shoulder.

"She attacked you!" Addison insisted.

He shook his head, swallowing a bite of pancakes like regret. "I never should have agreed to look at Heidi Rosenstein's breasts."

"Uncle Arnie, this is crazy. You can't take her back. She's a psycho."

"She's just . . . passionate. And I love her with my whole heart."

Addison looked concerned. "She's not right for you."

"My dear, I've dated a lot of women, and I've never met anybody else who makes me feel this way."

His niece put down her fork. "That's because you're dating airheads and bimbos and stoners with daddy issues. You need a woman of substance—someone who can challenge you without trying to kill you."

"If I ever found someone like that, I'd probably marry her in a second."

Addison bit her lip and went back to eating her pancakes. Arnie knew she didn't want to talk about it anymore, so he let it go. Besides, there was no sense in trying to defend Paulette. She was simply too complicated to explain.

They finished breakfast, and a short while later Addison thanked him with a kiss on the cheek and left to start her day. Then Arnie got busy tidying up, certain Melody Forrest would follow through on her promise to come by. After all, she didn't seem like the type to get cold feet. Then again, he knew that some women liked to tease—especially coming off a divorce, as they just needed to know they still had the goods to attract a man. Melody Forrest had it in spades, and if she let him, he'd do everything in his power to convince her of that.

A short while later, it looked like he would get his chance. Melody showed up at his door in a tight blue dress, wearing a big black purse and four-inch spike heels with gold straps. Her perfume was intoxicating.

"You look smashing, my dear," he said, and meant it. "But those might not be the best shoes for a long walk around the property."

"I don't intend to do much walking," she cooed, a hand on his chest.

Melody Forrest stepped in for a deep and hungry kiss. This woman moved as fast as a porn video, and for a moment, Arnie was taken back. But he returned the kiss and quickly found an excuse to slip into the bathroom and take a Viagra. When he returned, she was standing in the middle of his bedroom, stark naked except for the strappy high heels.

"Melody, you are one beautiful song," he said, and then moved in to do what he did best.

As it turned out, she had no interest in a tour of Beekman Towers and barely wanted to stay for a snuggle after they made vigorous love.

"I have tons to do today, babe," she said, wriggling back into her dress.

Arnie was struck by her use of *babe*, which people usually reserved for established relationships—not someone you met a few hours ago and jumped into bed with. But he didn't get himself worked up. It was probably just her sexy talk.

"You'll call me?" she asked.

"Of course," he said, and she picked up his phone to put her number into it. Then she gave him one last kiss and left.

Later, when his doorbell rang, he thought she had come back. But it was his elderly redheaded neighbor—the former movie star Sally Conrad, leaning on her cane. The poor dear was having trouble opening a pill bottle. The last time it had been a jar of preserves, and as always, she led with the same joke: "I heard you know how to get a woman's top off." She was a pistol, but one of these days Arnie would need to gently suggest she hire someone to look after her. For now, he was happy to help.

After that, Arnie finished reading his newspapers, went online to scan the medical journals his assistant had forwarded, and got ready for a late lunch with one of his golf pals. Before he left, however, something felt off, and Arnie stopped to look around. His eyes did a sweep of the place, and that's when he realized what it was. The Fabergé egg was gone.

Chapter 11
ADDISON

While growing up, Addison had never heard her mother say an unkind word about another person, with one exception. Her aunt Paulette.

There had been mutters about "that woman" throughout her childhood, but on the day of the phone call, the invectives came to a head.

"The bitch sent Uncle Arnie to the hospital," she heard her mother say to her father. "He might lose his eye."

"My god!" her father had replied.

"I could strangle her with my bare hands," her mother said.

Addison hadn't been more than eight at the time, but she remembered a good deal about the episode, as her mother had left Addison for the very first time, flying out to California with her grandmother—Uncle Arnie's sister—to "talk some sense into him." Addison loved her father but was young enough to find the situation unsettling, as she was so used to the precise way her mother cooked her meals, packed her lunches, and got her ready for school. Somehow, though, she'd screwed up the courage and persevered.

Mama and Nana returned from California with the news that Arnie's eye was saved but that the mission had failed. He wasn't pressing charges, wasn't leaving her. As it happened, the marriage only went on to last another few years, when "that woman" ran off to Europe with an

Italian designer. Addison's parents had huddled in the kitchen with her grandmother, unaware that she stood close by, listening.

"How's he handling it?" her father had asked.

"Terrible," her mother said.

"He'll get over it," her grandmother added, and it seemed she was right, as less than three years later they all flew out to California for his third wedding.

Now, as Addison thought about Paulette's return, all she could envision were the photographs she'd found stuck in an envelope in the back of the junk drawer in the kitchen, showing her uncle's bruised and swollen face with a line of gruesome black stitches angled down from the corner of his bloodred eye. It was all she needed to know about Paulette. Addison touched her heart necklace, which had belonged to her mom, and made a silent promise. She was going to find Arnie a love match before Paulette returned to the States.

She took a surreptitious look around the lobby of Beekman Towers, trying to scope out any suitable contenders.

"Am I going too fast?" asked her boss, Frankie. She was showing Addison how to use the software on her concierge tablet, where she would track every request from a resident, deployed or otherwise.

"I think I got it," Addison said.

"Good, let's walk."

Frankie gave her a brisk tour, introducing Addison to the doormen and porters on duty and explaining their responsibilities toward the residents, which included making deliveries of packages, dry cleaning, take-out food, flowers, and anything else that came into the building. Occasionally, when things got busy, some of these responsibilities would fall to Addison. Frankie also introduced her to Nikolai, the mountain-size security director, who promised Addison he would have her back if she ever had a problem.

Next they went to the pristine tennis courts, where there were three games and one lesson going on, balls thwacking back and forth in dizzying rhythm. They went back inside and entered the hushed quiet of the spa, followed by the chaotic hair salon, where it seemed everyone was trading loud gossip and beauty tips over the electric whir of hair dryers and the haze of cloying scents. When they reached the rooftop pool, they were greeted by a warm breeze. It was still early, and there were only a few sunbathers on lounges. The water was crystal blue and the surface so still it reflected the single cloud in the sky in glorious high-def. The day was heating up, and Addison was tempted to dive in, disrupting the glass-like perfection. But she would wait until after work, glad that Frankie had explained that her perks included free use of the facilities, as well as a discount at the overpriced salon and spa.

The lifeguard—a young guy with pale-blond dreads—was just getting set up for the day. He climbed to his perch and adjusted his visor.

"Jake!" Frankie called to him. "This is Addison, our new concierge."

"Nice to meet you!" Addison said.

"Bruh," he replied with a nod.

Bruh? That was the whole greeting? Addison looked at Frankie. "How old is he?" she whispered, as the kid didn't seem more than fifteen.

"Twenty-two."

When Addison's face registered surprise, Frankie explained, "You'll see that a lot in LA. People often seem much younger than they are. It was kind of a shock when I got here from Chicago."

Addison liked that Frankie was an outsider, like herself. She knew that she'd be a valuable ally . . . if Addison could manage to stay on her good side.

Jake gave two quick toots on his whistle to open the pool, and a slim figure emerged from the shadows, diving into the deep end with a quick and graceful slice. Addison did a double take. It was Zach Brody, and he was a hell of a swimmer.

She surmised he'd been able to get a good night's sleep after she left and wondered if he might thank her for the intervention. Addison glanced over as he came up for air and saw that he was looking straight at her. She gave a small wave, but he ignored her, diving back under the surface.

Earlier, Addison had told Frankie about what had transpired with Zach and his noisy neighbors. Frankie had nodded along to the story and seemed to understand that Addison had handled it as best she could under the circumstances. But Frankie explained that in the future, such issues could best be managed with a phone call, now that Addison had access to the contact information for all the residents.

Frankie showed Addison the Splash Bar, which was the closest thing the building had to a restaurant. It wasn't yet open for the day, but would serve meals like sandwiches, salads, hamburgers, and hot dogs, as well as soft drinks, wine, and beer. Addison knew just where she'd be having dinner most nights.

They were approached by an overly tan white-haired man wearing a bright-yellow bathing suit, matching bright-yellow pool shoes, and a scowl.

"Hello, Mr. Posner," said Frankie warmly.

He knit his brows. "I thought I had an appointment this morning!" he grumbled.

"I'm sorry?" Frankie said.

"My massage!" he said, sounding irritated that Frankie didn't know what he was talking about. "I showed up, and they said I wasn't on the schedule."

"I believe that's tomorrow," Frankie said calmly and turned to Addison. "Can you check?"

Addison swiped at the iPad Frankie had given her and looked up the spa appointments. "Yes," she said cheerily to the old man, "you're on for nine a.m. tomorrow."

The man glared at Frankie. "I want one today."

"I'll let them know to call you if they have a cancellation," she said. "How's that?"

He pointed a thumb at Addison. "Can she give me one?"

"Mr. Posner, this is Addison, our new concierge. She doesn't give massages, but she'll be happy to help you with scheduling."

"I don't see why she can't just take a few minutes and oil me up. I can lay down on a lounge in the shade. I'll make it worth her while."

"You know we can't do that, Howard," Frankie said, with the firmness of a schoolteacher. Addison couldn't help noticing she'd switched over to using his first name.

He hesitated. "She's a good-looking girl."

Frankie folded her arms. "Howard," she admonished.

"All right, all right," he grumbled, and walked away.

"Some of them are like children," Frankie said when the man was out of earshot.

"Like *entitled* children," Addison corrected, keeping her voice even. The guy was a shit, but it was nothing she couldn't handle.

Frankie nodded. "There are some residents who think they own the staff. That's why it's so important to establish boundaries."

"Got it," Addison said, taking a look around. Now that the pool was open, a few more people were trickling in.

"I still need to show you the gym and the indoor pool," Frankie said, "but let's take a walk around, and I'll introduce you to the residents."

As they approached the lounges surrounding the pool, Frankie's cell phone rang. She looked down. "I should take that."

"Go ahead," Addison said. "I'll introduce myself."

"You sure?"

"I'm fine," she said, and meant it. In fact, it would be a good opportunity for her to get a jump on interviewing prospects for Arnie. If she was going to find him a love match before Paulette's return, there would be no time to waste.

While Frankie moved into a shaded corner to take her call, Addison scoped the area for prospects. Of course, it was hard to assess the character of people lounging by a pool. Most were chatting with friends or scrolling through their phones, though there was one woman sitting on a chair in the shade, reading a book. Addison noted she was dressed in street clothes, not a bathing suit, which was curious.

Someone called her name, and Addison looked over to see a waving hand. She realized it belonged to the emaciated Julia Roberts look-alike who had greeted Arnie in the lobby the day before.

"Louise, right?" Addison said as she approached.

The woman gave a massive smile and introduced her friend, Fran Kennedy.

"I don't know if your uncle mentioned us," Fran said, "but we're very good friends."

"We worked out with him this morning," Louise added.

"Will you be at the concierge desk today?" Fran asked. "We were planning to ask for lunch reservations for Saturday."

"Happy to help," Addison said, then added, "Anything exciting on your agenda for today?" She knew it sounded like innocent chitchat, but she was probing for any indication these women might be deeper than the very first step into the pool. She had low hopes.

"I wanted to play tennis, but I promised my friend Nancy I'd help her pick out a new sofa," Fran said, hand to heart as if to illustrate her sacrifice.

"Didn't she just get a new sofa?" Louise asked her.

"That was for the guesthouse," Fran explained.

Louise looked up at Addison, shielding her eyes from the sun. "I'm having lunch with my daughter. Then we might do Rodeo Drive."

"Are you getting that handbag?" Fran asked her.

"I don't know. I was up half the night thinking about it."

Addison had heard enough. Even combined, Tweedledee and Tweedleditz didn't have the brainpower to hold her uncle's attention. She had higher hopes for the woman she'd seen reading a book. "Ladies, please let me know if there's anything I can do for you."

They thanked her and waved goodbye. As Addison turned, she was waylaid by Zach Brody, who was toweling his hair, his faded red trunks riding low on his hips. He had a boyish body—lean but taut. She smiled, anticipating gratitude for her intervention the night before.

"You never came back," he said, sounding petulant.

"I'm sorry?" she asked, confused.

"You said you were going to talk to them, and then you just disappeared."

She blinked at him. Was this guy for real? "I told you I was going to take care of it, and I did."

"How would I know you'd completed the task?"

"You didn't hear any more . . . noises, did you?"

"For all I knew, they could have been taking a respite. If you had told me you rectified the situation, I would have slept better."

"I didn't want to disturb you," Addison said, adding, "I hope you got enough rest. I know you have an important meeting this morning."

"Had," he corrected. "It was a Zoom meeting at six a.m."

"Wow," she said, "that's early." She expected a friendly shift in tone as he explained he was talking to Japan or Dubai or something, but he just stared at her.

At last he said, "I suppose you're still at the beginning of your learning curve," and it took Addison a moment to understand the reason for the observation. He was making a small concession—forgiving her for making such an egregious error.

"Today's actually my first day," she said, smiling. It was meant to soften him, to elicit a *congratulations* or *good luck*. But Zach rubbed at his hair with the towel again, causing it to spike out like it belonged to a cartoon character that had just been electrocuted.

"I'm sure you'll do better next time," he said, and turned to walk away.

As she watched him throw the towel around his neck, heading toward the men's lounge, she remembered something. "Hey!" she called. "Betty Snyder was the OG computer nerd!"

He paused and then turned to face her, his expression softening into that tiny smile again, but he caught himself.

"Pioneer," he corrected. "She was a programming pioneer."

Then he was gone, and Addison turned toward the other person she had wanted to speak to—the lovely woman reading a book. But she was gone too.

Chapter 12

Addison spent the rest of the morning sitting behind the concierge desk with Frankie at her side. A steady stream of residents stopped by on their way out and in, either to say hello and introduce themselves, or to make reservations for the salon, the spa, a tennis court, a personal trainer, or dinner at some posh Beverly Hills restaurant.

A man in a sleek gray sport jacket, black jeans, and expensive cologne stopped at the desk, commanding them to buy a birthday gift for his eight-year-old daughter and have it sent to her mother's house with a card from him.

"Please," he tagged on at the end, remembering his manners.

Addison wasn't exactly astonished by the request—working for Piper, she'd met more than one rich, entitled guy who couldn't be bothered with such trivial things as shopping for a child and thought everyone in his path was there to do it for him. But this man had the air of a power broker who was on his way to his office. Surely he had an assistant who could handle this for him.

Frankie took it in stride, getting the address and other pertinent information before asking him if there was anything in particular he wanted them to buy.

He shrugged. "Something under five hundred," he said.

"Do you know what she likes?" Addison asked.

"Likes?" He looked confused.

"Dolls . . . clothes . . . games . . . art . . ."

"Art!" he said. "She likes art."

"Very helpful, Mr. Stephens," Frankie said. "We'll have a package sent this afternoon."

"Thanks," he said, and knocked twice on the desk before walking briskly out of the building.

Addison didn't know how they would find art supplies for an eight-year-old that came anywhere close to $500, but with Frankie's guidance she called a Beverly Hills toy store and asked them to put together a package equaling that price and have it delivered this afternoon. Remembering the hours she'd spent at the kitchen table with a box of crayons and a coloring book, Addison imagined an eighteen-wheeler backing up to the little girl's house to dump an Everest of Crayolas.

Moments later, a petite woman with short blond hair came by the desk to ask about recommendations for a good plastic surgeon, and Addison was surprised when Frankie pulled open a file drawer and extracted a sheet of paper that listed the most highly rated Beverly Hills doctors with that specialty.

"Perfect!" the woman gushed, looking down at the page. "Thank you."

Addison didn't think the lovely blond looked like she needed to have any work done, but kept that to herself. She did, however, want to stall her for a quick conversation to assess her suitableness for Arnie.

"Good luck with it," Addison said. "I'm sure you'll look spectacular for whatever event you're getting ready for."

"The only event I'm looking forward to is my divorce."

"In that case," Addison said, "I hope he eats his heart out."

"Maybe if I show up with some stud on my arm," the woman said with a bitter laugh.

"What kind of stud are you looking for?" Addison asked, hoping she wasn't pushing it too far.

"Why? You know someone?"

Addison was about to say maybe, when she noticed Frankie glaring at her. "Sorry," she said instead. "I just got here."

"Well, keep your eyes open for me. I like them tall, dark, handsome, and breathing."

Addison laughed, but when the woman walked away, Frankie folded her arms and fixed her with a death stare.

"That was crossing the line," she said.

"I was just trying to make conversation," Addison protested.

"Listen, I know you have a background in matchmaking. Do *not* try to do that here."

Addison stalled, wondering how to explain her mission to Frankie. "Um," she began, but her boss jumped in.

"I'm serious, Addison. Do not get involved in the residents' private lives, and do not socialize with them."

"What about Arnie?"

Frankie gave her a look suggesting the answer was obvious. "Be serious," she said. "Of course you can socialize with your uncle. Just don't get embroiled with the other residents."

"But I'm trying to solve a problem," Addison insisted. "His ex-wife is returning from Italy, and he's thinking of—"

"Paulette?" Frankie asked, looking concerned.

"You know about her?"

"A bit."

Addison understood Frankie and Arnie were friendly—hell, her uncle was practically everyone's BFF—but she was surprised he'd opened up about Paulette. It made her worry that his obsession with the violent seductress was even worse than she'd thought.

"Do you know how terrible she was to him?" Addison asked.

"He didn't say as much, but I read between the lines."

Addison nodded, impressed that Frankie had intuited so much. This woman was as sharp as a surgeon's scalpel and just as formidable. Addison would need to watch her step.

"That's why I want to find a better match for him," she explained. "If he meets the right woman before Paulette returns—"

"No matchmaking!" Frankie insisted.

"But for Arnie . . ."

"Not for anyone. Am I clear?"

Addison opened her mouth to protest but realized it was a losing battle. Frankie was stubborn. Dug in. So instead of telling her boss she was being unreasonable, Addison simply said "Perfectly."

By the time the next resident approached the desk, Addison was prepared to be friendly yet professional. It was a man who needed them to arrange car service to an airport that was nearly two hours away. Addison thought it was peculiar to fly out of such a distant airport, but she kept that to herself until he walked away. Then she asked Frankie, who explained that some people in Los Angeles would do almost anything to avoid LAX.

A short while later, two distraught thirty-something women wearing white robes and the paper slippers of a fresh pedicure shuffled over to complain about the salon.

"I got the worst Brazilian wax of my life!" one of the women said, almost in tears. She began to open her robe, and Frankie stopped her.

"I believe you, Ms. Whitley," Frankie said. "You don't need to show us."

"I have a terrible rash," she said. "It's that new girl, Tameka. You should fire her."

"Yes," said the other woman, "fire her."

Oh, no, Addison thought, not Tameka. Though they'd met only once, there had been an immediate connection, and Addison had been taken by her kindness. Tameka was a sweetheart, a people pleaser. Plus, she had a kid and an ex-husband. But of course, that was nothing to these two entitled Karens.

Fortunately, Frankie didn't leap on it. She simply promised the distraught woman she would speak to the head of the salon and then offered to book her for a complimentary massage the next day. Addison took a slow breath. Part of her wanted to tell the women to get a fucking life, but Frankie had made it clear that her job was to treat the residents more sympathetically than a social worker talking to an anxious kindergartener. She could do this.

Later, a jumpy middle-aged man with a goatee stopped by the desk to say "Got another one for the suggestion box, Frankie." He took a seat opposite the desk, then got up again.

"What's that, Mr. Reed?"

"A cannabis dispensary in the building. It would be a great service to residents, and you'd make a killing."

Frankie promised him they would take it under advisement, and as the guy bounded away, she explained to Addison that he was usually pretty hyper and didn't seem able to contain the ideas bouncing around his active mind.

"No matter what he says, just tell him we'll consider it."

"Even if he seems high on coke?" Addison asked.

"*Especially* if he seems high on coke," Frankie said.

The next person at the desk was introduced to Addison as "Mr. Schlatter, one of our new residents."

"Nice to meet you," he said, as he self-consciously readjusted a baseball cap over a dense toupee.

"What can we do for you today?" Frankie asked.

He scratched at his neck. "I need a female escort for a business function next week—preferably blond and leggy, with a pretty mouth. Can you make those arrangements?"

Addison had to struggle to keep her jaw from unhinging. Was this guy seriously asking them to get him a prostitute? She feared his next request might be related to the woman's fellatio skills.

Frankie explained that they couldn't reserve escorts, due to liability issues, but she opened another file to produce a list of elite agencies serving the greater Beverly Hills area, complete with phone numbers and website addresses.

"Please understand this is not an official referral," Frankie said, "but feel free to contact these agencies on your own."

Mr. Schlatter rubbed a hand over his belly as he looked down at the page. "Do you think any of the ladies are aspiring actresses?"

Frankie paused, keeping her expression even, but Addison detected a subtle tightening around her mouth. "I wouldn't know."

He looked at Addison. "What do you think?"

"I think if you ask nicely, they'll be whatever you want them to be."

When the man walked away, Frankie looked at Addison, who struggled to hold back a grin.

"Okay," Frankie said, "you can have a little bit of fun, just not too much."

"Got it, boss."

At that, Frankie announced that she had to go back to her office for a while, leaving Addison to manage the concierge desk on her own. In Frankie's absence, Addison got two phone calls requesting spa appointments and one for the salon. Then the sunbathing ladies from the pool stopped by as promised, asking her to make a lunch reservation for Saturday, before heading out the door.

This is good, Addison thought as she called the restaurant and made the booking. She liked being busy and efficient. She texted the women to let them know the reservation was confirmed, and when she looked up, the young lifeguard was standing before her, presumably on his break.

"Jake," she said, "everything okay?"

"Totes," he said, and pointed toward the front door, where the two porters stood next to the doorman, staring straight at them. "Joaquín wanted to ask you something. I think it's about some dry cleaning that came in."

The request seemed odd, but she left her desk and approached the porters. For the life of her, she couldn't remember which one was Joaquín, so she addressed the two of them.

"What's up, guys?"

"A bunch of us are meeting at Rosebud's tomorrow around ten," said the tall one, whose name badge read *Lamar*. "It's a bar on Wilshire. You want to come?"

"It's kind of a regular Friday thing," said Joaquín, the shorter one.

"I work on Saturdays," Addison said, "so—"

"You don't have to stay that long," Lamar suggested.

Addison looked over at the lifeguard, who waved goodbye and headed back toward the elevators. She wondered why Jake the Dude, of all people, had been solicited to help make this connection. She realized, then, that for all his ostensible cluelessness, he might be one of the most clued-in staff members in Beekman Towers. After all, he had a direct line to the residents who visited the pool, which was just about everyone. She could only imagine the things he overheard in a day's work. And hadn't someone mentioned he did some freelance work in the security office, helping to keep the computers running? Perhaps she had underestimated him.

She turned back to Lamar and Joaquín. "How come you guys didn't just come over and ask me this?" she said. "Why the subterfuge?"

"The guests don't like it when we talk at the concierge desk," Joaquín explained. "They want you for themselves." He nodded toward the couch against the wall of the lobby, where Zach Brody sat, a faraway look on his face as he watched them. Addison shook her head. What was his deal?

"A lot of us are going," said Lamar, as if she might feel more comfortable with a big group. It wasn't that far from the truth. If she was going to make this new life work, she'd need friends.

"I can drive you," Joaquín offered, and she knew immediately he was interested. She decided he was pretty cute, with a pert nose and full cheeks. He had the broad build of a short guy who pumped a lot of iron to compensate.

Still, she didn't want to get herself into a situation where she was expected to get in a car at the end of the night with a guy who'd been drinking. So she said, "Thanks, but I'll just meet you there," and hoped an Uber ride wouldn't be too expensive.

"I promise we won't keep you out late," Joaquín said, as if that was the reason she didn't want to accept a ride.

"Trust me," Lamar added, "none of us wants to get on Frankie's bad side."

Addison nodded and agreed to meet them at the bar, explaining she wouldn't need a ride.

Joaquín looked disappointed, but he gave her a friendly smile, and with that, they exchanged numbers, and Addison headed back to her desk. When she got there, Dante was waiting for her. And across the lobby, there was good old Zach, still watching.

Addison took her seat. "Don't make trouble for me," she whispered to Dante. "That guy is watching me like a hall monitor, ready to rat me out to the principal."

"Don't worry, I'm here on official business," Dante said. He leaned in, putting his hands on the desk as if taking possession of it. Addison couldn't help but notice how enticing his olive skin looked against the crisp aqua shirt he wore.

She took a breath. "How can I help you?"

"I need you to make me a dinner reservation for Sunday night," he said.

"You're serious?" she asked, because it seemed like he was playing.

"Like an eight-point earthquake," he said.

Addison studied his coal-dark eyes, which gave nothing away. "Okay," she said, deciding it made perfect sense for someone like Dante to need plenty of dinner reservations—for work and play. She swiped to the restaurants page on her iPad. "Where would you like to go?"

"It depends."

"On what?" she asked.

"On what you're in the mood for."

She sighed. Clearly, Dante knew she was off on Sunday. "Don't do this to me," Addison said quietly.

"Do what?"

"Frankie doesn't want me fraternizing with the residents, and I'm trying to stay on her good side."

"But you're allowed to hang with your uncle."

"We covered that," she said. "It's different."

Dante brought his face close to her ear. "We have unfinished business," he whispered.

Addison fought the shiver that ran through her, and backed her chair away. She glanced across the lobby and could tell Zach had clocked the whole exchange.

"I can't go out with you," she said softly.

"Sure you can."

It was so tempting. This guy was gorgeous and charming, and she knew he'd take her someplace spectacular. But it could put this job in jeopardy, and then what?

"Dante . . . ," she said, "I'm sorry."

He folded his arms, thinking. "What if it was a double date?"

"A what?"

"I mean, let's say your uncle had a date and decided to bring his niece and another friend. What could be wrong with that?"

Addison thought about it, trying to imagine Frankie's reaction. Surely she couldn't object, despite what she had witnessed by the restrooms. And besides, Addison reasoned, it could be a good opportunity to try to find an appropriate match for Arnie and sneak in under Frankie's radar.

"Do you know if Arnie's free?" she asked.

"Only one way to find out," he said, and took his phone from his pocket to send a text.

While they waited for Arnie's reply, Addison said, "I'd want to pick his date."

"You have someone in mind?"

"That's the problem. I'm trying to find a woman in the building who isn't an airhead. But I need to do it on the down-low."

Dante nodded, taking that in. Then he looked around the lobby as if trying to find someone appropriate. A strikingly beautiful girl in a crop top and a very short skirt waved at him as she walked by, and he waved back.

"Not her!" Addison whispered.

Dante laughed. "Don't worry, we're not inviting Sage."

So that was Sage. No wonder Arnie was smitten. She was a knock-out, and guys his age didn't usually attract women like that. The door-man looked like he might have a stroke as she passed by.

The elevator doors pinged open, and a woman in a tight blue dress emerged, heading straight for the concierge desk, graceful but determined.

"Can I help you?" Addison asked, and Dante backed off, giving her space.

The woman raised her head imperiously before taking a seat. "I understand you can book me an appointment at the salon?"

"I'll be happy to." Addison offered a polite smile and swiped at the iPad to open the right page. "Special occasion?" she asked, figuring it was okay to probe a bit since Frankie wasn't there.

The woman looked to be in her late forties, which was technically too young for Arnie, but after seeing Sage, this regal diva seemed mature enough for the job. And she had the kind of commanding, high-energy presence Arnie responded to.

Also, she was attractive, though certainly lankier than the curvy Paulette. Yet there was something similar about the two women. Something beyond the charismatic presence. Addison studied her face and decided it was the intensity in her eyes. With a closer look, though, she feared it was something more than intensity. The woman appeared tightly wound. Like she might snap and shatter, exploding into dangerous bits.

Addison glanced at Dante and shook her head. This one would not do.

The woman cleared her throat. "Not really," she trilled, responding to Addison's question. "But I have a new boyfriend, and I want to look good for him."

Just as well, Addison thought as she found an available slot at the salon. She confirmed the time with the woman, got her name, and scribbled down the appointment on a business card.

"You're all set, Ms. Forrest," she said, handing her the card.

As she left, Dante moved back to the desk to call Addison's attention to a plain-looking woman entering the building. She wasn't unattractive—just trying hard not to be noticed, in a dull-brown sweater and loose jeans. Her hair was frizzy, with gray flya-ways, and she wore no makeup.

"She's a smart one," he whispered.

"How old is she?"

Dante shrugged. "Late thirties? Early forties?"

"Too young," Addison insisted.

"But this one seems like an old soul. Like she's *lived*, you know?"

Addison sighed. "Okay, introduce me."

"Carly!" Dante called across the lobby to the woman. "Come meet the new concierge."

The woman came over and offered a meek smile. Addison extended her hand and introduced herself. "Addison Torres," she said. "Nice to meet you."

Instead of responding with her own name, the woman muttered, "Oh, thank you."

"Addison," Dante cut in, "this is Carly Pratt. She's a writer."

Addison was intrigued. She sat up straighter and assessed the woman's appearance, deciding she was a diamond in the rough. A trip to the salon, a fitted outfit, and a cute pair of shoes would work wonders. She could imagine Arnie being attracted to her.

"What do you write?" Addison asked.

"It's not that exciting."

"I'm sure it is to some people."

"Technical journals, medical-product brochures, stuff like that," Carly said. "It's pretty boring."

Dante looked toward the entrance and then glanced back at Addison, as if trying to communicate something. She turned to see what he'd been looking at, and there was the mysterious woman Dante had identified as Maya Mayfield, the relationship guru who had apparently separated from her wife.

Carly Pratt followed their eyes to statuesque Maya and gasped.

"Are you okay?" Addison asked.

"I . . . I . . . yes, I'm fine. But . . ."

Addison could see Carly's eyes go moist and scared. "What's wrong?"

"I'm sorry. I just realized something I have to do."

Addison thought the woman looked pale and asked if she wanted to sit down for a minute. "Can I get you some water?" she added.

"No! I'm fine, really. I'm so sorry."

"Are you sure?" Addison asked, but Carly didn't answer. She just scurried off toward the elevator.

Addison and Dante looked at each other, silently acknowledging that Carly Pratt was an oddball in all the wrong ways. Dante sighed and lowered himself into the seat with a loud sigh.

"This is not going to be easy," he said.

Chapter 13
CARLY

Carly Pratt hurried into the elevator before the door shut, almost afraid to look up. Her heart thudded, and her palms went damp. She had never met a celebrity before—and certainly not someone who loomed as large as the exquisite Maya Mayfield, one of the brightest stars in Carly's late-night scrolling. She had to say something to this stranger who had sustained her through the darkest times. She just had to.

It was almost ironic, because one of the first things she had asked her brother when he moved her into this ritzy place was "Do you think I'll meet any celebrities?" Lenny had smiled gently and said, "Doubt it," yet here she was. Carly closed her eyes and pictured where she'd be right now if she hadn't had the gumption to leave Owen. She saw her kitchen table in Nashua, where she often sat in the deep night after he had gone to sleep. Sometimes she'd spend hours scrolling through Instagram, getting lost in people's lives. And no one seemed kinder, more centered, more insightful, more lovely, more glamorous than Maya Mayfield.

And her love story with Brianna! The way they met on *Single File*. You could tell it was love at first sight. Brianna's eyes had actually flooded. The loquacious Maya had gone mute. A week later, they were engaged. It was utterly breathless.

"Floor?" asked Maya, who was nearer the elevator buttons. It was that deep, sultry voice Carly remembered, and she had a hard time catching her breath.

"Five," she muttered, and Maya pressed it for her.

As the doors closed and the atmosphere compressed into forced intimacy, Carly bit her lip, almost losing her nerve. But she couldn't. She'd come too far from that life in New Hampshire to crumble at this moment.

"I'm sorry to bother you," she blurted, her voice breaking, "but I just wanted to tell you that I'm such a fan. I think you're . . . extraordinary."

A thick silence descended for several long seconds before Maya muttered, "Oh, shit."

Carly felt like the floor might give out from beneath her feet. "Did I say something wrong?" she blurted, feeling dizzy with dread. Would Maya call her an idiot? A moron? A rube who should have stayed in New England?

Did she deserve it? Carly took a breath and tried to choke the tendrils of self-hatred rising like weeds that wouldn't die.

Maya waved away the comment. "No, no. It's not you. It's just that I was hoping not to be recognized here."

Carly exhaled, relieved. In fact, if she wasn't so nervous she might have laughed. "You?" she said. "Not recognized?"

"My celebrity doesn't extend that far beyond Instagram," Maya said.

"But I used to watch you on television!" Carly insisted, her eyes wide in surprise at Maya's modesty. "Your relationship with Brianna was the most romantic thing I'd ever seen." The memory made her own eyes go damp.

Maya cleared her throat. "Listen, um . . . What's your name?"

"Carly."

"Listen, Carly, can I ask you a favor?"

"Anything!" Carly said, tingling. Maya Mayfield was about to ask for a favor!

"Could you please not tell anyone you saw me?"

"Of course," Carly promised. "I hardly talk to anyone here, so . . ."

Maya put a hand on her shoulder. "Thank you. That's such a relief."

When the elevator dinged and the doors opened on Carly's floor, she stepped over the threshold to block them from closing. "Do you mind if I ask why it's such a secret?" she said, still feeling warmth in the spot where Maya had touched her.

The glamorous influencer thought for a minute. "Well, let me ask *you* something," she said. "Why are you here?"

"On this elevator?" Carly asked, wondering if Maya realized she had rushed inside just to be near her. She felt her cheeks burn with shame.

"In this condo."

Carly let out a relieved breath. "Oh, well . . . I . . . I had a bad marriage. I mean, for years. I was miserable, my husband . . ." She stopped to wipe her eyes and realized she was nearly rambling. Maya wouldn't be interested in her sad story, after all, but she looked into the woman's eyes and saw no impatience, only sympathy, so she went on. "I was afraid to leave. I had nothing, you know? Nothing."

Maya put a gentle hand on her arm—that touch again—and stepped out of the elevator with her, letting the doors close. "You had yourself."

Carly felt her throat constrict. With the notable exception of her brother, so few people had been this kind to her. She let her eyes close, savoring this moment. Remember this, she coached herself. Remember every detail. She looked back at Maya.

"It didn't feel like enough. I thought I was nothing without Owen."

"Did he hurt you, Carly?"

Her voice was so compassionate Carly nearly choked on gratitude. She took a juddering inhale. "Not physically."

"But emotionally," Maya confirmed.

It was such a small remark, but the recognition felt like everything to Carly, and she let it all out in a rush. "He was always telling me I was worthless. He picked at me constantly. The way I shopped, the way I made the bed, the way I chewed and breathed. No matter what

I did, it was never good enough." She paused, reminding herself it had been exactly that bad, even though he had been kind to her after that first miscarriage, when he seemed to understand her sorrow, promising they could try again, assuring her they'd have a baby one day, no matter what. But of course, after the second miscarriage he was done, uninterested in taking any medical steps or even talking about adoption. *That shit's for rich people*, he had said.

Yesterday, when she got a text from Owen asking her to come back, promising he'd change—saying they could try again for a baby—she'd been tempted to believe him, almost forgetting how addicted he was to cruelty.

"That's abuse," Maya said. "I'm glad you got out."

"I never would have been able to do it without my brother," Carly admitted. The thought of Lenny's kindness formed a bulge in her throat. They hadn't been close as children. Lenny, five years older, had been so different from her—handsome, popular, ambitious. He barely seemed to notice her. But once they were grown, he kept tabs, always concerned. When he realized Owen had a temper, the calls became more frequent, even though she never told him just how bad things really were. To his credit, Lenny had never been harsh or judgmental, and she knew exactly how blessed she was to have such a brother.

"Don't give away all the credit, Carly," said Maya. "You're the one who found the courage to leave."

"I know, but Lenny, my brother . . . he's been incredible. And generous. He lives out here, and he's very successful. He was always trying to convince me to leave, but I didn't know where to go. He said I could come stay with him, but that felt awful, you know? He's got two kids and a wife. And I was in New Hampshire, and it all just felt so impossible." Carly couldn't believe how much she was rambling, but Maya seemed genuinely interested.

"How did he finally coax you out here?"

Carly took a breath. "One day he just called and said he bought this condo as an investment property, insisted I'd be doing him a favor if I came and lived here." It had been after another big fight with Owen over the baby thing. Since he'd insisted adoption was too expensive, she had looked into becoming foster parents, and he'd roared with indignation.

"Your brother sounds like a good guy."

Carly nodded. "And it was such a sweet lie. So irresistible. Then I just . . . did it. *I did it!* I thought Owen would shit his pants. He laughed and said I'd look like an old crone in Beverly Hills, that I'd have no friends. And now look at me—I'm talking to Maya Mayfield!"

Maya laughed. "I think you should feel proud of yourself every day that you had the strength to leave. Not everyone does."

Carly took a labored breath, and then she couldn't help herself. All those tears she'd been holding back finally escaped, along with a thin wail that turned into hiccuping sobs. It was so embarrassing, but Maya put a hand on her back and said, "This is so cleansing."

Carly dug into her purse and found a tissue, collecting herself. "You're very kind," she said. "I always knew you would be. I knew it."

"That's sweet of you to say."

"But you were trying to tell me something—about why it's a secret you're here."

Maya paused, studying Carly's expression as if to be sure she was okay. Then she brought her face closer and said in a softer voice, "I don't know if you saw it, but I was on Ellen DeGeneres one time and—"

"Of course I saw it!" Carly blurted, and felt immediately embarrassed. But if Maya thought she was a stalker, she didn't let on.

"Do you remember what she called me?"

"The Sherpa of love," Carly said softly, following Maya's lead. It was clear she didn't want anyone else to hear them. "She had it printed on a T-shirt."

"Right," Maya said. "It became my brand. Everyone comes to me for relationship advice. So how would it look if people knew I couldn't make my own marriage work?"

Carly nearly gasped. "You and Brianna split up?" she said, feeling her heart crack in two.

Now it was Maya's turn to tear up. "I tried everything. She fell out of love with me."

"I'm so sorry," Carly said, from the deepest part of herself. It was almost unbearably tragic. Such a fairy-tale romance was supposed to last forever.

"Thank you. Now I just have to figure out how to keep it a secret so I don't lose my career too."

Carly apprised Maya's face and saw the pain there. She couldn't imagine the ache of losing that kind of love and then feeling compelled to hide it. "I don't think you need to keep it a secret."

"But everyone assumes I managed to have this magical marriage. My life was . . . aspirational. That's what all my sponsors pay me for. Now I'm just another divorce statistic."

"No!" Carly said. "Listen, we've been talking for five minutes, and you've managed to make me feel better than my therapist and my big brother combined." It was true. This conversation had shifted her perspective so profoundly that she suddenly felt in no danger of forgiving Owen, of going back to try again. She felt . . . stronger. Better.

"I'm glad, but—"

"Maybe you could be the Sherpa of breakups," Carly interrupted, feeling proud. Smart.

"The Sherpa of breakups?" Maya repeated, holding the words in her mouth.

"People need help climbing *down* from the mountain too."

"Whoa. Yes. That's . . . I want to think about that."

Carly felt a prickle in her scalp. She'd given Maya Mayfield something to think about!

"I'll bet there are a lot of sponsors that would kill for your kind of influence in that market," she said. "You'd help so many people while launching a new career."

Then Maya Mayfield, the six-foot-tall beauty Carly had worshipped for years, hiked her handbag up on her shoulder and asked, "You want to grab a coffee or something?"

Chapter 14
ADDISON

By the end of the day, Addison hadn't met anyone more appropriate for Arnie than the crazy-eyed Melody Forrest. She did see the lovely woman who'd been reading a book by the pool but didn't get a chance to speak to her, as she'd waltzed right by the concierge desk and out the door.

Other than that, it wasn't a bad first day. There was a lot to learn, but Addison could anticipate getting the hang of things pretty quickly. For now—back in her apartment—she was ready to unwind. No more reservations, weird requests, nervous oddballs, or condescension. No more worries about impressing Frankie or finding someone for Arnie. It was Addison time.

She changed out of her work clothes and into a bathing suit, deciding she may as well take advantage of this luxurious building and miraculous Southern California climate. She'd go for a dip in that pristine rooftop pool—maybe she'd even have it all to herself, as the place seemed to go quiet after 7:00 p.m. Addison slipped on a cover-up and headed for the elevators, looking forward to a quiet evening swim under the moon and stars.

When she reached the top of the tower and pushed through the doors to the pool area, Addison realized why the lobby had seemed so deserted. Everyone was up here.

It was a party atmosphere, with people dressed in everything from cocktail casual to skimpy bathing suits. And nearly everyone held a glass of wine—even the people in the pool, who were standing by the edge, chatting. The sun was setting, and fairy lights threaded overhead gave the space a magical quality. She understood why everyone would want to be here instead of inside their units, eating dinner with no one to keep them company but Ryan Seacrest and Vanna White.

There was soft music coming out of speakers in the corners, and Addison strained to make it out. She almost laughed when she realized it was "You Can't Always Get What You Want," because these folks almost certainly did. Then she caught herself, because despite being rich and entitled, nearly everyone was here due to a failed marriage. She thought about Carly Pratt, who seemed to be experiencing exquisite pain. Perhaps most of these folks were simply better at hiding it.

"Addison!" called Arnie. He was sitting in a conversation pit, surrounded by friends. When she approached, he announced, "Everyone, meet my niece, our new concierge!"

After the greetings, Arnie told her to grab a glass of wine and join them.

"In a few," Addison said, because she was determined to slip into that velvety water and swim the length of the pool, feeling her strong shoulders propel her with graceful ease.

She pulled off her wrap, glad the center of the pool was empty, and dove in. The water was perfectly cool—not a single degree too warm or cold. She swam several laps, feeling her muscles flex, stretch, and finally relax. It was exactly what she needed.

Before she got too winded, Addison pulled herself up from the side of the pool, dripping wet as she stood. She wiped the water from her eyes and realized someone was standing before her, handing her a towel.

"Thanks," she said, pressing it against her face.

"You're welcome," said a familiar voice.

She lowered the towel and realized it was Zach Brody. Surprised by his kindness, Addison rewarded him with a smile. "I hope you aren't too mad I'm not wearing my red blazer," she joked.

Zach didn't laugh. He just took in the whole of her tankini-clad body, which seemed to elicit more discomfort than longing. "I'm not mad. The blazer isn't required when you're off duty."

"Good to know," she said, "because that would make it hard to swim."

The joke didn't seem to register at all. "In case you aren't aware," he told her, his face still, "you pick your head up too much."

"Excuse me?"

"When you swim. You need to rotate your whole body, not just your neck."

"I'll . . . try to remember that. Thank you for the critique."

"You're welcome."

"Anything else you want to criticize?" she asked.

"No, you're mostly fine."

"Mostly fine," Addison repeated, pretending to swoon from the compliment. "You'll make me blush."

"They don't call me a player for nothing."

Her eyebrows went up. Was Zach Brody making a joke? His face gave nothing away, so she said, "Are you really a player?"

He nodded. "*Minecraft . . . Fortnite . . . Call of Duty.*"

Addison laughed hard. The nerd humor was so unexpected. "Well, it's good to see you here," she said. "I didn't think you'd be into all this." She gestured around to indicate the crowd.

He nodded, acknowledging her observation. "I usually take my late swim in the indoor pool, but they're chlorinating it tonight."

She studied his inscrutable face, searching for a clue on his earlier behavior. "Can I ask you something?" she said.

"Of course."

"Why were you watching me today?"

He looked away and muttered, "I thought you might bring that up."

"It's not exactly something I could ignore."

"I apologize for my behavior," he said curtly, and turned to walk away.

"Mr. Brody, wait," she said, catching his arm. He froze, and she released him, speaking more gently. "Zach, please. Answer my question. Why were you spying on me?"

He turned back, his placid face turning angry. "You really want to know?"

"Yes!"

"Because you're not being careful," he pronounced, sounding so accusatory it confused her.

"Sorry," she muttered, "but I don't understand."

"Well, figure it out," he spit, and walked away.

She stared after him, wondering what he meant and why it inspired such hostility. Was he really warning her about something? Or was he just one of those tech geeks who aced every class but had no idea how to play nicely with others?

As he trudged to the deep end of the pool and dove in, Addison decided to let it go. Some people just weren't worth the trouble. Too bad, because he was really pretty cute.

She finished drying off, put on her cover-up, and joined her uncle's assembly, which included several of the folks she already met, as well as young Sage—who was sitting on the lap of an older gentleman—and Dante, who was drinking beer from a bottle and managing to make it look chic. She wondered if he had spoken to Arnie about Sunday night but didn't want to bring it up in front of the group.

Arnie was in the middle of relating a funny story about a med school mishap involving a pig cadaver when Melody Forrest arrived, wearing a gold bikini top and colorful sarong. She looked hot enough to turn heads. Even Jake, the lifeguard, couldn't take his eyes off her. But after stopping for a moment to survey the crowd, Melody walked straight toward their group and wedged herself between Arnie and his gym friend, Louise Wagner.

A bold move, Addison thought—especially for a woman who claimed to have a boyfriend.

"Hey, babe," Melody said to Arnie.

Addison studied her uncle for a reaction and thought he looked uncharacteristically uncomfortable.

Still, Arnie introduced Melody to the group. As she greeted everyone, she threaded her arm through his, staking her claim. Addison squinted in concentration. What was going on here?

Someone reminded Arnie to get back to his story about the pig, which he did, though he never recovered his prior ebullience.

At last—after having some dinner and a glass of wine—Addison announced that she was tired and needed to go to sleep. Dante put his hand to his chest, as if the news broke his heart. She shook her head at him, a silent admonition to keep their friendship—or whatever was going on between them—a secret.

"Good night, all," Addison said as she stood, adding, "Uncle Arnie, could I talk to you for a second?"

Looking relieved, Arnie stood and followed her to the elevator bank.

"Everything okay, sweetheart?" he asked.

"You tell me," she said. "I noticed how uncomfortable you got when Melody Forrest arrived."

Arnie let out a long breath and rubbed at his forehead. "I . . . uh, I met her this morning for the first time."

"The first time?" Addison said. "She didn't seem like a virtual stranger."

"Well, I offered to give her a tour, and she came to my apartment, and . . ." He shrugged.

Addison studied his face, and there it was. "You slept with her?" she said, incredulous.

He bowed his head, looking sheepish. "Melody comes on pretty strong."

Dear god, Addison thought, my seventy-five-year-old uncle is worse than I am. Then an even more disturbing thought occurred to her. Was Melody Forrest talking about Arnie when she said she had a new boyfriend? Was she really deranged enough to think one hookup constituted a commitment?

"That might not have been the smartest move," Addison said.

He held up his hands in surrender. "She seemed like such a great gal—sassy and smart."

"And batshit crazy," Addison said.

"It gets worse," Arnie said.

"Worse?"

He took a dramatic inhale. "I think she stole my Fabergé egg."

Addison was aghast. "Stole it?"

"I'm not sure, but . . . after we were intimate, she left pretty quickly. Then I had a little nap, took a shower, and that's when I noticed it was gone."

"Jesus! Did you call the police?"

"Of course not. I didn't want to raise a ruckus."

"But Uncle Arnie—"

"Look, I don't even have proof that she took it."

Addison stared at him. "Of course she took it!"

"Thing is, she didn't lock the door when she left. So maybe some-one came in while I was showering."

Addison paused. She knew her uncle hated to think the worst of people, but this was ridiculous. "Come on, no one broke into your apartment and snatched your Fabergé egg."

"But why would she do such a thing?"

"It's pretty valuable, isn't it?"

He shrugged. "I don't know. I haven't had it appraised in a while. Anyway, it's a replica, so it's not worth millions."

"But thousands?" Addison asked, recalling the heavy gold and embedded jewels. "Tens of thousands?"

"Maybe. But it doesn't matter—it's not something I would ever sell." He put his hand to his heart. "You can't put a price on sentimental value."

Addison shook her head. "You have to report this," she said.

"To the police?"

"Yes! Or at the very least to Frankie, or the security guy."

"I don't want to get Melody in trouble. She's recently divorced and probably going through a lot. I think I should give her a chance to return it."

"And how will you do that?" Addison asked, worried that he was treading dangerous waters.

"I'll speak with her."

Addison paused, wondering if she should try to talk sense into him about going to the police. But he seemed pretty immovable. "Do you want my help?" she asked.

"I can handle this, sweetheart. Don't worry about it."

"You sure?"

He kissed her cheek. "Get a good night's sleep. I'll be fine."

She studied his dear, kind face. "Be careful," she said.

"I promise."

With that, Addison got into the elevator and rode down the full length of the building to the subterranean level, where her apartment was.

A short while later, when she slipped under the covers of her new bed, Addison realized the jet lag had finally caught up with her, and drowsiness fell like a heavy tarp, dragging her under. When she was jolted awake by the buzzer at her door, she groaned.

"Go away, Dante," she mumbled. "I'm too tired."

He rang the buzzer a second time, and she continued to ignore him, though now she was fully awake. By the time he rang again, she wondered if maybe she should take him into her bed tonight. It wouldn't be the worst way to end her day. And then tomorrow she could start fresh, resetting her twelve-months-of-celibacy clock.

She stood and pinched her cheeks to add a little color to her sleepy face, then threw open the door, wearing only her T-shirt and panties.

"Okay—" she started to say, and stopped herself because the man at her door wasn't Dante. This one was elderly and familiar, but it took her a moment to realize who it was—the yellow bathing suit man who had grumbled about his spa appointment. Only now he was dressed in a bathrobe and monogrammed slippers.

"Mr. Posner?" she asked. "What are you doing here?"

He held up a bottle of scented oil. "I need my damned massage."

Addison put her hands on her hips, trying to decide whether he was doddering and senile or entitled and horny. "I'm not giving you a massage," she said.

He put his free hand in the pocket of his robe and pulled out a wad of bills in a money clip. "How much?"

"No!" she said, half shouting. "No massage! Not for any amount of money."

He looked her up and down. "How about if I give *you* one?"

She stared at him for a moment, trying to find the right words to put him in his place. Finally, she just said, "Go home, Mr. Posner," and slammed the door.

Addison waited there for several minutes until she heard him shuffle away; then she climbed into bed and went to sleep.

Chapter 15
ARNIE

"Isn't this romantic?" Melody said to Arnie, stroking his bicep.

The last of their assemblage had wandered off into the night, leaving the two of them alone. They stood by the railing at the edge of the rooftop, overlooking the twinkling lights of Beverly Hills and beyond. A cool breeze blew across the expanse, bringing with it the whoosh of traffic noises, including the insistent horn of an impatient driver.

To Arnie, the mood was anything but romantic. He was lost in thought, trying to figure out how to broach the touchy subject of his precious Fabergé egg and get it back without too much drama. If she refused or played innocent, what then? He supposed he'd have to report it to the police, and he couldn't even follow the thread of where that would lead. Instead, he came back to a scene with Paulette, where she would ask him what happened to it. He'd have to come up with some lie, because if she ever found out it was taken by a woman he'd slept with, she'd raise enough hell to set off the smoke detectors.

He cleared his throat, preparing to speak, but Melody jumped in to fill the silence.

"It's getting a little chilly," she hinted, moving closer, but Arnie backed away.

"Actually," he said, "I've been wanting to talk to you. It's pretty important."

She took a sip of her wine and set it on the ledge. "I think I know what this is about," she said, turning serious.

"You do?" Arnie was relieved. She was about to come clean—to explain why she'd taken the Fabergé egg. Maybe she'd confess it was an impulse—something to remember him by. Or perhaps she was in dire financial straits. If that was the case, maybe he could offer to help. Nothing wrong with being a hero to a woman in distress.

"I don't want to talk about it here," she said. "Will you come back to my apartment?"

"I don't know if I should," he said, though the memory of that morning was vivid enough to stir him. He simply had to stay focused. This was about getting that egg back.

She took his hand and looked straight into his eyes. "Arnie," she said, "there's something you're going to want to see."

He nodded. She was making it pretty clear she was about to confess and return the pilfered piece. Thank god this would all be over soon and he wouldn't have to worry about getting her in trouble. He could put the egg back in place on his kitchen counter, where Paulette would see it the moment she walked in the door. *Oh, Arnie*, she'd say. And in that moment, she'd know exactly how much she meant to him.

Arnie got in the elevator with Melody and followed her to her apartment.

"I haven't decorated yet," she said, opening the door to reveal a sparsely furnished living room, with an antique love seat, two rigid chairs, and no signs of an objet d'art in emerald green and eighteen-carat gold. "Just brought a few things from the house. When I have time— and get a settlement from my stingy ex—I'll put my stamp on it."

"I'm sure it'll be marvelous," Arnie said, and wondered if the stingy ex was the reason she'd pinched his precious keepsake.

"Can I get you a drink?" she asked.

"No thanks."

Melody sat on the sofa and patted the spot next to her. "Let's get comfortable."

Arnie remained standing. "You said you wanted to show me something."

"Ooh, you naughty boy," she said, and stood, untying her bikini top. "I'll show you whatever you want." She tossed the top aside, and Arnie tried not to look, but her firm small breasts drove him wild. She approached and pressed herself against him, burying her face in his neck.

He gently grasped her shoulders and pushed her away. "Why are we here, Melody?"

"Because we're crazy about each other."

"Honey," he said, intentionally softening his message with sweetness, "why did you take my Fabergé egg?"

"What?"

"Just give it back," he said gently. "I promise I won't make a fuss. No one has to know."

"Babe, I don't know what you're talking about."

"Come on, Melody, don't play games."

She glared at him, turning angry. "I don't play games," she said through her teeth, then grabbed her top and put it back on.

"Are you honestly telling me you didn't take my egg when you left? Seriously, you can tell me. I won't be mad."

Her face went red with rage. "Why would I want that ostentatious fucking egg?"

"You didn't take it?"

"Jesus, Arnie, I can't believe you think I would do such a thing."

"But—"

"But nothing!" she spit, her fury mounting. "Fuck you. Fuck you for thinking I would ever steal from you!"

"Okay, okay. I'm sorry. It's just . . . it was gone when you left. You didn't lock the door, so . . ." Arnie studied her, still not sure if she was telling the truth. She seemed so volatile, anything was possible. And god help him, it was getting him aroused. Even without Viagra.

"I can't believe you would accuse me of that." Her anger was turning to tears.

"When you said you had something to show me . . ."

"That was sexy talk, Arnie. I thought after this morning you would understand that. You're not going to break my heart so soon, are you?"

Her eyes were so vulnerable, so pleading. But he had to extricate himself from this, despite what was happening in his pants.

"Listen, Melody," he began.

"No!" she cried, clearly sensing he was ending this relationship before it even began. "Stop right there."

"You're such a beautiful woman," he tried.

She shook her head. "Do you have any idea how much my ex hurt me? I can't handle any more, babe. I can't."

She broke down in sobs, and he approached, taking her in his arms to comfort her and wishing it didn't get him so aroused.

After a few moments, there was a shift in her body, and he knew she felt his erection. She pushed her pelvis against him and opened her mouth to his. He started to succumb and caught himself. This would be such a terrible mistake. He backed away.

"Melody, I should go."

She nodded, looking chastised. "You're right," she said. "I understand. But can you give me one second? I really do want to show you something."

"Um . . . ," he stalled.

"Please. Just wait here. I'll be right back."

She dashed into her bedroom, and Arnie stood there, unsure of what to do. Maybe she'll return with the egg, he told himself as he paced, trying to think of something, anything, besides sex. Sports . . . politics . . . medical journals . . . but the memory of that morning's encounter was too fresh, flooding his hypothalamus. It was natural but shocking to him, this unaided arousal. It was also fierce. Forceful. Life affirming. Arnie felt like a young man.

Then there she was, stark naked except for those crazy high heels. And she held something in her hand, but it wasn't a Fabergé egg. It was a schoolhouse ruler.

"Dr. Arnie," she cooed, turning around for him, "Melody has been a very bad girl."

And then Arnold Glass, who graduated at the top of his medical school class from Johns Hopkins University and should have known better, was a very bad boy.

Chapter 16
ADDISON

On Friday morning, Addison sat in her boss's office, continuing her training. Frankie was showing her the lists of outside services they recommended to residents, including restaurants, stores, dry cleaners, interior decorators, feng shui consultants, florists, wedding planners, divorce mediators, babysitters, yoga studios, life coaches, holistic healers, astrologers, psychics, music therapists, art therapists, aroma therapists, pet therapists, colon therapists, plastic surgeons, dermatologists, dietitians, attorneys, accountants, private investigators, limousine drivers, AA groups, and more. Addison struggled to keep up with it all, grateful her predecessor had been so organized. Frankie was about to move on to safety and security when her phone rang.

Apparently it was Jake, the young lifeguard, informing Frankie that the day's towels hadn't been delivered to the rooftop pool. It seemed one of the porters was out sick and Raphael was in the middle of teaching an exercise class, so Frankie was going to bring the towels up herself.

"I'll do it," Addison offered, hoping for another chance to run into the lovely woman she'd seen reading, so they could have a little chat. So far, she was the only person Addison hadn't ruled out as a possible love match for Arnie.

Frankie agreed and gave Addison instructions for getting the towels from the loading dock, using the Tower A elevator, as the freight car was in use.

A short while later, Addison found herself pushing the massive towel trolley onto the elevator, where she discovered it took up half the space. She knew it was just the kind of thing that might anger the pricklier residents, but at least it had the pleasant smell of fabric softener.

When the elevator stopped on the fifth floor and a woman in a boldly patterned beach cover-up got on, Addison apologized, explaining the freight elevator wasn't available.

"Oh, don't worry about it, dear."

The woman was in her late sixties, with the same kind of dyed-black hair as Paulette. Addison thought she wore way too much makeup and jewelry, but she knew that wasn't the kind of thing that bothered Arnie. In fact, he liked high-maintenance types.

Addison introduced herself and learned the woman's name was Roberta.

"You on your way up to the pool?" Addison asked.

"I try to go for an early swim before it gets busy," she said, adjusting the bathing suit under her shift as she inspected her own cleavage.

Addison nodded. "I was surprised how crazy it gets at night."

"The wine-and-beer crowd," Roberta said with a sniff. "Too cliqueish for me."

The elevator stopped on the eleventh floor, and when the doors opened, there was Zach Brody. He looked from Addison to the massive towel trolley taking up half the space.

"You're supposed to use the freight elevator for that," he said.

Roberta tsked. "Just take the next car," she said, and pushed the Close Door button. Before they were even out of Zach's earshot, she added, "I can't stand that guy."

Addison smirked. This woman was bold and brassy—just the type Arnie liked. And yet, when she thought about it, something about Roberta seemed wrong. When they reached the roof, Addison understood what it was. The woman made a beeline for young Jake, peeling off her cover-up as she asked him if his whistle was ready for action.

Addison hated the term *cougar*, but with a heavy sigh she understood it was exactly the vibe she'd picked up on. Another contender crossed off the list.

Fortunately, the reading woman was back in her spot, absorbed in an oversize volume that could have been a textbook. Addison left the towels with the pool attendant and approached Arnie's prospective love match.

"Hi," she said, "I'm Addison, the new concierge."

The woman extended her hand. "Leyla Balik," she said with a soft accent.

"What a pretty name," Addison observed. "Is it Middle Eastern?"

"Turkish," she explained. "I'm from Istanbul."

"And you live here now? Or are you visiting?"

"Oh, I've lived here for almost thirty years. I came as a girl to study nursing."

A nurse, Addison thought. How absolutely perfect. The woman had a soft face with an arrow-straight nose, like an old movie star. And she was lusciously curvy. Addison could picture Arnie being instantly smitten.

"Is that a nursing book?" Addison asked.

Leyla shook her head. "Just something I found on neuroscience. I like to keep my mind active, you understand?"

"I do!" Addison said, impressed. Arnie, she knew, still read medical journals despite having been retired for years. These two were looking like an excellent match.

Leyla glanced past Addison's shoulder. "That young man is studying us like specimens under a microscope."

Addison turned to see Zach standing by the edge of the pool, trying to listen in on their conversation.

"Not again," Addison muttered, disgusted.

"He does this a lot?"

"He's made it his business to monitor me. My own personal warden, making sure I follow the rules."

"How terrible," she said, then signaled to Zach. "Young man! Come here." Her voice was stern, unyielding. When he hesitated, she got even flintier. "Right now!"

Chagrined, Zach approached, and Addison had a sudden hankering for popcorn. This could get interesting.

"Why are you watching this young lady?" Leyla demanded. She didn't even bother getting up from her seat, which she now occupied like a throne.

He shifted uncomfortably. "I'm not watching her."

"Don't lie!"

Zach's face reddened, but he said nothing.

"Well?" Leyla demanded.

He pointed at Addison like a child trying to shift the blame. "She's . . . she's very reckless."

"That's her business, isn't it?"

"Uh . . ."

"And don't point. It's rude. Didn't your mother teach you manners?"

"Yeah, but . . . she never told me not to point."

Leyla scoffed, disgusted, then stood up and slammed her book. "Well, from now on, try to behave yourself. This lady deserves some respect."

With that, she picked up her book and left.

"I don't like her," Zach muttered.

"I do," Addison said, feeling certain she had hit pay dirt. This was Arnie's love match—the very woman who could distract him from Paulette.

Chapter 17

The cars. Dear god, the cars. As Addison waited in front of the building for her Uber, she got to see the residents coming and going as they kicked off the weekend, keeping the valets busy with a parade of expensive vehicles. Even for Addison, who wasn't a car person, these were impressive machines—so much showier than the BMWs, Mercedes-Benzes, and Range Rovers driven by rich New Yorkers when they fled the city. There were Lamborghinis and Porsches and Bentleys and Maseratis and vintage Jaguars and a host of other cars she didn't even recognize. There were even a few restored antiques—the kind of cars that would have stopped traffic in New York, creating a jam on the Grand Central Parkway. Here in LA, though, everyone seemed utterly blasé about the whole thing.

"Hey, gorgeous," someone said, and she turned to see Dante exiting the building. He looked pretty gorgeous himself, in a black silk shirt, tan slacks, and shoes that probably cost more than she made in a month. The gold chain around his neck rested there like it was honored to be making contact with such rarefied flesh. And he smelled like a dream.

"Hot date?" she asked, indicating his appearance.

"Just taking out a client."

Addison laughed, imagining him telling that to his ex-wife just before she found a woman's panties in his pocket. "Yeah, right."

"What about you?" he said. "Those aren't the jeans of a girl who plans to stay out of trouble."

Addison knew damned well how hot her ass looked in her tightest black jeans. In fact, when she got dressed for the night, she had asked herself why she was wearing her fuck-me pants when she had no intention of going home with anyone. But old habits die hard. She was single and on her way out to a bar with some new friends. No one could blame her for trying to look her best.

"Just want to make a good impression," she said.

"Can't you save that for Sunday night?" he whispered, his eyes seductive enough to raise her temperature.

Addison had already decided there was no use trying to resist Dante. After their near miss the night of Zach's call, she knew they'd hook up again. In fact, she decided that sleeping with Dante wouldn't even count against her celibacy vow, as there was no danger of getting involved with him. He wasn't going to fall for her—he was too much of a player to want anything more committed than fuck-buddy status. And she wasn't going to fall for him—her orphaned heart could never open to someone so cocky. When it came to romance, Addison was more drawn to the wounded than to the warriors.

And that's why she needed to protect the world at large from herself. She was the unpinned hand grenade of relationships.

"Speaking of Sunday," she said, "I might have found a date for Arnie. Her name's Leyla Balik. You know her?"

Dante looked thoughtful but finally shook his head. "Don't think so."

"Weird," she said, "I couldn't find her on the residents roster either. I thought maybe her condo was under a different name."

"Possible she's a guest? Someone's girlfriend?"

"That would be tragic," Addison said. "She's perfect for him."

"Mr. D'Amico?" interrupted the valet.

They both looked up to see a polished red Porsche parked in front of them.

"That's me," Dante said. "Don't worry—we'll find someone for Arnie."

He gave Addison a chaste kiss on the cheek—lingering for just a moment too long—before getting into his car and speeding off into the night. Watching him go, she thought about the warmth of his lips on her face, his hand on her shoulder, the scent of his cologne hovering in the air. And then, almost on cue, Zach Brody emerged from the building. Addison braced herself for more recriminations.

"What now?" she demanded.

"Excuse me?"

"You have to stop following me," she told him. "It's creepy. And I don't give a fuck what you think about my friendship with Dante."

He stared at her, his expression blank. "I'm waiting for my car."

She folded her arms, certain he was lying. There was no way this awkward nerd had plans at ten o'clock on a Friday night. "Oh, come on."

"Mr. Brody?" said the valet, and Addison looked up to see a bright-yellow sports car—trimmed in black—that looked like it had just whooshed in from some portal to the future.

"Thank you," Zach said, shooting Addison a look.

That's when she noticed he was well dressed, in a blazer and jeans, with bright-white sneakers of a brand she couldn't identify—probably because they weren't sold at Foot Locker. She looked back at the otherworldly car. This guy was full of surprises.

"I . . . ," Addison started, not sure what to say. Weren't tech nerds supposed to drive Priuses? Or maybe Teslas? "What *is* that?" she finally asked.

"It's a McLaren," he said.

"I've never seen one before," she admitted, and tried to remember a conversation about this car she'd once overheard between two of Piper's rich clients.

"What do *you* drive?" he asked.

"I don't."

He stared at her for a beat, uncomprehending. "What do you mean?"

She shrugged. "I don't drive."

"You never learned how to drive?"

Addison wasn't about to explain her story to Zach Brody. But the truth was, she'd been learning how to drive right around the time her parents' car had been plowed into by a drunk driver on Queens Boulevard, pushing them into oncoming traffic, where they were hit by three more vehicles, including an eighteen-wheeler. When someone told Addison they had died instantly, she wasn't sure what instant they were referring to and spent far too many nights wondering about those last seconds of their lives.

After that, there was no one to teach Addison to drive, but also no motivation to learn. In fact, the very idea became terrifying. Now, though, she would need to overcome her fear. There was just no way to make a life for herself in Los Angeles without a car.

"I'm from Queens," she said to Zach.

He nodded, taking that in. "But now that you're here . . ."

"I'll take lessons, I guess." She stared off in the distance to look for her Uber, hoping to end the conversation, but Zach didn't move.

"Can I offer you a lift someplace?" he asked.

Addison looked back at his face, which had turned surprisingly kind. Open. So different from the seething resentment that had bubbled up by the pool. "Why are you being nice to me all of a sudden?" she asked.

"You have no car," he said, as if it were the most pitiable thing he could imagine.

Addison bristled. "I'm fine," she said, rejecting his misplaced sympathy. "I'm waiting for an Uber."

"*Mostly* fine," he corrected, and it took Addison a minute to realize he was joking. But she didn't laugh. She just watched as he walked around to the driver's side of his McLaren.

"Addison?" he called, looking over the roof of his car.

"Yes?"

"I can teach you."

"Excuse me?" she asked, certain she had heard wrong.

"I'm an excellent driver, I know all the traffic laws, and I'm very patient."

Suddenly, his pity felt like concern, and despite herself Addison was touched. He really wanted to help her. It wasn't something she had expected, and it formed a lump in her throat. For a moment, she considered accepting, but then she looked back at his car. There was no way she was getting behind the wheel of that thing.

"I can't possibly," she said, pointing to the vehicle.

"I also have a Prius."

She nearly laughed. "Of course you do."

He cocked his head. "Why does everyone say that to me?"

"It's the tech-nerd thing, Zach."

He said nothing—just stood there with that tiny smile again.

"Oh," she said, "you were joking."

"You're learning."

"So you're not offended at being called a tech nerd?" she asked.

Zach shrugged it off. "Of course not. But what gave it away?"

He seemed sincere. Forthcoming. So she said, "People talk. Also, you named your cat Betty Snyder. But even if I didn't know that about you, I'd know that about you."

He seemed to accept the answer, but almost immediately, it looked like he checked out, his mind wandering elsewhere. He appeared to be working out a problem in his head.

"You okay?" she asked.

He looked back at her as if he had momentarily forgotten where he was. "Just thinking about something," he said, and Addison suspected he did that kind of thing a lot—occupational hazard of the boy genius.

"Well, bye," he said abruptly, then got into his space car and drove off, leaving Addison wondering if she'd ever get used to LA.

Chapter 18

After the Uber came and whisked Addison off to the bar, things felt more familiar. It was crowded and noisy—with the occasional trill of laughter rising above the cacophony—and smelled of beer, sweat, and perfume. It could have been a bar in Manhattan or a million other cities. Her eyes swept the place, taking in the crowd, zeroing in on the flirting between strangers. This had been part of her training when she worked for Piper, and she strained to pick out the couples that would wind up together—at least for the night. She went to the bar to get herself a drink, then heard someone call her name.

It was Raphael, the personal trainer who doubled as Frankie's assistant. He was sitting at a small table with three of the women who worked at the salon. As Addison approached with her mojito, she saw that the next table was also filled with fellow staffers, including Joaquín, the guy who'd invited her to the bar. He called out to her, but Addison just gave a smile and wave, opting to make Raphael's table her first stop. After all, she'd barely met any of the other women who worked in the building, and she was hungry for female friendship. Things had gone pretty south with her bestie in New York just before she left. When Addison confessed that she'd cheated on Marco with a client, Courtney had said, *Girl, you're some piece of shit.* It was hard to come back from that, even after Courtney assured Addison she still loved her.

"Bitch, those jeans," Raphael said to her. "You could turn me straight."

"As if," said Naomi, the oldest one in the group. She had bright-red hair, and Addison seemed to remember that she was a divorced colorist.

The other young women at the table were Mei and Tameka. They all greeted Addison warmly, but Naomi's eyes kept darting back to a cute guy in a tight T-shirt. The kind of guy, Addison thought, who would be taking home a twenty-year-old.

"How's your first week going?" asked Tameka. She was pretty and petite, with a halo of soft black curls and a nose ring. There was an intelligence around her eyes that Addison was drawn to. She recalled the women in salon robes who had tried to get her fired, but she didn't want to bring it up now, in front of everyone. Later, in private.

"Full of surprises," Addison simply said.

Tameka nodded. "I hear you."

"Tell her about the old guy," Raphael said to Tameka.

Tameka laughed, embarrassed, then leaned in toward Addison. "This creepy old dinosaur came in to get his back waxed. Then he wanted me to watch him . . ." She trailed off, glancing around the group as she tried to find a way to finish the sentence. But she didn't need to, as Raphael mimed a hand tugging on a dick.

The whole group laughed, and when Addison asked "Was his name Mr. Posner?" they nearly fell apart, howling with glee.

"Not you too!" Tameka said.

"He showed up at my apartment with a bottle of oil and a wad of bills."

The group squealed even louder.

At that, Joaquín approached their table, leaning over Addison. She could smell the beer on his breath, and it reminded her of an ex-boyfriend.

"What am I missing?" he asked.

"Mr. Posner hit on Addison," Naomi said.

"Showed up at her *apartment*," Tameka clarified.

"That fucker," Joaquín said to her, and it seemed like Tameka was going to respond, but he cut her off, addressing Addison. "Did you call security?"

"I just sent him away. I think he's mostly harmless."

He put a heavy hand on her shoulder. "Just be careful," he said, then announced to the group that he was going to the bar and asked who was ready for a refill.

Only Tameka piped in, requesting a hugo spritz.

When Joaquín was out of earshot, Raphael looked at Addison and nodded in his direction. "You could get lucky tonight, girl. Unless, of course, there's another guy in the building you're busy with?"

He raised his eyebrows to suggest he knew something, and Addison felt her pulse race. Were people already gossiping about her and Dante? That was just the kind of thing that could find its way back to Frankie. She sipped her mojito and knew she had to tourniquet this gossip before another word was spilled.

"I am off men for the time being," she said, holding up her hands in surrender.

Tameka muttered a sad "Me too," but Mei's eyes lit up.

"Girls?" she asked, tucking her lavender hair behind her ears. She wore clown-pink lipstick and a vest that looked like it was made from a discarded Muppet.

"Not girls, either, I'm afraid. I plan to be celibate for a while."

"How come?" Tameka asked, looking genuinely curious.

"Just . . . dealing with some unresolved issues."

"I told you," Raphael said to the other three, "this bitch has got a dark past."

"Kind of," Addison admitted, wondering what else they said about her. She changed the subject. "What about Joaquín? What's his story?"

"Bitch thinks he's a screenwriter," Raphael said.

"He *is* a screenwriter," Tameka corrected.

Raphael scoffed. "Has he sold anything?" Tameka shrugged, and he turned to Addison. "He's aw'right. But he fucks anything that moves, and he drinks too much."

"Sounds like just my type." Addison sighed. In truth, she'd been involved with a drinker before she met Marco, and it was a mess. Sean was smart and funny as hell. Also crazy about her. So she kept making excuses for him but was in such terror every time he got behind the wheel of the car that she finally couldn't take it anymore and gave him an ultimatum: *me or the booze*. He picked up a bottle of Jack and said goodbye.

"I heard Joaquín slept with Sage Saunders," Naomi said, and Addison was surprised. She knew all the men lusted for smoking-hot Sage, but didn't think the girl with daddy issues would go for a guy in his twenties.

"I heard that too," Tameka offered. "Told her he sold a screenplay."

"I thought Sage only liked old men," Addison cut in.

"They got it all wrong," Raphael scolded. "He slept with Sage's *mom*."

Addison laughed, aware that she was only beginning to grasp what went on in Beekman Towers. Fortunately, she had tapped into the main artery of the gossip flow. "What have I gotten myself into with this place?" she asked.

"You haven't heard the half of it," Raphael said, leaning in. "You know Jake? The lifeguard?"

"Is he here?" Addison asked, looking around.

"He's too busy screwing old ladies," Naomi said.

"And they buy him shit," Tameka added.

Addison thought about the woman in the elevator who'd flirted with Jake, and wondered if they'd slept together. She also wondered how all this was happening under the boss's nose. Jake did not seem like he had the wherewithal to be discreet.

"Does Frankie know about this?" she asked. "Because she lectured me about *boundaries*."

"Frankie?" Raphael said with a dismissive wave. "If it makes the residents happy, she looks the other way." He stopped to sip his drink. "Usually."

"Usually?" Addison asked.

"It's different for the concierge," Mei said.

"I think it's because you're the face of the building," Tameka offered. "And Frankie's surrogate."

Raphael nodded. "You're here to set a good example for the children."

"That's what we call the residents," Naomi explained. "Children. Or sometimes brats."

"Speaking of brats," Raphael said, leaning in conspiratorially, "you have to spill what's going on with you and Mr. Wrong. Because I don't believe you're really celibate."

Damn. He knew something. Had someone seen Dante leaving her room? If so, she'd just have to tell them she sent him away before anything happened. For now, though, she'd play innocent.

"I don't know what you're talking about," she insisted.

"Come on," he said. "Dish. We won't tell Frankie."

Tameka caught her eye and gave her a warning look that said *You have a right to remain silent.* And Addison felt the warmth of knowing she might have found a friend.

"There's nothing to tell," she insisted.

"Come on, everyone sees you together. He follows you around like a puppy, watching your every move."

Like a puppy? Addison let out a laugh. They weren't talking about Dante. They were talking about Zach.

"What's so funny?" Mei asked.

"Remember the boy in elementary school who waited for you to mess up so he could go tell the teacher and score brownie points?" Addison said. "That's Zach Brody. Trust me, his only interest is in making sure I follow the rules and do my job." Even as she said it, though, Addison thought about the kindness in his face when he offered to teach her how to drive and wondered if she'd got him all wrong.

Raphael stirred his drink with a tiny straw, his pinky elegantly pointed. "Hate to break it to you, girl," he said, "but that freaky little boy wasn't trying to impress the teacher. He was trying to get your attention."

Chapter 19
ARNIE

He shouldn't have done it. He knew he shouldn't have done it. And now, well, extricating himself from Melody was going to be even harder. That morning, Arnie had awoken to one missed call from her and two texts. He didn't respond, as he needed to carve out some time to figure out how to handle her. Maybe on the golf course, once he was in the zone, it would all crystallize.

But as he drove there for his weekly game, another text came in. Great news, it began, and went on to explain that thanks to her PR connections, she had been able to get them dinner reservations that night at Spago.

As luck would have it, he didn't have to lie, as he already had plans for that night—a bar mitzvah in Los Angeles he couldn't possibly miss, as it was for the son of a young medical colleague—a former protégé who was now one of the best rhinoplasty surgeons in Southern California. He texted back to tell her he was busy, and shut off his phone.

He didn't turn it on again until he was back home and freshly showered. There were three more missed calls from her and a voicemail he couldn't bring himself to play back. But he knew it was time. Like ripping off a Band-Aid, he told himself. Just get it over with.

Arnie was glad he'd waited until after his long morning on the green. He was more relaxed now, and also grateful he could do this over the phone. If he had to face her, he'd be in danger of succumbing. God help him, but he found her devastatingly sexy. Almost as alluring as Paulette.

"Hey, babe!" she bubbled. "I've been trying you all morning."

"I know," he said. "I was golfing."

"Doctors and their golf!" she trilled with a laugh.

"Listen, Melody," he began.

"I'm so sad you're busy tonight!" she said. "Are you sure it's something you can't get out of?"

"It's a long-standing thing," he explained. "A bar mitzvah, actually. One of my colleagues—"

"Can't you bring a plus-one?" she interrupted. "I'd love to meet some of your friends."

"No," he said firmly. "I can't. In fact, this whole thing . . . Melody, I can't be in a relationship right now. I'm sorry."

There was a long pause, and Arnie tensed, waiting for a response. Give her time to process it, he told himself. She'll be fine.

"What do you mean?" she finally said, her voice accusatory.

"I mean, you're a wonderful gal. Really. It's just . . . the timing isn't good for me. I can't see you anymore."

"You're breaking up with me?" she said. "I can't believe it. I can't believe you're breaking up with me."

Arnie sighed, because it's not a breakup if you weren't together to begin with. "I think you misinterpreted what happened between us."

"Are you saying it was just sex?"

"Um . . ."

"Because I felt something, and you felt it too. I know it. I know you did. When I was in your arms . . . something incredible passed between us. Something *real*. Don't deny it!"

The woman's delusional, he thought, and tried to keep his voice sympathetic but professional, like he was handling a difficult patient.

"Listen," he said, aware that there was no good way to answer her question, "I think I'm getting back together with my ex-wife."

At that, she went quiet. Eerily quiet. Like the moment before an explosion.

"Melody?" he asked, not sure if she had hung up.

"Hang on a minute," she said, all business, and he heard a rustling sound, as if she were walking. After a minute or two, the phone went silent.

"Are you there?" he said, but there was no answer. Had she hung up or merely put him on mute? He wanted to disconnect the call but was afraid it might send her into a tailspin. So he went about his business, holding on to his phone as he looked into his closet, deciding what tie he would wear with his silver-blue suit.

The doorbell buzzed, and Arnie froze. Please, he thought, don't let it be her.

"Who's there?" he called, and when no one answered, he felt sure it was his neighbor Sally, the elderly actress, who was going deaf and didn't usually wear her hearing aids unless she was headed out. But when he swung open the door, there stood Melody, and she was a mess—her eyes red, her mascara running, her face wet with tears.

His heart sank—a combination of pity and dread. But Arnie stood in the doorway, blocking her entrance. He had to be firm.

"You shouldn't have come," he said.

"Babe," she pleaded, "look me in the eye and tell me I don't mean anything to you."

"I can't be your boyfriend," he said, looking past her, as he thought he saw Sally's door opening. "I'm sorry."

"I knew it!" she cried. "I knew you couldn't look me in the eye and tell me you don't care for me."

At that, Sally stuck her head out, her hair slick with wet henna. "Do you need me to call security, Arnie?" she asked.

Melody turned toward her in a fury. "Go fuck yourself, you old bag!"

Sally's door slammed shut.

"Oh, Melody, that was uncalled for," Arnie scolded her.

She pulled a tissue from her cleavage and wiped her nose. "But Arnie," she said, "*that's* who did it. That's who took your Fabergé egg."

"What?" he asked, certain he had misunderstood.

"It was her," Melody said, "and I have proof."

Arnie hesitated for a terrible second. And then, despite a voice telling him not to, he opened the door to Melody Forrest. Again.

Chapter 20
CARLY

Carly could barely think over the frantic thudding of her heart. She'd had coffee with Maya Mayfield. *The* Maya Mayfield. And (dared she even believe it?) they were practically friends.

Staring across the table into Maya's driftwood-gray eyes had been like a dream. They'd talked, joked, laughed, and even planned how Maya might relaunch her brand.

"You have so many great ideas," Maya had said, and for a magical moment Carly had actually felt valuable, like she had something to add. It was as if all those nights steeped in the lives of influencers—combined with her experience writing PR and marketing copy—had been preparing for her just that moment.

Now, Carly realized her chance encounter with her idol had shifted something profound in her heart. Just that morning, she'd been considering Owen's pleas to come back to him. When he said "I'll come and get you. I have the address," she'd pictured opening the door to him, letting him inside the apartment as she packed her things.

But now, well, it was unthinkable. There was so much on the horizon. It felt like anything was possible.

At the time, she had somehow convinced herself his comment was kind of romantic. But now that she thought about it, the message was borderline creepy, as she had never given him her address. In fact, when she first told him she was leaving and he pressed her for it, saying he would need to forward her mail, she had told him that mail had become irrelevant, as everything was online. He had snorted and called her an idiot, not bothering to clarify what was so stupid about her logic.

Still, she understood how he'd gotten her address, and it was her fault. She had let slip the name of the building. And since he knew the condo was under her brother's name, it would have been easy to look it up. Out of curiosity, Carly tried it herself, googling her brother's name, Leonard Gronek, and "Beekman Towers." And there it was, complete with her unit number, 506.

For a moment, Carly wondered if he might just show up. But no, she assured herself, it was ridiculous to even imagine Owen buying his own plane ticket, renting a car, and finding his way here. He'd always relied on her to make those kinds of plans, as he was a little dyslexic and it was a challenge for him.

"It's all about moving forward," Maya had said, and she was right. Carly had a new life now, and Owen had no part of it. The longer she went without seeing him, the more his presence would recede, until it was like a faded photograph she could tuck away forever.

It's all about moving forward. Such a simple line. So pithy. Carly repeated it to herself again and again, and it filled her.

Emboldened, she scrolled through her texts to find the one from her brother with the number of a divorce attorney. She'd been reluctant to take that step, telling herself it was the money. Lenny had already done so much for her, and she didn't want to run up some ridiculous tab with a high-priced lawyer. But now, well, Carly was ready. She would just take on more freelance work so she could pay him back. It was easier to find the time now that she didn't have to look after Owen.

Carly's finger hovered over the lawyer's number, trying to find her nerve. It was such a big step. I just need to take a minute, she thought, putting down the phone. She went to her laptop and sent emails to two clients, telling them she was available for more work. With any luck, they'd hire her for some big projects, and she'd be on better financial footing.

Now, she told herself. Just do it. She pictured making the call and then texting Maya the news. She'd hear from her right away. *Proud of you, girl!* she'd probably say.

And that was all the motivation she needed. Carly called the lawyer's office and made the appointment.

Then, instead of texting Maya the news, Carly decided she needed a walk—she'd take a stroll around the facilities, and maybe she'd even run into Maya. That would be better. Then she could mention it incidentally. *Oh, guess what*, she'd say, *I called that lawyer.* And then Maya would put a hand on her shoulder and give her that smile. Or maybe she'd even move in for a hug. Just the thought of it gave her the kind of warm rush she'd hadn't felt in years, maybe decades. She grabbed her keys and left.

Chapter 21
ADDISON

Sunday was Addison's first day off since starting this new gig, so she was damn well going to sleep in. The plan was to stay in bed until midday, then maybe spend the afternoon by the pool, reading a book, hoping she wouldn't be pestered by anyone. It would just be her, that glorious sun, and a tall glass of iced coffee she'd sip through a straw.

But that was still hours away. For now, she was in the middle of a luxurious dream, making out with some smoking-hot guy in an office building hallway. It was furtive, forbidden, exquisite. And then, just as the heat was about to consume them, two harsh buzzes jolted her awake. Rude. Addison rolled over and looked at the clock. It was 10:30 a.m., and someone was at her door.

"Fuck off," she muttered, and pulled the pillow over her head, trying to find her way back into the dream. She had nearly reached it when the buzzing came again. She felt certain it was some resident who didn't give a goddamn that it was her day off and needed her to schedule them a fingernail massage or chakra bleaching or some such entitled bullshit.

She got out of bed and pulled open the door, still wearing the tunic she'd fallen asleep in.

"What?" she demanded, only to discover she was facing Zach Brody, who looked freshly showered.

"You were sleeping?" he asked.

"It's my day off," she said. "What do you want?"

He held up something that looked like a key fob. "I was going to give you a driving lesson in the Prius."

"This early?"

"It's ten thirty," he said, "and you're normally at the concierge desk at ten, so I figured you would be up."

She realized that he'd pressed her buzzer at precisely ten thirty. Clearly, he'd planned this out like a rocket launch, except for one important detail. He hadn't told her.

"You've given this a lot of thought," she said.

"I wouldn't characterize it as a lot, but of course that's relative."

Addison rubbed her face. When he wasn't being a dick, there was something almost unbearably cute about his nerdiness. "I need to shower."

"I can wait for you," he said, without budging, and Addison knew he expected her to invite him inside. But she decided that would be a bad idea. Not that she thought he'd push his way into the bathroom while she was naked, but why open herself to temptation right after that steamy dream?

"Wait in the lobby," she said, "and then you'll take me out for coffee before putting me in the driver's seat."

As he nodded and turned to walk away, Addison felt a twinge of concern. Was this the kind of fraternizing that would piss Frankie off? She remembered the terrible moment Piper had fired her and shuddered at the thought of reliving that.

"Just one more thing," she said to Zach, "and it's important. We have to make sure Frankie doesn't see us leaving together. She doesn't want me socializing with the residents."

His face went tight in thought. "Is this against the rules?"

"Sort of."

Zach looked as if he were in pain.

"It's not like we're committing a felony," Addison said. "Frankie just wants me to keep my distance."

He scratched his chin. "Interestingly hypocritical," he said.

"How so?"

"She's playing tennis with residents right now."

"Right now?" Addison asked.

"It's Sunday," he said, as if that made the answer obvious.

"Frankie plays every Sunday?"

"Mixed doubles," he clarified. "With your uncle. You didn't know?"

She did not. Of course, Arnie had mentioned he was friends with Frankie, but Addison had assumed that was just part of his everyday charm—her outgoing uncle was chummy with everybody. The word her mother had used was *convivial*. Still, Addison was surprised to learn it was a real enough friendship to include a weekly tennis game, especially since Frankie had been so adamant about boundaries.

But Addison decided it wasn't worth working herself into a lather over. So she just explained to Zach that this was good news, as it meant Frankie wouldn't see them leaving together. And Zach—armed with the knowledge that Frankie didn't practice what she preached—decided he was amenable to breaking this one unjust rule. Addison rewarded him with a smile and got ready for her first driving lesson in LA.

Chapter 22

They picked up coffee at Starbucks, and Addison drank hers as Zach drove them to his chosen starting point for the lesson. He pulled over, and they switched places.

"Where are we going?" Addison asked as she buckled herself in.

"Just up the coast a bit," he said, and instructed her to keep her foot on the brake as she put the car in gear. "And don't forget to signal as you're pulling away from the curb."

Addison held tight to the steering wheel, hands at nine and three—not ten and two—recalling the driving lessons she'd taken ten years ago. Then she did as Zach said, clicking on the signal and easing out onto the Pacific Coast Highway. She was driving.

I can be chill about this, she told herself, even as her heart thudded and her forehead prickled with sweat. Totally chill. After all, it had been over ten years since her parents' car accident. She was a grown-ass woman now. She had gotten on with her life. Surely she could get on with this driving thing. She tried to relax her shoulders despite how tightly she gripped the steering wheel, desperate to avoid a crash.

"You can go a little faster," Zach said. "You're under the speed limit."

Addison looked down at the speedometer and noted she was going twenty-five miles an hour. Faster, she thought, and tried willing herself to press down on the accelerator, but her foot seemed frozen in place.

"I . . . I can't," she said.

"It's fine, I promise."

Addison didn't even know if she could speak about it without breaking down, and struggled to find her voice. "You don't understand," she muttered.

"So tell me," he said, his voice gentle.

Still holding fast to the steering wheel, she took a labored breath. "My parents died in a car crash."

It was the worst sentence in the world. She hated saying it and knew from experience that people hated hearing it. The car seemed to fill with a dark silence, and the coffee went sour in Addison's stomach.

Zach said nothing, and she couldn't bring herself to glance his way, even for a second. She kept her eyes epoxied to the road.

"I'm very sorry," he finally said, then went silent for a long time as if he were figuring out what to say next. "Are you okay? Do you want to pull over?"

She shook her head, done with the topic. "I'm fine."

"Okay then," he said, acknowledging her choice, and retreated again, clearly thinking about what to say. At last he announced, "You know, it's extremely unlikely you'll crash. Plus, it's nearly impossible to have a fatal accident at this speed."

Damn, this guy was logical.

"Okay," she said, and tried to fill her lungs.

"Also, remember that even the stupidest people drive. So surely it's a skill you can learn."

Despite herself, Addison laughed. "Is that supposed to make me feel better?" she asked.

"Yes, actually."

Addison realized, then, that it did, despite his clumsy phrasing. She *could* learn how to drive. Every idiot she'd ever met had a driver's license. She gave the accelerator a little more pressure.

"You're doing great," he said. "It's just a matter of practice."

"As long as I don't have to drive on the freeway," she said, "I think I can do this."

"Don't worry. I'm not taking you on the freeway today. Just go straight. It's a long road."

They drove for about ten minutes without talking, which didn't even feel awkward. She was too focused on steering. When a car came up on the left, driving awfully close to her, Addison tensed.

"It's fine," Zach said as if reading her mind. "He's not that close. You're perfectly safe."

It was the exact right thing to say, and Addison's fingers actually loosened their death grip.

"Did I even remember to thank you for doing this?" she asked. "It's so kind of you. So generous."

His response was an indecipherable mutter, as if he didn't want to talk about it, and she wondered if he was uncomfortable with her gratitude.

"Do you like the car?" he asked.

Relaxing a little into the seat, she realized that she did. It was the perfect vehicle for driving lessons. Solid but unintimidating, confident but not cocky. She never would have felt this way in his crazy sports car.

"I do," she said.

The car in front of her slowed down as they rounded a curve, and she did, too, despite how much distance there was between them.

"What made you decide to get the McLaren?" Addison asked, picturing the yellow-and-black spaceship she'd seen in front of the building. It was such a flashy, incongruous choice.

"That was Quinn, my former fiancée. She said we needed to project a certain image."

Of course, she thought. That made perfect sense—the choice hadn't been his at all. Addison resisted the urge to glance over to read his expression.

"What kind of image?" she pressed.

"We were trying to get financing for our business, and Quinn said we needed to look successful. In Los Angeles it's all about the car."

"Did it work?"

"Well, the financing came through, but . . ." He trailed off, and she managed to glance at him for a microsecond. He was looking out the window.

"But?" she prodded, her eyes back on the road.

"I don't want to talk about it."

He went quiet after that, and Addison let him sit with whatever he needed to work through. After several minutes, though, he told her to take the next right onto a small residential road. She used her signal, making a slow, cautious turn.

"Now a left," he said.

She made the turn more confidently and asked, "Where are we going?"

"Just up there." He pointed. "Turn on your signal and pull over."

She steered carefully to the side of the road, stopped the car, and put it in park.

"That was good," he said, and she looked over at his smooth, boyish face, with just a brush of stubble around his jawline. His nose and cheekbones had picked up a hint of sunburn from all his time in the pool, and it triggered a kind of tenderness that seemed to wriggle down her gullet.

"Why are we stopped?" she asked. "Are you okay?"

"See that house?" he said, indicating a sprawling glass-and-steel home on a cliff overlooking Malibu Beach. "That's where she lives."

"Your ex?" Addison asked as she took it in. The house rested on one of the most expensive pieces of real estate in the world and was designed for expansive views of the Pacific Ocean. There was no way she could estimate how much something like that might cost. Tens of millions, maybe?

"They just moved in," he said.

"They?"

"Quinn and Eli, my business partner. *Former* business partner."

Addison had already heard part of this story from Arnie, but she didn't want to let on. "Your fiancée and your former business partner are living together?"

Zach looked from the house back to Addison. "They scammed me. Out of everything."

Well, not everything, she wanted to say. Because he lived in a multimillion-dollar condo in Beverly Hills and owned a car that cost more than most people earned in five years. But she didn't doubt they ripped him off, so she just asked what kind of business it was.

"I invented an app," he said. "An aggregator of all the resale apps. So, like, if you were looking for a used couch and you lived in Cincinnati or wherever, the app would scan OfferUp, eBay, Craigslist, et cetera, and find all the couches in your area."

"What a smart idea."

"The coding was really complicated."

"You must have been so proud."

He nodded, thinking about it. For a long moment, he seemed lost in thought, and she waited for him to return.

"When I got it working," he said, "I was just . . . it was the greatest feeling. I can't even describe it. But just as we got set to launch, Quinn and Eli sold it to an investor and cut me out. They'll wind up making at least a billion dollars."

"Jeez," Addison said, trying to wrap her head around losing that kind of money. "Are you going to sue them?"

"I'm working on it."

"Is that what that early-morning meeting was about?" she asked. "Were you talking to attorneys?"

He shook his head. "That was something else," he said. "Another idea I'm trying to get financing for. Unfortunately, I'm not very good at that part. But Quinn was. Eli too."

Addison pictured the two of them as ruthless and charming, polished with oil. She wondered if Quinn's whole relationship with Zach had been part of the scam. Her heart broke for him.

"But you're going to keep trying," she said, "right?"

He pushed at a cuticle. "I'm up for a developer award. If I win, everyone will want to give me money."

"Great!" she said. "When will you know if you won?"

"Everyone says I'm a shoo-in, but I'll know for sure next week. There's an awards ceremony." He closed his eyes as if he were in pain.

"Oh, shit," she said. "Quinn is going to be there, right?"

"With Eli."

"Fuck."

"I was going to ask you," he said, "if you might come with me."

And just like that, Addison understood the offer to give her driving lessons. It wasn't magnanimous. At least not entirely. He needed a favor—a woman on his arm when he saw Quinn again.

Oddly, Addison didn't feel resentful. If anything, it put her at ease. Zach hadn't made some grand gesture of generosity. This was transactional.

"When is it?" she asked.

"Next Sunday."

She was off on Sundays and Mondays, so there was no reason to turn him down. "Okay," she said with a shrug, "I'll do it."

"You will?" He sounded incredulous.

"You want me to wear something sexy?" she asked, trying to get a pulse on his desire to make Quinn jealous. But he just stared back at the house, his beautiful green eyes so sorrowful it looked like it took everything he had to keep from crying. The guy was a brokenhearted wreck, and even his weird hostility made sense now. His feelings toward women were inexorably knotted in a dark tangle of betrayal.

And Addison, god help her, had never wanted to kiss anyone more.

Chapter 23

"You look *hot*," Dante said, taking her in.

Addison was glad he appreciated the outfit—a short flouncy skirt and silver heels to show off her legs. Still, she backed off so he wouldn't hug her out here in public. They were in front of the Beekman's circular driveway, where they had planned to rendezvous for their dinner date with her uncle.

"Where's Arnie?" she asked.

"He texted to say he and the mystery woman would meet us at the restaurant."

Addison glanced nervously around. She had intended to get into Arnie's car, which wouldn't have triggered a reprimand from Frankie. Now, she'd be sinking into Dante's flamboyant Porsche and speeding off into the night.

"Can you just pretend we're not together?" she said, turning her back to him. She looked off in the distance as if she were waiting for someone.

"Chill," he said, "it's a Frankie-free zone."

"You sure?" she said over her shoulder.

Dante gestured around, and Addison scanned the area. No Frankie. She tried to let that relax her but couldn't release the paranoia Zach had triggered. At this point, she was fairly confident he wasn't going to rat her out to Frankie, but there were other residents about, and these people loved to gossip. She wished the valet would hurry with Dante's car.

She sighed, frustrated Arnie hadn't realized the predicament he had put her in. But she supposed he was out with his "lady friend," as he called her, and had gotten caught up in whatever they'd been doing. Maybe that was a good thing. Maybe he found someone on his own who would distract him from Paulette. Addison was curious to meet her.

Until yesterday, she had been committed to finding Leyla Balik and asking her to join them tonight. In fact, she'd even abandoned the concierge desk to see if the woman was in her reading spot again. Her plan was to have a quick conversation and get back to her post before Frankie even noticed she was missing.

When she got up to the rooftop, though, there had been no sign of Leyla. Addison was ready to rush back to the elevator when Zach called out from the pool.

"She's not here!" he said, wiping the water from his face.

"What?"

"That lady you're looking for. She doesn't come on Saturdays."

"Thanks," Addison said, and turned to rush back to her post. But someone stood in her way. Frankie.

"What is going on?" she demanded, hands on hips. "Why aren't you at the desk?"

"I . . . ," Addison began. "There's somebody . . ." She trailed off, unable to think of a single lie.

"It'll be much simpler if you just tell me the truth," Frankie said.

But safer if I lie, Addison thought as she struggled to come up with a plausible excuse. Then Frankie's searing gaze bored a tunnel into her soul, and Addison felt the fight drain out. This indomitable woman would see right through even the cleverest fiction.

So Addison did exactly as her boss demanded. She told the truth, spilling it all and hoping for at least a little sympathy.

"I know you told me not to play matchmaker, but I'm so worried about Arnie. If you'd seen the photos of him after his fight with Paulette, you'd understand."

Frankie set her jaw. "Addison," she said sternly.

"Please," Addison cut in. "Arnie is my family. My *only* family. And I owe him so much."

"So you abandoned your post just to—"

"I met this woman named Leyla Balik. She's perfect for him! But she's as elusive as Cinderella, and I can't—"

"This has to stop," Frankie said, folding her arms.

"But my uncle—"

"It's not that I'm unsympathetic, but you're not a matchmaker anymore. You're a concierge. And anyway, your uncle is a grown man. Let him make his own decisions."

"But she sent him to the *hospital*. Did you ever notice that scar by his—"

"Addison, I mean it. If you want to keep this job, you have to stop this nonsense. I don't want you bothering the residents or chasing down Regina English's nurse. Am I clear?"

For a moment, Addison went mute. Because yes, Frankie's instructions were very clear. It was her motivation that confused Addison. Why was this such a big deal for her? After all, Frankie was dedicated to meeting even the most intimate needs of the residents. Why was matchmaking so verboten?

Then Addison remembered what she'd heard about her predecessor, Jenna, who ran off with one of the residents. Someone told her it had been a huge scandal, and Addison figured Frankie was determined to keep her on a short leash so it wouldn't happen again.

It was discouraging, because she felt like she owed it to her darling uncle—not to mention her dead mother—to do whatever it would take to protect him. Then a less discouraging thought occurred to her. Frankie had just inadvertently divulged the identity of Leyla Balik—she was the caretaker of the woman in the wheelchair. Plus, Addison recalled that Dr. English had said something about finding a love match for her beautiful nurse. It was all so perfect Addison couldn't help remembering a Yiddish word Arnie had taught her: *bashert*. It had something to do with destiny intervening to bring two people together. Addison even thought it was possible her mother was meddling from beyond. She simply had to see this through.

And so, with a chill, Addison knew what she had to do. She looked Frankie straight in the eye and said, "Yes, you're perfectly clear."

And that was why, several hours later—when Frankie was out at a meeting—Addison found herself pressing the buzzer of Regina English's unit.

"To what do I owe the pleasure?" Regina asked as she led Addison into the apartment. It was quiet except for some operatic music playing softly in the background. It didn't appear that Leyla was around.

"Your nurse isn't here today?" Addison asked.

"Not on weekends. And I do miss her." She brought her wheelchair to a stop in the living room, indicating that Addison should have a seat.

"That's actually what I wanted to talk to you about," Addison said, lowering herself into the plush gray sofa. "I believe I met her. Leyla, right?"

"Isn't she absolutely lovely? And such a force of nature."

"You said something about wanting to find a good man for her?" The doctor leaned forward. "Do you know someone?"

"That's what I wanted to talk to you about. It's my uncle, Arnie Glass."

Regina English looked surprised by this information. "I know Dr. Glass. I never considered him. Doesn't he have a string of failed marriages?"

Addison shrugged. "He's made a few mistakes. But I think he's ready to settle down now. And Leyla—she just seems perfect for him . . . smart, intellectually curious. And strong! Arnie loves strong women."

Dr. English nodded, bobbing her large head on her frail neck. "I hate to be indelicate, but I have to ask. Leyla is a very sexual woman, and Dr. Glass is over seventy, so . . ."

"Oh, that's definitely not a problem."

"You're certain of this?"

Just ask half the women in the building, Addison wanted to say, but thought that might be overselling it. "He's . . . vigorous."

"A doctor and a nurse," Regina mused. "Lord knows it's worked before."

"Do you think she might be free tomorrow night?" Addison asked. "I've arranged a sort of double date."

"I'm afraid not. She's going out with Geoffrey tomorrow."

"Your son?"

Dr. English looked exasperated. "He's absolutely besotted."

Besotted? Addison went on high alert. "Wait a minute," she said, hoping the strange thought that just came to her was utterly and completely wrong, "is Leyla the woman who . . . the other night . . ."

"Didn't you know? Yes, cookie. Leyla is Geoffrey's lover."

Addison reeled. "I don't understand," she said. "Why do you want to find a man for her if she's involved with your son?"

"Trust me, she has no interest in Geoffrey outside the bedroom. But he's so madly in love he imagines proposing one day. If I can find someone for Leyla before it gets that far, it will save him from so much heartache."

The stars hadn't aligned after all. Addison sunk with disappointment. Leyla had seemed so perfect for Arnie. But there was no way she'd match him with Geoffrey's dominatrix. She gave Regina English her apologies and explained that under these circumstances, she didn't think they would be a match. Then she rushed back to her post before she got into even more trouble for this fool's errand.

Now, she worried that finding a match for Arnie would be impossible, as Frankie would be laser focused on her efforts. But perhaps her uncle had found someone on his own. He'd seemed excited when he told her he had a date for tonight's dinner.

The valet pulled up with Dante's bright-red Porsche, and Addison took a quick look around before approaching the car. That's when she noticed that Joaquín, who stood next to the doorman, was looking straight at her. He gave a knowing wink as she lowered herself into the passenger seat. And Addison understood that keeping secrets here would be nearly impossible.

Chapter 24
ARNIE

Arnie knew it was absurd to suggest that elderly Sally Conrad had stolen his precious egg. The woman walked with one of those quad canes and couldn't open her own pill bottles. It was hard to imagine her sneaking into his place, tucking the purloined valuable under her arm, and shuffling out the door at the speed of a grand piano being inched across a stage.

"I'm telling you, Arnie," Melody had said. "It was *her*. She was in the hallway when I left."

Arnie shook his head because he knew that Sally had been hobbling toward his door to ask for help. "She didn't take it. Trust me."

"Well, somebody did, and it wasn't *me*." She paused, hand on chest, for a dramatic breath. "Though god knows I could use the money." At that, she broke down into sobs and fell against his chest.

Arnie stood rigidly, but when her sobs increased, he relented, patting her gently on the back. "It's okay, honey. Everything is okay."

"No." She sniffed. "You don't understand."

"Just hang in there. Once the dust settles on your divorce—"

"It's not that. Oh, Arnie. I was fired from my job. Me, fired! I've been too embarrassed to tell anyone."

Her dismay was genuine and palpable, and it seeped into him. "Oh, dear," he said. "I'm so sorry."

"It happened right after I closed on the condo. We lost a big client, and they slashed half the senior staff. It was a bloodletting."

"I'm sure you'll find another job," he said, hoping to cheer her up. "A better one, I'll bet."

Melody looked up at him with her mascara-streaked face. "You believe in me. Oh, Arnie!" She burrowed into him again, sobbing.

"If there's anything I can do to help," he said, and immediately regretted it. He'd given her the proverbial inch, and that could be trouble.

"Really?"

"I mean—"

"Because I've been sleeping on an air mattress, and it's miserable. How am I going to find a new job when I'm a sleep-deprived wreck?"

Arnie felt a rush of panic. Was she going to ask to move in? "Well," he said, "we must get you a proper bed."

She gasped. "I knew you'd help! You're the sweetest, most generous man in the world. When can we go shopping? Tomorrow?"

That was how Arnie found himself spending his whole Sunday with this emotionally desperate woman. And later, after he'd swiped his credit card for a luxury adjustable king-size bed, along with a headboard, a dresser, two night tables, and a velvet side chair, Arnie told himself it wasn't so bad. He could afford it, after all, and it made her beam with joy. Maybe, he decided, it wouldn't be such a terrible thing to bide his time with Melody while he awaited Paulette's return. The larger problem, he realized, would be reuniting with his Fabergé egg. Because he still thought she was the likely culprit.

But for now, he felt buoyed by her gratitude and adoration. So when he waltzed into the restaurant with Melody on his arm, Arnie smiled.

Chapter 25
ADDISON

Oh, no, Addison thought as she saw Arnie enter with crazy, egg-stealing Melody Forrest. Please, no. Anyone but her.

Oddly, Arnie seemed to be in a jovial mood, unconcerned that the woman had manipulated her way into his life. Then Addison found out they had spent the day together, and she hoped it hadn't been a shopping excursion. She imagined him reaching for his wallet again and again and hoped he hadn't bought anything expensive for this unhinged femme fatale.

Just try to enjoy the meal, Addison told herself as she took in the surroundings. The restaurant was a softly lit Mediterranean place in the heart of Beverly Hills. And it smelled delicious—like lemon and garlic and olives and briny fresh seafood. A hostess led them to a comfortable banquette.

"Well, this is wonderful," Melody said after they sat. "I'm so happy to be spending time with Arnie's darling niece and her handsome beau."

"Handsome *fuck buddy*," Addison corrected.

Melody laughed and turned to Dante. "Is that true?"

"I certainly hope so," he said.

"You guys are too cute!" Melody gushed, then brought her hands together. "Now that we've got sex covered, what else should we talk about? Anything but politics, am I right?"

"Right," Arnie said, and Addison understood that Melody would be taking up most of the oxygen that night.

As Melody asked a passing waitress for a glass of wine, Arnie leaned over and whispered to Addison, "She's not too bad, right?"

"Oh, Uncle Arnie," she said quietly, "you can't do this."

"Don't worry," he said, patting her hand, "I'm a big boy."

But she did worry. And suddenly, dominatrix Leyla Balik didn't seem like such an unreasonable alternative.

"Why don't you tell us about your first week on the job," Dante said to Addison. "Is it everything you expected?"

"It is *nothing* that I expected."

"How so?" Melody asked.

"No one told me about the whole Divorce Towers thing. I thought it would be a bunch of snotty rich folk who kept to themselves. Instead it's like Camp Horny for the Wayward Wealthy."

"That's pretty accurate," Dante said.

"What do *you* do?" Melody asked him.

"I'm a talent agent."

Her eyes went wide. "You must have some great stories!"

"I do," he said, tapping his head, "but I keep them up here. I never dish about clients."

"Can you at least tell us who some of them are?"

He went on to list some major names in movies and television, and Melody was breathless with delight. Addison noticed that something or someone had caught Dante's eye, and she followed his line of vision to see a lithe sixty-something man heading for their table. When he got closer, she realized who it was. Kevin Bacon. With zero degrees of separation.

"Dante," Kevin said, extending his hand, "good to see you, man."

"I didn't know you were in town," Dante said as they shook.

"Got in today. We were just talking about you—Kyra and I ran into Cassandra yesterday."

Dante ran his hand through his hair. "I didn't know," he said, then added, "Let me introduce you to my friends—Melody, Arnie, and Addison."

Kevin Bacon said it was good to meet them, gave a charming smile, then left to join his group.

"Is he as nice as he seems?" Melody gushed.

"He's a sweetheart."

"Who's Cassandra?" Addison asked, curious about whether she was someone he represented, someone he slept with, or both.

"Just a mutual friend," Dante said quickly, and Addison suspected there was more to the story, but she wasn't going to press it. In truth, she had no right to the information.

They looked at their menus, and when Arnie made a tired joke about the sea bass, Melody laughed like it was the wittiest, most original thing she'd ever heard.

"Your uncle is so *funny!*" she said to Addison.

"Hilarious," Addison replied.

"He really is," Melody insisted. "But also generous. We spent the whole day shopping for furniture, and he put everything on his credit card. *Everything!*"

Furniture? Jesus. Addison shot him a look, and he gave a sheepish shrug. She knew how stupid men could be when they thought with the brain in their pants, but she never expected her uncle to be such a sucker. Not at his age, and not after all he'd been through.

"Great," Addison said. "I'm sure you kids had a blast at Ikea."

Melody, Arnie, and Dante laughed the laugh of rich folk who thought the idea of sitting on the floor with an Allen wrench and numbered instructions was the height of hilarity. Addison sighed.

"Having fun?" Dante whispered, close to her ear.

"I think I forgot how."

He put a warm hand on her bare thigh. "I can remind you."

She didn't remove his hand. In fact, she wanted him to edge it higher, to feel his breath on her neck again. And just like that, her mood turned from annoyed to thirsty.

"Sounds like a plan," she said.

At the end of the meal, Arnie and Dante did the usual macho thing, bickering over the tab, and when her uncle gave in faster than he normally would have, Addison understood he was likely thinking about his credit card bill.

"Ready to go?" Melody cooed, and Arnie gave her the grin of a guy who had a pocketful of Viagra and knew how to use it.

"Let's stay awhile," Dante said to Addison, and they lingered at the table.

"What now?" she asked him.

"I'm going to take you to my favorite club," he said, "and we're going to dance and drink and stay out late. Then, we'll get back to the Beekman after everyone else has gone to sleep, sneak into your apartment like a couple of nasty ninjas, and finish what we started."

Chapter 26

Her apartment. Yes, that made sense. If they went to his place, she'd wind up in the elevator sometime in the middle of the night—or the wee hours of the morning—dressed in her evening clothes. It would fuel the exact kind of gossip she needed to avoid.

The doormen, valets, and porters were all off duty by the time they got back to the building. So Dante parked his car, and they hurried inside, greeted only by Nikolai, the head of security who had promised to have her back if she ever had a problem.

He put his hand in front of his eyes, discreetly signaling that he was blind to their presence, and she believed him. The guy had a distinct KGB air about him. A vault.

Alone in the elevator, Addison and Dante stood inches apart, staring at each other. How, she wondered, could anyone be so fucking sexy?

"I want so badly to kiss you," he said.

"Then why don't you?"

He nodded toward the ceiling, where a camera was mounted, and Addison wondered how much Nikolai had witnessed over the years.

They were barely through the door of her apartment when she tore off her shirt and he unhooked her bra, his face in her neck. She pushed herself into him, desperate for his pulsing erection. She started unbuttoning his shirt.

Dante kissed her on the mouth, long and deep, and she felt her insides going liquid. She needed him. She needed this gorgeous, sexy man. Right. Fucking. Now.

"I'm kind of torn," he said.

"Torn?" she asked, barely finding the breath for the single syllable.

"Yeah," he said, "because I want to fuck you so fast, but I also want to fuck you so slow."

"Why not both?"

And that's what they did, clawing their way to the bedroom in frantic, breathless desperation, coming together, flesh against flesh, hot and frantic, her body wanting more and more and more and more.

He teased her to the precipice, and when at last her back arched in exquisite release, they fell together, panting and sated but not spent. Not really.

And later, they came together again—this time slowly, tenderly, lovingly—and her orgasm was a prolonged chord, a diva holding and holding and holding that final note, that crescendo, that promise, that nearly intolerable climb to the peak.

Then they were naked, falling asleep in each other's arms as he stroked her hair. He put his lips so tenderly to her forehead that Addison felt her eyes go moist. In that small, affectionate gesture—chaste and grateful—she understood that something had shifted. This was more than sex. For both of them. And all Addison could think was oh, shit.

Chapter 27

Dante left during the night, explaining that he had to get up early for work. The excuse was unnecessary, as Addison had wanted him out of there. She simply couldn't face the kind of lingering, lazy morning of two people falling for each other. No, she wanted to recapture her belief that this was just about sex. And if it wasn't, well, they would not be doing it again. She couldn't possibly get involved with someone like Dante. He was too slick. Too much of a player. She could never relax into a relationship with such a man. Besides, she was sticking to the plan. No involvements for at least a year, so she could figure out why she was so bent on sabotage.

But Arnie. He was someone who needed a relationship, and needed one now, before he got in any deeper with the nutty, manipulative, gold-digging Melody Forrest . . . and before he picked up again with the nutty, manipulative, violent Paulette Davenport-Glass.

And the more Addison thought about it, the more convinced she was that Leyla Balik was the right choice. Of course, she didn't know if Arnie was particularly attracted to S & M, but she was pretty sure a woman who had the personal power to be a dominatrix would make his head spin. So Addison, once again, went up to see Regina English.

This time, the door was answered by Leyla herself, who was surprised to see the concierge coming to call.

"Oh, hello again. Is everything well?"

"Yes, fine," Addison said, deciding Arnie would be instantly attracted to this beautiful woman. Even plainly dressed, there was something softly glamorous about her face—like an old movie star. Or a Turkish Jennifer Lopez. "It's not an official visit or anything," she went on. "I just wanted to talk to Dr. English, if that's okay."

Leyla invited her inside and led her to the doctor, who suggested they talk in her study. Once the door was closed, Addison got right to the point.

"I've changed my mind," she said. "I want to get Arnie and Leyla together. I think they'd be perfect for one another."

"I'm glad you've come around," said Dr. English in her husky voice. "Geoffrey is getting in deeper by the minute. How should we proceed?"

Addison had a plan. She didn't want to fix them up on a date—better to let them get acquainted with each other in a more organic encounter. This way, they wouldn't know it was part of an effort to separate Leyla from Geoffrey.

"I thought we could arrange for them to visit the salon at the same time," Addison said. "I know that Arnie gets manicures, so maybe you could treat Leyla to one, and we could coordinate the appointments."

Regina English looked thoughtful but dubious. "It's a large space. How can we assure they would even cross paths while there?"

"I can arrange to seat them next to each other. And if you could encourage Leyla to bring one of those medical texts she likes to read, I can almost guarantee he'll strike up a conversation."

As Dr. English smiled, her crow's-feet seemed to fan out in delight. "Let's make it happen."

A short while later, Addison went down to the salon to talk to Tameka about the plan, confident her new friend would be willing to help by ensuring the prospective lovebirds sat next to one another.

"You think Dr. Arnie's going to fall in love with Nurse Leyla?" Tameka asked.

"Stranger things have happened."

Tameka gave a cynical shrug. "I'm happy to help," she said, "and I hope it works out. But I have to admit I've lost faith in true love."

Addison studied her face. "Your ex?" she asked.

Tameka heaved such a massive sigh Addison thought she might deflate.

"He was worse than I ever could have imagined." The pain in her eyes looked so fresh Addison asked if she wanted to talk about it.

"There's not much to say. When I suspected he might be sleeping with a woman from work, I sneaked a look at his phone."

Addison was surprised at the bold move from someone so . . . sweet. Clearly, there was more to Tameka than she realized. "Risky business," she observed.

"Tell me about it."

"And you found out he had a girlfriend on the side?"

"Three," Tameka said, shaking her head. "He was sleeping with three different women he met online. And I had no idea. I feel like an idiot."

Addison could see misery fill her whole being. "I'm sorry," she said.

Tameka waved it away, indicating she was done with the subject. "I actually wanted to talk to you about something else," she said, and pulled Addison to an empty corner of the salon.

"What is it?"

"I thought you should know people are talking about you and Dante," Tameka said quietly.

Addison tensed. "Seriously?"

"Someone saw you leave with him last night, and they're drawing all sorts of conclusions."

Addison put her face in her hands. "Shit."

"Are they wrong?" Tameka asked.

For a moment, Addison wondered whether it was wise to fess up, but one look in Tameka's face and she knew she could trust her. "I wish," she muttered.

"Girl, you got to be careful. This is just the kind of thing that would make Frankie go batshit. From what I hear, she's still reeling from what happened with the last concierge."

"I know. I know."

There was a long pause, as if Tameka were deciding whether to push. Then she leaned in and whispered, "Was it worth it?"

Addison flushed with the memory. "Doesn't matter. I'm not going there again."

"Good. And I don't just mean about Frankie. I wouldn't trust that dude for a hot minute."

Addison nodded—she knew Tameka was right. She simply couldn't let herself fall for this guy. He wasn't even her type. And if she could maintain healthy boundaries with Zach—who actually *was* her type— surely she could do the same with Dante.

Today she'd be taking another driving lesson and had already decided she would get through it without flirting with Zach or sending any signals, despite how eager she was to spend time with him. But when she thought about meeting Zach in front of the building in the middle of the day, she realized it could be yet more tinder for the gossip fire. And another reason to ignite her combustible boss.

"I think I might have another problem," she said.

"Tell me."

Addison explained the arrangement she'd made and asked Tameka if she thought it would be bad if anyone spotted her getting into Zach's car.

"*Very* bad," Tameka said. "These folks would love to accuse you of sleeping with half the residents."

"I guess that's it for my driving lessons," Addison said, her disappointment heavier than it should have been.

Tameka tsked. "We can work this out," she said, and explained that she needed to take her daughter to a gymnastics class that afternoon, and it would be easy to give Addison a lift to a rendezvous point where she could meet up with Zach. Addison was delighted with the idea. Tameka really was some kind of angel.

"How does that sound?" Tameka asked.

"Sounds like your ex didn't know how good he had it."

"No shit," Tameka said. Then she announced that her next client was waiting, and Addison left.

When she got back to her apartment, Addison was surprised to see that something had been left in front of her door. It was a massive bouquet of flowers, spreading out three feet wide and four feet tall, like a centerpiece you'd see in a hotel lobby. It was ridiculous. Over the top. And of course, it was from Dante.

Chapter 28
CARLY

For years, Carly had avoided thinking about her appearance, as it had been impossible to make even the slightest effort without opening herself up to Owen's teasing and derision.

Bozo called, he wants his clown paint back.

Oh, please stop with the tight pants—you'll embarrass yourself.

Only whores and idiots whiten their teeth.

So she had mostly avoided mirrors and tried to keep herself invisible. It worked pretty well, as she had spent the last decade or so slipping in and out of rooms like a phantom, unnoticed. It almost felt like a superpower.

Since meeting Maya, though, Carly couldn't help reevaluating. She examined herself in the mirror, wondering how she looked to her new friend. Did Maya think she appeared intelligent, thoughtful, above the petty concerns of vanity? Or did Carly simply look like someone who had given up?

It was time, she decided, for a makeover. Well, maybe not head to toe, but surely she could start with a manicure. She thought about Maya's lovely hands and how it would feel to admire her own nails as she held a coffee cup, pointed to an item on the menu, adjusted a necklace on her clavicle.

As she was about to leave her apartment, Carly's cell phone rang with an unfamiliar number. She answered it, hoping it was a client calling with a new assignment. But when she said, "Hello," no one answered, even though she could hear noise on the other end. For a moment, she wondered if it was Owen but realized that was ridiculous. She knew his number. And this wasn't even from a Nashua area code. Probably just a pocket-dialed wrong number.

Still, it put her on edge, and as she walked toward the salon, Carly couldn't shake the feeling she was being watched.

Stop it, she told herself. For once in your life, things are going really well. Don't let anxiety and your hyperactive imagination ruin it.

By the time she approached the salon, Carly was thinking about Maya and her mood had lifted. Everything was fine. Better than fine, actually. It was all more than she ever dared to dream.

Inside, as she waited, Carly overheard the manicurist talking to Addison, the concierge. There was something about an ex-husband, and it sounded troublesome. Even hostile. Carly wondered if this Tameka was the kind of person Maya would be able to help. Maybe she could even be the first client to experience her friend's rebranding as the Sherpa of breakups. Carly imagined gathering intel and delivering it to Maya, who would shower her with delight and gratitude, and it would feel like the cleansing spray of a summer rain.

"What are we doing today?" Tameka said, examining Carly's nails.

"You think I'd look good with a French?" she asked. Carly had always admired that type of manicure, but even now, after finally understanding how unfair Owen's cruelty had been, a part of her expected to be laughed at. *You? A French manicure? You think you're fancy now?*

Maybe if she hadn't received that pocket dial—and if Owen hadn't been texting her and leaving phone messages—it would be easier to move on. But he still felt like a constant presence in her life.

"I think it would look great!" Tameka said.

As the woman got to work, Carly considered how to broach the subject of what she'd overheard. She wasn't going to pitch the idea of hiring Maya as her life coach—that wasn't Carly's place—but she would gather enough information to start a dossier. She tingled with excitement. This was a perfect project for her.

As she considered how to probe the manicurist for information, Carly's phone buzzed with a text, and she glanced over just in case it was from Maya. But it was Owen. Of course. Almost all her texts were from Owen.

"You have to get that?" Tameka asked.

Carly shook her head. "My ex. He's *pathetic.*"

It felt good to say that out loud—like a belt of whiskey sliding down her gullet. It was a warm burn—loosening her muscles for a fight. And it was true. He really was pathetic, begging her to come back, to talk to him, to start over.

"I hear you," Tameka said.

"Are you divorced?" Carly asked, and it felt so organic. This was exactly the kind of conversation women had with their manicurists. She had to keep herself from shifting in her seat with excitement.

"In the process."

"Does he still call you a lot?"

"Not like in the beginning. He used to beg me to take him back. Now he knows it's never happening."

Carly wondered when Owen's calls and texts would taper off. So far, they had only escalated. In fact, lately there seemed to be more urgency to his pleas. She was grateful they were three thousand miles apart, a whole country between them.

"Did you kick him out?" she asked Tameka, wondering if the woman's ex was like Owen. Did he hurt her with words? Did he wear her down with a slow and constant assault on her ego? Or maybe it was physical. Maybe he was the kind of man who talked with his fists, like her father had.

"He was a serial cheater, and he'll never change."

Oh, that, Carly thought, and made a mental note to research the main causes of divorce. She figured infidelity topped the list, though she recalled reading that money issues were the main cause of marital strife. She imagined researching that for Maya.

"I'm sorry," she said to the manicurist. "That's rough."

Tameka gently pushed at Carly's cuticles with a wood implement. "Yeah."

"Are you . . . doing okay?"

"I guess," Tameka said. "I'll never trust another man again, that's for sure. You?"

"I feel a little stronger every day. I made a very special new friend, and that helps."

Tameka looked up and raised her eyebrows suggestively. "Special friend?"

"Oh, no. Not that," Carly explained, blushing. "Not a man. Not a romantic friend. Just a friend friend. A woman—here in the building."

"Good for you," Tameka said. "Friends are more important than men, anyway."

Carly thought about Maya's laugh, her perfect white teeth, the warmth of her smile. She imagined their next encounter—over lunch, maybe—where Carly would present her plan about helping Tameka get past her heartache and learn to trust again. Maya would listen intently and seriously. Then she'd express her gratitude and maybe even compliment Carly on her manicure.

"Friends," Carly agreed, "are everything."

Chapter 29
ADDISON

"I really appreciate this," Addison said as she opened the passenger side door to Tameka's Honda. She was in the middle of lowering herself into the car when her friend reached over and snatched a plastic elephant from the seat.

"Sorry!" Tameka chirped, tossing the toy into the back.

Addison watched it land between a child's booster seat and a baggie of Cheerios. She sat and buckled herself in, nodding toward the back. "How old is she?"

"Four," Tameka said, and scrolled to a picture on her phone, which she handed to Addison. "This is Jada."

The child was gorgeous, with delicate features like her mother but massive dark eyes, like a doll. Or an anime. "Too bad she's not good looking," Addison said, confident Tameka would get the sarcasm.

"Right? People tell me I should get her an agent or something, but come on. Life is tough enough without that kind of pressure. I wouldn't do that to her . . . or to me."

Addison tried to imagine navigating motherhood as a twenty-something without a partner. "Must be hard to juggle it all," she said.

Tameka exhaled. "I never thought I'd be a single mom. Never."

Addison nodded. Tameka's life had been as upended as her own. But Addison only had herself to worry about and couldn't imagine how hard it would be with a child. "Are you doing the joint custody thing?" she asked.

"So far. And I'll say this about the prick—he's a good father. He loves the shit out of Jada, so I guess I'm lucky in that regard. And I have my mom, who helps."

"Good to have family," Addison said, hoping she didn't sound as rueful as she felt.

"You close to your uncle?" Tameka asked as she backed out of the parking space.

"Yeah. I mean, he's pretty much all I've got," Addison said, nearly choking on the sentiment. She loved Uncle Arnie with all her heart and sometimes panicked at the thought of losing him. Again and again, she told herself it was the trauma of her parents' death that made her dwell on such things. Seventy-five wasn't even that old, especially for someone so vital. She looked back at Tameka, trying to pull herself out of it. "And he never had kids, so it kind of works both ways."

"He seems like a sweetheart."

Addison nodded. "He's amazing," she said, thinking about all he'd done for her. After her parents died, her mother's friend Cynthia had stepped in to help her navigate the estate, paying for college, and figuring out her next step. But it was Arnie who kept tabs on her, sending money when she needed it, making sure she was okay, letting her know she wasn't alone in the world. Addison didn't know what she would have done without him.

"And this Leyla woman?" Tameka pressed. "Why are you trying so hard to set them up?"

Addison exhaled. It was a long story, but she filled Tameka in on the basics of Arnie's terrible history with Paulette and his excitement at her return.

"I was hoping to find someone he could fall head over heels in love with before she got back, but then Melody Forrest appeared."

"That skinny whack job who just moved in?" Tameka asked. "I saw the lifeguard looking at her like a desperate puppy."

"I don't know about the lifeguard, but it doesn't surprise me. Jake's got a thing for older women. And she's pretty hot." Addison went on to tell her what happened with Arnie's Fabergé egg.

Tameka's eyes went wide. "She stole a Fabergé egg?"

"A replica," Addison clarified, "though it's still pretty valuable."

"Arnie must be wigging out."

Addison shook her head. "He seems pretty convinced she didn't take it. Or maybe she's so good in bed he doesn't care anymore."

"He's got to want it back," Tameka said.

"He does! But he doesn't want to go to the cops, in case they take Melody away in handcuffs."

Tameka considered that for a moment. "What about Nikolai?" she said, referring to the building's head of security.

"What about him?"

"You should ask him for help. He's very discreet. And I know he can get to the bottom of it. He's got those elevator cams."

The elevator cams! Addison hadn't thought of that. "You really think I can go to him?"

"I'll come with, if you want."

"Actually," Addison said, warmed at the idea of having a friend at her side, "yeah. Thanks."

"No problem." Tameka slowed to make a turn and changed the subject to Zach Brody, asking Addison how she'd wound up approaching him for driving lessons.

"He offered," Addison said, "when he realized I didn't drive."

"He must want to hook up."

"It's nothing like that," Addison insisted. "I swear."

Tameka shrugged, as if she didn't quite believe it. "He does seem a little . . . weird."

"He's a lot weird," Addison said, "but not in a bad way. Not really. He had his heart broken, and that messed him up. The rest is just plain old awkwardness—the whole nerdy-genius thing. But he's got this dry sense of humor. And he's also patient and calm—a good driving instructor."

"You make him sound kind of perfect."

Addison considered that. "Do I?"

"Come on, you must be at least a little interested in him."

"No!" she blurted. "I mean, he's all right, but—"

"He's really cute," Tameka said, putting on her signal to change lanes.

"I've noticed."

"He must like you, though," Tameka observed, "even if he hasn't come on to you . . ."

Addison shook her head. "He needed a favor. We've got a quid pro quo thing going on." She thought about the dinner she'd be attending with Zach and realized there was exactly one dress in her closet that was formal enough. It was black and silver—with a plunging back. She'd always felt sexy in it but wondered if it was a little too much for a tech industry event.

Tameka focused on the road as she passed a slow truck, then glanced at Addison. "What kind of favor?" she asked.

"His ex really fucked him over. She ran off with his business, his money, his partner. Now he's up for some tech award, and she's going to be at the ceremony."

"So you agreed to be his hot date."

"Yup."

"And you have absolutely no romantic interest in the guy."

"Correct," Addison said emphatically.

Tameka laughed. "If you say so."

"You don't believe me?"

"Addison," Tameka said patiently, "you agreed to be his date in exchange for driving lessons."

"So?"

"And today you got frazzled when you realized you might not be able to keep your appointment with him."

"I really want to learn how to drive!" Addison insisted. "I need to."

Tameka approached a red light and slowed the car to a stop. "Your beloved uncle," she said patiently, "is a retired man with a driver's license, a working car, and a niece he'd do anything for. If this was only about driving, you'd be making arrangements with Arnie."

Addison went quiet, thinking about it until the light turned green. Tameka, she realized, was absolutely right. After blowing up her relationship with Marco—and shattering his heart in a million pieces—Addison had vowed she wouldn't get involved with another man until she figured out why she kept behaving so badly. And now there were two men in her life she couldn't stay away from.

Tameka turned onto La Cienega Boulevard and drove toward the green awning of the designated Starbucks. Zach was waiting outside, leaning against his parked Prius as he stared down at his phone. He had the casual slouch that lanky models tried to affect when they wanted to look cool and unselfconsciously sexy. On him, it was genuine, endearing, vulnerable. Addison was pulled to him like a train heading downhill and felt like there were only two options: she could keep going until they crashed . . . or derail at high speed.

Chapter 30

Addison's phone buzzed with a text from Dante just as she was getting into the Prius. She sneaked a glance, angling it away from Zach.

Can't stop thinking about you

No, she thought. Please. Don't do that. No more texts. No more flowers. You're supposed to be a player. Just move on to the next girl and forget about me. She slipped the phone into her purse without responding.

"You know, you might be able to get that repaired," Zach said.

"'Scuse me?"

"The cracked screen."

Oh, that. Addison shrugged. "It's a crappy phone. I'm just going to wait until I can afford a new one. Where are we going today?"

"You'll see," he said, and instructed her to head north, then make the next right.

Addison drove slowly and cautiously, getting honked at repeatedly. To settle her nerves, she kept reminding herself of what Zach had said the last time—that even the stupidest people learned how to drive. She could do this. The car behind her beeped three times.

"You're not doing anything wrong," he assured her. "Ignore them."

"Easier said than done."

"I'll have to get one of those *student driver* signs for the back of the car. That would be useful."

He took out his phone and started tapping at it. Addison glanced over. Surely he wasn't ordering one on the spot, was he?

"Don't worry about it," she said.

He slipped his phone back in his pocket. "It'll be delivered tomorrow. Make a left here."

She stole a quick glance at his face. What a naturally generous soul he had. "You're so *nice*," Addison observed.

"So are you," he shot back, as if she had insulted him.

Her, nice? As she considered the word, Marco's pained face appeared before her, in that terrible moment when confusion gave way to understanding. She had betrayed him. She had cheated. The hurt was as deep as anything she'd ever seen.

"No," she said to Zach, her eyes going damp. "I'm not. I'm not nice." She paused to swallow against the hardness in her throat.

"Why would you say that?"

Addison stopped at a yellow light, prompting a long and hostile honk from the car behind her. She held tight to the steering wheel, avoiding eye contact with Zach. "You know that terrible thing Quinn did to you?"

"What about it?"

She took a sharp breath. "I did the same thing to my ex-fiancé."

Zach looked at her, then back at the red light. "You stole his business and ran off with his partner?"

He was trying to lighten the moment, but she was too ashamed to release her misery. "I mean I cheated on him. And he didn't deserve it." There. Now Zach would know she was trouble. And he would keep his distance, no matter what.

"Is that the reason you abandoned New York?"

Addison nodded, unable to speak as she tried to erase the image of Marco's wounded expression. She never again wanted to see that look on anyone's face. Ever. She took a juddering breath, and for some reason the memory of that terrible moment after the accident came back to her. *In the ambulance on the way here,* someone in the hospital had said, but Addison couldn't hear. Not really. She had floated out of her body to a place where words couldn't reach her. Her mom's friend Cynthia had collapsed into tears, holding tight to Addison, who just kept saying *I don't understand* until at last she did.

But why was she thinking about that now? Surely the harrowing memory had no connection to what she'd done to Marco. Or did it? Once again, Addison didn't understand.

The light turned green, but it wasn't until she heard a short honk from the car behind her that Addison took her foot off the brake.

"You okay?" Zach asked.

"I could use a tissue," she croaked.

Zach glanced around the car and then grabbed something from the back seat. "This will suffice," he said, handing her the sleeve of his jacket.

She glanced at him and then back at the road. "I'm not wiping my nose on your sleeve, Zach."

"It's not a problem—this is a washable item."

"No," she said adamantly. "I'm not doing it." She fought the urge to reach over and shake him. No wonder he'd wound up with someone who took such terrible advantage of him. He made it too easy. And he didn't deserve it.

"I'm sorry I don't have a tissue," he said, tossing his jacket into the back.

"You don't have to apologize."

He pointed out the windshield. "Make a right at the next light onto Hollywood Boulevard."

"Hollywood!" she said, glad for the distraction. She'd heard that people were always disappointed to learn that it was seedy and touristy—not glamorous at all. But Addison was eager for seedy and touristy. She'd take the grittiest or cheesiest reality over a glitzy veneer any day. Even that, however, turned out to be a myth, as the street she steered onto was a fairly ordinary residential road, with squat apartment buildings and palm trees.

When she came to a major intersection with a street called La Brea, Zach said, "Just continue straight here," and that's when the surroundings turned more urban, and certainly more touristy, with places like Madame Tussauds and the Hard Rock Cafe—the Hollywood version of Times Square. At one point, she stopped at a light only to realize she was at the famed corner of Hollywood and Vine. It was, well, *nothing*. Just an ordinary corner. No glamorous stars or sleazy hookers or even menacing drug dealers, as far as she could tell.

"That's it?" she asked Zach.

"Disappointed?"

"I was expecting more squalor."

"You want squalor?" he said. "That can be our next excursion. Trust me, there's no shortage of it in LA."

"Where to now?" she asked.

"Left up ahead, then go straight."

She did as he said and found herself driving over a winding road.

"Just continue," he instructed.

At last, when she came to a grassy area on her right, Zach told her to pull over into a parking spot.

"Why here?" she asked, getting out of the car.

He pointed up in the distance, and there it was. The iconic Hollywood sign that she'd seen a million times in the movies. She looked back at his face, and he was smiling.

"Thank you," she said. "I've been dying to see it in person."

"I expected as much," he said. "Would you like to go for a hike and get closer? Or should we just sit on a bench?"

"Let's sit," she said, because she needed to finish the conversation they had started.

Zach led her into the park—carefully navigating around a small area with a KEEP OFF THE GRASS sign—until they found a secluded bench in a shaded spot. He brushed away the leaves and dust.

"Okay," Addison said as she sat, "there's a reason I told you about the thing with my ex." She bent over, avoiding eye contact as she watched some leaves swirl in an eddy of wind.

"You wanted to warn me," he said.

She looked over at him, surprised, and reminded herself not to underestimate this guy. He could be awkward, but he wasn't oblivious to social cues. "Look," she said, "I don't want to make any assumptions. Maybe you're not even attracted to me, but—"

"Of course I am."

"Okay, well—"

"Are you attracted to *me*?" he asked.

She gave him a quick glance and looked away. It was pretty clear he knew the answer and just wanted to hear her say it. But Addison didn't want to get anywhere close to that icy slope.

"Thing is," she said, "it doesn't matter."

"Because you only want a platonic relationship."

"Right."

"I understand," he said.

"You do?"

"I'm a broken mess—malfunctioning and possibly unrepairable. Who would want to deal with that?"

"I actually kind of like that you're a broken mess." She paused. "God, that sounds so fucked up."

He laughed. "A little."

"Truth is," she said, "it's me. And I know that sounds like bullshit, but I mean it. I can't subject myself to the world at large until I figure out why I keep hurting people. That's why I decided to be celibate for a year. I just . . . I have to figure out why I'm such a fuckup in relationships."

"You're celibate?" he asked.

"Yes."

He exhaled. "That's a relief. I thought you were having relations with Dante."

"What?" Addison felt herself flush.

"That guy is a miscreant, Addison. I'm really glad you're not sleeping with him."

"Yeah, me too," she said, swallowing hard against the lie as she looked toward the Hollywood sign. When she glanced back at him, Zach was checked out again, and she wondered what went on inside his head when he did that. Was he working out code? Doing high-level mathematics? Designing some new software program?

She gave him the space to think as she took in the scenery and the people. One small child, who walked between two parents, literally jumped for joy when one of his dads pointed out the Hollywood sign. His little squeals broke Zach's reverie, and he finally turned back to face Addison. His expression was calm, earnest, trusting, and it gave her heart a jolt.

She looked away and stood. "How about that hike?"

Chapter 31

Tameka set her phone on the table in front of her. "I spoke to Nikolai," she said softly. "He told me he'd send a text as soon as he finds the elevator-cam videos we're looking for."

Addison and Tameka were sitting under an umbrella in a sunny corner of the rooftop. It was Tuesday, and they had arranged to meet there during break, buying lunch from the Splash Bar with their employee discounts.

Addison looked around to be sure they were out of earshot of any residents, noting that the two Karens who had bitched about Tameka were sitting by the pool. They didn't look over, and Addison understood that as far as they were concerned, the two employees having their lunch were all but invisible.

"Thank you," she said, reaching over to give Tameka's arm an affectionate squeeze.

Her plan was to show her uncle the video proof of Melody's crime so that he could no longer deny it. Surely he would come to his senses about being involved with her once the evidence was clear. And then there was the egg itself. If Arnie couldn't get it back from her, Nikolai almost certainly could.

Tameka smiled and dug into her salad. "How was your driving lesson yesterday?"

Her expression conveyed that the question was loaded—she wasn't really asking about driving. But Addison just swallowed a mouthful of turkey sandwich and said, "I'm getting better."

It was a tease, of course, and Tameka gave her a good-natured shake of the head. "You know what I mean."

A wind blew across the rooftop, and Addison slapped her hand on the napkins before they were carried off. She tucked them under her sweating iced tea. "We had a very frank chat."

"About?"

Addison leaned over and sucked on her straw. "I told him I'm celibate."

"No shit?" Tameka said, surprised. "And how did he take that?"

"He was relieved."

"Relieved?"

"Because he thought I was banging Dante, who he thinks is bad news."

"News flash: you *are* banging—"

"Shush!" Addison interrupted. "That was once." She paused to think about their night together and added, "Okay, twice. But it'll never happen again."

"So it was . . . a moment of weakness?"

"Not really," Addison explained. "I just thought I could sleep with him and it wouldn't really count since he's not my type."

Tameka laughed. "You thought you could get laid and be celibate at the same time?"

"When you put it like that . . ."

"And how is that snack not your type? He's everyone's type. Even old Sally Conrad thinks he's the whole meal."

"I didn't mean physically. Because trust me, Dante is one of the hottest guys I've ever met. I meant in terms of an emotional connection. I thought he was safe because I would never develop feelings for someone like that. And he just didn't strike me as someone who developed feelings at all. Too messy in terms of his sex life."

"But now that you've slept with him?"

Addison sighed. "I don't know. It didn't feel like just sex, though. And check this out." She retrieved her phone and opened the text message from Dante, turning it toward Tameka.

"What are you showing me—your cracked screen?"

Addison shook her head. "The text from Dante."

Tameka leaned forward for a better view. "'Can't stop thinking about you,'" she read out loud.

"And there's this." Addison showed her a photo of the flowers he sent, and Tameka moved back, as if making room.

"Jesus. How big is that thing?"

"Like a small car."

"You might be in trouble, girl," Tameka said.

"Also," Addison confided, leaning in, "after we had sex, he kissed me here." She pointed to the spot on her forehead.

"Damn. What did you do to that boy?"

"I don't know," Addison said, "but I'm not going to do it again."

A few minutes later, Tameka's phone buzzed with a text from Nikolai, telling them to come down to his office. Excited, they quickly finished their lunch, threw out the trash, and hurried down to the security office.

Nikolai pulled open the heavy door before they even had a chance to knock.

"Videos are gone," he said, in an unmistakably Russian accent.

Addison looked up at the mountainous man. "What?"

"The files have been deleted."

"Why?" she asked. "By whom?"

"I don't yet know the answer to these questions. But only files missing are from Tower B elevators on Thursday morning."

Tameka and Addison looked at one another, confused.

"A cover-up?" Addison asked.

"I think this, yes," Nikolai said.

Tameka shook her head, as if trying to get her mind around this development. "Did you tell Frankie?"

"Maybe best if Miss Frankie doesn't know," he said, folding his massive arms.

Addison reeled. Was someone in the building protecting the thief? "Do you have a way to investigate?" she asked.

"I think deleted files perhaps can be recovered. My computer technician has not enough expertise. He is very good but not professional—mostly amateur. Works for me part time."

"Are you talking about Jake, the lifeguard?" Addison asked, recalling she heard he sometimes worked in the security office.

"After last one quit, young lifeguard said he can do job."

Tameka looked surprised. "Jake with the blond dreads is your techie?"

"These young people," Nikolai said with a shrug, "they understand technology. But for this job I need smarter person, more expert."

Addison thought for a second. "I might know someone."

Chapter 32
ARNIE

Arnie had been clear—very, very clear—that he intended to reconcile with his ex-wife. Melody said that she understood and was happy just to have him to herself for the time being. It was, he reassured himself, a reasonable arrangement.

That night, after they made love at his place, he held her in his arms for nearly an hour before dropping a hint he hoped wouldn't offend her.

"Wow," he said, looking at the clock, "I didn't know it was so late." His arm had gone numb by that point, and he extricated it from under her head.

"Do you mind very much if I stay the night, babe?" she asked, rubbing her hand up his thigh.

He did mind, actually. Spending the whole night together was a level of intimacy he didn't want to reach with Melody. But he couldn't think of a kind way to throw her out at this hour, since her new bed hadn't yet been delivered and she'd complained several times about the air mattress she'd been sleeping on. No, this brittle, broken woman required a gentle approach. And anyway, he supposed it couldn't hurt, just this once. Besides, he reasoned, it had been so long since he'd made love in the morning.

"You know we can't make a habit of it," he cautioned.

"I understand," she said. "But this bed is comfortable. And you make me feel so . . . *wonderful.*" The last word was uttered with such grateful enthusiasm he stored it away to recall when his ego needed a little . . . stimulation.

Arnie ran a thumb down her pretty cheek. "Okay," he said, and then rolled over and fell into a deep sleep.

He was awakened sometime later by his cell phone. It was making a strange noise he couldn't quite identify in his groggy state. He picked it up and studied the screen, suddenly understanding what it was. A video call over Facebook, from Paulette.

He bolted out of bed and grabbed his boxers from the floor.

"Everything okay?" Melody asked, rolling over.

"It's . . ." He hesitated, trying to find a plausible lie. Then he realized it was best to be honest. After all, he'd told her about Paulette again and again, and maybe this would solidify the reality for her. He pulled on his boxers. "It's Paulette, calling from Italy. I have to take this."

In the dark, he couldn't read her expression, but it didn't matter. Arnie brought his phone to the bathroom and shut the door, then quickly looked around for a good place to answer the call. If he sat on the toilet lid, she'd know he was in the bathroom and might surmise that there was a woman in his bed. He decided to lean on the ledge in front of the large window, so Paulette would see nothing but the Beverly Hills night sky behind him.

He swiped at his phone, then ran his hand through his messy hair. When her image appeared, he nearly choked on gratitude. Paulette! His beautiful bride. His whole heart.

"Is it really you?" he said, grinning so hard his cheeks ached.

"My silver fox," she observed, because the last time she'd seen him his hair was dark, with only a few strands of gray.

"You like it?" he asked.

"It suits you. Very distinguished."

"You look as beautiful as ever. Like the day we met." She did, in fact, look older. But it only made him love her more. There was a vulnerability to her now, and he ached to take care of her, to show her exactly the kind of man he could be.

"I've been thinking about you lately," she said.

"I've been thinking about you too."

Paulette leaned forward as if to get a better view of his surroundings. "What time is it there?" she asked.

"A little after midnight," he said, and could see that it was early morning in Italy. She was on some kind of veranda, surrounded by potted flowers. Her black hair, cut in a bob now, blew in the wind.

"It's morning here," she said, raising a cup of coffee as if to prove it.

"And Sergio?" he asked.

She shook her head. "He moved out. Things were getting . . . messy. How about you?"

"I'm unattached, Paulette."

"But playing the field?"

"Not too much," he said, shielding her from the truth. He couldn't bear for her to know how active his sex life had been. It might derail any chance he had. She could be so very, very jealous.

She laughed, able to see through him. "You never were a very good liar."

He offered a sheepish shrug. "Point is, there's no one like you."

"That, I believe," she said, and gave him her ten-million-dollar smile.

He experienced it in his whole body, and it was a special kind of joy, almost religious, as if someone had flicked a switch that lit up the whole universe. If Arnie didn't know better, he'd worry his heart might burst. "How about you?" he asked. "Are you seeing anyone?"

"Oh, hell no," she said.

"And you're coming home soon? Back to the States, I mean."

Paulette nodded. "Winona is helping me find a place in LA," she said, referring to her younger sister.

"You can live here!" he blurted, a rush of dopamine coursing through his bloodstream. "With me."

"Arnie," she said, and took a juddering breath as tears spilled. "Oh, Arnie. I never should have . . . oh, god." She covered her face with her hands.

"Sweetie, are you all right?" he asked, concerned, but also excited by what this outburst might mean.

She pulled a tissue from her cleavage and dabbed her cheeks, cleaned her mascara. "You ever wonder what would have happened if I never left?"

"Constantly," he told her.

Paulette sniffed and attempted a brave smile. "You really want me back?" she asked.

"It's all I think about."

Arnie heard a noise coming from the bedroom. His pulse accelerated, but he tried to keep his expression even, telling himself Melody knew enough to behave herself while he was on this call.

"Everything okay?" Paulette asked.

"Yes, I—"

The doorknob rattled, and Melody cried, "Let me in!"

Oh, no, Arnie thought. No no no!

"You have a woman there?" Paulette asked, her eyebrows tight.

Melody banged on the door. "You can't talk to her while I'm here, you fucker!"

"Jesus Christ, Arnie," Paulette said, her expression turning dark, "why didn't you tell me you had a woman in your bed! Are you in a relationship?"

"No!" he said. "It's nothing like that."

"Yes it is!" Melody screamed through the door. "Don't listen to him, Paulette. He's lying!"

"She knows my name?" Paulette demanded, her fury climbing.

A current of panic shot through him. Paulette was about to explode. "Sweetheart, it's not what you think," he said, "I swear. I'll call you back and explain everything." Arnie disconnected the call, then sat on the toilet lid, catching his breath. Melody banged on the door.

"What are you doing in there!" she demanded. "Jerking off?"

With a heavy sigh, Arnie got up and opened the door to face Melody, who was stark naked, her body illuminated by the bright light flooding in from the bathroom.

"What the fuck, Arnie!" she screamed. "What the actual fuck!" She knocked a ceramic lamp off the night table, and it crashed to the floor, shattering.

"Melody! Jesus, calm down."

"Don't tell me to calm down. You take a call from your ex-wife while I'm naked in your bed? Who does that!"

"I told you. I told you I was getting back together with her."

"That's not the point, and you know it!"

Arnie felt his anger rising. This deranged woman could ruin everything. "You called me a liar!" he seethed. "Now she'll think I'm seeing you."

"You *are* seeing me."

Arnie took a long breath as his eyes went from his shattered lamp to this unhinged woman, naked and panting like an animal. He had to fix this. Right now.

"No," he said coolly. "Not anymore. This is over."

They stared at each other for a heated moment, and her body got so tight he stepped back, fearing she might scratch at him. Then, as quick as a cat, she lunged forward and yanked the phone from his hand.

"I'm calling her. I'm going to tell her the truth. She deserves it."

Arnie grabbed her wrist and pulled the phone away. She yelped like a wounded dog.

"You hurt me!" she cried, holding her wrist.

"Knock it off," he said, well aware that he hadn't done any damage. He'd taken his own pulse with a firmer grip.

"I could have you arrested."

"If anyone's being arrested," he said, "it's *you.*"

Melody narrowed her eyes. "Is this about that damned egg again? I told you—I didn't take it."

He glared at her, unwilling to continue the charade. "We both know that's a lie, don't we?"

"You are despicable," she spit.

"You'd better go now," he said.

"Or what?"

He thought for a second. "Or I'll call security."

"I hate you," she said. Then she picked up her clothes, got dressed, and left.

Chapter 33
CARLY

Carly had been happy. Gloriously, deliciously, uncharacteristically happy. She even felt like she deserved it, which was the most surprising part of all. Carly Pratt was starting to love herself, and the future seemed to glimmer with hope.

That is, until she got a text from Owen that was unlike any he'd sent before, and her world went from sunshine to gloom.

After her manicure—which looked so beautiful she could hardly stop staring at it—Carly had called Maya to tell her about Tameka, the young divorcée who needed life coaching from the Sherpa of breakups.

"Maybe we can meet for lunch and talk about it," Carly had suggested.

"I have a better idea," Maya said. "Why don't you come over for dinner tomorrow. I'll cook. You like salmon?"

Carly breathlessly accepted, unable to believe her good fortune. She was having dinner with Maya Mayfield! Just the two of them. Like a couple of gal pals.

And if that wasn't enough, Carly had heard from one of her clients, who hired her for a huge project. She would be writing all the materials for a new product rollout. It wasn't exactly glamorous—a new type of hospital gurney—but the money was a windfall. Carly was so proud that she'd had the gumption to pitch for more business from them.

In the past, she would have worried they'd say *Who does she think she is?* Now she knew who she was—an excellent copywriter with finely tuned instincts! It made perfect sense they'd hire her for this lucrative assignment.

Carly had looked at her reflection in the entranceway mirror. No more excuses, she had told herself. It's time to make an appointment at the Beekman's pricey hair salon. Normally, such an indulgence would have made her nervous, but she was excited for the transformation and could imagine Maya telling her she deserved the self-care.

That lovely concierge, Addison, had been able to get her an appointment for early the next morning, which meant that Carly could show up at Maya's with her freshly coiffed new look.

Carly left her apartment, locking the door behind her. She stopped, noticing something odd. There were deep scratches on the doorframe, close to the lock. She ran her finger over them, trying to recall if she'd seen them before. Surely they'd always been there and she was only noticing them now due to being more engaged with the world around her. Hadn't Lenny said something about the previous tenant forgetting to turn over the keys before disappearing? Clearly, that's all this was— evidence of a locksmith's efforts to replace the cylinder.

Don't work yourself into a frenzy just because your life is coming together, Carly told herself. You deserve happiness!

When she arrived at the salon, the colorist told her she'd rock some auburn highlights, and Carly agreed. She refused to look in the mirror until they were finished blowing it dry, and then she stared, transfixed. After a moment, Carly shook out her straightened hair, watching it catch the light like spun silk. The shine was extraordinary. Her eyes filled with tears.

"You like it?" asked the stylist.

"Are you kidding?"

After she left the salon, Carly took a walk around the property, holding her head up, feeling like she actually belonged. People smiled and said hello. She even thought a man checked her out, looking up from his phone to watch her. Carly had never felt more beautiful. She floated back to her apartment.

But there was no time to indulge in preening. The deadline on this new project was tight, and she had made a schedule for herself that left little room for goofing off. She put in several hours of work before getting up from her desk, realizing it was almost time to get ready for her dinner with Maya.

And that's when she saw the text from Owen that made her blood run cold: **That's some haircut.**

It was only three words, but she reread it several times. How on earth had Owen known? Was he here, in Beverly Hills? Impossible. Owen was afraid to fly and wouldn't know how to book a ticket, anyway. The farthest he'd ever traveled from Nashua was to Boston, except for the one time they drove to Maryland for his cousin's wedding.

No, someone was spying on her for Owen. There was no other explanation. He must have hired a private investigator who was reporting back to him—maybe even sending pictures. She imagined him feeling angry and powerless after she'd ignored his messages, and this was his way of getting back at her. He wanted to scare her.

It was working.

Carly thought about the scratches she'd noticed on the doorframe but assured herself they'd always been there. After all, the building had security, and the manager had even assured her there had never been a break-in. But what about all the people she'd passed after leaving the salon? Had one of them been Owen's spy? Perhaps the man she thought was checking her out was actually a private detective. She shuddered at the thought of someone snapping a secret photo of her prancing through the grounds and texting it to Owen. Maybe they'd even sent a video.

By the time she left for Maya's apartment, Carly was feeling desperate and paranoid, wondering about every person she passed along the way. When she got into the Tower B elevator, a man stepped on with her, and he looked so ordinary—so *nondescript*—it was suspicious. Average height, brown sweater, black glasses. Okay, his glasses were round like Harry Potter's, which was a little unusual, but other than that, he was just the kind of man you wouldn't notice . . . except that she'd thought she'd seen him before. When he stared down at his phone, it seemed like a ruse, as if he were only pretending to be reading something.

She pushed the button for eight—Maya's floor—and the man continued staring down at his screen.

"What floor?" she asked him.

"Eight," he said evenly, and her heart skittered. Just before the doors closed, she jumped off the elevator and saw the man glance at her, then quickly look back down.

Her pulse pounding, Carly counted to sixty before she pushed the call button for the next elevator. Calm down, she told herself. This is probably all your imagination.

But then, when she got off the elevator on the eighth floor, the nondescript man in the round glasses was lingering in the hallway, still looking at his phone. There was nothing for Carly to do but hurry to Maya's door.

Chapter 34

"Are you okay?" Maya said when she saw Carly's face.

Unable to speak, Carly merely shook her head, and Maya pulled her into the apartment, shutting the door.

"What's wrong?"

"Look," Carly said, determined not to cry. She held out her phone. "It's from my ex in New Hampshire."

Maya read the text, covering her mouth as she took it in. "Ay!" she said. "Does he know anyone here?"

Carly almost laughed at the thought. "No way," she said.

Maya paused, concern filling her eyes. "Then he must have hired a private investigator."

Exactly, Carly thought as she gulped against a bulge in her throat. "I'm freaking out."

"Of course you are," Maya said. "Come here."

She put her arms out and wrapped Carly in a firm hug. For a quick second, Carly resisted, nervous, but Maya's hold was insistent, so she gave herself into it. Completely. And it felt . . . exquisite. Maya's embrace was firm, tender, soft, loving. Carly breathed in her scent, and it felt like nothing she'd ever experienced before. It felt like home.

Carly pulled herself away, trying to process what she was experiencing. You're just vulnerable, she told herself. That's all this is. That's all.

She looked into Maya's beneficent face—her almond-shaped eyes soft in concern—and told her about the man on the elevator.

"He might be the private eye, or he might not," Maya said, adding a bit of perspective, and Carly understood that she was right. He could have been someone who lived on Maya's floor, or just an ordinary guest coming to visit a friend. Still, it was hard to shake the fear.

"Point is," Maya continued, "that fucker of an ex is trying to get in your head, to intimidate you."

"It's working."

Maya held her shoulder. "Listen," she said, "I don't think you're in danger. I really don't. I mean, you'll want to report this to security, but in the meantime, you have nothing to worry about. Think about it. What can Owen really do with these photos of you? You're not doing anything wrong."

Carly took that in. It was true. So what if Owen had pictures of her living her best life? Screw him. She looked down at Owen's contact information in her phone. Do it now, she told herself. Before you lose your nerve.

Maya released her shoulder. "What are you doing?" she asked.

"I'm blocking him," Carly said, her finger hovering. It felt momentous. Brave. A final severing of her ties to the obdurate Owen.

"I'm proud of you!" Maya said. "I know how significant that is."

Carly tapped the screen to confirm that yes, she did want to block the number, and a shiver of relief coursed through her. She was done with Owen. Done!

She looked up at Maya, her eyes watering. "This feels . . . like freedom."

Maya took Carly's face in her hands. "You're a superstar. I hope you believe that." They stood quietly for several moments—their faces close, their pulses synchronizing—before Maya finally released her and took a step back. "And your hair! I didn't even tell you how great it looks. The color is stunning on you."

Carly felt herself flush from the unexpected proximity. For a split second there, she had thought Maya was going to lean in and kiss her. What, she wondered, would she have done? It was almost too much to process. Besides, it didn't matter. Maya was her friend, and that was enough. More than enough, really.

Carly touched her own hair. "You really think it's okay?"

"Better than okay! It's like a whole new you."

"I *feel* like a whole new me." She closed her eyes for a second, imagining the life opening up to her, free of Owen's invectives. "It's like the longer I go without seeing Owen, the better I feel."

"You know what else will make you feel better?" Maya asked with a smile. "Wine! Come."

She led Carly deeper into the apartment, which was colorfully decorated in artsy bohemian style, with rich blues, pale pinks, rustic rusts, a sprinkling of purple and yellow, and lots of throw pillows—a perfect mélange of hues and textures. The effect was soothing, charming, romantic.

"Did you decorate this?" Carly asked, in awe. She couldn't imagine how someone could picture all this in their mind as they chose colors and made choices. How on earth did she know it would all come together? It would have taken Carly years to make so many decisions, and even then she'd never be able to pull it off. The whole thing seemed like magic. But Carly understood she had never been a particularly visual person. She was better with words than images.

Maya smiled. "You like it?"

"I love it!" she gushed. "Maybe you can help me decorate my place?"

"My pleasure," Maya said, and Carly realized she might have spoken out of turn. After all, her brother had furnished her apartment, and no matter how much money she made freelancing, she'd never be able to afford such luxe furnishings.

"I mean, one day, when I can afford it."

"You'd be surprised how much thrifting is involved in all this," Maya said, with a sweep of her hand.

They went into the kitchen, which had green-painted lower cabinets, a checkerboard floor, and a patterned mosaic backsplash. "This is so dreamy," Carly observed. "I don't know how you do it."

"Still a work in progress," Maya said, pulling a cork from a bottle of white wine. "I hope you like Riesling."

"Love it!" Carly said as Maya poured. She accepted a glass and held it up. "What should we drink to?"

"To the new Carly," Maya said, "who will never have her wings clipped again!"

Carly loved the image of growing wings and soaring. They tipped glasses and sipped. Then Carly held hers up again. "To the Sherpa of breakups . . . the shepherd of second chances . . . the star of starting over!"

Maya clinked on it and laughed. "I want every one of those on a pillow!"

They drank; then Maya announced it was time to make dinner and got busy with preparations. Carly wanted to make herself useful and assumed lemon-slicing duty. As they worked, side by side, she relayed the details of the conversation she'd had with Tameka, and Maya listened intently.

"I'd like to speak to her," Maya said. "If she's open to it. Can you make the introduction?"

Even though she knew it might be awkward, Carly said "Sure," because she also knew she could push past Owen's voice in her ear telling her she was making a fool of herself.

"If I'm able to help her," Maya said, "I'll come back and ask her for an anonymous endorsement. It might be enough to kick this thing off."

"And then you'll have a built-in client base right here in Divorce Towers!"

Maya laughed. "Maybe I'll set up a desk next to the concierge!"

Carly knew it was just a joke, but she also understood that Maya was dead serious about this rebranding. She was so proud of the role she'd had in it she felt ready to burst.

"I'm happy to help in any way I can," she offered.

"I might take you up on that," Maya said. "I made some notes, but I could use help putting a press release together. You have experience with that?"

"I do!" Carly said. "I'd be happy to write *anything* for you." She felt immediately embarrassed by her excessive enthusiasm. It was too much, too gushing. More like a starry-eyed fan than a friend and equal. But Maya didn't seem to notice.

"I'll pay you, of course," she said.

"Don't worry about it. I don't—"

"Absolutely not!" Maya said. "You're a professional writer, and your talent is valuable. I don't want to hear any arguments."

"Okay!" Carly said with a good-natured laugh. "Point taken."

"One of the things I'm trying to work out is how to explain that you can be sad after a breakup, and that's okay. But it doesn't mean you can't also embrace looking at it as an opportunity for growth, for happiness, for fulfillment."

Carly held up half a lemon and wiggled it for emphasis. "Does this help?" She squeezed it into a measuring cup.

"Lemons into lemonade!" Maya said. "That's perfect. I can work that imagery into my logo." She laughed with joy. "Oh man, that's so good! I love you, Carly!"

"Love you too!" Carly said, as casually as she could. Inside, however, it felt like she'd just experienced her first earthquake. Stop it, she told herself, blocking the shock waves before they could begin. That's just the way people talk in California. She took a deep breath and, feeling more settled, picked up another lemon to slice. But when she reached for the knife, her hand was shaking.

Chapter 35
ADDISON

Addison and Tameka made arrangements to meet Zach and Nikolai at the security office at 9:00 p.m., when the building was quiet. It hadn't been that difficult to talk Zach into helping them. When he heard someone had thwarted security by illegally deleting video files, he was eager to right that wrong.

Addison was feeling optimistic about their little caper, as Zach had seemed confident he could retrieve the deleted file. That meant Addison would have proof that Melody had stolen Arnie's Fabergé egg. Nikolai would then pressure her to return it, and Arnie would at last come to his senses about breaking it off with the tightly wound manipulator. Once that was accomplished, he might just be open to the charms of Addison's chosen love match for him. She was certain that if anyone could distract Arnie from dangerous Paulette, it was Nurse Leyla, healer and dominatrix.

First, though, Addison and Tameka went out for a casual dinner and fell into an easy conversation about their lives. Addison learned that Tameka had an associate's degree in hospitality and had been hoping to go for her bachelor's, though that plan got derailed when she threw Vin out for cheating. Her goal was to get a job at a hotel and work her way up to management. She'd taken the gig at the salon because the hours were flexible, the tips could be pretty decent, and it seemed at least hospitality adjacent.

To Addison, Tameka's ambition to be in hospitality made perfect sense. She was a people pleaser, with a cool head about problem-solving—just the skills to make her a great concierge. Addison decided that once she was settled into the job and on solid footing with Frankie, she'd suggest Tameka as a fill-in, so the desk wouldn't be empty on her days off.

"For now, the job works," Tameka said. "Besides, it gave me a great idea for a screenplay I almost finished writing."

"Seriously?" Addison asked. She had no idea Tameka had writing aspirations.

"Don't tell anybody."

"Why not?"

"You saw how everyone ribbed Joaquín about it. Besides, it's such a punch line in LA. Everybody and their manicurist has a screenplay."

"The concierge doesn't have one," Addison said.

"Give it time."

"Don't do that," Addison insisted. "This is a big freaking deal. You've got a job and a kid, and you wrote a script. It's impressive as hell."

She asked Tameka to tell her about the story, which was a mystery that involved a confession to a manicurist, a Bitcoin conspiracy, and the murder of a client's husband. Addison thought it was a great plot, and they continued talking about it as they ate. The time flew by, and she was just finishing her chicken kebab when her phone buzzed with a text from Nikolai.

New plan. Meet at 8.

"Shit," she said to Tameka, "he wants to meet an hour earlier."

"Did he say why?"

Addison shook her head. "It's *Nikolai*," she said pointedly.

Tameka laughed. "Right. He could tell us, but then he'd have to kill us."

"Your next screenplay," Addison offered.

Addison sent Zach a text about the change in plans, and while the women waited for a response, they paid for the meal and left. By the time they got into Tameka's car, there was still no answer.

"He's probably in the pool," Addison said. "He likes to go for an evening swim."

"We'll find him," Tameka assured her.

But when they got to the building and checked the indoor pool, which Addison knew was his preference in the evening, they found it was overrun with kids. Apparently, Wednesday was a popular night for divorced dads to have custody, and the indoor pool had become the unofficial playground of Beekman Towers.

That meant Zach was probably in the rooftop pool, so the two women took the elevator up, emerging into the unofficial happy hour of Divorce Towers. By now, Addison was able to recognize nearly half the residents and made a quick note that crazy Melody was nowhere to be seen.

But Arnie was there, tucked into a corner with her boss, Frankie, where they seemed to be having a serious private conversation.

"There's Zach," Tameka said, nodding toward the pool.

Addison could imagine approaching Zach to tell him the meeting had been moved up, only to get a stern lecture from her boss. She pulled Tameka toward the Splash Bar. "We have to play it cool. Frankie's here."

"So what's the plan?"

"We either have to wait until she leaves, or until Zach spots us, so we can give him some sort of signal."

"Can I buy you ladies a drink?" came a voice behind them. It was Dante. And he looked spectacular in an unbuttoned white linen shirt and swimming trunks, his black hair still wet from a swim. He wasn't just sexy, he was Hollywood sexy, like a scene from a movie complete with perfect lighting and background music designed to make every girl drop her popcorn. Addison was determined to hold tight.

"Don't get me in trouble," she said.

"Hey, I'm just a guy hanging out by the snack bar. That's not against the law, is it?"

Addison sighed. He knew damned well how good he looked. "Just behave yourself."

"Where's the fun in that?" he asked, then leaned in closer to whisper, "I'd like to come by later."

"Don't," she said, backing away.

"You're wasting your time with that chick!" came a booming voice from the other side of the pool. "She doesn't put out." It was the elderly Mr. Posner, and he got the attention of everyone on the roof deck, including Frankie. All eyes were trained on them as laughter rippled around the clots of happy drinkers.

"You'd better go," Addison muttered, and turned her back to him.

"I'll text you," he said, and started to walk away, but Tameka interrupted.

"Wait a second," she pleaded. "Can you do me a favor? Can you tell Zach Brody I want to speak to him by the elevators?"

Impressed by her friend's resourcefulness, Addison turned back in time to see Dante raise an eyebrow.

"A budding romance?"

"Something like that," Tameka said.

Dante gave her a salute. "I'm on it."

Chapter 36

The security office was a windowless room not much bigger than a closet. It was equipped with a gray desk, a computer, a plug-in air freshener that made Addison's eyes water, and a wall of monitors showing live images of the building's entrances and six elevators.

After a brief conversation with Nikolai, Zach sat down at the desk and got to work, taking a quick look at the stored files before downloading some state-of-the-art data recovery software he said hadn't yet hit the market. The other three stood behind him, trying not to hover. Addison wished they could prop the door open for some air but understood this mission was top secret.

"Is everything okay with you?" she asked Nikolai.

He furrowed his brow. "Of course," he said, as if the question was absurd.

"Then why did you need to move up this meeting?"

"Frankie," he responded.

"Frankie?" she asked, and wanted to tell him he wasn't going to get in trouble with the KGB if he answered in complete sentences.

"She need to see me at nine."

Addison considered the conversation she'd witnessed on the roof between Frankie and Arnie. They'd seemed pretty intense, and she wondered if he'd finally told her about his missing egg, and if that was why Nikolai had been summoned.

"Did she say what it was about?"

"No," he said, and that, apparently, was the end of the conversation.

Several minutes later, Addison's phone buzzed with a text from Dante: OK to come by around 11?

She let out an exasperated breath because she desperately wanted to say yes but knew it would be a terrible mistake. Be strong, she told herself. Definitive. She tapped out a simple, Nikolai-like response: Sorry, no

Zach stopped clicking at the computer and glanced at her, as if sensing a shift in the energy. Addison kept her expression even, and he went back to work.

Moments later Dante responded.

Midnight?

Addison stared down at the single word, plus the praying hand emoji he had added, wondering what she could say to signal that he had to back off—not just tonight but for good.

"You okay?" Tameka whispered to her.

Addison rolled her eyes and mouthed "Dante."

Tameka leaned close to her ear and whispered, "Just ignore him."

"Can't," Addison said, because she knew how persistent Dante could be. If she didn't respond, he'd just show up at her apartment again. Maybe with two bottles of Dom Pérignon this time. Or a bouquet the size of a VW bus.

"Why not?" Tameka whispered, and Zach tsked.

"I'm trying to concentrate here," he said.

"Okay, ladies, outside," Nikolai said. "Too many bodies for small room."

Tameka and Addison happily exited the tiny office and leaned against the wall in the hallway, where Addison showed Tameka the texts.

"What should I write back?" she asked.

"Can't go wrong with no," Tameka said.

Addison nodded at the advice and then followed it. Moments later Dante responded.

What's wrong?

Addison didn't know what to say to that. Nothing? Everything? *Sorry, but when I fucked you I had no idea I might actually develop feelings for you?* She finally wrote: It's complicated

He replied: So let's talk about it

She knew she owed him an explanation, but not alone, at night, in her apartment. So she simply wrote: Not tonight. Then she silenced her phone and dropped it into her purse.

A few minutes later, Nikolai cracked open the door and signaled them back inside.

"Did he find something?" Addison asked him.

Nikolai shut the door. "Yes," he said, and then addressed Zach. "Proceed."

Zach clicked on something, and two of the monitors revealed the inside of an elevator from opposite angles. Seconds later, there was Melody Forrest, who fussed with her hair as she rode the elevator up to the sixth floor, where Arnie lived, and exited. There was a time jump of about an hour; then she got back on the elevator. Unfortunately, she was carrying a tote-size purse, and it was impossible to tell if the egg was inside.

"Damn," Addison said. "Is there any way to zoom in to see if her purse looks larger than it did before?"

"Wait," Nikolai said.

Moments after Melody exited the elevator, a man in a white base-ball cap got on, his face mostly obscured under the brim.

"Do we know who that is?" Addison asked.

"He is not resident," said Nikolai.

"Is he the thief?" asked Tameka.

"Please," said Nikolai. "We watch, then talk."

The room went quiet as the man glanced down at a piece of paper in his hand, which he folded and put in his pocket. He got off the ele-vator on the sixth floor, and there was a time jump again, but this time it was less than five minutes before the man reappeared. Now, his hand was in his jacket pocket. After a moment, he pulled it out to look down at what he was holding: Arnie Glass's Fabergé egg.

"Who *is* that?" Tameka asked, just as Addison gasped at the realization that Melody was not the culprit.

"I will find out," Nikolai said.

"The doormen would know, right?" Tameka said. "I mean, they announce every visitor."

Nikolai heaved a weary sigh. "I tell Miss Frankie all the time we need security improvements. But the residents—they like everything easy."

Still reeling from the surprise of learning that the sticky fingers were not Melody's, Addison wondered who else might have known about the pricey trinket. She turned to Nikolai.

"You mean there's a chance they don't even have a record of this visitor?" she asked, before turning her attention back to the screen.

"This is likely, yes," said Nikolai.

"Why were the files deleted?" Zach piped in. "Does this guy have a friend inside who's protecting him?"

"Very concerning," Nikolai said.

Addison moved her face closer to the monitor. "I wonder why he's wearing hiking boots," she said. "That's pretty unusual in Beverly Hills, right?"

"Please," Nikolai said to Zach. "Close-up of boots."

Zach zoomed in on the black-soled boots on both screens, showing them from different angles.

"Not hiking boots," Nikolai said. "Steel-toe working man's boots. For outdoors."

"You mean like construction work?" Addison asked.

"Perhaps."

"Could it be someone who works on the grounds here?" she asked.

"Maybe yes," he said. "Or maybe no."

"You think you can find out?"

"I will catch thief," he said, and then ushered them out of this office.

Chapter 37

"I told you not to come," Addison said when Dante showed up at her apartment several hours later, carrying a bottle of wine. He had roused her out of bed, but this time she'd taken pains to pull on a baggy sweatshirt and shorts before opening the door.

"Can't we just talk?" he pleaded from the hallway. "I want to know what's wrong." He had changed from his bathing suit into street clothes and was now wearing a black microfiber T-shirt and jeans. She knew he meant to look casual, but no matter what he wore, the guy was as polished as a Cartier diamond.

"It's not a good time," she said.

"Please," he begged. "I'm leaving for New York tomorrow and won't be back until next week. Can't you just give me ten minutes?"

She shook her head, resolute. "I can't let you in."

"You're driving me crazy, Addison."

He looked genuinely pained as he tried to reach for her hand, and she was struck by the vulnerability of his admission. Still, she pulled back, thinking about that feeling she got in his arms. She also thought about how very badly she wanted to kiss Zach Brody, that nerdy, adorable weirdo. It was all too much.

"Look," she said, "I just . . . I have to go back to being celibate. *I have to.*"

"What did I do wrong?"

"Nothing."

"Didn't you like the flowers?" he said. "Were they too much?"

"Yes, Jesus. They were way too much. What were you thinking?" She was tempted to open her door to show him how they took up half her living room, but didn't want to encourage him to come inside, because she couldn't trust either of them . . . but especially herself.

"I wanted to be sure you knew how much that night meant to me. But if you don't like flowers—"

"Stop," she said. "This is not about flowers."

"Then tell me, so I can fix it."

Addison rubbed her forehead, trying to figure out how to explain her decision. "Dante," she began, but took such a long pause, he jumped in.

"I think about you all the time," he admitted. "I never expected to feel like this."

Me neither, she thought. And that's the problem. But his eyes were so pleading Addison felt her resolve softening. No, she warned herself. You cannot.

"Everything about this is too risky," she said.

"You mean Frankie?" he asked. "Because I can talk to her."

Was he kidding? If Frankie thought Addison was swimming in the same waters as her predecessor—ready to run off with a resident and create an ocean-size scandal—she'd be as merciful as a tiger shark.

Addison imagined losing her job and her apartment in the same stroke and felt a wave of nausea. Arnie, she knew, would swoop in to the rescue, but it was a worst-case scenario. She was a grown-ass woman and did not want to rely on her elderly uncle to save her. Again. It was humiliating, not to mention unfair to Arnie. The last thing he needed was to live his golden years supporting his dead sister's loser grand-daughter. She couldn't do that to him.

"No, Dante, for god's sake. Don't go to Frankie about us."

"You might be underestimating my charm."

"I'm begging you," she said.

"What else is going on?" he pressed. "Because I don't think this is just about the job."

She looked into his dark eyes and once again felt something powerful and dangerous pass between them. That tender kiss on her forehead was like a warning bell. They were headed someplace too intense for either of them to handle, and it could not possibly end well.

"Dante," she said slowly, "there's a reason I can't get involved with anyone right now. And this . . ." Addison paused to point between the two of them. "This is why."

"That makes no sense."

"Even if we could manage to hide it from Frankie, I can't be in a relationship," she explained. "I thought it was just going to be sex, but then . . . I don't know what happened, but something shifted."

"Let me get this straight," he said. "You don't want to sleep with me because you feel something here." He pointed to his own heart.

She nodded. "Because we both do," she said, locking eyes with him. "And I'm just not good at this shit."

"You're thinking about your ex."

"Yes." During their night together, she had told him what happened with Marco. At the time, she didn't know why she was opening up to him, but now she realized she'd been trying to warn him.

"You're worried about breaking my heart?" he asked.

"Well . . . ," she began, because that was only part of it. The other part was that in some strange and twisted way, sleeping with Dante already felt like cheating on Zach. It made no sense at all. She and Zach were not involved. In fact, as far as she could tell, he was still in love with the ruthless Quinn. But in Addison's heart, a bond had formed. It was all so damned confusing.

"Because let me assure you," Dante said, "I'm a tough son of a bitch. I have to be in my business. I don't get hurt."

"You're bulletproof," she said, "like Superman."

He nodded and smirked, giving her that single killer dimple. And damn if it didn't do something to her insides. She grew warm, needy.

The yearning to press against him almost overwhelmed her. Addison looked at the flesh of his neck, his beautiful hands, the longing in his coal-dark eyes. That was the part that could shatter her resolve. His desire. This gorgeous man, who spent his days surrounded by beautiful starlets, wanted her. It was intoxicating.

"Yes," he said, moving in for a kiss, "like Superman."

Addison gathered all her strength, then stepped back and shut the door, panting. It took so much out of her that she leaned against it as she struggled to catch her breath, wondering which one of them was kryptonite.

Chapter 38
ARNIE

Paulette wasn't responding to his texts and emails, and Arnie thought his heart might break in half. It couldn't be over. It just couldn't.

He pulled out his phone and composed a new text: My love, that woman is gone. I made a clean break. Can we talk?

He hit send, certain she wouldn't respond, and pondered what else he could say to get through to her. To his surprise, though, his phone began to cry out with that special high-pitched ring. Paulette was calling!

He sat by the kitchen island so that the expanse of his living room appeared behind him, and tapped the answer button. Her lovely face came into view. It was dinnertime in Italy, and she seemed to be dressed for going out—fully made up, wearing a black low-cut dress and a spectacular emerald-and-diamond necklace. She wore a dusky color on her full lips, and it stirred him.

"My beautiful darling!" he said. "Thank you! Thank you for calling me. I've been desperate."

"Oh, Arnie. You fool. You stupid fool!"

"What did I—"

"I'm not angry that you were *dating* someone," she chided. "I'm angry that you lied to me."

"Yes, of course, but—"

"And you took the call while she was in your bed! My god. It's perverse."

"I understand. And I'm so sorry. But I was overjoyed to hear from you. And that woman, she meant nothing to me. I didn't even want to get involved with her, but she was aggressive. I'm so glad that's all over. There's no one but you. There never has been."

"You're still such a little boy, Arnie Glass."

He knew she was trying to hurt him, and he understood. She was wounded and lashing out. "I can be exactly the man you need me to be," he said. "Please, let me prove that to you."

She shook her head. "I don't know anymore."

He could feel the disappointment in her voice, and it crushed him. In their last call, she'd wept, nearly admitting it had been a mistake to leave him. He wanted to bring her back to that moment, to forget about what she'd witnessed with Melody.

"Isn't there any part of you that still loves me?" he pleaded. He recalled the look on her face as she held his hand in the ER after that accident with the coffee table. When she asked the doctor if he'd be okay, she'd looked terrified, and he'd understood how fiercely she loved him. He wanted to remind her, to bring her back to that moment, but the incident was too fraught with other emotions, like her guilt over his injuries and the jealousy that had started the whole fight. So he just added, "I think the love is still there, deep in your heart."

At that, her face softened. "Of course it is," she said. "I've never stopped loving you, Arnie. You should know that."

Despite himself, Arnie felt his eyes water. This would all work itself out. It had to—they were meant to be together. She just needed reassurance.

"I can make you happy, my love. Just give me a chance."

Paulette fingered her necklace as she considered it. "I have one condition."

An opening! His heart flooded with hope. "Anything."

"You need to promise you'll be completely honest with me from now on."

"Of course!" he said, sitting up straighter.

"I mean it, Arnie."

Good lord, she was forgiving him! It was really happening. "Completely honest from now on, I swear."

She peered at him so hard he felt her presence, and it was as if she were there in the room with him. "But there's something else," she said, "isn't there?"

"Something else?" he echoed, but he knew. He couldn't get anything by this extraordinary woman.

"You're keeping something from me. I can tell."

Arnie nodded and swallowed. "I am," he said. "You're right."

"Tell me."

He took a deep breath. It was time for a confession. This way, she'd know he wasn't holding back. "You remember that Fabergé egg you gave me?"

"How could I forget? It was a replica, but it still cost more than my car."

"I treasured it all these years because it reminded me of you. And I kept it out where I could see it, so you would always be with me."

"That's very touching," she said, but her expression was dubious, because she knew something was coming.

"That hysterical woman," he said, "Melody . . . she stole it."

"Stole it?"

"She was here in my condo, and when she left, it was gone. She says she didn't take it, but I'm not so sure."

Paulette's eyes turned dark with anger. "That little bitch has my Fabergé egg? You have to get it back, Arnie!"

"How?"

"For god's sake, do I have to tell you everything? Do what it takes! Press charges, have her arrested."

"You're right, darling. Of course. I'll get it back."

"Listen, I have to go. But if you want me back, you get that Fabergé egg from that horrible woman, you hear me?"

"I'll get it back, Paulette, I promise."

She disconnected the call, and Arnie put his head in his hands, wondering what to do. He had to get that egg back. He had to.

His phone pinged to remind him he had a manicure appointment, but he ignored it. He was in no mood to sit still and get his nails tended to. Then his phone buzzed again with a text. It was from Addison, who had made the appointment for him.

Just a reminder about your 10:00 manicure! ♥

Arnie tapped the little microphone icon to dictate his reply. "Sweetheart," he said, "please cancel . . ." He stopped to think, picturing Addison's disappointment. She'd been so enthusiastic about helping him schedule this appointment—so cheerful and devoted—that it seemed unkind of him to cancel at the last minute for no reason. It was also unfair to the manicurist, who'd be left with a hole in her schedule. Besides, he had nothing else to do this morning, and it would almost certainly clear his head to be around other people. It was something Arnie understood about himself—he was a social animal, at his happiest surrounded by people, especially women. He backspaced over the message and started again. "I'll be there."

Chapter 39

Arnie was met at the salon by a young lady named Tameka, who was not his usual manicurist.

"Nice to see you, Dr. Glass," she said with a genuine smile, and Arnie could feel his mood lifting. This woman had such friendly energy about her that he was reminded of his favorite receptionist from his old office. She'd always made patients feel so at ease.

Tameka led him to a station next to a woman he'd seen in the building but never spoken to. She was an exotic and natural beauty, and he'd even asked around about her, but no one seemed to know who she was. He told himself he wouldn't flirt—not too much, anyway—but was delighted for the opportunity to solve the mystery.

"Hello!" he said as he took his seat next to her. The woman gave him a smile that lit up her face, made her even prettier. He decided she looked like an ethnic version of Ingrid Bergman at the height of her beauty.

"Hello," she said back, and he thought he detected an accent.

"I'm Arnie Glass," he said, not extending his hand, because her fingers were in the possession of the manicurist. "I don't think we've met."

"Leyla Balik," she said. "Delighted to make your acquaintance."

He grinned, charmed by the old-school introduction. It was, no doubt, something she learned in a classroom. "Turkish?" he asked, because he had a good ear for accents and thought he might have once met a man named Balik at a medical conference in Istanbul.

"Impressive," she said.

"My goodness, what are you reading?" he asked, pointing to the book on her table. It was a thick hardcover with a photo of a surgeon in an operating room.

"Memoir of an adventurous neurosurgeon," she said. "Interesting reading."

"Are you in the medical field?" he asked.

"I'm a nurse."

This was getting more intriguing by the second. And since both her hands were on the table in front of her, it was easy to see she wasn't wearing a ring.

"I'm a doctor," he said. "Well, retired doctor."

"What field?"

"Plastic surgery. Not as interesting as neurosurgery, I suppose."

"No!" she protested. "It's *very* interesting."

"You mean you'd read my memoir?" he said with a teasing smile.

"Oh yes, Dr. Glass."

It sounded like she was flirting, and it buoyed him. "Please, call me Arnie," he said, then added, "What's *your* specialty?"

"I was an OR nurse for many years—first in Cleveland and then here in Los Angeles, at Good Samaritan. But the pressure was so great, you know? And I decided, *Leyla, you deserve an easier life with time for fun.* So now I'm a private nurse to a woman here in the building."

"And you have time for fun?"

She glanced at him out the corner of her eye. "I make the time, Arnie."

It wasn't his imagination. She was coming on strong. The woman looked back at her nails and saw the manicurist swipe bright-pink polish onto her pinkie nail.

"No, my dear!" she said firmly. "That is the wrong color. If you please, find the one I asked for."

Arnie grew warm. Nurse Leyla wasn't just smart and flirty but strong. Outspoken. He knew he should be focused solely on Paulette right now, but she wasn't here. And hadn't she said she didn't care that he was dating someone? Right now, he couldn't see what harm there would be in seeing if this bright, luscious beauty might consent to a romantic dinner. She'd look so lovely by candlelight.

Her cell phone rang, and she carefully pressed answer with the tip of her finger, putting the phone on speaker.

"Geoffrey," she said, "I am at the nail salon."

"I was wondering if I should make us a dinner reservation for tonight," he said.

She huffed, exasperated. "I told you already."

"Mario's?"

"The seafood there is not fresh. You know this."

"I thought you liked Mario's."

"Geoffrey," she said, in a tone of voice that was clearly intended to let him know she was running out of patience.

"Okay, I apologize. I'll find another restaurant that can accommodate us."

She disconnected the call without saying goodbye, and Arnie pondered what he had heard. It didn't sound like a loving relationship.

"Having dinner with your boyfriend tonight?" he probed.

"Boyfriend," she repeated, as if she hadn't considered the word before. "He thinks he is my boyfriend."

"But *you* don't think so?"

"I'm still deciding."

It was, Arnie knew, a perfect opportunity for him to ask if she was open to seeing other people, but a voice in his head—one that sounded very much like Paulette's—warned him not to. If he was committing to Paulette, he needed to be serious about it. The other voice in his head—one that sounded more like his own—reminded him that it would be unfair to this lovely woman to get something started with her. Apparently, she was already in a knotty relationship and didn't need to get entangled with a man who was in love with someone else.

"That sounds complicated," he said to Leyla.

"Yes, I suppose so. What about you? Do you have a girlfriend? I thought I saw you with that woman who wears the very high heels."

"I'm not seeing her anymore," Arnie said, "but . . . it looks like I might be reuniting with my ex-wife." He exhaled, proud of himself for doing the right thing.

Leyla nodded, taking in his pronouncement. "Love is difficult, no?"

"Always," he said.

Chapter 40
ADDISON

Addison had time to kill. After getting the lowdown from Tameka about the conversation between Arnie and Leyla at the nail salon, she knew she needed to find other opportunities to bring them together, because they had clearly hit it off. Tameka even insisted that sparks flew. But Arnie, unfortunately, was just too stuck on Paulette to make a move. So Addison had arranged to meet him by the rooftop pool at the exact time she knew Leyla would be up there reading. Her plan was to be just late enough to give them time to chat.

Sure enough, by the time she arrived on the rooftop, Arnie was stretched out on a cushioned lounge in the shade, right next to Leyla, who had a book on her lap. They were so engrossed in conversation they didn't notice her.

Addison stood and waited until at last Arnie looked up and waved her over. "Sweetheart," he called, "do you know Leyla?"

Addison approached, and the two women exchanged greetings.

"What are you two kids talking about?" Addison asked, pointing to the book. "Neurosurgery? Brain hemorrhages?"

Arnie laughed. "We were actually talking about a waiter at a restaurant in Glendale."

"Mr. Friendly," Leyla said.

"Mr. Nosy is more like it," Arnie added.

"I had to shoo him away from our table!" Leyla said, amused. "He made it so terribly awkward."

She and Arnie shared a laugh, and it was clear these two had chemistry. Addison tingled. It was a perfect match, just as she had predicted. She wanted to pat herself on the back.

Leyla announced that it was time for her to go to work, and when she picked up her book and left, Addison watched Arnie watching Leyla. Yes, she thought. This woman could be just the person to distract him from Melody and divert him from Paulette. She sat on the side of the vacated lounge, facing her uncle.

"Everything okay with you?" Addison asked. "I saw you having a serious conversation with Frankie last night."

Arnie thought for a long moment as his expression turned serious. Then he sat up straighter, as if he needed to be upright for this particular conversation. "It was about Melody."

"Oh?" Addison probed, eager for more. Now she was pretty sure that conversation was the reason Nikolai had been summoned. In any case, she hoped Arnie was close to severing his relationship with Melody. Thief or not, the tightly wound manipulator was not a good match for him.

"She still denies she took my Fabergé egg, but I just don't believe her."

Addison stayed quiet, wondering where this was going. She knew she would need to tell her uncle that Melody wasn't the culprit after all, but she didn't want to say anything that might encourage the relationship.

"I've been trying to figure out a way to get it back from her," he added.

"I see," Addison said, keeping her expression even.

"I went to Frankie last night for help." He rubbed his forehead, as if in pain, then looked at Addison. "Did you know there are security cameras in the elevators?"

"Mm," she said noncommittally.

"You know," he said, "I really wanted to protect her at first. But now . . ."

He trailed off, and Addison studied his pained expression. She had always thought there was something endearing about his savior complex when it came to women. Sure, it was sexist, but he was from another generation, so it was understandable. Besides, his reverence for women was so extreme it was hard not to be charmed by it, especially since she couldn't really disagree. Women were strong, glorious, capable of anything. Even the unhinged Melody Forrest probably had some inner goddess.

"Did something happen with her?" Addison prodded.

"We had this massive fight. Over Paulette. And Melody was so awful, so crazy. It was like she was determined to ruin my life. So I ended it."

Addison exhaled, relieved. One down, one to go, she thought. "I'm glad you did."

"Only, I need that egg," he said, "or Paulette won't take me back. I still would rather not involve the police. I mean, what good does it do anyone to throw Melody in jail? Frankie had a perfect solution. She said the elevator-cam videos would give us all the proof we need, and we can use them to force Melody's hand. She told me she'd talk to Nikolai about it."

"Have you spoken to either of them today—Frankie or Nikolai?"

"Not yet."

Addison let out a long breath. "Uncle Arnie," she said, "I have something to tell you."

He looked up at her with his clear blue eyes. "Yes?"

"I saw the elevator-cam videos."

"You did?"

Addison started at the beginning, telling him about her motivation of hoping the video evidence would compel him to break it off with Melody, only to discover the files had been deleted.

"Deleted?" he said. "My god! Melody must have a friend on the inside who's helping her."

"That's what I thought," Addison said. "But Zach Brody was able to recover the files, and it turns out it wasn't Melody."

Arnie looked shocked. "Who was it?"

"A man in work boots."

"Are you certain?"

"Saw it with my own eyes. He had it in his hand."

Arnie looked confounded by this news. "But who was he?"

"Nikolai's trying to find out," Addison said. "He's questioning the doormen and following any clues." She opened her phone to an image of the thief that Zach had sent her. She turned it toward her uncle. "Do you know this man?"

He shook his head, but stared for a long while, losing color. "He was in my apartment?"

"Apparently."

He handed the phone back to her, looking dejected. "Now I'll never get that egg back," he mumbled.

"I know it had sentimental value to you," she said, "but it's just a thing. What's important is that no one was hurt."

"That's not the way Paulette's going to see it."

Addison wanted to protest that she was sure Paulette wouldn't be angry once she understood the egg had been stolen by some strange man who got into his apartment, but decided that was the wrong framing.

"Uncle Arnie," she said gently, "if she would let something like this come between you, is she really the person you want to spend the rest of your life with?"

"I love her," he said.

"Don't you think you could fall in love with someone else? Someone less . . . volatile?"

"Frankie said the same thing. But Paulette is my person, Addison." He pointed to his chest, looking stricken. "She lives right here."

He was so earnest that for a moment Addison was ready to abandon her pursuit of a love match for Arnie. After all, if the feeling was this strong, maybe he and Paulette really did belong together. But then she closed her eyes and saw that photograph her mother had stuck in the kitchen drawer. She saw Arnie's bloodred eye and his terrible scar, freshly sutured. She recalled her mother's distress over the awful marriage.

And also, she knew deep down he could be happy without Paulette. In fact, his life had been so cheerful and carefree before he learned she was coming back to the United States. Surely he could recapture that . . . especially if he found the right match.

She looked in the direction Leyla had gone, then told her uncle she had to get to work, letting him assume she was talking only about her concierge job. But in her mind, she was already three steps ahead, thinking about the ways in which she and Regina English could get to work, conspiring to put Arnie and Leyla together.

Chapter 41

As Addison sat at the concierge desk answering questions and making appointments, she found herself looking at the feet of every man who passed to see if anyone was wearing black-soled work boots. But in Beekman Towers, all the men wore designer sneakers (or tennis shoes, as they called them here), designer leather loafers, designer boat shoes, designer lace-ups, or designer sandals. She even saw designer flip-flops, and one pair of flamboyant designer cowboy boots.

Addison noticed a familiar pair of black shoes and looked up to see they belonged to Dante, who had a travel bag slung over his shoulder. She remembered that he said he was heading to New York, so she gave him a surreptitious wave goodbye, as she was sitting with a resident who had asked about tennis lessons. He waved back, flashing his killer dimple. Then he walked through the glass doors to a waiting car and was gone.

Addison's attention returned to scoping out male footwear, and the only shoes she saw that fell short of high-end designers belonged to staff members, a couple of repairmen, and one resident in round glasses who took a seat on the lobby sofa and pulled out his phone. Addison didn't know who he was, but aside from his scuffed loafers, there wasn't anything particularly suspicious about the guy, so she went back to work.

A few hours later, Joaquín approached the desk holding a small black box. "This came for you," he announced.

"For me?"

"Hand delivered," he said, putting it on the desk.

She looked down to see a label that said **ADDISON TORRES, CONCIERGE EXTRAORDINAIRE, BEEKMAN TOWERS.**

"Thank you," she muttered, and slipped it into her purse, sensing it was something she shouldn't open in public.

"Looks like you've got a rich admirer," he said with a wink. Then he put his finger over his lips to indicate he'd keep it a secret, and walked away.

Later, in the privacy of her apartment, Addison opened the box to find another box inside. This one was Tiffany blue, tied up with a white silk ribbon. Next to it there was a small card inside an envelope. She pulled it out and read the message.

Still thinking about you.

It wasn't signed, but she knew who it was from. Addison put the Tiffany box on the table in front of her, almost afraid to open it. Everything at that store was expensive. Insanely expensive. There was no way she could accept such a gift—it was just too fraught. And sure, he probably thought it was just a sweet, romantic gesture, but to Addison, it felt like she was being bought.

She left the box there as she had dinner and tried to relax. Finally, just before bed, she decided she had to open it or it would haunt her all night.

Addison untied the ribbon and eased off the lid, hoping to find something very small and very plain. A token. She extracted the velvety drawstring pouch, holding her breath. And then, at last, she saw what was inside: a rose gold bangle bracelet, embedded with real diamonds.

No, she thought, taking it out to examine it. I simply cannot accept this. But as she slipped it back in the pouch, she saw something delicately inscribed on the inside.

Always, Dante

Chapter 42

Even on her day off, Addison couldn't imagine a way to sneak out of the Beekman in a gown without attracting the kind of attention that would almost certainly find its way back to Frankie. So on the night of Zach's award ceremony, she arranged to take her things to Tameka's house and get dressed there.

It was a first-floor garden apartment, with windows overlooking lush landscaping. The walls were painted a pale buttery yellow, making up for the lack of sunlight, and the living room was crowded with a blue leather sectional and piles of toys.

To Addison, the best part of the arrangement was that she got to meet four-year-old Jada, who was even prettier than her photographs, with big round eyes and her mother's delicate bone structure. She had clinging arms and ebullient energy and took to Addison immediately. The feeling was mutual. Jada sat on Addison's lap, having her snack at the kitchen table, as the two women chatted.

"You ready for some show-and-tell?" Addison asked her friend. She hadn't told anyone about the bracelet and needed some perspective.

"Born ready," Tameka said.

Addison opened her purse and rooted around. "I got a package on Thursday. Special delivery."

"From?"

Addison found the tiny envelope and pushed it across the table.

As soon as she saw the Tiffany & Co. logo, Tameka answered her own question. "Dante," she said, then extracted the card and read it. "Oh, lord. This boy's not playing. What did you get?"

Addison readjusted sweet Jada on her lap, then pulled out the aqua jewelry box and handed it to her friend. Tameka opened it and gently freed the bracelet from its pouch. Her mouth opened in awe as she held it toward the light, watching it sparkle.

"Diamonds," she whispered with a kind of reverence.

"Let me see!" said Jada.

"Sorry, baby," her mother said. "This is for grown-ups."

"I want it!" cried the little girl.

"Me too," her mom said with a laugh, then squinted at the inscription. "*Always*? That's like half a step from *I love you*. Maybe a quarter."

Addison grimaced. "This is exactly what I didn't want. *Exactly.*"

"Give me your wrist."

Addison dutifully reached across the table, and Tameka opened the delicately hinged bangle and clicked it closed on her wrist.

"What should I do?" Addison asked, holding up her hand to examine the bracelet. "I mean, I can't possibly keep this."

"Of course you can."

Addison frowned. "It feels . . . transactional."

"Don't even," Tameka said. "The man gave you a gift. A gift he can clearly afford. You keep it, you enjoy it, and you owe him nothing."

"Nothing?"

"Nothing," Tameka said adamantly.

Addison shook her head as she examined her own wrist. "I almost wish it had been another ridiculous bouquet of flowers."

"Flowers die," her friend said. "Diamonds—"

"I know," Addison cut in, "but the truth is, I don't even like diamonds. Aesthetically or ethically."

"You're thinking too much. Just enjoy it. And enjoy that someone thinks you're worth it."

Addison studied her friend, whose demeanor seemed a little brighter than usual. "What happened to your cynicism?" she asked.

"Strangest thing," Tameka said. "I had a long conversation with this woman in the building—Maya Mayfield. You know her?"

Addison nodded. "The Sherpa of love and marriage, right? I thought she was trying to keep a low profile."

"Not anymore. She's rebranding herself as the guru of breakups or whatever, and she offered me a free life coaching session, though I'm supposed to keep it on the down-low until she makes an official announcement. You want some tea?"

Addison nodded, and Tameka rose from the table to put the kettle on.

"Did it help?" Addison asked. "The life coaching?"

"A lot. She walked me through my own feelings, gave me some perspective."

"Mommy, I'm done," Jada announced. She picked up a napkin and wiped her little mouth, illustrating that it was time to move on.

"You want to watch something?" Tameka asked her.

Jada, clearly bored with the grown-up talk, was ready for some cartoon about puppies, so her mother set her up in the other room, then came back into the kitchen and finished making the tea.

"Anyway," she said, handing Addison a cup, "I'm thinking about putting myself out there again after the divorce is final. Maybe try a dating app."

"That's terrific," Addison said. "But you don't need an app—you've got a building full of eligible men."

Tameka rolled her eyes. "No, thank you," she said. "I wouldn't mind a diamond bracelet, but those guys are the worst."

"What about the staff?"

"Like who?"

Addison thought for a moment. "How about Joaquín?"

"Didn't Raphael say he fucks anything that moves and he drinks too much?"

"Raphael," Addison dismissed with a wave, as if the building's personal trainer and resident gossip hound wasn't worth taking seriously. "He just loves drama, loves trashing people. I can only imagine what he says about us behind our backs."

Tameka leaned back as she considered that. "Joaquín *is* pretty cute."

"And you both write scripts," Addison observed. "Maybe you could be one of those screenwriting couples, like Dorothy Parker and Alan Campbell. And you could act out your most lurid scenes."

Tameka rewarded her with a smile. "Fine, I'll consider it. But until the divorce is final, I can't even think about getting laid. Speaking of which, let's get you ready for your hot date with Zach Brody."

"It's not a date, Mom," Addison said.

"Sure it isn't. Finish your tea, young lady."

Later, after Addison was dressed and Jada had her bath, the girl sat by the window at the front of the house, looking out. She didn't understand what was going on but had picked up on the electrified energy of the grown-ups.

"Is that a real car?" she asked, pointing at the street.

Addison put on her earring as she looked out over the girl's head. Zach had just pulled up in his yellow-and-black McLaren.

"I think it's safe to call that a toy," said Tameka, joining them at the window. "A rich man's toy."

Zach emerged from the car, and Addison took a sharp breath. God help her, but she thought there was something almost painfully sexy about a tall nerdy guy in a tuxedo and sneakers.

"He cleans up nice," Tameka said.

Addison straightened herself and smoothed out her black gown. It was a shimmery silk charmeuse halter dress that showed off her broad shoulders. Subtle beading around the neckband offered just enough bling. Tameka looked her up and down, then motioned for her to give a spin. When she saw the plunging back, she gave a whistle.

"You're going to give that boy a heart attack."

The doorbell rang, and Tameka opened it. "Well," she said instead of hello, "you two are going to be the best-dressed couple at Taco Bell."

"I wouldn't go to Taco Bell dressed like this," Zach said with such earnestness Addison nearly cut in to explain it was a joke, but he wasn't done. "We're going to In-N-Out Burger."

"Goody," Addison said, "another first for me."

He turned to look at her and seemed to lose his breath. "Oh," he murmured.

"This is when you say something nice," Tameka told him.

He nodded, still staring at Addison. "You look . . ."

"Hot?" Tameka suggested. "Drip? Drop-dead gorgeous?"

"Keep going," Zach said.

"What about me?" Jada demanded.

He bent to face her. "You look drop-dead gorgeous too," he said. "Those are the best pajamas I ever saw."

The girl looked down at the printed pink-and-green pattern, then back at Zach. "I want to come to In-N-Out Burger."

"Maybe next time," he said. "Maybe we'll all go."

"We're going to read a book now," Tameka said to her daughter, then looked at Addison and promised she'd drop her things off the next day.

"Don't stay out too late, you kids," she added.

Addison picked up her clutch bag. "Let's get out of here before we get a lecture on leaving room for Jesus when we dance."

Tameka moved in for a hug and whispered to Addison, "I slipped a condom in your purse. Just in case."

Addison laughed, but Tameka said, "I'm actually serious."

Addison laughed even harder. "I always have condoms," she whispered back.

Chapter 43

"That dress," Zach said as they drove toward the Beverly Wilshire for the Innovations in Software awards ceremony. "It's . . ." He tapped his lip as if trying to shake free the right word.

"Too much?" Addison asked.

"No!" he insisted. "It's perfect."

"But will it outshine Quinn?" she asked, not quite sure it would. Addison had googled the woman and knew she was beautiful and dramatic, with short platinum hair she often wore streaked with pink or blue. In the photos, she appeared to be a fashionista, and there was no doubt she'd be dressed in something Oscar-worthy for this event. She could certainly afford it.

"That's of no consequence," Zach told her.

As if, Addison thought. "It's okay," she said. "You don't have to pretend this isn't about Quinn."

He held tight to the steering wheel, looking lost in thought. "I just . . . I want to see her expression when I receive that award."

"You know for a fact you're going to win?"

He shrugged. "It's difficult to keep a secret in this industry."

"In any industry, I think," Addison said, realizing there was nothing more universally loved and hated than gossip. "You think Quinn knows?" she added.

"Probably. But it'll still infuriate her to see me amassing offers she can't get her claws into."

"Offers?"

"Innovator of the Year is the top prize for an individual. Whoever wins that never has to worry about financing their next project. Investors virtually throw money at them."

"Your dream come true," Addison said, recalling that he'd complained about the challenge of wooing investors. "Quinn will eat her heart out."

He nodded, retreating into himself, but came back quickly. "Tell me about that dress," he said.

Addison looked at him. It was such a lovely question for a guy to ask. And sure, he was changing the subject, but he wasn't playing her, like when a guy compliments your shoes because he read an article that said it scores points. Zach was truly curious.

She didn't want to tell him that she'd worn the dress only twice and the second time was at Marco's brother's wedding. They'd been dating only two months when he asked her to be his plus-one, and it had accelerated their relationship—partly because he had the kind of warm family that had immediately welcomed her into the fold. But mostly, it was because that night, for the first time, he'd said "I love you." And Addison, for the first time ever, had said it back.

She patted her chest, as if assuring herself she could keep all that private. But she could certainly share the dress's origin story, which began before she even met Marco.

"I needed something spectacular for a client's wedding at the Plaza," she said. "When I found this dress, I thought it was perfect. But even on sale it was more than a week's salary, so I asked my boss if she could buy it for me, since I was invited through her company."

"Did she?"

"The tightwad *loaned* me the money—took a bit out of my paycheck every month until it was paid off."

Zach shook his head. "That's a legitimate business expense," he said. "She could have written it off on her taxes."

"She thought she was teaching me a lesson. That's the problem with entitled people like Piper—they think the problem with poor people like me is that we just don't work hard enough or have enough ambition or understand what it means to sacrifice. It's so twisted. They think we'd be as rich as they are if we were just as good as they are."

"I know people like that," Zach said. "They belong to country clubs, make massive political donations, and never leave tips."

"You've met Piper," she said.

"Her type, for sure."

Addison looked out the car window. Driving through the city of Beverly Hills at night, she could easily imagine she was back in New York—except for the palm trees, of course—and it made her homesick, stirred regrets. She wondered what she'd be doing right now if she hadn't been so impulsive with Logan Kinkaid. Would she and Marco be making plans for the future? Would she be shopping for a wedding gown with his mom and sister?

She had ached for that day, for the bittersweetness of relying on Elena, Marco's mom, as a surrogate for her own. But had she really ached for a happily ever after with Marco? Even during the best of times, it had been hard to picture a future with him. Addison had assumed it was her own lack of imagination. But now she wondered if it was ever the right path for her. Maybe she'd been more swept up in the idea of having a new family than in her love for Marco.

And maybe—just maybe—it was why she cheated. On some level, blowing up the relationship was a shortcut to the exit.

But no, that didn't feel right. She'd broken up with guys before Marco. Something else had compelled her to destroy her own future. She understood it was all tied to her parents' accident, but it was hard to connect the dots. Why would she want to continually recreate the worst day of her life? The very bottom of her world had fallen away, leaving her with nothing.

She recalled the astonishment of the moment. It hadn't been just the shock of her parents' death but the realization that there was nothing she could do about it—no way to roll back time and stop the accident from happening.

Addison turned her attention back to Zach, tired of the imponderable puzzle. "Tell me about the awards ceremony," she said.

Zach got into the left lane as he considered the question, slowing as he approached a red light so he could coast through when it turned green. He was such a good driver—so confident and in control. Those were the skills she'd need to learn.

But of course, they wouldn't protect her from getting hit from behind by a truck. After all, her parents had both been good drivers. She imagined riding down Queens Boulevard, both hands on the wheel, as a truck barreled up from behind, trying to make the light. Would it really be impossible to prevent the accident? What if she sailed through the yellow light even as it turned red? Or what if she glanced in the rearview before stopping?

Zach broke her reverie. "Expect a sizable gala," he said. "There will be dinner and dancing, as well as a number of boring speeches. They rearrange the agenda sometimes, but usually you have to sit through it all before they give out awards."

Addison felt like she was on the brink of a breakthrough, almost understanding something profound about her compulsion to sabotage her relationships. But it had just slipped through her fingers. So she focused on the conversation.

"And you're sure Quinn is going to be there?" she asked.

He nodded. "With Eli. Homebuoy is up for Best New E-Commerce App."

"Homebuoy?"

"That's our company. Or actually, *their* company." His jaw went hard.

"I thought you said they sold it."

Zach exhaled, and she could see he was trying to release some of his fury. "Sold most of it. They worked out a deal where they still run it, still extract a percentage."

Addison shook her head. "Shit. People like that get every damned thing they want."

"And have to crush everyone in their way. Because to them, you're not truly winning unless someone else is losing."

And yet you're still in love with her, Addison thought. But she understood. Sometimes you simply fell for the wrong person.

A short time later, they walked arm in arm into the ballroom of the Beverly Wilshire Hotel. The tables around the perimeter were dressed in blue to match the curtains on the stage at the back of the room. The chairs were draped in white, like a heavenly choir, and each table had a tall glass vase with long-stemmed white calla lilies reaching for the heavens. Oversize screens bookended the stage, lit with a graphic that read "Innovations in Software 19th Annual Awards Ceremony."

Only a few people were seated at the tables—most were crowded in the center of the room, talking and drinking. It didn't take more than three seconds for Addison to spot Quinn. Her hair was dyed purple, and she wore a dramatic white dress with cutouts over the shoulders and midriff, creating the effect of wearing a white bra out in public. It certainly got attention, as nearly all eyes were on her. Addison knew her own gown—as sexy as it was—didn't stand out nearly as much, since a lot of women wore black. But heads turned as she and Zach made their way through the horde. There were enough murmurs for Addison to get the gist—this crowd knew what Quinn and Eli had done to Zach.

She looked at him as they walked and could tell he was keeping his eyes averted, as if glancing Quinn's way would turn him into a pillar of salt. It seemed like he was trying to move through the crowd invisibly.

Despite his efforts, Zach had enough celebrity status to create his own buzz. Guys clapped him on the back as he passed, saying things like "I voted for you, man" or "Congratulations, dude, you got this."

Zach was chatting with one of these guys when Addison saw a nearby woman point at Zach and nudge the redheaded man she was talking to. "Ask him," the woman said urgently.

The man—who was nerd-cool, with a thick red beard and multi-colored polka-dot bow tie—turned to Zach. "Good to see you, Brody."

"Nate!" Zach said, giving him a half hug before introducing him to Addison. In turn, Nate introduced his wife, Maria.

"Listen," Nate said to Zach after Maria gave him a look, "I was just wondering . . . Are you nervous about Jared Einbinder?"

"Not at all," Zach said.

"It's just that . . . I mean, people are talking."

Zach patted his shoulder. "I'm unperturbed."

"You're sure?"

"Absolutely."

As a waiter with a tray of champagne glasses approached, Nate and Maria disappeared into the crowd.

"What was that about?" Addison asked Zach.

"Jared Einbinder was also nominated for the innovator award, but his app turned out to be buggy. He doesn't pose a threat."

But he could, Addison thought. Surely there was a reason that couple had been so concerned. She wondered if there was a way she could track the gossip trail and get more information. Because if it was true—if this Jared Einbinder was a real threat—Zach would need to prepare himself. Otherwise, he'd be devastated.

When he was fully engaged in an arcane conversation about coding, Addison whispered that she was going to take a walk and would be back soon.

She started with the ladies' room, lingering as she tried to engage a few different women in conversation. But software development was still such a boy's club that most of them were wives or partners of the industry insiders and had little to offer.

Addison went back into the ballroom and situated herself by the bar. She struck up a conversation with a curly-haired guy, using the same opening she had tried with the women in the bathroom.

"I've never been to this event before," she said. "I had no idea it was such a big deal."

"It's huge," he said.

"Do you know how they choose the winners? Is there a panel or something?"

"It's a straight-up vote by the members."

"So it's like the Oscars?" she asked.

Two guys nearby stopped talking and started listening in on their conversation. Addison could tell they were dying to offer their own expertise. This mission was starting to feel almost too easy. Guys loved a chance to mansplain. And if a girl was wearing a sexy dress with a naked back, they were positively compelled.

"Yeah," the curly-haired guy said. "Kind of like that."

"Are there ever any surprises? I mean, I heard that Zach Brody is a shoo-in for the innovator award. But someone said maybe not."

"Oh, I think Zach's got it in the bag," he said.

"I don't know about that," one of the eavesdroppers offered.

Addison turned to him, affecting a fascinated expression. "Really?"

"His ex-partner, Quinn McLeod, has been stumping for another guy."

Quinn? Addison nearly choked. Poor Zach, she thought. This was a worst-case scenario. Legitimately losing to another guy would be bad enough, but getting burned by Quinn yet again would be devastating. Her stomach tightened in worry.

"Why would she do that?" Addison asked.

The other eavesdropper—who seemed drunk—cut in. "Because she's a stone-cold bitch."

"She thinks it'll take attention away from her company if Zach wins," his sober friend said. "She wants all the glory."

"Like I said," the drunk guy added, "stone-cold bitch."

"Come to think of it," the curly-haired guy mused, "a lot of people I spoke to said they voted for Jared. Said it would be nice to see the underdog win for a change."

The drunk guy laughed. "Fucking sheep. That's exactly the line Quinn's been feeding them. Stone-cold—"

"What about the other guy, Eli?" Addison asked. "What's his role in all this?"

"He does whatever Quinn tells him to," said the sober one.

The drunk added "Pussy whipped," and Addison bristled. She hated that expression, even when applied to that monstrous couple. But she wasn't going to get into it with these guys. There was something more important to do.

So she simply said "It was nice meeting you all." Then, with a sputtering heart, she disappeared back into the crowd to find Zach.

Chapter 44
CARLY

Carly didn't usually find herself working on a Sunday night, but after spending three days on Maya's press release—rewriting it at least a dozen times until it shone like polished gold—she realized she was falling way behind on her freelance work for the medical products manufacturer. She muted *60 Minutes* and got to work, losing herself in the uninspired yet satisfying task of learning all she could about hospital gurneys so she could write about them with confidence.

It reminded her of doing homework as a child. Though she never admitted it to anyone, Carly had actually enjoyed it. She liked being smart enough to sail through the assignments or determined enough to hunker down and figure it all out. In the end, she almost always felt proud of herself. That was something no one could take from her—not her father, who was even crueler than Owen, and not her classmates, who teased her for being the odd, quiet girl who always seemed to know the answers to the teachers' questions.

She learned early on not to raise her hand and call attention to herself, and certainly not to express pride in her hard work and good grades. It had all been so very private, pushing Carly more and more inward.

She placed her fingers on the keyboard and started writing her copy about the Pro-Care 3000, which the manufacturer insisted was the best in the field. She stopped and stared at the opening, trying to find an elegant way to rewrite it so that "health care" and "patient care" didn't appear in the same sentence. It was like a puzzle, and when she finally nailed it and moved on to the next paragraph, Carly thought again about school, recalling the precise moment she'd known she had a talent for writing. It had been prompted by her eleventh-grade English teacher, who had a pointy goatee and wore paisley vests and had been universally despised by her classmates. She understood why—he was smug and affected and made no secret of the fact that he thought the students were a bunch of useless, semiliterate idiots. But in the margin of her midterm paper he had scribbled *These are well-written paragraphs, Miss Gronek.* From anyone else it would have been mild praise, but from Mr. Linhardt it felt like a revelation. Yes, Carly had realized, they are! And from that moment on, she thought of herself as a writer.

She'd been at work on the project for nearly an hour when her phone buzzed with a text from Maya. Despite her vow to continue working well into the night, she grabbed for it.

Come join me for a glass of wine on the roof! Wear something cute

Carly read it three times, trying to quiet the flutter in her chest. Wear something cute? Why on earth would Maya say such a thing? Surely she wasn't flirting, yet Carly felt herself flush.

Stop it, she told herself. Stop it right now. You are not sixteen, and Maya is not the captain of the football team. You're just a silly fan reacting to her celebrity. That's all this is.

She picked up her phone and typed a message:

Would love to, but I have a ton of work. Next time!

There. It was the sensible, responsible thing to do. Because if she took a break now, she'd never have enough energy to get back to work tonight, and she'd fall even further behind.

Before hitting send, Carly reread the text, and an uneasy feeling wormed its way inside. What if she was just looking for an excuse to stay in her stagnant life? Surely she could just work twice as hard tomorrow and the next day. Maybe this was what she was supposed to be doing—engaging with the world, being a social creature, having fun. She was an almost-divorced woman living in Beverly Hills, after all. She had a new haircut and an adorable dress she had bought from Amazon hanging in her closet, tags still dangling. It was short, feminine, youthful. The kind of thing she never wore because Owen would make her feel like a joke. But here, no one would laugh.

She backspaced over the text and typed:

Will do. Thanks!

Excited, Carly studied the emojis looking for something appropriate to add. A smiley face? A heart? She settled on the pretty cocktail and hit send. Then she cut the tags off her new dress, slipped it on, and examined herself in the mirror, even turning around to check the back. There was nothing wrong with the outfit. The shoes worked. Her arms and legs looked slim and smooth. But somehow she felt naked. The dress was so formfitting to the waist, and there was so much skin. Carly grabbed a cardigan from her closet and put it on. Yes, that felt more comfortable.

When she arrived on the rooftop, it was like a party. The bass beat of a Beyoncé song throbbed and trilled, and the area around the pool was clotted with people chatting and drinking under the twinkle of fairy lights outshining the stars. Several heads turned to look at her, and Carly tucked the hair behind her ear, smoothed out her dress. She heard someone call her name and looked up to see Maya by the railing, talking to two men. Dressed in a sunny yellow bikini top and flowing skirt, Maya was clearly coming out of hiding. Carly surveyed the crowd again and noticed several men staring at the tall beauty. And why wouldn't they? She was a goddess.

Carly approached and felt like a celebrity herself when Maya moved in for a hug, as several people watched the exchange and a murmur undulated through the crowd.

"Take the sweater off and flaunt that bangin' body," Maya whispered before releasing her. Or maybe Carly had imagined it. It just didn't seem possible that Maya would say such a thing. At least, not to her, Carly Pratt from Nashua. But, nearly hyperventilating, Carly did as she was asked and accepted the glass of white wine Maya thrust in her hand.

Maya introduced her to the two men, explained to them that Carly was a gifted and inspired writer. One of them wore a Hawaiian shirt open over a bathing suit and was apparently an entertainment attorney. The other, who was taller than Maya and wearing a preppy polo shirt and slacks, was some kind of entrepreneur.

"What do you write?" he asked Carly.

Maya gave her a surreptitious wink as she excused herself and headed toward the Splash Bar. Carly watched her go, disappointment shrouding her like a dense cloud as she realized why Maya had told her to wear something cute. She'd wanted Carly to make a good impression on these divorced men so that at least one of them might ask her out.

Carly felt something shrivel inside as she joined the crowd in watching the beautiful Maya Mayfield cross the patio to approach an attractive, athletic-looking woman at the bar whom she seemed to know. They kissed each other on both cheeks, like Europeans, and shared a quick laugh.

"I write . . . I write pretty boring stuff," she said to the polo shirt guy, still focused on the bar. When she saw Maya brush a strand of hair from the woman's face—a gesture so filled with tenderness it nearly choked her to watch—Carly moved a hair from her own face and could feel the cool touch of Maya's fingers. She took a juddering breath, and a pang of jealousy formed a fissure in her heart, threatening to break it in half. And at last, Carly Pratt admitted to herself that she had fallen in love with Maya Mayfield.

Chapter 45
ADDISON

By the time somebody took the microphone and asked everyone to please find their seats, Addison still hadn't told Zach what she'd learned. He had been too engrossed in conversation with one person or another, while Addison stood silently by, holding on to a glass of champagne.

"Are you the plus-one?" came a voice behind her, and Addison turned to discover she was face to face with the notorious Quinn McLeod and her white bra-dress. Up close, the woman wasn't as attractive as she'd looked from a distance. Her makeup was too heavy, and her purple lipstick—the exact same shade as her hair—couldn't hide the unnaturalness of her overplumped lips. Still, Addison understood why Zach had been so intoxicated. The treacherous schemer had a fierce energy about her—like the sun itself—and she could imagine Zach being pulled into her orbit.

Addison couldn't ignore the passive-aggressive implications of Quinn's question. Not *Are you the girlfriend* or *Are you with Zach*. The plus-one. Not even *his* plus-one. Dehumanizing. Dismissive.

"I'm the girlfriend," she said, immersing herself in the role. "Addison Torres."

Addison extended her hand, but the woman pretended she didn't see it and sipped her champagne. "I'm Quinn."

No last name, of course. This diva thought she was Beyoncé, Madonna, and Cher all rolled into one. But Addison simply said "I know."

"Aren't you going to say it's nice to meet me?" Quinn sneered.

Addison took a sip of her own champagne. "I don't like lying."

"Me neither."

"And yet you're so good at it," Addison marveled.

Quinn shrugged. "I have many talents."

"I don't doubt it."

"What do *you* do?" she asked, with such disdain it was clear she couldn't wait to hear it was something trivial, something that would never amass the kind of fortune that would let her purchase a $50 million house in Malibu overlooking the Pacific Ocean.

"I'm a cashier at Walmart."

"Funny," Quinn said, looking Addison up and down as if tallying the cost of what she was wearing, "but I bet it's not too far from the truth."

Refusing to be intimidated, Addison glared at her, and Quinn responded with an amused grin, as if she were winning whatever this stupid game was.

"Did you want something?" Addison asked. "I mean, something you didn't already help yourself to?"

"I just want to wish Zach good luck," she said, with such a smug expression that Addison wanted to slap her. Quinn seemed completely confident she had ruined his chances of winning and was reveling in it. The drunk had been right. She was a stone-cold bitch.

"I'll pass it along," Addison said; then she turned her naked back on the woman and took Zach's arm, leading him away.

"I have to tell you something," she whispered as they walked toward their seats, but before she could get another word out, a gushing couple approached.

"I think we're at the same table!" the woman said.

Zach introduced them to Addison, who promptly forgot their names. But she shook their hands and exchanged pleasantries before trying to get Zach's attention again.

"I really need to talk to you," she said. "Now." Addison glanced across the room and saw Quinn watching her as she hung on the arm of some man, presumably Eli, Zach's former business partner.

The emcee approached the microphone again and pleaded for everyone to find their seats.

"Can it wait one minute?" Zach asked Addison.

"I guess," she said, understanding it would attract a lot of attention if Zach walked away from the table at that moment.

They took their seats, along with everyone else, and the man at the microphone announced that the program would begin shortly, starting with the Innovator of the Year award, followed by an address from the president of the board, the keynote speech, and then the industry awards.

"Outstanding," Zach said, rubbing his hands together. "They're leading with the innovator award."

"That's what I wanted to talk to you about," she insisted, as the others at their table studied their menu cards. "I heard that Quinn—"

A man came up behind Zach and grabbed his shoulders. "Yo, Brody. You excited?"

Zach turned to face him, and they launched into an excited conversation about some new notepad-type app that was in development. With a sigh, Addison took out her own phone with its cracked screen and opened the soon-to-be obsolescent notepad app. She typed out: Quinn has been campaigning for Jared to win.

Then she interrupted his conversation. "I need you to see something," she said, and passed him her phone under the table.

While the man was still talking, Zach glanced down at his lap and read her message. Addison watched as the color drained from his face. He stood and told the man he had a small emergency he had to take care of; then he grabbed Addison's hand and led her outside the ballroom.

"What's going on?" he asked her when they were alone. "I don't understand."

"It's Quinn," she said. "I just wanted you to be prepared."

"She's been campaigning for Jared Einbinder?"

Addison nodded. "I heard it from numerous sources."

"And are people . . . I mean, is she succeeding? Did they vote for him?" He looked terrified.

"Zach," she said gently, touching his arm.

He ran his hand through his hair and walked around in a circle, dazed. "What the fuck?"

"I know," Addison said. "I'm so sorry."

"But . . . do you think she really swayed a majority of voters?"

"I don't know," she said. "I just wanted you to be prepared, in case she succeeded."

He put his face in his hands. "My fault," he muttered. "This is on me."

Addison thought he looked emptied, bereft, like a refugee who had lost everything he had in the world, and she hurt for him.

"That's not true," she said, and touched his arm again, but he was rigid, impenetrable.

"It is! I knew exactly who she was when I got involved with her . . ."

"Don't blame yourself for this."

"Why not!" Zach insisted. "I knew she was ruthless. I'd seen her burn other people again and again. And yet I let myself get sucked in. I was so flattered that she'd picked me. Like I was anointed or something. What an idiot."

"You're pretty far from an idiot."

"I'm ruined," he said.

He looked so sad, her own eyes went moist. It reminded her of how she felt when Piper fired her and then she had to confess to Marco about what she'd done. Addison had felt that her life was over and she had no one to blame but herself.

"You'll get past this," she reassured him.

"You really believe that?"

"Of course! You're a brilliant man. You'll figure it out."

He went silent for a long moment. Then Zach took a breath, straightened his shoulders. "Quinn McLeod was the worst lapse of judgment in my entire life. It was like I sold my soul just to be near her. But I promise you this—I will never compromise my integrity like that again."

"There you go," Addison said, acknowledging his vow with a smile. "You've already won. Let's go back inside."

By the time they returned to their table, a waiter was taking dinner orders, and a short while later, the emcee was back at the microphone, introducing last year's Innovator of the Year—Julia Chen—to give out this year's award.

Julia went to the microphone holding an oversize envelope in bright purple—the same shade as Quinn's hair—and Addison understood it was not a coincidence. The conniving narcissist had appropriated the organization's trademark color to position herself as the queen of the Innovations in Software 19th Annual Awards Ceremony.

Julia opened by explaining that winning the award had changed her life, and she thanked all the members and the organization itself. Then, as she wedged her finger under the flap of the envelope, she congratulated the nominees and wished them all luck.

"The winner of the Nineteenth Annual Innovator of the Year Award goes to . . ." She paused to open the envelope and pull out a card. Addison reached for Zach's cold hand, and it seemed the molecules in the air stopped moving as a roomful of people held their breath. Julia Chen put her mouth right up to the microphone and loudly announced "Zach Brody!"

Despite herself, Addison burst into tears, and before she knew it, she was swept into Zach's arms, getting the best kiss of her life.

Chapter 46

It was 4:00 a.m. by the time they got back to the Beekman. The weekend security guard was on duty at the door and acknowledged them with a discreet nod as they sauntered past into the deserted lobby.

Giddy and a little buzzed, Addison stopped in the middle of the vast and barren space, feeling like she and Zach had landed on the surface of the moon, where they could plant a flag to mark his victory. The perfect ending to an unforgettable evening. He stopped to look at her, as if trying to read her mood.

"Rooftop?" he asked, holding up the bottle of Bollinger champagne that had been in his swag bag. "I'm too wired to go to sleep."

She understood. It had been a magical night for him, and he didn't want it to end. It had been a magical night for her too. There had been something freeing about playing the part of his girlfriend. She wasn't her real self, yet she inhabited the role. She liked the way that felt. It was also intoxicating to be walking through the building when it was so deserted, no fear of running into Frankie . . . or anyone.

"Why not?" she said.

A little unsteady, Addison slipped out of her high heels and held on to his arm as they got into the elevator. It was a familiar gesture. Intimate. But they'd been through so much together that night, her guard had evaporated. His win. That kiss. Their shared delight at Quinn's rage when Zach was surrounded by well-wishers. Then there was the dancing—fast and exuberant, followed by the lingering closeness of a slow dance, their bodies damp and loose. She could still feel his warm hand on her naked back.

The rooftop was also deserted, and the fairy lights had been turned off. Addison liked it better this way. She could see the glinting flickers of Los Angeles in the distance, the stars overhead, a silvery crescent moon hovering cinematically on the horizon.

Zach looked around. "They put the chairs away."

"It's okay," Addison said, then hiked up her dress to sit on the edge of the pool, her feet dangling in the water. Zach struggled to do the same, finally managing to hike his pants legs up to his knees. He took off his tuxedo jacket.

"You want this?" he asked her.

"I'm fine," she said. The October night in Los Angeles was warm enough to remind her of summer in New York. If it had been a little more humid, she could have told herself she was in a friend's backyard on Long Island.

Zach popped open the champagne, then took a seat next to her, his legs in the water. He passed Addison the bottle, and she was just drunk enough to forget that she was sipping something carbonated, and the surprise made her cough it out onto the patio. He laughed, and as soon as she caught her breath, she did too.

"You okay?" he asked, patting her back.

"Just a little drinking problem," she joked, wiping her mouth. Addison tried again, taking a more prudent sip before giving the bottle back to Zach.

They sat like that, passing the champagne back and forth several more times before she finally put it down and moved in closer to him. He took the cue and put his arm around her.

She closed her eyes, taking in his scent—not heavily perfumed, like Dante, but soapy and fresh, despite all the dancing. There was a part of her that knew this should be the end of it. She had played her role, and now it was time to let him go so he could deal with his win and use it to get over everything that had happened with Quinn and his ex-partner.

He did not need the complication of an entanglement at this point, especially not with someone like her.

And yet. This all felt so good. So right. So . . . romantic. She looked at the reflection of the night sky in the pool and stirred the water with her foot to animate the stars. She glanced back at him, and his stare was intense, his lids heavy. She knew that look. He wanted her.

Just one more kiss, Addison thought. That's all. Just one perfect kiss under the stars and she would set him free. Then she'd stay right here on earth and watch him soar.

Addison tilted her head back, moved her mouth toward his, and then, for the second time that night, they kissed. This one went on and on, but it wasn't enough. Not nearly.

He pulled away and looked at her. "What happens now?" he asked.

He was leaving it up to her, and Addison knew what to do. Still, she ran through the choices. They could go to his apartment. Or hers. Or they could do the right thing and part this very instant. But she wasn't quite ready. The air was too velvety. The moon too vivid. Zach's nerdy passions and bright optimism too endearing.

"I don't know," she said. "I . . ."

"A swim?" he asked, his face lit with a smile.

Addison laughed, because it was perfect. "Yes!"

"Wait," he said, as if something had just occurred to him, "are we allowed?"

Clearly they weren't. There were at least three signs warning against swimming when the lifeguard wasn't on duty. "Do you care?" she asked.

"A little," he admitted. "But fuck it."

It was so uncharacteristic, Addison laughed. Then she slipped out of her dress even though she wasn't wearing a bra. No one could see them up here, anyway.

Then they both stood in their underpants, facing each other.

"Ready?" he said, holding out his hand.

She took it, and they jumped in together, the cold water shocking her warm flesh. They surfaced, then dove under, swimming the length of the pool as their bodies adjusted to the temperature. When they reached the end, Addison came up for air, her hair dripping, but Zach pushed off the edge and swam another length before coming back and surfacing.

"Show-off!" She laughed. "You're just trying to impress me."

He shook the water off his face and smiled. "Did it work?"

"Always," Addison said, and meant it.

He pushed her against the edge of the pool and kissed her again, their slick wet bodies fusing. They pressed closer together as his erection stirred and pleaded, and it was nearly too much. Her breath went shallow and quick, and she knew it would be just so easy for them to slip out of their underpants and come together, right here, right now, in this corner of the pool under the night sky.

"I don't know what to do," she admitted.

He looked dubious. "You seem like you know *just* what to do."

"I'm serious," she said, ignoring the pulsing urgency of her own body.

"The celibacy vow?"

Addison nodded. "I just think this would be a bad idea."

"You're afraid you're going to hurt me," he said.

She studied his boyish face. There was a tenderness about him that nearly broke her. "I am," she said, swallowing against a thick warning in her throat. Why did she suddenly feel like crying?

"But you're not Quinn," he said, "and I'm not as fragile as you think."

"Until I can figure out why I always fuck things up," she told him, "I need to keep my distance."

Even as she said it, Addison knew she was on the brink of figuring it all out. Again and again, she'd felt compelled to recreate the trauma of losing her parents. And the reason was so close to the surface, she could sense it about to come up for air.

"For how long?" he asked.

"A year?" She made it sound like a question because it suddenly seemed like an unreasonably long period of time.

"How about six months?" he countered, as if reading her mind.

"Are you negotiating with me?"

He nodded. "Would you like to hear my terms?"

Addison studied his eyes to see if he was joking, but he was dead serious. "Okay," she said.

He moved a lock of wet hair from her face. "No one else," he said. "For either of us. And in six months, we give this relationship a try and see if it can work."

He ran his finger along the sensitive part of her neck, and his touch was so gentle she shivered. Her head rolled to the side, her eyes closing, her body pleading for him to keep going. Then she looked back at his earnest, handsome face, and waiting even one more minute seemed impossible. But she pushed away from him and held out her little finger.

"Six months," she agreed, and they locked pinkies.

Still, they couldn't part. Not yet. So when they got out of the water, Addison put on his tuxedo jacket and Zach put on his trousers, and they sat on the edge of the pool, watching the sun rise.

Chapter 47
ARNIE

After finishing his early-morning workout, Arnie showered and headed for the spa. He didn't usually schedule a massage for a Monday morning, but Addison had insisted it would help him deal with his stress about the missing egg. Also, Frankie had apparently poached some extraordinary European masseuse from the best spa in Beverly Hills, and she was getting booked up fast.

He looked forward to a massage from someone so skilled. "Magic hands" was the phrase Addison had used. He was grateful to her for snatching one of the last available appointments for him, and to Frankie for being such an efficient and dedicated manager. She really wanted the best for the residents and approached the task as fiercely as a mother bear looking after her cubs. It was, he thought, admirable.

The day before—just prior to their doubles tennis game—he had spoken to Frankie again about the missing Fabergé egg. She had already heard from Nikolai about the elevator surveillance video and knew their assumption about Melody had been incorrect. Unfortunately, Frankie didn't know who had tampered with the computer files, nor the identity of the mysterious man in work boots.

"Still, I'm relieved it wasn't one of the residents," she had said to him, then asked what he wanted to do.

After some back-and-forth with her, Arnie decided to let Nikolai proceed with his investigation before involving the police. Apparently, the enigmatic security man had some methods that could be effective, if not entirely legal. Arnie chose not to focus on what that might mean. He needed that egg back, after all, and Nikolai seemed like the man for the job. They could, he understood, go to the police later.

"We're going to get it back," Frankie had said to him with such certainty he believed her. And when they crushed their doubles opponents—thanks to smart teamwork and Frankie's killer serve— he felt even more confident. He was one step closer to reconciling with Paulette and wondered if she might even agree to remarry him. The thought made him giddy.

Arnie arrived at the spa and approached the full-cheeked girl at the reception desk. "Arnold Glass for Katrine," he said pleasantly.

The receptionist smiled and asked him to have a seat, explaining that Katrine would be available in about ten minutes.

"Arnie?" came a voice behind him, and he turned to see Leyla in one of the waiting room chairs. She looked soft in a pink sleeveless blouse and a demure strand of pearls. Then he noticed something that belied the girlish sweetness of her outfit—a black corset showing discreetly through the fabric. This woman was getting more interesting by the minute.

"What a happy surprise!" he said. "Are you waiting for a massage?"

"I'm waiting for Dr. English," Leyla explained. "She's in with Katrine now."

Arnie took a seat next to her and noted she was carrying a different book. "More light reading?" he joked, pointing to the thick tome.

She showed him the book—a deep dive into the complicated history of pandemics—and let him riffle through it. He ran his finger down the table of contents and could see that it was grim stuff, bordering on macabre.

"You're a serious reader, my dear," he said, handing it back to her. "Does Geoffrey share your interests?"

"Unfortunately, no. He is interested only in modern art."

"That's not so bad," Arnie said.

"He's very knowledgeable, but his passion is narrow. All he wants to do is go to museums and galleries. I like that, too, but . . ." She shrugged.

"But you'd like to do other things as well," he offered.

"Of course. Yet he refuses."

He could tell she was exasperated and wondered about the nature of their relationship. Didn't she realize she could have almost any man she wanted?

"I'm sorry to hear that," he said.

"I told him, 'We don't have to go skydiving, but perhaps another type of museum. Like that medieval one.' You know the place I mean, Arnie?"

"The one on Hollywood Boulevard?" he asked, thinking he had to be wrong.

She nodded. "Geoffrey said it is for tourists."

"You're talking about the Medieval Torture Museum?" he said, for clarification, because he didn't know many women who would be interested in such a place.

"Doesn't that sound intriguing?"

"It does, actually," he said, because human cruelty fascinated him. As someone whose guiding force in life had been helping people, he was mystified by this historically pervasive behavior. And as a physician, he was horrified but impressed by the medical creativity of these primitive torturers. "I've thought about going but could never interest anyone in coming with me."

"I'll go with you," she said.

"That would be marvelous," he gushed. "Do you think Geoffrey will mind?"

"It doesn't matter. I'm my boss, not him."

Arnie beamed with pleasure. "How's tomorrow?"

She gave him a subtle smile. "You're very kind," she said, evoking Ingrid Bergman again, and Arnie's heart thudded with pleasure.

"So it's a date?" he asked.

"It's a date."

Chapter 48
ADDISON

Tameka poured Addison a cup of coffee. They were alone in the break room of the salon, settling in for the debriefing on Addison's night with Zach.

"No holding back," Tameka said as she sat down. She pushed the cup of coffee across the table, and Addison yawned.

"Come on," Tameka begged. "Dish."

Addison took a sip, welcoming the caffeine into her bloodstream. She had slept deep into the afternoon and was still trying to jettison the hangover of fuzzy slumber and fizzy champagne . . . still reliving that kiss in the pool . . . still trying to reconcile her feelings.

She looked at Tameka, who clearly sensed there was a lot to tell. But it was hard to jump right into the thick of it, so she led with the easy stuff, describing the venue and the people, especially Quinn.

"I think I know the dress!" Tameka said, excited. "Vera Wang. Mindy Kaling wore it to the Oscars. It's hot!" She took out her phone and found the image, passing it to Addison.

"That's the one. I bet Quinn saw it on the red carpet and placed a direct call to Vera herself."

"I wouldn't have pictured something like that at a techie event," Tameka said.

Addison recalled the way Quinn stood out in a room of tuxedos, black gowns, and the kind of vintage dresses that bordered on cosplay. "Trust me, Quinn was the only woman dressed for the Oscars."

Tameka leaned forward. "What was she like?"

Addison exhaled, trying to find the right words. "Monstrous. Narcissistic. Toxic."

"Rad," Tameka said, "let's invite her for dinner."

"Only if you have raw meat. Otherwise she'll eat us alive." Addison went on to explain how Quinn had tried to orchestrate Zach's loss, and her friend's expression went from shocked to disgusted.

"What did he ever see in her?"

"For one thing," Addison said, "she's beautiful, in a fierce sort of way. Real sexual charisma, you know? The kind of woman who makes even a smart man stupid."

"But once he got to know her . . ."

"It was like she had him hypnotized."

"His dick," Tameka corrected. "She had his *dick* hypnotized."

Addison laughed. "I don't know. I think it was more than that. She's a hell of a manipulator."

"You think he's still in love with her?"

Addison had been wondering that herself. "Not sure," she said. "Last night should have been the last straw, but some demons are hard to exorcise."

"And the two of you?" Tameka asked, raising an eyebrow.

Yeah, that, Addison thought, and tried to quiet the current of anxiety that had started today, when she felt an almost irresistible impulse to knock on his door and tell him she needed him right now, to hell with their agreement to wait six months. He would have taken her in his arms and swept her inside. And then what? Addison tried and tried to imagine a happy ending, but she simply couldn't get there. Every scenario ended with her screwing up and leaving him with gaping wounds.

"I have to show you something," Addison said. She reached into her purse and pulled out the gift that had been left at the door of her apartment. It was the latest top-of-the-line iPhone. With a screen still intact. She passed it to Tameka, who turned it over, examining it.

"Sick! I didn't even know this was out yet. Where did you get it?"

"It's a thank-you from Zach."

Tameka shook her head in wonder. "Does he have a friend for me?"

"I thought you didn't go for nerdy guys . . . or rich ones."

"Are you kidding? I'd kill for a dude like this. He was paying attention. He knew what you needed."

"Unlike Dante, you mean."

"Zach's the one who gets you," Tameka said.

Yes, damn him. Addison nodded and put the phone back in her purse.

"Now tell me the good stuff," Tameka said. "Did you use that condom I slipped into your clutch?"

"I was tempted," she said, "after we kissed, and then kissed again." Addison felt like her body was still reliving that feeling in the pool, their slick wet desire turning cold skin into hot flesh. "Really, *really* tempted," she added.

"Was it that good?"

"Better," Addison said, her heart heavy with concern.

"So why do you look miserable?" Tameka asked. "Is it that stupid vow of celibacy?"

"That stupid vow is the only thing standing between me and disaster." Addison stared down into her coffee. "No matter how hard I try, I can't imagine this ending well."

"Why not?"

"Because I'm like a toxic cloud."

"That's not true, Addison."

"I keep thinking about what I did to Marco, and that look on his face. The shock of disappointment. He was just . . . crushed. Devastated. And I did that."

Tameka's mouth went tight as she nodded. "Not going to lie. Nothing hurts worse than betrayal."

"How are you even friends with me?" Addison asked, tears spilling.

"Stop it. You're nothing like Vin," she said, referring to her ex.

"But I am."

Tameka shook her head. "He was a cheat and a liar. You're just a cheat."

Addison gave a bitter laugh. "I guess that makes me a saint."

"I'm not saying you didn't fuck up, because you did. I'm saying you don't have a dark nature. You're not a schemer, like my ex. Or like Quinn. Going forward, you can do better. I know you can."

Addison wasn't so sure.

Chapter 49

"I have some good news, cookie," Regina English said when she opened the door. "Come in."

Addison had expected as much when she'd been summoned to the apartment through another ruse involving the delivery of a package. And it had brightened her mood. She was still in turmoil over her feelings for Zach. He was a bright and delicate canary, winging toward the future. She was a dark and dangerous coal mine.

Dr. English took the envelope from Addison and laid it on her lap, then led her into the living room.

"Can I get you something?" she asked.

"I'm fine," Addison said, taking a seat. She was eager to get the good news, as she had to get back to work. "Are we alone?"

"We are indeed. Geoffrey is working, and Leyla . . ." She paused to smile. "Leyla is on a date."

"Right now?" Addison asked, delighted. "With Arnie?"

"It seems our most recent effort paid off."

Yes! Addison thought. This could be exactly what Arnie needed. She imagined him falling so head over heels for Leyla he'd forget all about Paulette. She touched the heart charm on her neck, connecting with her mother, promising she would see this through.

"That's great news," she said.

"I agree. Geoffrey seems so close to proposing. He needs a dose of reality before he gets in over his head."

"You're so sure she'd turn him down?"

"To be frank, I don't think she even likes him very much. She tolerates him."

From what Addison had heard through Zach's bedroom wall that night, those two shared something more than tolerance. But even if the sex was mind blowing, there had to be something more to sustain a relationship. Maybe Arnie would be the right man at the right time.

"Do you know where they went on their date?" she asked.

Addison hoped Arnie had swept Leyla off her feet, taking her someplace romantic for their daytime excursion. She pictured a gourmet picnic on the top of a hill overlooking some magnificent vista. Or a boat ride on a still lake, surrounded by lush trees and a dreamy soundtrack.

"The Museum of Medieval Torture," Dr. English said.

Addison blinked at her. It sounded like a joke, but the doctor didn't look like she was kidding. "Seriously?" she asked.

"Leyla was very interested in it, and Geoffrey would never take her. I think he was afraid to be seen there."

Afraid he might get too aroused is more like it, Addison thought, but she kept it to herself. "I can imagine," she muttered.

"I know it doesn't sound romantic," Dr. English said, "but Leyla was very impressed that he shared her interest."

Addison could barely wait to check in with her uncle to see how it went. "Do you know what time she'll be back?"

"I told her to take the whole day off. I didn't want her to feel there was any rush."

Addison heard the door open and turned to see Geoffrey walk in, wearing a garish windowpane plaid suit with a silk pocket hankie, like he was auditioning for the cover of British *GQ*. His checkerboard glasses gave the whole thing a clownish effect.

"Is everything all right?" he said when he saw Addison.

"I was just delivering a package," she told him.

He looked around, concerned. "Where's Leyla?"

"I gave her the day off," his mother said. "She had plans with a friend."

Geoffrey arched his back, straightened his glasses. "Which friend?" he demanded.

"How should I know?"

"Mother," he chided, "I want the truth."

She sighed and turned her wheelchair away from him. "Oh, Geoffrey," she said, "don't be so tiresome."

At that, Addison excused herself and left.

Chapter 50
ARNIE

Arnie was in shock. He hadn't expected to wind up in his bedroom with Leyla after their date at the Medieval Torture Museum, and he certainly hadn't expected the kind of wild jungle animal she turned into once the door was closed. She was a tigress—feral and insatiable. Every time he thought he caught up, giving her the pleasure she so desperately demanded, she wanted more. By the time they were done, he felt like he'd finished—and won—a triathlon. Now, alone in his bathtub, he was still chafed, raw, breathless. His jaw ached, and the skin on his buttocks stung from her repeated slaps.

He was enraptured.

Dear god, he thought, what a woman. He'd been with so many, but this one. There was simply no way to keep up with her. And the pleasure! The nearly excruciating ecstasy! He'd never reached that level before. Not even with Paulette.

"When can I see you again?" he'd asked when she was getting dressed.

"Oh, Arnie. You are a very sweet man, but I don't think we should do this again."

He sat up. "What do you mean? Didn't you enjoy that?"

She approached the bed and put a tender hand on his cheek. "Of course I did. You were a very good little boy."

What a tease she was. "Leyla," he said, grabbing her wrist, "don't go." He thought it might entice her to get angry and excited again, but she was done. She pried his fingers off.

"This is finished, dear man."

He searched her face, hoping she didn't mean it. "But when can I see you again?" he begged.

"I am with Geoffrey. You know that."

He felt so changed from this experience, like everything was different now. Surely she felt the same.

"But do you love him?" he asked, certain she didn't. They had so little in common, after all. But he and Leyla seemed meant for each other. When they wandered through the museum, marveling at the horrors and the oddities, they were in complete sync, stopping to understand the mechanisms and the kinds of injuries they would induce. They even shared a few dark jokes. But that wasn't all. Just like him, she loved to read, to keep up on the latest medical advances, to constantly broaden her knowledge.

She cocked her head at his question about Geoffrey. "I suppose I love him a little," she said thoughtfully.

"Is that enough for you?"

"He and I are well suited in many ways."

"What about you and me?" he said.

Leyla smiled. "You are already in love with someone else," she said. "Did you forget?"

He had, god help him. Because as much as he loved Paulette, this woman had stirred something inside him he didn't even know existed.

"I'll leave her for you!" he blurted, and meant it, though he knew it was crazy, that he was completely and utterly bewitched.

"I am not your soulmate, Arnie Glass."

"How do you know that? Can't you give us a chance?"

"Thank you for a lovely day. It will be a sweet memory for me."

A sweet memory? After all that panting and bucking and screaming? After climbing the heights of pleasure and reaching paradise?

"How about dinner this weekend?" he asked. "I'll take you any-where you like."

"You need a nice warm bath, dear boy. Then put some ointment on your bottom. By tomorrow you'll be thinking about Paulette again."

"I'll be thinking about *you!*" he insisted, but it was too late. She had gone.

This can't be the end of it, he thought, even as he limped to the bathroom to take the warm soak she had prescribed. Later, as he relaxed in the tub, his body as loose as it had ever been, Arnie heard the unique trill of a video call from Paulette. But instead of grabbing for his phone, he leaned back in the water, closed his eyes, and let it ring.

Chapter 51
ADDISON

After work, Addison lingered in the lobby for the Chinese takeout her uncle had ordered, then brought it upstairs to his apartment. She'd been delighted when he suggested they have dinner together, as it would be the perfect chance to hear all about his date with Leyla.

She rang the buzzer and waited, then waited some more. "Uncle Arnie?" she called, her ear to the door. "You in there?"

She heard some noise and then "Just a minute!"

When the door finally opened, he wore an enormous grin, his face as flushed and happy as she'd ever seen it.

"Sorry, sweetheart," he said, as he leaned in for a peck. "I got a little injury that slowed me down a bit."

"You okay?" she asked, though he certainly seemed fine. "How did it happen?"

Arnie seemed to redden at the question. "Oh, I just . . . I fell in the shower. It was nothing. I'll be as good as new by tomorrow."

"Are you going to see a doctor?" she said as she followed him into the apartment. It was pretty clear he was in pain.

"I *am* a doctor, and I promise you, it's just a little friction burn."

"Why don't you sit and rest," she suggested, "and I'll get us set up."

He didn't argue, easing himself gently into a chair at the table.

"When did this happen?" she asked, trying to imagine him limping around the museum for hours.

"Just a little while ago."

She took that as good news. It meant he'd been feeling well during his date. "How was your day going until then?" she asked coyly as she retrieved plates from the cabinet.

"To be honest," he said, "it was one of the best days of my life."

Addison nearly dropped the dishes. "Seriously?" This was so much more than she could have hoped for.

"I went out with a woman today. You've met her—Leyla Balik. She's Regina English's nurse."

It took all Addison's self-control to keep an even expression instead of breaking out into a touchdown dance. "Uh, yes. I know who Leyla is," she said. "What a lovely woman."

"The face of an angel," he agreed. "I never thought I could fall so hard and so fast. Not at my age."

Barely breathing, Addison got the table set up, then unpacked the food. "I want to hear everything," she said, passing him the cold sesame noodles. When she looked at his face, that blush was back, like he was a kid with a crush.

"I took her to a museum," he said.

"An art museum?" she asked, playing dumb.

"I know this is going to sound peculiar, but she wanted to go to the Medieval Torture Museum, in Hollywood."

"It is a little odd, I guess."

"We're both medical people interested in history, so it was kind of fascinating." He drew some long noodles up from the container and dropped them on his plate.

"Sounds like you really hit it off."

"The connection was electric." He stopped to blink, as if the memory was nearly overwhelming. "I never met a woman quite like her."

"Not even Paulette?"

"I'll always love Paulette. Always. But Leyla . . . she . . . she changed me."

Addison puffed with pride. This was the most successful match she'd ever made, and she almost wished Piper was there to witness it.

"I'm so excited for you, Uncle Arnie!" Addison said, only too happy to steer the conversation away from Paulette. "When are you going to see her again?"

He chewed and swallowed. "That's the problem," he said. "She's dating someone."

"Maybe she'll break up with him for you. I mean, if there was such chemistry between you . . ."

"What's the expression you kids use when someone comes into your life and shakes everything up?"

She thought hard, trying to figure out what he was going for. "She rocked your world?"

"That's it!" he said. "She rocked my world. And then she left, like it meant nothing. She said she'd never see me again."

Addison sunk. "Oh, no!" she said.

"The woman broke my heart, kiddo."

"So . . . the other guy . . . Is she madly in love with him?"

"No! That's the crazy part. I didn't get the impression she even liked him that much. I can't understand what the attraction is."

"Money?" Addison ventured, hoping it wasn't the kinky sex that kept her tethered to Geoffrey.

Arnie gestured around the well-appointed condo. "I don't know the other guy's situation, but I think she understands I could probably buy her whatever she wants."

"Maybe she's afraid to hurt his feelings. Sometimes people get caught up in relationships out of pity or something."

He spooned some chicken and broccoli onto his plate as he considered it. "I don't think she's the type to tiptoe around someone's feelings."

"You want my advice?" Addison asked.

"Sure."

"I think you need to keep pursuing her. Convince her you're the better man." Even as she said it, though, Addison had a sinking feeling about Leyla's connection to Geoffrey. It was entirely possible she needed a man she could control with absolute power. And if that was the case, Arnie was not her match.

But he nodded for several long beats as he considered Addison's suggestion. Then he reached across the table and patted her hand. "My dear," he said, "I think that's a splendid idea."

Chapter 52

Addison and Arnie were in the middle of their meal when she got a text from Dante, who had just returned from New York and wanted to know if she was free for dinner.

"Everything okay?" Arnie asked when he saw her looking down at her phone.

"Dante is back, and apparently he's hungry," she said.

"Tell him to come over! We have plenty of food."

"Oh, Uncle Arnie," she said. "I don't know. Things are a little complicated with him right now."

"Sweetheart," he said, "you could do a lot worse than Dante D'Amico. He's handsome, he's successful, he's hardworking, and apparently he's crazy about you."

"He's a player," she insisted. "Besides, how do you know he's crazy about me?"

"He told me."

Addison put down her fork. "Dante talked to you about me?"

"He came to me for advice before he left for New York," Arnie said with a shrug. "I didn't know if I should say anything. You're not mad, are you?"

"Of course not," she said, her mind reeling. It was hard to reconcile her image of cocky, confident Dante with this lovesick man who approached her uncle for counsel. She thought again about the feeling she got in his arms, that kiss on her forehead, and everything that had followed—the texts . . . the flowers . . . the bracelet. He was in even deeper than she had thought. This wasn't supposed to happen, and it rattled her nerves.

But also—if she was honest with herself—it puffed her ego with so much helium she could barely hold on to it. This man lived in a candy store of beautiful women, yet he had chosen her. Was it simply because she made herself unavailable? Or was there something special about her, something that drew him in?

"What did he say to you?" she asked.

"He wanted to know if I could see you two together, if I thought it could work."

"And what did you tell him?"

"I said of course, but he needed to be patient." Arnie stabbed a piece of broccoli and put it in his mouth.

"I don't think he's wired for patience," she said, pushing the food around on her plate, feeling almost dizzy from this information.

"Do you know any man who is?"

Addison thought about Zach's vow to wait six months. "Maybe," she said.

Arnie took that in as he wiped his mouth. "Fair enough. But Dante lives in an aggressive world. He's a fighter, you know? He couldn't make it as an agent if he wasn't."

"I don't want to feel pressured."

"And you shouldn't!" Arnie reassured her. "Especially if you don't think he's right for you."

Addison went quiet as she considered that. She tried to take a step back and wondered who'd she choose for herself if she was a match-maker. Then she realized it didn't matter. Regardless of whatever boxes Dante might tick on a dating profile—or his strong feelings for her—Zach was the one she'd fallen for.

"I don't," she told her uncle. "I don't think he's right for me."

"That's that, then," he said, dusting his hands to illustrate that he wouldn't press the issue any further.

Addison held up her phone. "But what about tonight?"

Arnie waved away her concern. "Tell him you're with me. He's a big boy. He'll get his own dinner."

Addison felt a pang of sympathy. Dante had just returned from a long flight and was hungry and alone and eager for company. How would it hurt to invite him up for a bite? She opened the text message and started tapping out a response.

"I'm inviting him up," she said.

"Are you sure you're okay with that?"

"Not even a little," Addison said as she hit send.

Ten minutes later, Dante arrived, freshly showered and carrying a bottle of white wine. He gave Arnie that half hug that men did, then embraced Addison with his whole being.

"I missed you," he whispered into her hair. She nudged him away and took a seat at the table.

The threesome fell into an easy conversation over dinner. Dante told them his New York trip had been jammed with meetings and he was glad he'd gone. One of his clients had just landed a starring role in an HBO drama he was certain would be huge.

As the conversation went on and moved through several different topics—including the streaming shows they'd been watching—Dante kept looking at her, offering that killer dimple, but Addison wouldn't connect. She was determined to keep her promise to Zach.

The threesome moved to the living room, chatting amiably until it was so late Arnie started to yawn.

"I'm sorry, Uncle Arnie!" she said. "I wasn't paying attention to the time."

She and Dante left the apartment, and he waylaid her in the hallway. "Can we talk?" he asked.

She shrugged and leaned against the wall. "Sure."

The neighbor's door opened, and old Sally Conrad stuck her head out. Addison waved to her, and the woman went back inside.

"Someplace more private," Dante pleaded.

"Not my apartment," she said.

"Where, then?"

Addison didn't want to risk the chance of being seen alone with Dante—especially by Zach, who might get the wrong idea—so she suggested the benches behind the tennis courts.

"Why don't we just talk in my car," Dante suggested. "They're predicting rain."

Addison hadn't heard anything about rain, but she agreed. It seemed like a perfect spot for privacy, since the parking valets were off duty.

"Look," he said after they got into his car. "I know I've been coming on really strong. To be honest, I don't know any other way." He turned on the radio as if trying to set the mood, blasting a song by Halsey. It seemed like a move to Addison, a way to prove he was evolved or something.

"It's not fair to me," she told him.

"Occupational hazard," he said instead of apologizing. "It's what I do. I push people until they say yes."

"But why *me*?" Addison said, even though she knew it sounded like she was fishing for compliments. The question was simply too important to go unasked.

"I don't know," he said. "And that's the truth. I just feel connected to you. Like we *need* to be together. Don't you feel the same way?"

"No."

He chuckled, as if amused by her bluntness, and took her hand again. "I don't believe it."

"I think this," she said, pointing between them, "might just be chemistry."

"But that's everything!" he insisted.

"It isn't!" she protested, thinking about the look on Zach's face when his mind took him away and how badly she wanted to go there with him.

Dante went quiet for a long moment, as if he were wrestling with something. Finally he said, "Can I be honest? Like, *really* honest?"

"Please."

He nodded, chewing on his lip, and finally took a long breath. "I've been with a lot of women, Addison. I mean a *lot*."

"Shocking," she muttered, despite the gravity in his voice.

"But I don't think about them," he said. "That's the thing. We have a good time and then . . . that's it. But you. Jesus, I think about you all the time. It's driving me crazy."

Addison let out a sigh, because this just felt like more pressure. It got inside her head, made her question her own feelings. Focus, she told herself. Focus.

"Come on," he said, "don't you think about me too?"

She shook her head, getting clarity. "There's someone else," she blurted, because she needed to be definitive.

"Who?"

"Zach Brody."

"Brody!" he repeated. "I knew it! I knew you had a thing for that weirdo."

"Stop it, Dante," she said. "You don't even know him."

"But I do," he insisted. "I once tried to do a business deal with him, but he's always off in the clouds like a space cadet. And he's got a *cat*."

"Well, let's call in the National Guard."

"Seriously, Addison, he's a nice guy. I get it. But he's just a boy. That's not what you need."

"I like him," she whispered.

"You'll break him right in half. He's no match for you."

She nodded. He wasn't wrong. Zach was so damaged. Addison wondered if it was really fair to make him wait for someone like her. Would it be better to set him free and let him find someone better suited?

"I know," she admitted.

"With me, you'll never have to worry about that. I'm unbreakable."

"Bulletproof," she said, remembering their last conversation. "Like Superman."

"Like Superman," he repeated, putting his thumb under her chin to tilt her head toward his. For a quick moment, she was ready to succumb, but before he could move in for a kiss, Addison pushed him away. She wasn't going to do this to Zach. She'd made a promise, and she was damn well going to keep it.

Dante turned the music way up, blasting a Halsey song Addison knew well, as she'd been obsessed with it for a while. It was called "Control," and it had been her go-to whenever her life was spiraling and she'd felt the need to remind herself of the singer's challenging question: "Who is in control?"

Hearing it again, Addison felt haunted by her obsession with the song. She closed her eyes, wondering why she had been so drawn to that refrain, pulling it deep inside her. She knew it was directly tied to her need to recreate the trauma of her past, but what was the connection? With a gasp, she finally understood. It was all about control, or lack of it. Addison hadn't been able to control what had happened to her, so she'd been playing out the pain of her upended life again and again, almost as a redo, a chance to control the outcome. It wasn't rational, but it had been driving her, and it was time to stop.

Suddenly, Dante was on her, mouth to mouth. She shoved him away.

"What the fuck?" she said, as she clicked off the radio.

"You closed your eyes," he said. "I thought—"

"You thought wrong," she said, and opened the door to leave. That's when she saw another car tearing out of the parking lot. A yellow-and-black McLaren.

Chapter 53
CARLY

Carly sat back in her chair, flooded with relief and ready to celebrate. She had just finished her massive copywriting project and sent it off to the client, aware that she had never worked harder or better or faster. It was a revelation that she could accomplish so much when she was free of Owen's relentless assault on her ego.

But he still wasn't letting her go. Since she had blocked his phone number, Owen had shifted over to emailing, and there were three new messages from him today. Delete. Delete. Delete.

Feeling buoyant, Carly picked up her phone and texted Maya: I'm done with my project!

She put the phone down on her desk and stared at it, willing it to buzz with a response, hoping Maya would want to celebrate in person. When the phone rang instead, Carly jolted like a skittish cat. Was it Maya?

It was! A soothing purr moved through her.

"Congratulations!" Maya said. "You must feel great."

"I'm so proud of myself."

"Of course you are! I'm proud of you too. We should celebrate. I have a little good news myself."

"You want to tell me over dinner?" Carly asked. "I'm feeling flush, and I'd love to take you out."

"Tonight?" Maya said uncertainly, and Carly deflated. She'd been so pumped up, she'd lost sight of solid earth. What foolishness to think Maya would say yes to a date. Carly warned herself that she was going to have to learn to self-regulate. There was a middle ground between the dark depths of self-hatred and the blinding folly of soaring too close to the sun.

"Um, yeah," she said. "I was, uh . . . if you're free—"

"You know what?" Maya said. "Fuck it, yes. I was thinking of popping in on my old book club tonight, but I'd much rather see you. Should I make a res? I know a place in Malibu that will give us a private table on the deck, away from any would-be paparazzi."

It sounded like such a dream that Carly's heart thudded with joy. She quickly agreed and arranged to meet Maya in the lobby at seven o'clock. Then she called Addison, who found her an open slot at the salon so she could get her hair done before dinner.

Three hours later, Carly stood in the lobby, hoping she didn't look ridiculous in her low-cut green silk blouse and black skinny jeans. She had tried so hard to look like she wasn't trying too hard and couldn't tell if she'd pulled it off.

Carly breathed deeply, calming herself, as she waited for the elevator doors to open. Then she heard the soft ding and looked over to see Maya emerge, willowy and breathtaking in a flowy ivory dress and matching hat. She strode straight toward Carly, a smile wide across her face.

"You look beautiful," Maya said. She kissed Carly on one cheek and then the other.

"So do you," Carly sputtered, and felt like this could be the most romantic night of her life.

As they walked toward the exit, though, Carly had the feeling they were being watched. She glanced behind her, and there on the lobby sofa was the man in the Harry Potter glasses—the one she'd been on the elevator with. At first, she told herself not to be paranoid. He had just as much right to be in the building as she did. But of course, she had concrete evidence Owen had hired a spy, so maybe this ordinary-looking guy was a private eye. Fine, Carly mused. Let him send a picture of me leaving the building with the famous and fabulous Maya Mayfield.

Carly hooked arms with Maya and waltzed away, thinking, Owen, eat your heart out.

Chapter 54

It was sunset, and Carly looked out over the Pacific Ocean in awe. The sky was striped in shades of vivid blue and golden orange, soft indigo and a brilliant, beckoning yellow. The breath caught in her throat. How very far she had come! Carly pictured the sunset in Nashua at this time of year, the spindly trees looking freshly barren, with their black branches spreading eerily against the icy-blue horizon. Here, the sunset was warm and plump, ripe with promise.

"Beautiful," she whispered, almost afraid to break the spell of this magical sight.

After a moment, she looked back across the table at Maya, who was also admiring the view. The women smiled at each other.

"You look happy," Maya said.

"I am," Carly confessed. "Very."

The waitress came to their secluded section of the deck to take their orders, and when she left, Maya asked Carly to tell her about the project.

"You first," Carly insisted, eager to hear whatever Maya had to say. "You told me you have news."

Maya shook her head. "I want to hear all about your accomplishment."

"You sure?" Carly asked with a laugh. "It's pretty boring."

"I bet you can make it sound interesting," Maya said, and so she did. As they sipped wine, Carly explained that after reading the manufacturer's notes about the hospital gurney and following it up with a phone call to ask questions, she was fully sold on the quality of the product. That made it easy for her to write about it, tapping into the difference it would make for patients and hospitals. She told Maya about the scope of the project, which required writing the product brochure that would accompany the delivery of each bed, as well as website content, ads for three different publications, brochures that would be handed out at trade shows, two different press releases, and a three-page article for a hospital-products journal.

"The best part is that it looks like it'll lead to a lot more work."

Maya beamed at her. "See? When you're passionate, you make it fascinating."

Carly shook her off, embarrassed by the praise. "Enough," she said. "Tell me your news. I want to hear."

Maya leaned forward. "Well," she said, bringing her hands together, "it looks like I'll be hosting a podcast."

"A podcast!" Carly echoed, almost embarrassed she hadn't thought of it. "What a great idea."

Maya explained how it had come to her—she'd been researching self-help books on breakups to see what was out there when she realized that one of the leading authors in the field had a podcast. She listened to a few episodes and thought it was dreadful.

"Now *that* was boring," Maya explained. "He interviewed all these dull experts who had nothing new to say. And I thought, He's doing this all wrong. He should be taking calls and giving advice. Then I realized it was a need I could fill. The more I thought about it, the more right it felt. So I reached out to an advertiser—one of those online-therapy companies—and spoke to their marketing person. She was really enthusiastic about it."

Carly shook her head in wonder at the grit it took to pick up the phone and call a potential sponsor. "This is going to be huge," she said. "I can feel it."

They talked for a long while about how the podcast could be for-matted, and when there was a lull in the conversation, Carly found the gumption to broach a subject that had been troubling her.

"I was meaning to ask you," she said, "who was that blond woman you greeted at the Splash Bar the other night? She looked so familiar to me."

It was a lie. The woman hadn't looked at all familiar. But Carly was desperate to know if Maya was involved with her and couldn't think of any other way to approach the topic.

Maya explained that the woman had been a producer on *Single File* but that she'd had a small, recurring role on a network sitcom for a few years before that. "So maybe that's how you know her," she suggested.

"Maybe," Carly said, still unsure about Maya's relationship with the woman.

"She's a trip, though. Separated from her husband last month and is already thinking about moving in with her boyfriend."

Carly exhaled, relieved, and looked up to see the waitress approach-ing with their food.

"Anyway," Maya said, "I wanted to talk to you about the whole idea of writing a self-help book for people going through breakups. I know I'll need a hook, and I'm still thinking about that, but once I get the pod up and running, it's something I want to get to work on."

Carly grinned. "You're unstoppable!"

"I hope so! I mean, this is a long game, and the book will only work if the podcast is a success. But there's one moving part I need to discuss with you."

"I'm all ears," Carly said, happy for an excuse to put down her chopsticks. They were eating sushi, and Maya had made it look so easy.

"Like I said, it's a tentative project, but here's the thing: I have no writing skills. I think you know that. But fortunately, I now have a dear friend who's a fucking rock star with words. So Carly, I was wondering if you might be willing to coauthor the book with me. I know it's a lot to ask, but I'd split the profits fifty-fifty, if that sounds good to you."

Carly stared at her, unable to speak. "I, uh . . ."

"You'd be doing the bulk of the work. I should make that absolutely clear. We'll talk about what I want to cover, but I'll rely on you to organize the thing and get it written. If it's too much and you'd rather not, I understand."

"Are you kidding?" Carly said. "It's like a dream come true."

"You sure?"

"I've never been more sure of anything."

They began brainstorming ideas about the podcast and the book, their voices rising with excitement. Concerned about being overheard by the diners on the other side of the partition, Carly glanced over and saw something that shocked her—a camera held above it, pointed down at them.

"What the hell!" she said and bolted toward it, grabbing the camera from whoever was holding it. It was completely out of character for her, but she wasn't about to let someone invade her famous friend's privacy.

"Hey, that's mine!" came a man's voice.

Carly peered through the slats to see the man in the round glasses—Owen's private eye. "You!" she said. "I should call the police. This is stalking."

"I have every right to be here," he insisted.

"You can tell Owen I'm not getting back together with him, ever, no matter how many pictures you take."

"Who is Owen?" he asked.

"The man who hired you!"

"I work for TMZ," the guy said, and in a terrible rush, it all became clear. He hadn't been some random Maya Mayfield fan, nor Owen's hired detective. He was a gossip reporter, and he'd been spying on Maya for days.

She looked over at her friend, whose face was in her hands, and Carly felt an overwhelming desire to protect her from this jackal.

"Leave us the hell alone," she said to him.

"Give me back my camera or *I'll* call the police," he insisted.

Maya sighed, resigned. "Give it back to him, Carly."

Carly hesitated but realized she had no choice. She handed the man his camera, and moments later he was thrown out of the restaurant. Maya received profuse apologies from the management, which comped their meal. Of course, the women were in no mood to continue their ebullient conversation, so they left.

Chapter 55

In the car on their way back to the Beekman, Maya looked dispirited. "The timing couldn't be worse," she said. "TMZ will probably run the story tomorrow or the next day, before I even get a chance to make the public announcement about my breakup and new direction. I'll be on defense, and it'll ruin everything."

"No, it won't," Carly said. "We can get ahead of it—go public before they have a chance to paint a terrible picture." Even as she said it, Carly understood what the terrible picture would look like—Maya Mayfield out with another woman, cheating on Brianna with a nobody.

"Is there time? I don't even have my new website designed."

"That doesn't matter. I've already written the press release. You can break the news across social media tonight."

Maya thought for a long moment, holding on to the steering wheel. "It's going to be a hell of a lot of work."

"I'll help you."

Maya gave her hand a grateful squeeze, and it was settled. From there, an eddy of activity swirled as they went back to Maya's apartment and got busy. They laid out a plan, then shot a video of Maya explaining that Brianna had left her and that it had been difficult for a while but that she was doing okay now, was moving on, and would always be grateful to Brianna for what they'd had together. Now, her attention would be focused on helping people like her who'd gone through a difficult breakup and struggled to heal. It was spoken from the heart, and when Maya teared up, Carly did too. She could also feel the strength and determination to continue having a fulfilling life. It was all perfectly imperfect.

And yet. Recording the video had taken so much out of Maya that she looked drained.

"Are you okay?" Carly asked.

Maya shook her head, took a juddering breath. "That was hard."

Carly thought she looked like she was about to break and felt the pain shoot right through her. "Can I make you some tea?" she asked.

"I'll be fine," Maya said. "I just need a minute."

She sat on the couch, and Carly brought her a box of tissues. She took one, blew her nose, whimpered.

"It's okay to cry," Carly said.

Maya nodded and let it flow. "I really loved her," she choked out, and reached over to grab Carly's hand for strength.

"I'm here for you," Carly said, her voice cracking in sorrow and compassion. She wished she could absorb Maya's pain and take it away.

Maya inhaled deeply, exhaled slowly, and announced that she was fine.

"You sure?"

Maya gave her a quick hug. "More or less," she said. "Let's get back to work."

And that was it. There was still a lot left to do, but together they moved through it quickly and efficiently. They created appropriate announcements for all Maya's social media accounts and then went into launch mode, sending them all out almost simultaneously. And finally, Maya emailed the press release to all her favorite reporters.

"Done!" she announced. She shut off her computer and told Carly she wouldn't look at it again until the morning.

"What now?" she said to Carly. "Wine or champagne?"

Carly hesitated, ready to choose wine, as if she weren't important enough for a real celebration, but stopped herself. "Champagne!" she announced. "This is a momentous night."

Maya agreed and poured them two glasses. They clinked and toasted to success.

"Should we move to the sofa?" Maya asked, and Carly swallowed hard. If a man had said that, Carly would assume he was putting the moves on her. But with Maya, she couldn't tell. She took a long breath, both hoping and fearing it was true.

"Oh, wait a minute," Maya said. "I want to give you something. I have a necklace that would look spectacular with that blouse."

"You don't have to do that," she said, disappointed that Maya thought she needed to repay her in some way.

"It's not compensation or anything," Maya said, as if reading Carly's mind. "Just a gift from one friend to another. Be right back."

Carly sat on the couch amid all the throw pillows and waited while Maya went into her bedroom. She rubbed her sweaty palms on her pants, wondering what would happen next. Perhaps Maya would emerge from the bedroom with the necklace, smiling in anticipation of her reaction. Carly would gasp at the beauty of the lovely piece, and Maya would insist she try it on. Then she'd gently touch Carly's neck and tell her how beautiful she looked.

With her eyes closed, Carly let the fantasy go further, imagining a longing look from Maya as she said something like *I never thought I'd feel this way again.* Carly would respond *Me neither.* Then Maya would ask Carly if it was okay if she kissed her.

Shivering, she opened her eyes.

"Here it is," Maya said, emerging from the bedroom with a white box.

She handed it to Carly, who lifted the lid to see a delicate gold chain with tiny emeralds spaced an inch apart. It was almost ephemeral in its lightness, like it could float away.

"It's beautiful," Carly gushed. "Are you sure you don't want this?"

"It's not really me," Maya said, touching the chunky Berber necklace she wore. "Can I put it on you?"

"Please," Carly said, lifting her hair.

Maya went behind her, and Carly nearly gasped as she felt the graze of warm fingers on the back of her neck.

Maya spun her around. "Stunning!" she said. "Come look." She led Carly to a mirror in the entranceway and stood behind her.

Carly touched the delicate strand, admiring how perfect it looked on her neck and how beautifully it complimented her blouse. She glanced at her friend's face in the mirror and noted that she beamed expectantly.

"I love it," Carly said.

"Do you really?"

"It's perfect. Thank you."

She turned around and embraced her friend, holding tight as she breathed in Maya's floral scent. This is my life now, Carly thought. This is my moment. This . . . is my person.

She pulled back from the embrace just enough to plant her lips on Maya's. For an almost imperceptibly quick moment, Maya returned the kiss. But then she stiffened and pulled away.

"Oh, no, Carly! No! You misunderstand."

"What!" Carly said, feeling like the life was draining out of her.

"Oh, god. I'm so sorry if I gave you the wrong impression. This is all my fault."

Carly closed her eyes and wanted nothing more than to die at that very moment. But when she stared at Maya again and saw the stricken look on her face, she knew she wouldn't get that wish, or any wish at all. And so, without a word, she ran for the door and fled.

Chapter 56
ARNIE

As he swam his second lap in the pool, Arnie willed himself not to look at the lounge in the corner—the one he thought of as Leyla's chair—where he had left a bouquet of flowers as well as a book on biological weapons he thought she might find interesting.

When at last he came up for air, Arnie heard someone call his name. He looked over to see young Sage on a lounge in the sun, oiling herself.

He glanced toward the other end of the patio, and there was Leyla, just taking a seat, as she examined the book he had left. The flowers had been moved to another chair.

"Haven't seen you in a while, Papa Bear," Sage called, shielding her eyes from the sun.

"Good to see you too," he said, pretending he hadn't heard her correctly. Then he lifted himself from the water, toweled off, and approached Leyla, who was dressed for work in printed scrubs. She managed to make it look beautiful.

"I see you left me some presents," she said.

He nodded. "I've been thinking about you."

"You must stop that," she admonished.

He sat on the edge of her lounge. "Leyla," he said, "I want you to consider giving us a chance. Life is so short, and we have something special, you and me."

"It was very special, Arnie, but it was only that one time."

"Please," he begged. "Let me take you out to dinner just once. Any place you like. If you decide that I'm not the man for you, I won't bother you again. Let's just try it. Don't we owe that to ourselves?"

She shook her head and gave him a sad look. "I've already made my decision. I'm so sorry."

Arnie heard more women call his name, but he didn't turn around.

"Is it Geoffrey?" he said. "Are you really committing yourself to that man?"

At that, Leyla held up her left hand, and showed him the ring she now wore. It was a massive round diamond, set in a circle of smaller ones. "I really am," she said, "but thank you for the book."

Chapter 57
ADDISON

It was a busy day at the concierge desk, thank goodness. Addison was feeling edgy about what Zach might have witnessed in the parking garage, despite Dante's assurance that there was no way he could have seen them. To quell her anxiety, she'd sent Zach a friendly text but hadn't heard back. Surely he was just busy, she told herself. She'd hear from him any minute.

Addison focused on her job, wearing a concerned expression as she listened to a tedious resident complain about the Pilates class schedule. She promised the woman she would talk to Frankie about it and then checked her phone again to see if Zach had responded. Nothing.

A short time later, Arnie's chatty gym friends, Louise and Fran, stopped by the desk to book a tennis court and then complained that they hadn't seen Arnie at the gym that morning.

Addison knew he had gone for an early swim instead. "I need to nurse this injury," he had told her.

"I think you've got another kind of nurse on your mind," she had teased, and he'd laughed.

"Guilty," he'd said, and she hoped he'd run into Leyla at the poolside.

But she didn't think any of this was Louise or Fran's business. So she simply informed the women that he was fine and promised she'd tell Arnie they'd asked about him.

When they left, Addison looked across the lobby to see Zach watching her. Finally, she thought as she tried to read his expression. But he was inscrutable. She smiled and waved him over, hoping for the best, but his face looked still and serious.

"Everything okay?" she asked.

"No." His voice was even, but there was something about his demeanor that sent a chill through her.

"What's wrong?" she asked.

Zach said nothing, just turned his phone toward her, practically shoving it in her face. She had to move his hand back to see what he was showing her. It took Addison a second to realize what she was looking at. Then she went cold. It was a picture taken through the window of Dante's car, capturing them at the moment he had tried to kiss her.

"No," she whispered as her world crashed down around her. "No, no, no." She looked into Zach's face and saw the bitter hardness of a broken man.

"Even after everything I've been through," he said with slow precision, "I believed you."

"I was telling the truth . . . ," Addison began, not sure how to defend herself and explain she hadn't broken their vow.

"But you're just like her. A liar and a cheat."

"No," she protested. "I meant everything I said to you."

He put his hand up to stop her. "It's fine," he said, with exaggerated nonchalance.

"It's not," she protested.

Zach shook his head, his eyes going moist. "You and Dante are perfectly suited. I hope you're happy together."

"Don't do that," she said. "Nothing happened between us. Nothing! You're the one who . . ." Addison didn't even bother finishing the sentence. Zach was gone.

Chapter 58

After Zach left, Addison tried to focus on her work, keeping her voice light and pleasant as she answered questions and booked appointments, wondering if anyone could hear the strain. All the while, she kept her eye on the clock, counting down until she could leave the desk so she could go someplace private to call Zach and try to get him to understand.

"How's everything here?" Frankie asked when she arrived to relieve Addison for her break.

"Wonderful," Addison lied. She wanted to make a quick exit but knew Frankie would request a debriefing on the day's highlights, especially anything that might require follow-up, like the complaint about the Pilates class schedule. As Addison sorted through her digital notes, she heard people approaching the desk and looked up to see Leyla pushing Dr. English in a manual wheelchair with Geoffrey walking alongside. They made an odd threesome. Leyla looked purposeful, Geoffrey looked eager, and Dr. English, inscrutable.

"May we have a seat?" Leyla asked. "We have something to discuss."

"Of course," Frankie said. "How can we help you?"

Leyla put the brakes on Dr. English's wheelchair, made sure she was comfortable, and then took a seat. Geoffrey hesitated as if waiting for permission, and Leyla tsked. "Sit down," she told him, and he did, smoothing out his pants and straightening his back.

Addison studied the disparate threesome, wondering what was going on. Were they there to register a complaint? She caught the eye of Dr. English, who gave an apologetic shrug Addison couldn't interpret.

"We have news," Leyla said crisply.

"This lovely lady and I are getting married," Geoffrey pronounced.

"Married?" Addison blurted, wondering how it could possibly be true. "To each other?" She looked at Dr. English, who had been so certain this would never happen, and the woman gave a small nod of confirmation.

"Congratulations," Frankie piped in, clearly trying to cover for Addison's inappropriate response. "That's wonderful news."

"Yes," Addison said, trying to collect herself, "wonderful." She looked across the desk at Leyla's left hand and saw an enormous diamond ring catching the light of the overhead chandelier.

"We would like to have the wedding in the Beekman," Leyla said.

"We met here," Geoffrey added, "so we thought it would be romantic."

Leyla gave a small, tolerant smile, and Dr. English folded her hands in her lap. She looked from Frankie to Addison. "They'd like to have the whole affair on the rooftop—a cocktail party followed by a small ceremony and then dancing."

"Under the setting sun," Geoffrey said as he turned to Leyla and attempted eye contact. She gave his hand a pat.

"It sounds like a lovely idea," Frankie said. "We've never done a wedding in the building. It will be our first!"

"We would like to invite all the residents," Leyla said.

"That was Geoffrey's idea," Dr. English added. "He thought it would be more festive with a lot of witnesses."

Witnesses? Addison glanced his way and understood this was all about his ego. He needed everyone to see him marrying this exquisite woman, like she was some kind of trophy. He adjusted the glasses on his face, holding on to them for a moment as if the sheer force of his pride could send them hurtling forward.

Addison looked back at Leyla, wondering what she got out of the relationship. Was it simply the kinky sex? Or was this controllable man her soulmate—the crooked lid that fit her heat-warped pot?

"How very generous!" Frankie said. "I think that will be lovely. Don't you, Addison?"

"Lovely," Addison echoed, thinking about poor Arnie and his broken heart. She also thought about that scar by his eye and wondered if this would send him running back to Paulette.

"We can certainly help you with the catering and any other arrangements," Frankie said. "What date did you have in mind?"

"Next Sunday evening," Leyla said.

The room seemed to leak oxygen. Addison and Frankie exchanged a look as if to confirm they'd heard correctly.

"You mean . . . ," Frankie began, clearly trying to wrap her head around what would be required to plan a wedding in less than two weeks.

"It's eleven days away," Leyla said. "I know that's terribly close, but we don't require much."

"Geoffrey's afraid she might change her mind," Dr. English said.

"Please, Mother," he said. "It's not that at all." He reached over and took Leyla's hand, then turned to Frankie and Addison. "It's very simple. I have tickets for a gallery opening in Paris, and we'd like to make that trip our honeymoon."

"It's not a problem," Frankie said. "I'm certain we can pull all the details together." She looked at Addison and pointed at her tablet. "Let's start with the catering."

Chapter 59

We need to talk, Addison texted to Dante. Her plan was to demand that he speak to Zach and explain exactly what had happened between the two of them in his car.

Still at work, he texted back. Meet me for dinner in an hour?

She wrote back: Rather not

My only window, he texted. Leaving for NY later

Addison sighed, wondering what she should do. But before she could respond he texted again: I'll send a car

Addison was sitting at the Splash Bar, sipping an iced tea and ignoring the crowd that was beginning to gather. She glanced across the pool and saw Melody Forrest posing on a lounge, her back arched like a porn star's. She wore a bikini, as if sunbathing in the twilight. Jake, who was still in his lifeguard chair, stared at her, transfixed. He gave a toot on this whistle, letting the swimmers know he was going off duty. Then he climbed down from his perch and made a beeline for Melody.

Bruh, she wanted to tell him, *be careful what you wish for.*

Addison felt someone hovering and looked up to see that Mr. Posner was standing over her, his Hawaiian shirt open over his bathing trunks, which he adjusted as if getting ready to make a move.

Addison turned her back to him and responded to Dante: Fine

A short while later, the hired car took her to a restaurant called Musso and Frank—a steak house with a retro exterior. Addison wondered if he was trying to impress her. When she got inside and greeted him, she got her answer, as he proudly told her that the place had been a legendary Hollywood haunt for a century.

"And it has more literary cred than anyplace in New York," he added, and started ticking off on his fingers the famous writers who had eaten there. "Faulkner . . . Hemingway . . . F. Scott Fitzgerald . . . Dorothy Parker . . . Raymond Chandler . . ."

Addison refused to be impressed. "Ever hear of the Algonquin?" she said.

He laughed. "You don't make this easy," he said as they were led to a table in the back. Addison noted that the restaurant looked as historic as promised, paneled in dark wood, with leather banquettes and waiters in red jackets. She also noticed the diners surreptitiously eyeing them as they strode through the room. That, she imagined, was the main sport at this place—trying to scope out celebrities without being obvious about it.

"The filet mignon is pretty good," Dante said after they were handed menus, "if you're in the mood for steak."

Once their orders were placed, Addison looked straight into Dante's face. "I have a problem," she said, "and I need your help."

"Anything," he told her, "as long as it doesn't involve Brody."

"How did you know it was about Zach?" she asked, wondering if this whole thing was a fool's errand.

He shrugged. "A hunch."

A waiter brought over a bottle of wine and went through the ritual of showing the label to Dante, pouring him a taste, and then waiting for approval before filling their glasses. This was beginning to feel very much like a date, and Addison was growing impatient.

"It turns out," she said when the waiter left, "that he got a good look at us in your car."

"So what?"

"He thinks we were kissing! You have to tell him it's not true, tell him what I said about choosing him over you."

Dante made a face. "Why would I do *that*?"

"Because it's true and I'm asking you to. Please. He doesn't believe me."

Dante looked unruffled. "Come on, Addison," he said dismissively. "Is that really what you want—a heartsick little puppy who falls apart when he thinks you've been unfaithful?"

It's exactly what I want, she thought, because that's what happens to a committed heart. It breaks. But someone who's bulletproof wouldn't understand that.

"He's hurting, Dante."

"He *wants* to hurt. That's his thing."

"No, it isn't."

Dante waved away her objection. "Then why did he take a picture?"

Addison opened her mouth to respond but stopped herself. How did he know Zach had taken a picture? At the time, Dante had assured her Zach hadn't seen a thing. She studied his face, and the truth became clear.

"Oh my god," she said. "You did it on purpose. You knew he was there, and you moved in on me at that moment to give him the wrong idea."

He folded his arms. "That's ridiculous."

"No," she said, her fury rising. "It isn't. You wanted him to come to the wrong conclusion."

He went quiet for a long moment, as if deciding whether the truth or a lie would make a stronger case. "So what if I did?" he finally said.

"That's . . . monstrous!"

"Don't be naive. This is what men do. We stake our claim."

Addison felt nauseated. "Is that what I am? A claim?"

"You know what I mean." He reached for her hand again. "I want you all to myself. That's not so bad, is it?"

She thought about Zach's pain and understood that it didn't trouble Dante at all. In fact, it made him feel more powerful, more victorious. Addison recoiled. This wasn't simply a man who needed to win. He needed to crush, to destroy. For Dante, cruelty was part of the fun.

"You're the worst mistake I ever made," she said, and stood, thinking about the Tiffany bracelet in her purse, which she had intended to give back to him. Instead, she turned her back and left the restaurant. Then she walked two doors down to an Irish pub, where she took a seat at the bar and called Tameka to ask if she could come pick her up.

Chapter 60
CARLY

Her brother was worried about her. "I called you three times," he said.

"I know. I'm sorry. I guess . . . I haven't really been feeling that well." Carly plumped the pillow under her head, almost regretting picking up the phone. She had considered letting it ring—again—but knew he'd keep calling. Besides, he'd been so good to her. It just wasn't fair to ignore him, no matter how awful she was feeling.

Maya was another story. She'd been texting, expressing "concern," but Carly hadn't responded. It was all too humiliating.

She'd also ignored an urgent email from her client about making a last-minute change to the press release. There was just no chance she could focus on anything other than her wish to disappear. Carly picked up the glass of water by her bedside, doused her dry throat, and lay back down again.

"Did something happen?" Lenny asked. "You sound depressed."

"I'm okay," she lied.

"No, you're not."

Carly turned away from the aggressive beam of light sneaking past the closed curtains. "I really don't want to talk about it."

"At least agree to come over this weekend. Diksha and I want to see you."

"I don't know, Lenny."

"The kids miss their aunt Carly."

The kids. Reya and Samira—two beautiful girls. A lump of longing formed in Carly's throat, and she wondered what would have happened if she'd been able to have a child. Maybe Owen would have changed, softened. It was possible. People changed all the time. It hurt to think about the life she might have had—one where she didn't humiliate herself in front of Maya Mayfield, the most beautiful, the most accomplished, the most extraordinary woman who had ever lived. As if Carly had a chance with her! What a fool. What an idiot. What an addle-brained loser. Owen had been so right about her.

"We'll barbecue," Lenny said. "I'll invite our neighbors, Greg and Donny. You'll love them."

Carly hesitated, feeling so tired she could no longer hold up her head. "Maybe."

"Maybe?" he repeated.

"If I have the energy," she said, and then rolled over and went back to sleep.

Chapter 61
ADDISON

Fortunately, it was Jada's night with her father, so Tameka had been happy to pick Addison up and drive her back to the Beekman after the terrible dinner with Dante.

"This is so nice of you," Addison said, grateful she had made such a dear friend.

"I'm glad you called me."

As Tameka drove, Addison explained everything that had happened and asked for her advice on what to do about Zach.

"He's not responding to my texts," she explained.

"Just call him."

"He won't pick up. I'm sure of it."

"So leave a voicemail."

Addison didn't know if he would even play it back but decided it was worth a try. So she did it right there in Tameka's car, leaving a long message that explained everything, including the part about Dante orchestrating his move at the precise moment Zach was looking in the window.

"I didn't sleep with him, I didn't kiss him, and I didn't lead him on," she said. "I told him about you, about us. I hope that you can believe me. I . . ." She paused, wondering if she should tell him she loved him.

"Say it," Tameka whispered, but Addison worried it would scare him off, since he was still so raw from his breakup with Quinn. Besides, she felt vulnerable enough as it was. So even though it was the truth, Addison simply said goodbye and disconnected.

Then she took the diamond Tiffany bracelet from her purse and gave it to her friend.

Chapter 62
CARLY

Carly wasn't contemplating suicide. Not really. But as she stood by the railing on the rooftop at 3:00 a.m., the fantasy felt freeing. She could imagine it—a release from the hurt and humiliation. But she didn't think she was ready to leave this world. Not when there were still so many sunrises and sunsets. Not while there was air that Maya Mayfield had breathed. She just had to get through another day, and then another.

Carly thought she heard a rustling sound and turned, alarmed. Who else would be on the roof at this hour? But of course it was just her frayed nerves reacting to the wind.

Leaning over the railing, Carly gazed out at the twinkling in the darkness. The headlights of cars, the streetlamps, the flickering of life inside homes and apartments. So many people. So much heartache and joy. So much triumph and disappointment. So much life and death. She leaned back and looked up at the stars. Was the bright one Venus? It was hard to contemplate the vastness and her own insignificance. Even her mountainous pain was a small thing.

From the corner of her eye, Carly saw a shadow move among the shadows, and she jumped back from the edge.

"Who's there!" she called, but there was no answer. Then she heard the door to the elevator vestibule open and close.

Someone had been up there watching her, and Carly went cold in fear. Had they meant to push her? She covered her mouth to keep from retching and tried to understand. Had it been Owen's private eye? Someone else? It could be nothing, she tried to reassure herself. Maybe another resident had come up to the roof and seen her there, then left to give her privacy. There wasn't much she understood except that despite her pain, she didn't want to die.

Carly went back to her apartment and didn't even bother trying to sleep. She knew it would be impossible after the fright she'd had. Besides, this was the demon hour, when depression was joined by anxiety and the two stomped around in her brain, pillaging and plundering, wreaking havoc.

She spilled out the tea she hadn't finished, made another cup, and set it next to her laptop. With dread, Carly opened her email and saw another urgent message from her client. She knew they were getting frustrated with her—even angry—but she still couldn't bring herself to respond. What could she say? Was there even a plausible excuse for why she had been ignoring them?

There was also another email from Owen, of course. This one had been sent only minutes ago, and had a subject line with a typo: I just want to tlak. She ignored it and hovered her cursor over the bookmark to Instagram, which had always offered her such glorious respite—a chance to delight in the beautiful lives of her favorite influencers. Now, it felt like rooting around in an open wound. She clicked.

Carly scrolled past a post from an old friend recommending an exciting psychological thriller, a reel of bloopers from *The Office*, a gloriously unflattering photo from Jamie Lee Curtis, and a beautiful image of a glistening tomato salad from a food influencer, and then there it was—a new post from Maya Mayfield. It was an image of a sunset—one that looked very much like the view from the restaurant in Malibu. Beneath it was the message: I have a friend who is going through a hard time right now, feeling alone and sad. If that sounds like you, please know you are loved. Don't cut yourself off when you need people most. Let them in.

Carly read it through four times, certain Maya was talking about her. She began to weep. I *am* alone, she thought. And there's no one but you I want to let in. But I can't. It hurts too much.

Carly grabbed a tissue and wiped her eyes, but the tears kept coming as the pain roiled through her. How could she have been so stupid! Maya Mayfield, for god's sake. She had tried to kiss Maya Mayfield! And in that single moment, she had destroyed her one chance at a magnificent friendship, at a better life. It was all over now. She was just Carly Pratt from Nashua, married to Owen Pratt, who worked as a lineman for the electric utility company. And it was all she'd ever be.

Carly reached around, opened the clasp on the delicate necklace from Maya, and dropped it on the table. Then she clicked over to her email and opened the message from Owen. Inside, it said: I can do better. I know it. Can we talk?

Carly stared at the message. She'd always heard that people don't change, but she knew that wasn't true. Leaving Owen had changed her in so many ways, and maybe—just maybe—it had changed him too.

Carly hit reply and typed out: I'll think about it.

Then, at last, she got into bed and went to sleep.

Chapter 63
ADDISON

Frankie had instructed Addison to make sure someone from each unit in the building received a hand-delivered invitation to Leyla and Geoffrey's wedding. Fortunately, Addison was able to get through nearly half the list just by sitting at the concierge desk all morning and presenting them to people who passed.

"A Beekman wedding," she announced to each resident as she handed over their invitation, "and everyone is invited! We hope you can make it."

This was usually followed by questions about the couple, whether they'd met here in the building, and whether "no gifts" really meant "no gifts."

When Melody Forrest emerged from the elevator, Addison was tempted to pretend she didn't see her, but the instructions had been clear.

"I have something for you," Addison said, calling her over, and when she explained about the wedding, Melody's eyes went wide.

"And they met here, in this condo?" she asked.

"Yes," Addison said, not bothering to explain that Leyla was a hired worker, not a resident.

"It's the most romantic thing I've ever heard," Melody gushed, and Addison understood that if Leyla threw a bouquet, this woman would dive off the railing for it.

In the late afternoon, Frankie came back to the desk to announce that the two of them would divide and conquer, knocking on the rest of the doors to deliver the remaining invitations in person.

"You take Tower A," Frankie said, "and I'll take Tower B."

Addison drew a long breath. Zach was in Tower A. He had never responded to her voicemail, and she didn't even know if he had played it back. She certainly didn't know how he would react to seeing her again.

And then there she was, in front of his apartment, wearing her red blazer and carrying a stack of wedding invitations. She rang the buzzer.

"Zach, it's Addison," she called.

She could hear him approach and hesitate for only a moment before opening the door, Betty Snyder liquid in his arms. He was in the same green T-shirt he'd worn the first time they met, his hair so askew Addison was tempted to reach out and straighten it. As if sensing her thought, he finger-combed it with his free hand.

"I was working," he said, readjusting the cat. "What is it?"

She hoped he'd step back and invite her in, but he didn't budge. "Sorry to bother you, but I have official business." Addison tugged on her lapel. "See? Red blazer."

He remained serious. "Did you need something?" he asked, petting the cat.

"Well, yes, I . . . Leyla and Geoffrey are getting married." She nodded toward the apartment next door. "Everyone in the building is invited."

She handed him his invitation, and he took it, thrusting the cat at her so he could read the cordial message.

Addison wordlessly accepted the animal, knowing she'd pay for it later with itchy eyes, runny nose, scratchy throat, and hours of flu-like misery. She welcomed the suffering, feeling like it would put her on equal footing with Zach.

He pulled the invitation from its envelope and scanned the card. "Does this mean they'll move?"

"I don't know," Addison said, realizing she should have thought to ask them.

"Because if I have to put up with that disturbance every night—"

"I understand," she said. "I'll . . . talk to them." Addison hoped they'd tell her they were moving to Bel Air or Paris or something, so she wouldn't need to broach the awkwardness of addressing their aggressively loud sexual habits.

His eyes went back to the card. "The wedding is here in the building?" he said.

"On the roof," she confirmed. "Next Sunday. Can you make it?" Addison began petting the cat in gentle strokes. She was such a soft thing. Then, when the purring started, Addison was tempted to hold her even closer, to welcome the vibrations into her own chest.

Zach slipped the card back in the envelope. "Maybe . . ."

Addison waited for him to continue, but he disappeared into his reverie. She handed back the cat, hoping it would get his attention and prompt him to invite her inside, but he didn't move. "Did you listen to my voicemail?" she asked.

He shook his head. "I deleted it."

"I wish you hadn't done that," she said, her throat starting to itch.

"Why?" he asked. "I knew exactly what it said without even listening to it—that nothing happened between you two—"

"Nothing *did* happen!"

"I know what I saw."

"But Dante staged that! He knew you were watching, so he lunged for me. He's that awful, Zach. I told him about us, how I felt about you, and he wanted to ruin it."

Zach took a step back, as if he needed physical space to take that in, going silent for a long moment. "And you have no interest in him?" he finally said, squinting dubiously. "None at all?"

"God, no. He's a monster."

He went quiet again, disappearing into his thoughts, and Addison waited for him to come back. At last he said, "I suppose he told you, then."

"Told me what?" she said, her voice going hoarse.

He studied her face, as if searching for a clue. "You really don't know?"

It was getting hard to speak, so she just shook her head.

"Are you okay?" he asked.

Addison pointed to her throat and managed to croak out, "Do you have a Benadryl?"

Chapter 64

No Benadryl? Addison had assumed everyone kept a box in their medicine cabinet. Now, she panicked, because this was no longer just about suffering—it was about anaphylaxis. She was sinking fast, and if she didn't get some antihistamine soon, she'd need an EpiPen. As it was, she had to breathe through her mouth, as her sinuses had swollen shut. When Zach saw her expression, he understood. In a microsecond, he dropped the cat and grabbed her arm. "The nurse!" he said, and pulled her toward the apartment next door.

"What's wrong?" Leyla asked, as she opened the door to his pounding.

"Benadryl," Zach said. "She's having an allergic reaction."

Leyla rushed them inside. "Sit," she commanded, and ran to another room.

As Addison tried to relax and catch her breath, Dr. English wheeled into the living room, inserting her hearing aids. "Everything okay?" she asked.

"Leyla's getting her some Benadryl," Zach explained.

Concern swept the doctor's face as she assessed the scene. "I have an epinephrine pen, but I think it's expired," she said.

"I'm okay," Addison managed to whisper, though she didn't know if it was true.

Leyla emerged and dropped two pills in Addison's hands, then gave her a glass of water. "Drink the whole thing," she instructed.

Thank god, Addison thought, and tossed the pills toward her throat. As she drank the water, the three of them watched as if they thought she might perish at any moment. Leyla took the empty glass from her and went into the kitchen to refill it. Addison drank that one down too.

Leyla grabbed her wrist and took her pulse. "A little fast," she said. "Was it that stupid cat?"

"I didn't know she was allergic," Zach said.

Addison cleared her throat again. "My fault."

"Don't be ridiculous," Leyla said.

It was still difficult to speak, so Addison tapped Leyla's arm to get her attention and mimed holding and stroking the cat.

"Oh, you fool!" Leyla admonished. "Go wash your hands. Face too."

Addison did as she was told and emerged from the bathroom feeling better, though she couldn't tell if it was the Benadryl kicking in already or her panic easing off. Either way, she knew she would recover. The medication was making its way through her bloodstream, blocking those dander-triggered histamines.

"Thank you," she said to everyone in the room, and meant it. They had literally saved her life. She relaxed into a chair.

Zach looked from the doctor to the nurse. "Is she going to be okay?"

Leyla picked up Addison's wrist again and counted, then nodded at Dr. English. "She'll be fine."

"Stay as long as you like," the doctor told Addison.

"I just need a couple of minutes."

"I'll stay with you," Zach said.

She looked at him, and a feathery vapor of hope lightened her heart. This wasn't guilt talking—he was genuinely concerned.

"If you need to go back to work . . . ," she said, and trailed off.

Leyla gave a judgmental cluck. "Let him stay. He likes you."

Addison was pleased it was that obvious. But of course, it wasn't the whole story. "He doesn't know if he can trust me," she admitted.

A tiny smile played on Leyla's face. "Even better," she said.

Chapter 65

A short while later, Addison was back at work, hand-delivering the rest of the invitations. The Benadryl had done its job, leaving her free of symptoms but sluggish and sleepy. Still, she was buoyed by Zach's concern for her well-being, especially since they hadn't had enough time to finish their conversation about what he had witnessed in the parking garage.

Addison took the elevator one floor down and noticed a blond young man at the end of the hallway. Groggy, she tried to make sense of what she was seeing. It was Jake, the lifeguard, slipping something under a door. For a dull moment, she thought he'd been tasked with helping to deliver invitations.

"Jake?" she called. "What are you doing here?"

He straightened up, looking embarrassed. "Me?"

Even for Jake, who was as dumb as a pool noodle, it was a stupid question. Clearly, he was stalling for time. Addison approached him. "Were you sticking something under the door?"

He looked down, pouting. "She never pays any attention to me."

"Who?"

"Mrs. Forrest."

"Melody Forrest?" Addison asked, trying to understand.

"She's the most beautiful woman I've ever seen."

Addison studied his forlorn expression, surprised. She had assumed the older women chased after him, not the other way around. And she certainly never expected him to develop lovesick crushes.

"You really like her?" Addison asked.

"No matter what I do, she acts like I'm just some kid. Some . . . lifeguard."

You are, Addison thought, but didn't want to be cruel. "You left her a note?"

"I wanted to tell her how I feel."

"Oh, Jake. I think you're barking up the wrong tree with Melody."

"Because she likes older men?" he asked.

And because she's batshit crazy and will eat you alive, Addison wanted to say. Instead, she told him, "I think there are a lot of women who are better suited for you."

"You mean younger ones."

"Well," she began.

"Because I'm very mature for my age."

"Mature?"

"I listen to Aerosmith, Kiss, Black Sabbath . . . even the Beatles. Girls my age—you wouldn't believe the music they like."

"Wow, you really are an old soul," she lied, because the conversation was getting just too ridiculous.

"Right?" he said, excited, as if someone finally saw him for who he really was.

"Well, good luck with Melody," she said, and told him she needed to finish handing out the invitations.

"Thanks," he said, as he headed for the elevator. "Good luck with Zach Brody."

Addison stopped and stared after him, wondering if he was really as stupid as she'd thought.

Chapter 66

When she reached unit 806 and rang the buzzer, Addison looked down at the top envelope in her hand, admiring the elegant way the calligrapher had penned the capital *H* and capital *P*. It was only then that she realized who the recipient was—Howard Posner, the disgusting old guy who didn't understand boundaries. Please don't be home, she prayed. Please.

"Who's there!" he called.

Addison sighed. Be strong, she told herself. Be assertive. Don't take any shit from this horny old nutcase.

"It's the concierge, Mr. Posner."

At that, the door swung open, and there he stood in his tighty-whities, his bare feet planted far apart, like some Wild West gunslinger in a pair of chaps.

"You changed your mind," he pronounced. "Come in."

"No, I'm just here to give you something," Addison said, holding out the invitation.

He folded his arms over his naked chest. "Not a massage?"

"No," she said sternly, aware that there was no room for social pleasantries with this guy. "I will never give you a massage. You need to stop asking me that. It's creepy and inappropriate." There. She had laid it all out as concretely as she could. "You need to behave yourself," she added for good measure.

Addison watched as he took it in with a nod, internalizing her censure. After a moment, his arms dropped, and he hung his head, chastened. "I should have put on pants," he mumbled.

"Yes, you should have."

He looked up and made eye contact. "I'll never do it again," he promised, and Addison could read the loneliness in his face. Despite herself, she felt sorry for him.

"That's good, Mr. Posner," she said.

He took the envelope from her hand. "What is this?"

"A wedding invitation. Geoffrey English from 1104 is getting married a week from Sunday, up on the roof."

He pulled out the card and looked at it. "I'm invited?" he asked, sounding surprised.

His tone was open, guileless, and Addison's heart began to fissure. He really was a lonely old man who had no one. "Yes," she said. "You should come. It'll be lively."

"You think I'll get laid?"

For a moment, Addison went mute. The old dog just couldn't stop himself.

"Goodbye, Mr. Posner," she said, and walked away.

"Wait!" he called after her. "I have cash!"

Addison hurried off to the elevator.

Fortunately, the residents she encountered on the next couple of floors were so boring Addison had to suppress several yawns. By the time she worked her way down to the fifth floor, she was ready to lie down in the hall and take a nap.

Still, she remained in work mode when she encountered a man she didn't know waiting by the elevators. Addison introduced herself as the concierge and asked if he lived on that floor.

"Uh, yeah," the man said, scratching the back of his neck. "Apartment 506."

"Great," Addison said, tapping at her tablet to find him on her list. "Mr. Gronek?"

"That's right. Lenny Gronek. Leonard, I mean." He pressed the down button on the elevator and adjusted his baseball cap.

"Here you go, Mr. Gronek," she said, handing him an envelope.

"What's this?"

"A wedding at the Beekman!" Addison told him, struggling to sound upbeat. "Everyone's invited."

He stared at the envelope without opening it, then slipped it into the breast pocket of his jacket. "Well, thanks," he said, and pressed the elevator button again.

"You're welcome! I hope to see you there."

"Sure," he said, as the elevator doors opened. He stepped inside. "See you there."

Addison thought it was odd that he hadn't looked at the invitation or asked about the date, but she didn't think much of it. She just assumed he was in a hurry to get someplace and didn't want to be bothered with her. As she watched him adjust his white baseball cap, Addison had a strange feeling of déjà vu, as if she'd lived through this very scene before. Then, as the doors closed, severing their connection, she noticed something that gave her a chill, and Addison understood why the scene felt so familiar. She had watched it on the security cam. The man was wearing black-soled work boots.

Chapter 67
ARNIE

Momentary madness, Arnie told himself. Fear of his own mortality. That's what his obsession with Leyla had been. She'd ignited a spark he hadn't felt in years, and he'd thought he had recaptured his youth. Now, he understood that what they had together lacked the depth and maturity of his connection to Paulette. Sure, the physical attraction to Leyla was intense, but Paulette was the one he belonged with, his happily ever after. He just had to get that egg back, and all would be well.

"Don't disappoint me, Arnie," she'd said in their last video chat.

"I promise," he'd responded, and meant it. He would move heaven and earth to prove himself to her. He had even ordered a new off-white sofa to replace the black leather sectional he knew she'd dislike.

Now, he looked down at a text from Frankie, his pulse rising.

We've identified the culprit. Can you come to my office?

Identified. It didn't mean they'd caught him, but they were close. Arnie filled with hope. His holy grail was in sight. Soon, he would recover his egg and win Paulette back forever.

To show his appreciation, he made Frankie a cup of coffee from the special imported blend she liked, poured it into an insulated cup, and headed to her office.

When he arrived, she was in a meeting with Nikolai, and Arnie had to apologize for only bringing one coffee. The security guard stood, rising like a Caucasus mountain, and waved off his apology.

"I don't drink American coffee."

"If it doesn't disintegrate the cup, he's not interested," Frankie said, reaching for the coffee. "Thank you, Arnie."

Nikolai didn't smile at the joke. "We have break in case," he said.

"So I heard." Arnie took a seat and glanced from the giant security man to Frankie, who looked so petite by comparison. She was such a formidable presence—both as the building manager and as a tennis partner—he didn't often notice how tiny she was. "What happened?"

He listened while Frankie recounted a story about Addison running into the man who had stolen the egg, recognizing him from the elevator-cam video.

"She was a little out of it," Frankie explained, her small hands wrapped around the oversize cup. "By the time she realized who he was, the man was gone."

"I would have locked down building," Nikolai said.

"It took Addison a while to find us," Frankie clarified. "So the guy got away."

"Wait," Arnie said, concerned about his niece. "Why was she out of it?"

"She's okay," Frankie assured him. "She just had an allergic reaction to a resident's cat and needed to take an antihistamine."

"She wasn't anaphylactic, was she? Should I check on her?"

"She was just tired. I sent her back to her apartment for some rest. I'm sure she'll call you later."

Arnie had seen enough allergic reactions to know how dangerous they could be and made a mental note to ask Addison if she carried an EpiPen in her purse. If not, he'd insist on it. That kid was everything to him.

"You okay?" Frankie said.

Arnie understood why she'd asked. No doubt he'd gone pale at the idea of losing Addison. "Yeah," he breathed. "I just need a second."

Frankie handed him one of the water bottles she kept behind her desk, and he sipped at it. This is just about a silly egg, he reminded himself. Okay, a silly egg and his future with Paulette. But nothing was more important than Addison. He tried to relax, knowing she was okay.

He looked from Frankie to Nikolai. "How do you know the guy got away?" he asked.

Frankie turned her computer monitor to face him and played a video from the security camera over the building's freight entrance. He could see a man in a white baseball cap scurrying through the door and out of frame. Arnie's heart sank, wondering if they'd ever find him.

"Do we know anything about the guy?"

Frankie and Nikolai shared a look. "We know his name," she said to Arnie.

"You do?"

"It's Leonard Gronek. He owns unit 506, but he doesn't live there. He bought the place for his sister, Carly Pratt."

Arnie sat back, trying to digest the information. "What do we do now?"

"Police," Nikolai said.

Frankie nodded. "I think it's time to involve law enforcement. They can find this guy, arrest him."

"But why would he do it?" Arnie asked, trying to imagine what might drive a man to steal his property like that. "I mean, if he's affluent enough to afford a condo for his sister . . ."

"Maybe rich-guy money problems," Nikolai offered.

"Or maybe," Frankie said, leaning forward, "someone told him about the egg—someone who didn't know it was a replica."

Arnie took that in and decided it made sense. If anyone had seen that bejeweled piece in his apartment, they might have assumed it was one of the actual eggs from the House of Fabergé, worth tens of millions of dollars.

"If I had an original Fabergé egg," he said, "I'd probably keep it under lock and key. Did you know there are only sixty of them in the whole world?"

Nikolai folded his arms. "Fifty-seven," he corrected.

Arnie turned back to Frankie. "So, an inside job?" he asked, thinking about the people who had been inside his place and seen the egg. Friends . . . lovers . . . workmen . . . porters . . . his decorator . . . his cleaning lady. It was a long list.

"It's just a theory," she said.

But a good one, he thought, impressed.

The three agreed there was no reason to put off calling the police, so Frankie picked up her phone and spoke to someone at the LAPD, then announced that a detective would be arriving in about an hour. At that, Nikolai left, and Arnie stood.

"You hungry?" he asked Frankie.

She nodded. "Let's go to the Splash Bar. I'll let you buy me a sandwich."

Arnie gave her a smile and a bow. "I'd be honored."

Chapter 68
CARLY

What now? Carly thought when the buzzer rang. She was lying in bed, watching an old episode of *Property Brothers* on her phone. It was how she'd been passing the time lately, avoiding calls, texts, and emails. Lenny, her brother, had tried phoning her again the night before, but she wasn't in the mood to deal with his pressure to come over for a barbecue. Carly just couldn't face putting on a polite smile while sitting in the beautiful yard behind his beautiful house, being entertained by his beautiful wife and beautiful children.

The buzzer rang again, and she dragged herself out of bed.

"Who's there?" she called, hoping she could send away whoever it was without opening the door.

"Carly, it's Lenny. I've been trying to reach you."

"Lenny," she said, pulling open the door. At once, she was awash in guilt. He was worried, and she should have answered his calls.

"Jesus," he said, taking in the sight of her. "You look terrible."

It was true. Her face was drawn and pale, with dark-purple crescents under her eyes. Since she hadn't showered in days, her hair was a matted, dirty mess. She wore her most comfortable clothes—the gray sweatpants she had used for gardening and a grease-stained T-shirt of an indeterminate beige color that matched her pallor. In contrast, her brother was in a crisp blue button-down that looked like it had never been worn before. His light-brown hair was cut stylishly short, and a bright, fresh fragrance wafted off him.

"I didn't know you were coming," she said, as if it were an excuse for her appearance.

"Didn't you get my text?"

She hung her head, ashamed. "I haven't really checked."

"Carly, listen. We have to get you out of here for a few days. I spoke to Diksha, and we want you to come stay with us."

No, no, no, she thought. She needed her bed, her blanket, her pillow. These were her friends, and she couldn't possibly leave them.

"I'm fine, really," she said. "I just . . . I need to work through a few things."

He walked past Carly into the living room, then stopped and turned toward her, his face twisted in worry. "You're not safe."

"Oh, Lenny," she said, "honestly, I'm not suicidal. I'm just blue. It'll pass."

"I'm not talking about that," he told her.

"What then?"

Lenny asked if they could sit down for some tea and offered to make it while she got herself dressed. A short while later, Carly emerged from the bathroom—scrubbed clean and wearing the extravagantly plush robe her sister-in-law had bought for her as a housewarming gift—to join her brother in the kitchen. He had made them each English breakfast tea with a small splash of milk, the way their mother used to drink it.

"Has anyone in the building spoken to you?" he asked as she sat.

"About what?"

He took a long breath. "Carly, the police showed up at my house."

"The police?" She sat up straighter, concerned.

"Apparently, there was a thief in this building. He made off with someone's Fabergé egg."

Carly looked at him, trying to understand. She got that it was a terrible crime, but beyond that she was stumped. "What does it have to do with you?" she asked.

"Before he escaped, he gave them my name. Said he was Leonard Gronek and lived in unit 506."

Carly rubbed her eyes at the crazy puzzle. Why would some random thief rattle off that information? Then she thought about the mysterious presence on the roof. Were these things related? With a shiver, Carly tightened her robe.

Lenny sipped his tea. "Thank god the police had a photo of the guy," he continued, "or they would have arrested me."

Carly pictured Lenny opening the door of his home to two uniformed police officers, Diksha and the girls behind him. "What an ordeal for you," she said.

He waved away her concern. "I'm fine, but I need you to pack a few things and come stay with us a few days, just to be safe."

"You're being overly cautious," she said, even as she wondered if she might be in danger. "I'm sure the thief won't dare show his face here again."

"Carly, you don't understand. The guy who—"

"I can't leave, Lenny!" she insisted, envisioning Maya here in the building—working out at the gym, getting her nails done at the salon, having a white wine up on the roof. She simply couldn't sacrifice that proximity. But there was no way to explain all that to her brother. Carly's eyes filled with tears.

Lenny reached across the table and grabbed her hand. At first, she thought he was comforting her, but when she looked into his eyes, she realized he was trying to make sure she was listening.

"Carly," he said, "they showed me a picture of the thief. It was Owen."

Chapter 69

Owen?

Carly tried to put the pieces together as she packed her things and rode to her brother's house. She thought back to the creepy message that made it clear Owen had been spying on her. She'd assumed he hired a private investigator, but now she realized he'd been there on the property, watching her. Owen—who'd never been farther west than Silver Spring, Maryland—was here in Beverly Hills. And very likely he'd been watching her on the roof. It was the most vulnerable she'd ever felt, and Owen had been right there. Carly shuddered.

When she probed a little deeper, she realized his messages had increased in desperation and frequency just days before his disturbing text, and she guessed that the change in tone marked his arrival in town. Carly wondered what his game plan had been, or if he'd even thought that far.

She also wondered how Owen had managed the travel on his own—booking a flight, a hotel, and probably a rental car. He'd always insisted that his dyslexia made those types of arrangements too difficult for him. Now she realized he was capable of pushing his own limits—it had simply been easier for him to make Carly do absolutely everything.

The most perplexing part of the puzzle was the burglary itself. She'd never known Owen to be a thief. In fact, he found burglars, vandals, and trespassers—with their disregard for private property—the lowest form of life. She supposed his desperation had pushed him to cross that line. Maybe he'd figured a windfall would help him win her back, not to mention pay off the trip itself. Still, that didn't account for how he knew about the Fabergé egg in the first place. She wondered if he even understood what it was. It didn't seem likely.

"You think they'll catch him?" she asked her brother as they turned into his community. Carly had never been afraid of Owen—not physically, anyway. She'd always thought of him as benign, in his own awful way. Kind of like a migraine. But perhaps *benign* was too kind a word. *Cowardly* may have been closer to the truth. This changed everything, though, and she could no longer guess what he might be capable of.

"The police have his photo and his name, so I'm pretty sure they'll find him. He's not exactly a mastermind."

"You think they'll want my help?"

"Almost definitely," Lenny said. "We can probably expect a visit from a detective in the next day or so."

Good, Carly thought. She'd be happy to give them whatever they needed to track Owen down and arrest him before his behavior got any worse. And sure, part of her prickled at the thought of him in prison, but when she recalled the intentionally terrifying text he had sent, that tiny vestige of sympathy resorbed into tougher tissue. An orange jumpsuit seemed about right.

Lenny pulled up in front of his property and pushed a remote control that opened an imposing black metal gate leading to the driveway. He and his family lived in a sprawling seven-bedroom Spanish-style house set back from the road and neatly landscaped. Lenny popped the trunk and grabbed Carly's bag, then led her inside through the arched doorway.

She'd been there before, of course, but Carly was always struck by the view from the entrance foyer, complete with sixteen-foot ceilings and an impressive winding staircase with an ornate iron railing. There was a straight view through the living room to the glass doors at the back, where a shaded swimming pool was surrounded by verdant drought-proof landscaping. Carly wondered if Lenny still saw the splendor when he walked inside or if he had become inured to it.

Diksha emerged dressed in yoga pants and a pink tank top, her silky black hair tied in a ponytail. She wrapped Carly in a hug. "I'm so glad you're safe."

"Thank you for letting me stay here," Carly said.

"Of course! We're delighted to have you."

She showed Carly to her room—the guest suite at the end of the hall, complete with a queen-size four-poster bed—and did her best to make Carly feel comfortable. Still, in these resplendent surroundings, it was hard not to feel like an old worn shoe.

That night, after they had dinner and the kids went to bed, Diksha and Lenny gently pressed Carly about what had happened to trigger her depression, but she told them she didn't want to talk about it.

"It's too painful," she insisted, still feeling the hot burn of humiliation. Besides, she wouldn't even know where to begin. *I think I'm a lesbian*, she could say, or *I might be bisexual*. Either way, the deeper truth—the one that counted—was that this wasn't about women or men; it was about Maya. She'd simply fallen madly and hopelessly in love.

Over the next few days, Carly gleaned small bits of information about Owen. From the detective, she learned that he had booked a rental car but not a hotel, which meant that he was either staying with a friend or sleeping in the car. Carly couldn't think of a single person Owen might know in Los Angeles and told the detective as much. From Lenny—who had been in touch with Frankie Wilcox, the building manager—she learned that the stolen egg belonged to Dr. Glass, who lived in unit 605. That solved a key piece of the mystery for Carly. She believed Owen had been looking for her in 506 and had inadvertently transposed the numbers. Since the door was unlocked, he'd waltzed inside to confront her, quickly realizing he was in the wrong place. But before he left, he'd snatched the bejeweled prize, believing he could sell it for cash. And knowing Owen, he'd probably found a way to justify it to himself. She wouldn't even be surprised if he managed to make it her fault.

Carly also learned there would be a wedding in the building on Sunday and that everyone who lived there was invited. Immediately, she pictured Maya in a soft sand-colored gown, standing in the middle of the crowd as everyone mingled, sipping champagne. She could see herself there, too, right next to Maya, in a new blue dress. They looked so right together. Carly could feel her heart collapsing all over again.

She considered going to the wedding, reasoning that she'd be perfectly safe with all those people around, but her brother insisted it was too dangerous. "Owen could be lurking about, waiting for you."

Carly didn't put up a fuss, as the idea of seeing Maya again was just as terrifying as it was exhilarating.

Then, on Saturday, everything changed. Lenny got a call from a friend who had a connection at the LAPD and gathered some inside intel. Apparently, Owen had booked a seat on an American Airlines flight from Los Angeles to Manchester-Boston Airport for the very next day, and the police planned to intercept him at the departure gate.

Carly was relieved. She didn't know why Owen had given up on stalking her but decided it didn't matter. This whole episode was nearly over. Best of all, it meant she'd be safe to go back to her apartment, and Lenny agreed.

Still, she was undecided about attending the wedding, even though it was fun to imagine dancing with Maya at the same time Owen was being dragged out of LAX in handcuffs.

"Maybe you *should* go to that wedding," Diksha said over dinner.

"I agree," Lenny added. "Might do you some good."

Carly shook her head. "I don't know," she said, so anxious about seeing Maya it was hard to eat.

"If you don't feel safe," Diksha said, "I understand."

"It's not that."

"You don't like parties?" asked Samira, who had just turned thirteen and discovered she didn't enjoy them as much as she used to. The kid had always struggled with shyness, but puberty had added a whole new dimension.

"Not very much," Carly admitted.

"Why not?" asked Reya, who was nine and adored parties. Good thing, too, because she seemed to have at least one every weekend.

Carly reached over and touched her smooth cheek. "Not sure. I used to. I guess I need to find my courage."

"Maybe you left it in New Hampshire," Reya joked.

Carly laughed. "Definitely not in New Hampshire!"

"You took it with you, Aunt Carly," Samira said.

It sounded so loaded, so meaningful, that Carly put down her fork to study her niece's earnest face. "How do you know that?" she asked.

"Because you moved all the way across the country by yourself!"

Carly sat up straighter. Her niece wasn't wrong. It did take acres of courage to make that trip. She recalled exactly how she felt boarding the plane. She had been nervous, anxious, even terrified. But she'd also been empowered. She'd been so proud of herself for having the gumption to face those fears and move on. Carly missed that feeling and wondered if she'd ever get it back.

"I think you should go to the wedding," said the thirteen-year-old, sounding unexpectedly bold.

"And why's that?"

"It'll be fun!" Reya piped in.

Samira and her mother shared a poignant look; then the girl turned to Carly. "Every time we face our fears, we grow a little bit."

Carly looked at Diksha, who beamed with pride. Clearly, they'd had this exact conversation, and it had helped Samira with some of her social anxiety. Carly went back to that image of Maya at the wedding reception and understood how desperately she wanted to see her again. They would need to have a difficult conversation that might leave Carly feeling even more rejected. But she needed to face it and get on with her life. She took a jagged breath.

"You okay, sis?" Lenny asked.

Carly gave a sharp nod, then looked at her sister-in-law. "I'm going to need to buy a new dress."

Chapter 70

The day of the wedding, Carly emerged on the rooftop, shocked she'd found the courage to wear such a dress. When Diksha had taken her shopping, all she knew was that she wanted something in blue. She tried on several and was leaning toward a cobalt number in a summer-weight crepe, off the shoulder, with a high-low hem, but worried it was a little young. Then Diksha brought in a sequined dress that shimmered between indigo and navy, on delicate spaghetti straps.

Carly had sucked air. "I don't know. I was thinking Kate Middleton and that's . . . Tina Turner?"

"Try it on," her sister-in-law had said.

Carly was stunned by the slinky, sexy woman staring back at her in the changing room mirror. The dress was short and formfitting, with a bold slit to show even more of her thigh.

"If you want to make him eat his heart out," Diksha said, "that's the dress."

Carly made pointed eye contact. "*Her*," she corrected, and her sister-in-law raised an intrigued eyebrow.

"She must be pretty extraordinary."

"She's . . . everything." Carly choked up, and Diksha handed her a tissue.

Now, in this crowded space, Carly became aware that heads were turning toward her. If only Owen could see me now, she thought before catching herself, because it wasn't Owen she wanted to impress. She closed her eyes and envisioned him in the back of a police cruiser, cursing her all the way to the station house.

Enjoy the ride, you son of a bitch, she thought.

Carly opened her eyes and took a deep breath. Then she straightened her dress self-consciously as she looked over and around the men eyeing her, but Maya wasn't there. Just as well, she thought. Best to fortify with some liquid courage first. She headed to the busy bar that had been set up on the far side of the pool, beside a makeshift dance floor, and ordered a vodka gimlet on the rocks. She hadn't had one in years—not since she used to go out with her friend Lilly, before she married Owen. Carly brought the drink to her mouth. The first sip was sharp and gutsy, but she remembered it would go smooth and mild as the ice melted. She told herself that by the time she finished her drink, Maya would arrive. She forced herself not to glance at the door.

The night before, Carly had finally texted Maya, asking if she was coming to the wedding. She'd responded: Yes! Will you be there? When Carly said that she would, Maya wrote: Great. Can't wait to see you and talk

As Carly nursed the last sip of her drink, a man in a black suit and a lavender tie appeared at her side. He wasn't bad looking, but she had no interest.

"What are you drinking?" he asked.

"Excuse me?"

"I'd offer to buy you a cocktail," he said, "but it's an open bar." The man laughed like it was a funny joke, and his teeth were so white it looked like he'd swallowed a halogen lamp.

"I'm waiting for a friend," she told him.

The man gave a tight nod, retreating, and Carly downed the last watery sips of her cocktail. She turned back to order another and noticed that Tameka from the nail salon was one of the bartenders. She knew that Maya had counseled her and wondered if the woman was feeling better, stronger, more positive about her future. Carly liked her and could imagine striking up a friendship. It wasn't something that had come easily to her in the past, but maybe now she could. It would just take a little effort . . . and courage. But after humiliating herself in front of Maya, Carly was pretty sure she could handle just about anything.

Before she could even say hello to Tameka, though, she was waylaid by that handsome talent agent who always dressed so impeccably. Today, his expensive cologne was mixed with the scent of alcohol.

"Carly!" he said just a little too loudly, and kissed her cheek. "You look wonderful. Wow!"

"Thanks, Dante."

He stepped aside so she could see the man next to him, who had a shaved head and a dark beard. "This is my friend Freddie," Dante said, clapping the man's shoulder. "He wanted to meet you."

Carly extended her hand, wondering if she was emitting a vibe of desperate loneliness or if it was all about the dress. In either case, it made her uncomfortable. She wondered how Maya could feel so at ease moving about the world with no chance at anonymity.

"Dante tells me you're a writer," Freddie said.

"That's right." Carly knew it was rude not to reciprocate by asking what he did for a living, but she didn't want to get any deeper into this.

"My sister just self-published a novel," he said. "I didn't read it, but I understand it's very good. I'm in awe of people who can write. I'm sort of a numbers guy."

It was an even more blatant hint to ask him what he did, but she looked across the patio and saw Maya emerge, wearing a flowy bohemian print dress in pink, blue, and turquoise. It was the gown of a goddess, confident and divine. All heads seemed to turn at once, as if sensing her presence.

"Is that the bride?" Carly heard someone ask, and had to stifle a laugh.

She waved, and Maya smiled when she caught sight of her.

"You know her?" Freddie asked, impressed, as Maya strode toward them.

"We're business partners," Carly told him, not sure if it was still true.

"Whoa," the guy said. "She's the biggest thing on the internet. I see that video of her every place I look."

It was true. Since launching her news, Maya's star had gone supernova. Carly couldn't help feeling pride in her role in that. Even if she never spoke to Maya again after this night, she'd be able to hold that close to her heart.

Feeling awkward, she gripped her drink tightly as Maya reached them. Would they hug? Do that European kiss thing? Shake hands?

Maya moved right in for an embrace. "Look at you!" she said, backing up to admire Carly's dress. "You're *breathtaking*."

Carly felt herself flush. Maya thought she was breathtaking! "You too," she stammered.

Maya signaled the bartender and asked for a dirty martini. When she turned back, Carly introduced her to Freddie and Dante.

"Would you guys excuse us?" Maya said, taking her drink from the bartender. "Carly and I need to have a private chat."

Before they could answer, she led Carly away to the far corner of the empty dance floor. They stood by the railing between two potted trees.

Carly wanted to speak first, to body block any pity before it had a chance to land. Of course, she already knew Maya felt sorry for her, but she couldn't handle seeing it all over her face.

"Listen," she began, her heart banging in her chest, "I want to apologize. I'm sorry I put you in that position. It wasn't right." There. It was exactly what she had wanted to say. She took another sip of her drink and hoped she could get through the rest of this without crumbling.

"Stop it," Maya said. "You didn't do anything wrong."

"I did!" Carly insisted. "And I feel terrible. I know I misread the situation so badly." She looked up into Maya's beautiful face, her skin glowing in the waning light. The pain was nearly exquisite.

"You didn't misread a thing."

"Of course I did!"

"Carly, hear me. Please. I was giving off flirty vibes. It was one hundred percent my fault."

And there it was—the charity. Carly wanted none of it. "I was an idiot," she insisted. "I got carried away with my feelings . . . like, I don't know. It was like I was trying to be someone else."

"I don't think so," Maya said gently. "I think you were being true to your feelings. Maybe for the first time."

Carly stared at her, feeling so exposed it was as if she'd been cracked open. Yes, she thought. Dear god, yes. In her entire life, she had never once been more true to her own emotions.

Despite herself, she dropped her head and started to cry. Maya gave her the cocktail napkin she'd been holding.

"Here's the thing," Maya said, as Carly wiped her face. "I was developing feelings for you. Really strong feelings. But I didn't trust my own heart, coming off my relationship with Brianna. So I kept telling myself, 'Carly is just a friend. And she's straight. Don't push this to be anything more.' Then you kissed me, and . . . I almost felt like I made you do it."

"You didn't!" Carly protested. She felt so lightheaded she had to hold on to the railing. Maya had strong feelings for her? It felt like a dream.

"It took me a while to understand that," Maya admitted. "I was feeling guilty, like I had somehow tricked you into being attracted to me."

"Oh, god, no," Carly said. "It wasn't a trick. Those feelings grew from in here." She put her hand over her diaphragm, because it felt like the center of her being.

"I get it," Maya said. "And I'm sorry I reacted so badly."

Carly rubbed her forehead, feeling like she needed to do something physical to ground herself. "This is not how I expected this conversation to go."

"Come here," Maya said, and pulled her into a long embrace.

Carly held on, feeling like it was exactly where she was supposed to be—right here, on this night, in this woman's arms, receiving nothing but love. Carly tried to recall a single moment with Owen—or with anyone—when she'd felt this special, this appreciated, this authentic. And god help her, but she was certain Maya was experiencing it too. Maybe not in the exact same way, but they were wrapped in a current of energy, sharing a connection.

"What now?" she whispered so softly she wasn't even sure Maya heard. But she pulled away and nodded.

"Good question."

"I mean, we're both coming off of painful situations," Carly said, aware that they were each emotionally raw in their own way. "So . . ."

"So we should wait," Maya said.

"I think that's smart," Carly agreed, though she wasn't sure either of them would want to stick to this agreement for very long.

She heard a murmur ripple through the crowd and turned to see the bride and groom emerging through the doorway. Geoffrey English was dressed in a black tuxedo with a single silver earring dangling, and Leyla wore a shimmery white satin gown that looked couture, hugging the curve of her hips in elegant parentheses. It didn't look especially bridal, yet it was perfect for this remarkably beautiful woman. Even her black high heels with leather gladiator straps—an odd accessory for a bride—seemed to suit her.

As they stepped toward the crowd, the door opened again and a man entered, casually dressed in a tan windbreaker and a baseball cap. At once, Carly's breath caught in her throat. It couldn't be him. *It couldn't.*

"Are you okay?" Maya asked.

Carly swallowed against an egg-size lump that had formed in her throat, and it took her a long moment to find her voice.

"No," she finally said as a chill poured down her scalp, "I'm not."

Chapter 71
ADDISON

The cocktail reception was in full swing when Addison arrived, and she glanced around the crowded space, taking it all in. It was late afternoon, approaching dusk, and the sun was low in the sky, casting long shadows across the patio. Gold-draped bistro tables with tall chairs had been set up around the pool, which had white rose petals floating on the surface. The twenty-five ficus trees, which had arrived so late Frankie nearly had a coronary, had now been threaded with fairy lights and placed all around the perimeter. The effect was magical.

Addison's eyes swept the clots of people, looking for one in particular and not finding him. At last, she smoothed out her strapless little black dress and headed for the bar at the far end, where she knew Tameka was working.

A small crowd had formed, and Tameka was too busy to have an extended chat. But she made Addison a drink and, without being asked, told her she didn't think Zach had arrived yet.

Of course she'd been right to assume Addison was looking for him. The night of the allergy incident, he'd called her over FaceTime to see how she was feeling. Knocked out by the Benadryl, Addison had just woken up from a three-hour nap.

"Fine," she had said. "Just tired."

"Why didn't you tell me you were allergic to cats? I wouldn't have thrust Betty Snyder at you like that."

"We were having in important conversation," she said, "and I didn't want to change the subject."

"We can talk about it now, if you want."

And they did. Zach told her he believed the incident in the car had happened exactly as she had said and he was relieved she wasn't involved with Dante.

"What about us?" she had asked, feeling hopeful.

Zach went quiet for a long moment, his face stony in pain. "I went to a very dark place after I saw you together," he admitted. "I thought you betrayed me. I thought it was Quinn all over again."

"I'm sorry," she said. "I'm sorry you—"

"It was excruciating!" he interrupted, his voice cracking as if some kind of internal battle was wreaking havoc.

Dante, she thought, feeling Zach's pain whirl through her like a storm. This was Dante's fault. "I hope you know you can trust me," she said gently. "Maybe after we wait six months . . ."

Zach shook his head. "I don't think we should have made that agreement."

Addison's throat tightened, and her heart went leaden in her chest. She struggled to fill her lungs. "Why not?" she pleaded.

"Because I'm not ready," he said. "Because I crumble too easily. I can't put myself in that position again. I think I should just concentrate on my work for now."

She nodded. He was breaking up with her before they even began, and it made perfect sense. She pulled a tissue from her nightstand and blew her nose. "I understand."

"I release you from our agreement," he said, without any sense of irony. "And of course, you're free to date anyone you like, but—"

"But stay away from Dante," she filled in.

"He's bad news. And that's not just jealousy. That's a fact."

"Don't worry. I plan to stay as far from him as possible."

And that was it. She saw Zach in passing several times after that, but they were like cordial acquaintances. It was nearly unbearable.

Addison scanned the crowd again to see if he was there, and her eyes landed on Arnie, who seemed to be trying to extricate himself from a conversation with two of his female gym buddies. At last he tore himself away and approached.

"Sweetheart," he said to her, "you look marvelous."

"How are you doing with all this, Uncle Arnie?" she asked, concerned about how he was coping with Leyla's wedding.

"Like a champ," he said.

"Are you sure?"

"I'll admit I was enthralled, but it was a passing infatuation. She's quite a gal, just not for me." He looked around. "Have you seen Frankie? She said she had some news for me about those missing videotape files."

Addison pointed toward an area near the entrance, where Frankie was giving instructions to a couple of waiters. "Go ahead," she told him. "Report back if there's anything interesting."

As Arnie walked off, Addison turned back to Tameka, who caught her eye and nodded toward the other end of the bar. There was Dante, sipping a drink while talking to a bearded man. Addison hadn't seen him around since the day she walked out of the restaurant and supposed he'd been in New York the whole time.

When Dante sensed her gaze, he looked up. She tried to avert her eyes quickly, but it was too late. He said something to the man, then left him to approach Addison, a glass of what looked like scotch in his hand. His swagger was more pronounced than usual, and she realized he was at least a little drunk.

"I have nothing to say to you," she told him when he got close.

He put his drink down on the bar and moved his face toward her ear. "You look like a million bucks," he cooed, and ran his knuckle down her naked shoulder.

She moved away. "Back off, Dante."

"You're still mad at me?"

Addison shook her head, exasperated. It wasn't as if they had some little tiff. He'd shown his true nature, and it was appalling.

"Not mad," she said, "I just don't like you."

"Come on, Addison," he pleaded, "you don't mean that."

"Like hell I don't."

"That breaks my heart," he said, grabbing her wrist. "Tell me how I can make it up to you. I'll do anything."

"No," she said firmly, and tried to pull her arm away, but he held tight. This drunk side of Dante wasn't one she'd seen before, and it was even worse than the rest of him.

"Give me a chance, at least."

"Leave me alone!" she demanded. As she struggled against his grip, Addison saw Zach emerging through the crowd. Dante noticed him, too, and was distracted enough for Addison to yank her wrist away.

"What do *you* want?" Dante sneered at Zach when he reached them.

"I want you to leave her alone."

"She's a big girl."

"And the big girl wants nothing to do with you," Addison sneered.

Dante scoffed. "And you want *him*?" he said, barely nodding toward Zach. "He's a child. A nothing. A fucking geek who lets people walk all over him."

"At least I'm not a liar and a cheat," Zach said.

Dante turned and took a sip of his drink. "Asshole," he muttered.

Zach stood still, seething, and Addison could tell he was deciding what to say. Finally, he leveled a gaze at Dante and asked, "Did you tell her the truth?"

"Leave us alone," Dante said.

"What truth?" Addison pressed.

"I can't believe you didn't tell her."

Dante downed the last of his drink and signaled for another. "I don't know what you're talking about."

As the bartender poured Dante a scotch, Zach turned to Addison. "Ask him why he keeps going back to New York."

"Business," Dante said, taking his drink. "She knows that."

Addison looked from Dante to Zach, wondering what he knew that she didn't. "Does he have a girlfriend there or something?" she asked.

"You going to tell her, or should I?" Zach said to Dante.

Addison folded her arms, waiting for an answer, but Dante kept his back to them, focusing on his drink. "Fuck off."

Zach took a deep breath. "Not a girlfriend," he said to Addison. "A wife. Cassandra D'Amico. And twin girls. They live on the Upper East Side."

Married? Impossible. Surely Arnie would have known such a thing. And then there were the flowers, the bracelet, the inscription: *Always, Dante.* She thought about that kiss on her forehead, his insistence that they had a future together.

"That's a lie," Dante spit.

"Problem is," Zach said, "when you try to invest money with a 'fucking geek,' it takes him about ten minutes to dig into your background and find out you're leading a double life." He pulled his phone from his pocket and tapped at it, then held it up for Addison to see.

She stared, shocked, at an image of Dante with a beautiful brunette woman with two little girls, standing in front of the marquee of a new Broadway show.

"This was posted on her Instagram two days ago," Zach said. "They went to the premiere."

Addison took a step back, trying to wrap her mind around it. Dante was married. He had a family in New York. Everything he'd said to her was a game, a seduction, nothing more. And Addison hadn't seen it. She felt like throwing up.

Dante grabbed Addison's naked shoulders. "It doesn't change anything. You and me, Addison, we're so good together!"

"Get off me!" she said, and shoved at his chest, sending him staggering back toward the bar.

"You all right?" Zach asked her.

She peered into the distance as she tried to get her bearings. The bride and groom had entered the party and were making their way through the crowd. Behind them was a man dressed inappropriately in a baseball cap and casual jacket. He looked up, and Addison froze.

"It's him," she whispered.

"Who?" Zach asked.

"The man from the video. The one who stole Arnie's egg."

Addison looked around for Nikolai but didn't see him. There was nothing to do but confront the man herself, because she was not going to let him get away a second time—not when he had her uncle's precious egg. That is, if he hadn't sold it yet. Addison pushed her way through the crowd until she stood facing him.

"What do *you* want?" he sneered.

She looked him straight in the eyes, her rage boiling over. Dante had taken so much from her, and now here was this smug, entitled thief who had taken so much from her uncle. "I want the Fabergé egg you stole," she said.

"Is that all?" He scoffed and shook his head, as if the demand were ridiculous. Then he reached into his pocket—the same one she'd seen him slip it into in the video. Thank god, Addison thought. At least there's that. But when he pulled his hand out, he wasn't holding an egg. He was holding a gun.

Chapter 72
ARNIE

"You made a hell of a party," Arnie said to Frankie. "Everyone's having a splendid time."

"I'm amazed we pulled it off," she admitted.

"I'm not," he said, and meant it. The woman was a marvel. "You're capable of anything, Frankie Wilcox."

"You got that right," she said. "There was just one last-minute glitch."

He glanced around, searching for an imperfection, and could find nothing. The decor was beautiful, and neatly dressed servers threaded discreetly through the crowd with trays of wine and hors d'oeuvres.

"You could have fooled me," he said, wondering if the problem was related to the deleted computer files. "Everything looks fabulous."

"Not that," she said. "I had to fire Jake."

"That young lifeguard?"

She pointed toward Arnie's drink. "May I?" she said. He nodded as she took a sip before handing it back. "Turns out Jake was the one who erased those videos."

Arnie's eyes went wide in surprise. "Why on earth?"

"Apparently he had the hots for Melody. And since that perch of his was like a front-row seat to Beekman gossip, he heard some rumor about her stealing your egg. He had access to the security system computers, so he went in and deleted the files, thinking it would score points with her."

Arnie shook his head at this news, unable to imagine Melody going for the young surfer dude. He was practically a child. "Did it?"

"God, no. She thinks he's an idiot. She came straight to me with the story. And it took about thirty seconds for me to get him to confess."

Arnie glanced around, looking for Melody, and saw her talking with Nikolai, who was too busy scoping the area to make eye contact with her. When his eyes narrowed, Arnie turned and saw Addison marching purposefully through the crowd, like she was on some kind of mission. She said something angry Arnie couldn't quite make out, and he shifted his gaze to the object of her scorn.

He couldn't quite believe what he was seeing and had to shake off the cognitive dissonance to understand. There was a man with a gun, and it was pointed right at the person he loved most in the whole world.

Arnie felt his universe turn upside down. For a moment that seemed to exist in a molasses of memories, his love for Addison played out in vivid images, starting with the call from his sister, telling him her daughter had a baby girl and named her Addison. He'd wept, and then wept again the first time he held her in his arms, tightly bundled and smelling like cornstarch and warm milk. He saw her at age five, with paint on her face when she was in that silly day-camp show, beaming with pride, and again at nine, when she had her leg in a cast after falling from a handrail she'd thought she could balance on. He saw her at age eighteen, after losing both her parents, feeling so certain her life was over, and at twenty-nine, walking toward his car at the airport.

Now, as he laser-focused on that handgun, nothing mattered but Addison. Not Leyla, not Paulette, and certainly not that stupid egg. Good lord, why would anyone care about such a thing? It was nothing. A trinket. A useless imitation of a coveted collectible. But even if it were a real Fabergé egg, it would be nothing to him.

Before he knew it, Arnie was diving between his niece and the gunman. Shoot *me*, he thought. Shoot *me!* And in that suspended second, the truth crystalized. Paulette was not the one. What a fool he'd been! What an obsessive, romantic fool! If he survived this, he'd need a woman of substance. Someone who understood what was important in life.

Then, there was a bang, and Arnie was on the ground. I'm hit, he thought, and that means Addison's okay.

Arnie felt nothing but peace as he recalled his father and the Hebrew prayer he should be saying at this moment. But wait. Had he really been shot? Arnie was able to prop himself up on his elbows and look down at his torso, his legs, his arms. He felt his head. No stickiness, no blood. He looked up and saw the gunman in a headlock, Nikolai's beefy arm around his neck. The security man's other arm held the thug's wrist, forcing the weapon to point skyward. That's when Arnie realized what happened. No one had been shot—the bullet had gone straight up in the air. Nikolai wrested the gun from the man's hand, pocketed it, then brought the guy to the ground in one swift movement.

"Call police, please," he said, his knee on the man's back.

Zach Brody, who was standing nearby, whirled around and said, "I'm on it," his phone already to his ear.

Arnie looked around. Where was Addison? He had a moment of panic, but then there she was, looming over him, safe and whole. Tears flooded his eyes.

"Are you okay?" she asked.

"I wasn't hit," he said.

"No," she confirmed, "you weren't."

"And you?"

"Not a scratch, I promise."

He realized, then, that Nikolai had knocked him over to get to the gunman. As Arnie wept in relief, he felt a gentle hand on his shoulder and saw Frankie standing over him, looking even more beautiful than usual, the fairy lights creating a halo around her.

"Let's get you up," she said as she and Addison helped him to a chair.

He glanced over and saw that Nikolai didn't need any assistance in keeping the gunman subdued until the police arrived, but several men helped anyway, piling on to ensure that he couldn't move.

"What happened?" Arnie asked Addison.

"I thought I could get your egg back," she explained, "to make you happy."

"He doesn't care about that anymore," Frankie said.

Arnie looked into her deep, dark eyes. "How did you know that?"

"You dove in front of a gun to protect your niece. That's not the action of a man who gives a crap about some silly ornament."

As he studied her face, Arnie realized that Frankie understood him better than he understood himself. A strange warmth flooded his heart, and it took him a minute to realize what was happening. This wasn't anything like his feelings for Paulette or Leyla or Melody or any of the others. It was more real. More solid. It was rooted in the firm, sweet earth.

He looked into her eyes and saw it. She was in love with him. And though he hadn't realized it until that very moment, he was in love with her too.

Chapter 73
CARLY

"Is that him?" Maya asked. "Is that Owen?"

"He . . . he wasn't supposed to be here."

Carly was in shock, standing frozen in place as her husband of fifteen years lay face down on the patio, blubbering and weeping and calling her name.

"Please, Carly," he cried, sounding like a wounded dog. "Please! Don't let them take me away. You have to help me!"

Have to? A fury rose up in Carly as she realized he was expecting her to save him, after everything he'd done. It was an unfamiliar emotion, this outward anger, and it felt like she'd downed a jigger of righteous rage.

"It's your own damned fault!" she called, and the crowd parted, creating an open corridor between the two of them. Still, Carly remained rooted in place, next to Maya.

"Is that you?" he said, unable to see her from his vantage point, held flat against the hard ground.

"What are you even doing here?" she demanded. "You were supposed to be flying home today."

"Your email," he called.

"What email?"

"You said we could talk. I thought you might come back to me."

Of course, she thought, recalling his message: I just want to tlak. She'd told him she'd think about it.

"And if I didn't?" she asked, feeling a chill. Had he planned on killing her if she'd said no? She glanced at the door to the elevator bank, wondering when the police might arrive.

"I didn't think that far."

That tracked. Owen existed in a world of *right now*. He had no ability to play things out in his head and figure out what might happen. And yet, he'd come armed.

"What about the gun?" she demanded.

"I wasn't going to hurt anybody, I swear." He started to blubber again. "You have to believe me. I wasn't going to shoot anyone."

"Man who points gun means to shoot," said Nikolai.

"No!" Owen cried. "I just . . . I got scared. I didn't know what to do."

"Where did you even get it?" Carly asked.

"I . . . someone gave it to me."

"*Gave* it to you?" she said, incredulous. Owen had always been a terrible liar.

"I traded it for something . . . something I found."

It took her less than a second to connect the dots. He was talking about the Fabergé egg. "You mean stole," she corrected.

"I was running out of money," he said. "These people here—they're so rich. They don't even care if you take something. They always come out on top anyway."

"Oh, Owen."

"I tried to pawn it. Then this guy offered a trade, and I was so desperate. Please, Carly. I still love you. Don't let them arrest me."

At that, the door opened, and a uniformed police officer entered, followed by three more.

"I am security," Nikolai said. "This is gunman."

It seemed to take less than a second for the officers to cuff Owen and get him on his feet. At last, Carly was able to see his face. He looked worn and haggard, one cheek reddened by the rough paver of the patio. His hat had come off in the scuffle, and she could see that his hair was overgrown and dirty.

He looked her up and down, in the same appraising way he always did before saying something cruel. But now, he looked small and chastened.

"You're not really going to let them take me," he cried, his eyes desperate and pleading.

"Goodbye, Owen," she said.

As the police led him away, he turned back to her. "You look like a whore!" he called, and then he was gone.

Chapter 74
ADDISON

After the police took Owen Pratt away in handcuffs, Frankie had a confab with the bride and groom, who decided to go ahead with the wedding. Apparently, Leyla thought the high-stakes drama was a perfect way to start a marriage.

Frankie asked Addison to help her herd the guests toward the draped chairs at the side of the patio, where a makeshift chapel had been set up in the spot that was normally sectioned off for towel bins and stacks of lounges. Now, there was a spired altar built from white-painted wood and billowy fabric, with an art deco stained glass window hung against the back. An aisle had been created from an unfurled red carpet with flowering shrubberies in white baskets placed alongside it.

Once the guests had settled into their chairs, Frankie told Addison to take a seat. She nodded but held back, scanning the rows. Most of the seats were filled, and she watched as Frankie sidled into the empty chair Arnie had been saving for her. He turned back toward Addison and signaled toward another empty space two seats away from him. Addison shook him off, as she knew he would make everyone move down for her, and she didn't want to create a fuss. Besides, she was looking for Zach.

She saw one tall man seated toward the back, but it was Nikolai. Next to him, a swooning Melody Forrest—who had witnessed his brave takedown of the gunman—was trying to get his attention.

A lot of eyes were on Maya Mayfield, whose presence in the building had recently become more public, as she had announced her split from Brianna on social media. Smiling, Maya indulged a couple of people who wanted selfies with her, all the while holding the hand of Carly Pratt, who was almost unrecognizable now. That was one match Addison couldn't have predicted. She smiled as she saw them sit together, ready to enjoy the wedding ceremony.

Zach was nowhere to be found, and Addison knew why. After the gun had gone off, she had whirled around to discover he was right behind her. Grateful they were both alive, she'd thrown herself into his arms. He'd held tight for only a quick second, then backed off.

"You're okay?" he'd asked tersely.

When she nodded, he'd turned away from her, and she understood. The brush with death hadn't changed anything. He was simply not ready to even think about a relationship. So after the gunman was taken away, Zach had left, overwhelmed by her aggressive affection.

With a sigh, Addison took a seat in the last row and waited for the ceremony to begin.

As the music started, she sensed a presence looming over her and looked up to see Zach's tall figure silhouetted against the overhead lights. Heavily shadowed in the semidarkness, his features seemed rendered in black and white, like he was a swoony 1940s movie star. He motioned for her to shift to the empty seat next to her, which she did, trying to keep her excitement in check.

"I thought you'd left," she whispered as he sat.

"I did."

She understood. He had indeed been overwhelmed and needed some space but ultimately decided he didn't want to miss the wedding. "I'm glad you came back."

"As am I," he said softly, then put his finger to his lips to indicate that they needed to stop talking, as the ceremony was about to begin. But Addison had one more thing to say.

"I'm sorry I threw myself at you like that."

"What?"

"Honestly," she said, "I respect that you need space. I didn't mean to pressure you. I'm so sorry—I promise I won't do that again."

A murmur rippled through the crowd as the groom began his walk down the aisle beside his elegantly dressed mother in her motorized wheelchair, a small bouquet in her lap. Geoffrey helped her get situated in the front row and took his place at the altar.

Addison knew from the planning meetings that this was to be a very simple ceremony. There were no bridesmaids or groomsmen, no flower girl or ring bearer. The next person to come down the aisle would be the bride, on the arm of her father.

The wedding march began, and the crowd turned, but Leyla wasn't there. They waited, then waited some more. People began to whisper, wondering if the bride had taken off. But Addison was pretty sure this was Leyla's way of adding a bit of torture to the ceremony. Once her groom began to sweat in utter desperation, she'd make her appearance.

Addison glanced toward the altar, where Geoffrey shifted uncomfortably, straightening his glasses. After several more minutes, he bent and whispered something to his mother, then took his place again.

Enough already, Addison thought, sending a silent message to Leyla. The poor guy is about to have a heart attack.

The wedding march started up again from the beginning, and then, after another long, dramatic pause, there she was, clutching a plump white bouquet splattered with tiny red buds. Geoffrey looked like he was about to burst.

A short while later, after they had both said "I do" and the officiate pronounced them married, there were sniffles and tears throughout the crowd, and Addison wondered if people would continue to call this place Divorce Towers.

"Aren't you glad you decided to come back?" Addison asked Zach.

He looked at her quizzically. "I was always coming back."

"You were?"

"I just had to go feed Betty. She's very particular about her fresh food."

"Oh," Addison said, trying to readjust her thinking. "I thought I scared you off."

Zach went quiet, that faraway look shrouding his face again. But after a moment, he returned, making eye contact that pierced her. "I'm not scared anymore," he said.

"You're not?" She studied his emerald eyes as they softened.

"Well, maybe a little, but . . . I missed you so much."

"I missed you too."

"When I saw that gun, Addison . . ." He trailed off and shook his head, his eyes going damp.

She nodded. "It was scary."

"But that's the thing," he said, peering hard into her face to be sure she understood. "I don't want to live my life scared."

"Me neither," she whispered.

The guests remained in their seats as the bride and groom made their way back down the aisle as a married couple. In the midst of that, Zach leaned in and kissed Addison, who kissed him back, losing herself so completely she forgot where she was. Or nearly forgot, because deep down she knew. She was right where she belonged.

"You're sure you're okay with this?" she asked when they came up for air.

He nodded, and she was so overwhelmed by his faith she nearly started crying. It was like he was jumping off a cliff, confident she would catch him, willing to go down if she didn't.

"Are you worried about Frankie finding out?" he asked when he saw her teary expression.

Frankie. With everything going on, she'd slipped Addison's mind. This was going to be a hell of a relationship if it had to be clandestine.

She imagined sneaking off with Tameka to rendezvous with Zach in secret, again and again and again.

"Maybe I'll tell her the truth about us and hope for the best," she said.

Zach's mouth edged into the smallest grin. "I don't think Frankie is going to be a problem."

"Why's that?"

He nodded toward the front of the makeshift chapel, where Arnie and Frankie were still in their seats, gazing into each other's eyes. He said something to make her laugh, and then they came together for a soft, sweet kiss.

Holy hell, Addison thought. Frankie and Arnie. Yet another match she hadn't predicted. But of course, now that she saw them together, it made perfect sense—Frankie was everything her uncle needed in a partner. Also, it cleared up the mystery of why Frankie had been so angry about Addison's efforts to find a match for Arnie. She had wanted him for herself.

"They seem happy," Zach said, "but it's too bad that egg is still missing."

Was it really too bad? Addison pondered the question as she looked into the starry horizon, recalling the sunrise she and Zach had witnessed after that kiss in the pool. She realized she was facing east, toward her past, and thought about all the miles from this spot to the place she had left. A lightness filled her as she understood how very far she had come.

"Maybe not," she said, still peering into the night sky. Then she turned back and they looked at each other, sharing a thought neither of them needed to say out loud: they had all found something much more valuable.

"Can I ask you something?" she said.

"Always."

"When you do that thing where you drift away, where do you go?"

He nodded, as if acknowledging it was a reasonable question, one he had anticipated. "The future," he said.

"You go to the future?"

"It's something I've always done. I play out what might happen next, and how I should respond or react. When I was a kid, I assumed everyone did it."

"And do things always play out the way you expect them to?"

The people around them started to rise from their seats, but Addison and Zach stayed put. "Only sometimes," he said thoughtfully, "but recalibrating is half the fun."

That took Addison by surprise. "The place you go is fun?"

"When I want it to be."

"Can I come with?" she asked.

Zach's eyes went wide in delight—exuberant and grateful—as if it were the best question he'd ever heard. Then, as the other guests shuffled past them toward the starlit dance floor, he rose and held his hand toward hers.

Smiling, Addison took it and knew she had her answer. It was time to dance.

Acknowledgments

Writing is a lonely endeavor, so I consider myself lucky indeed that I had such a wonderful creative partner in Pete Harris, who was always ready to talk through any idea and explore its myriad possibilities. His energy, inspiration, and support were the fuel that kept me going.

Huge thanks to Maria Gomez for believing in this book and its appeal to readers. From the very beginning, she was an enthusiastic champion whose smart advice and spirited encouragement motivated me to revise and polish until my beloved manuscript was even better than I thought it could be. I'm so grateful *Divorce Towers* found the right home!

My developmental editor, Andrea Hurst, understood exactly what this book needed, and I'm so thankful for her skills, intelligence, wisdom, and guidance. She's a treasure.

Thanks to my beta readers, Saralee Rosenberg and Rook Mogavero, who weighed in with excellent input, insights, and confidence boosters. Their help was invaluable. A special shout-out to Bonnie Berry LaMon, Susan Henderson, Arielle Eckstut, and David Henry Sterry for their sage advice and counsel. Also to Annelise Robey, for believing in me with unwavering faith.

An extra big thanks to my family for their patience and good humor through the long journey of this book. Most of all to Mike, my rock, the only man I know who could stick by a wife as she wrote a book called *Take My Husband*, then one called *Divorce Towers*, and keep on laughing. Love you, Mike!

About the Author

Ellen Meister is a novelist, book coach, screenwriter, and creative writing instructor who started her career writing advertising copy. Her novels include *Take My Husband*; *The Rooftop Party*; *Love Sold Separately*; *Dorothy Parker Drank Here*; *Farewell, Dorothy Parker*; *The Other Life*; and more. Meister's essays have appeared in publications such as the *New York Times*, *Newsday*, the *Wall Street Journal* blog, the *Huffington Post*, the Daily Beast, *Long Island Woman*, *Writer's Digest*, and *Publishers Weekly*. Career highlights include appearing on NPR, being selected for the prestigious Indie Next List by the American Booksellers Association, having her work translated into foreign languages, and receiving a TV series option from HBO.

Meister lives in New York and publicly speaks about her books, fiction writing, and America's most celebrated literary wit, Dorothy Parker. For more information, visit https://ellenmeister.com.